RAPUNZEL IS LOSING IT

PRINCESS CROSSOVER SERIES
BOOK 2

DILAN DYER

IMPORTANT AUTHOR'S NOTE

This is **book two** in the Princess Crossover series.
It should be read in a duet with CINDERELLA IS FAKING IT.

This book is <u>not</u> meant to be read as a stand-alone.

In *Cinderella*, Delilah is hired to be Cordelia's body double. While pretending to be Cordelia, she falls for Beck, who had his eyes set on Cordelia's family fortune.

The events in *Cinderella* directly trigger the plot of *Rapunzel*.

Rapunzel IS LOSING IT

PRINCESS CROSSOVER SERIES
BOOK TWO

DILAN DYER

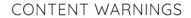

CONTENT WARNINGS

Heavy

Ableism & Internalized Ableism • Gun Violence • Kidnapping • Panic Attacks • Physical Violence • PTSD flashbacks • Sexually Explicit Content

Moderate

Alcohol Abuse • Car Crash

Minor

Discussions of Fertility (in relation to Disability) • Dismemberment • Mentions of Abuse through Parent • Mentions of Death of Parent • Mentions and threats of Sexual Abuse and Exploitation

For a full list of themes, tropes and kinks explored in this novel, please visit

WWW.DILANDYER.COM

Dicktionary

These chapters get spicy.
Do what you will with this information.

Playlist

WILD HORSES • Grace Power
SCARY PEOPLE • Georgi Kay
I CAN SEE YOU • Taylor Swift
SPIRACLE • Flower Face
SAD DREAM • Sky Ferreira
SPARKS FLY • Taylor Swift
DIRTY THOUGHTS • Chloe Adams
TAKE ME THERE • Delta Rae
I CAN'T BREATHE • Bea Miller
QUEEN OF THE NIGHT • Hey Violet
DAYLIGHT • Taylor Swift
DO IT FOR ME • Rosenfeld
ALWAYS • The Veronicas
EXHALE • Sabrina Carpenter
5 OUT OF 6 • Dessa
EYE FOR AN EYE • Rina Sawayama
INVISIBLE STRING •.Taylor Swift
BUZZCUT SEASON • Lorde
PERFECT • Ed Sheeran

For all the girls who should have had a childhood
but got *backstory* *instead.*

CHAPTER ONE

VICTOR

SIX YEARS AGO

Whatever I had expected to step into, it hadn't been a cotton candy glittering Barbie fucking dream house. I'd never seen this much pink in one room, and I'd barely made it past the doorstep. Even the damn ceiling had been painted pink, with a pink glass chandelier dangling above the entryway.

"What agency are you with?" the guy in the wrinkle-free gray suit asked, tapping his finger against a tablet. I should have looked at him to give my eyes a break from the pink onslaught, but the whole place was a train wreck. Not even just the color. But this was a nice house. An old house. And that antique-looking side table had to be even older than the house. Some French general was rolling over in his grave, knowing his desk was now decked out

1

with a glittering pink vase overflowing with pink ruffled flowers. Tasteless.

"No agency," I finally answered, dragging my eyes away, "I'm freelancing."

"I'm sorry but I'll have to ask you to leave. Everyone who walks through this door has undergone extensive background checks."

I blinked at the man and his receding hairline, then at the door that was firmly shut behind me. I had walked through without a hitch. No wonder this girl needed to beef up her security.

Before I had to phrase a response, the door behind the man opened. An old guy with a sweater vest under his suit jacket, built like an inflatable-noodle-man, walked out. He was closely followed by a young blonde, clad in a shimmery blouse and a fucking *pink* mini skirt. She was tall, but not spindly like the noodle man. The only *long* things about her were her hair and her legs.

Cordelia Montgomery.

Better at hiding in plain sight than any spy, and exactly the woman I had to talk to. "Thank you, we'll call you when we've made a decision," she told the noodle man, all the warmth of a rose-colored glacier in her voice. As the dismissed guy shuffled past me, Cordelia's cool blue eyes landed on me. She didn't say anything yet, her gaze traveling up and down my body. I was used to being assessed. People usually tried to kick the shit out of me afterwards though. Cordelia just shook her head.

"I'm Victor. I'm here to interview for the-"

"Sorry to have wasted your time, Victor," she cut me off, "but you're not getting this job."

"Has the position already been filled?" I asked, raising my brows at the noodle man exiting the pink nightmare house. If he was anyone's security detail, they were lucky to still be alive.

"No, you're just not the right fit."

I couldn't leave. Not getting this job wasn't an option unless I wanted to die, either by my uncle's hands or the freezing cold.

This was one of the few places in Boston where neither could slip through the cracks. "With all due respect, Miss Montgomery-"

She grimaced. "Cordelia."

"Miss Cordelia, I deserve a chance."

She sighed and gestured for me to follow her into the room. It was an office space with even more shades of pink. At least the monotone color was somewhat broken up by the piles upon piles of paper on her desk. Maybe she should hire a housekeeper instead of a bodyguard, just to get that mess sorted.

I took the seat across the desk from her. The man with the iPad stood in the door, his stare heavy on the back of my neck. I could glean his reflection in the window behind Cordelia, and made sure to keep one eye on him, while I waited for her to speak.

"I was very specific in what I was looking for and you don't fit the bill. You're too young to forfeit your life."

"Forfeit my life? Do you expect a lot of bullets to come flying your way? If so, I'm probably faster to jump in front of you than Mr. Rogers out there."

"No, not like that." She ran her hands through her long hair, twirling the ends around her pinky. "This is an around-the-clock kind of position. You'd spend 70% of your time glued to my side."

"I don't need a lot of sleep."

"I don't leave my house."

"Do I get my own room?"

"Yes, but-"

"I can start right now."

"No."

"Tomorrow?"

"Victor, you're too young. You'll want to take nights off, meet friends, go on dates. You probably want to start a family at some point. I can't build a trusting relationship with you, only for you to up and leave twelve months from now because this job is too much."

"That won't be an issue." I cut a glance at the reflection of her guard dog. "I would like two minutes alone with you."

"Why?"

"To explain why I want this job more than any of the walking midlife-crises on your list."

"120 seconds. Exactly." She nodded at the man in the suit, who pulled up his watch as he stepped outside. "You won't change my mind."

I waited for the door to shut before I sat up and focused completely on the girl in front of me. Fuck, I hoped I wasn't about to ruin this. "My family is involved in organized crime. I want out. You give me this job, it's my chance to disappear from the world. From *their* world."

To her credit, Cordelia Montgomery merely blinked and crinkled her nose. "Organized crime?"

"Gambling, extortion, drugs, murder, you name it."

"Do you do drugs?"

"No."

"Did you ever kill someone?"

"Yes."

"Hmm." Again, nothing but a slight nose crinkle. Everyone knew that Cordelia's mother had been shot in front of her when she'd been a kid. It had been all over the news. That kind of violence changed you. For all the rosy, fluffy exterior, she had to carry a pretty dark spot inside if she didn't even flinch at murder. "Maybe you should disappear from the world by going to prison then."

"Prison would be more of my family's shit, just behind bars. Bribing guards and cutting the throats of anyone who could rat out my uncle. Then once I got out, back to business as usual."

"You want *out*-out."

"I want out."

She shifted her hair to her other shoulder and continued

4

combing her fingers through it. "Do they know where you are right now?"

"No," I lied. Technically, Luka knew. Luka had found this place for me and had helped me disappear from my uncle's radar. Luka would die before ratting me out.

"If my well-being was compromised, would you be comfortable using violence?"

"Yes."

"Do you have a gun?"

"Multiple."

"You cannot bring *anyone* into the house."

"No problem. I'm here to lie low. You allow me to stay, this house will be the safest house in the city. For me and for you."

"Can you cook?"

"No."

"Where are you staying?"

"My car."

The door swung open behind me, but the suit didn't wait in the doorway this time, walking straight up to the desk. "Two minutes are over." He gave me a pointed stare as if he expected me to stand and leave.

"Victor moves in tonight," Cordelia announced. Never had four words sounded better. My chest expanded in a silent sigh of relief.

"Cordelia, we should discuss-"

"Victor, this is Thomas," she said, not letting him finish. "You'll be taking over for him. He'll stick around for a few days to show you everything."

I just nodded at the guy, whose face was turning a splotchy pink to match the walls, and the curtains, and the rug. And all three mugs on her desk.

"At least meet with the other applicants," Thomas pleaded.

Fuck Thomas. Fuck the other applicants.

I got the job. I got the only safe haven on the east coast.

"Victor, flex your arms." Cordelia turned her storm-colored eyes on me. I did as I was told. My shirt stretched tight over my biceps. "See?" she said, as if that one moment was enough to win their argument. "Does what he's told and has the muscles to do the job. We're good."

She breezed past me into the hallway, and with a clear voice dismissed whatever applicant must have walked in after me.

I almost felt bad. Almost. It could be six days or six months for Luka to get me safely out of the country. Until then, the Montgomery house would do just fine.

CHAPTER TWO

Cordelia

"Where's Victor?"

I stared at the man standing in my door, and the bundled up young woman unconscious in his arms. I'd only seen Julian Beckett in pictures, but the Beckett brothers shared features sharp enough to recognize anywhere. That just didn't explain why he was here.

Victor had gotten the call that *I* had been delivered to the ER with Beck, the other brother, because Victor was my emergency contact, and because Delilah had been acting as my stand-in all summer. Del, who currently lay unconscious in Julian's arms.

Julian stared at me for a heartbeat.

Of course.

7

Two Cordelias.

I glanced past him, but no-one else was there. Not Victor, not Beck.

"Let me in," he huffed and adjusted his grip on Del.

"Of course." I shuffled aside, pulse hammering in my ears. Why on earth was he bringing Del here? She had a thick cast around her arm and the medical gown still on.

Someone at the hospital must have found out that she wasn't me.

Victor had to be dealing with the fall-out.

There was no other explanation.

"Whereto?"

I shook my head, trying to clear it, and tossed the door shut behind Julian. "This way." I jogged up the stairs, opened the door to Del's room and quickly shuffled aside the mountains of books and pillows on her bed. "Is Beck okay? What's going on?"

"I feel like that's a question I should be asking you."

He set Del down on the bed. She looked even paler than usual, and so small in that boxy plastic gown.

"I should get her more comfortable," I said before disappearing into her closet and digging out the softest, largest shirt I could find.

"So, you're the real Cordelia Montgomery." Julian squinted at me, but it wasn't a question.

"I don't think that matters right now. What happened? Is Del going to be okay? Do we need to call a doctor? Does she need medicine?"

"She'll be fine. I have an IV-drip for her in the car. I'll go get it while you do this." He waved at the shirt in my hand.

I waited until I heard his footsteps at the bottom of the stairs, before I collapsed onto the bed next to Del's still form, and let out a squeaky whimper. "Oh my god," I mumbled and shakily untied the hospital gown, "oh no, no, no. No. This isn't happening."

There was a man in my house, and Del was hurt, and I didn't

know where Victor was, and it was all wrong. Every single instinct was screaming at me to run and hide. I couldn't go through this again. I couldn't be responsible for another person getting hurt. But Del was here, and she needed help, and I couldn't hide under my blankets until the nightmare passed.

Julian wasn't back by the time I'd changed her. Maybe he was just waiting for the signal that she was decent again.

"Julian?" I called out for him, and when I didn't get a reply, I checked the hallway. Empty. Del probably needed those meds sooner rather than later, right? I rushed downstairs, only to find a huge bag of what looked like medical equipment at the foot of the stairs. "Julian?"

"In here!" His voice came from the back of the house. I followed the noise of drawers banging shut to the kitchen.

"What are you looking for?"

"Found it." He waved a butter knife through the air - but instead of using it for whatever medical stuff he'd brought, he stepped up to the kitchen island where he'd already laid out bread, mustard, turkey and lettuce.

"What are you doing?"

"What does it look like?" He raised his brows at me, one side of his mouth contorting into a strange grin.

"Are you making yourself a sandwich right now? You can't be serious."

"You're right." He set the knife down.

Thank god. I knew people had strange reactions to distressing situations, but food was not a priority right now.

"I think *you* should make me a sandwich," he said. "You're the woman of the house, right? It's your kitchen."

"What?"

"I said, you should make me a sandwich." Julian reached behind his back, and my world froze. Everything zeroed in on the gun in his hands. The black metal gleamed in the kitchen lights. The gaping black hole of the barrel pointed straight at me. I shut my eyes for a moment as I forced myself to stay calm. The memory of an old familiar blood stain took shape behind my lids, but when I opened my eyes again, there was just Julian with his gun. "Chop chop."

If there was one rule engraved on my brain, it was that you didn't argue with the men holding you at gunpoint. That kind of rule became part of your very being once you saw your mother shot in the chest.

My feet somehow moved me to the kitchen counter, and I stared at the ingredients before me. I'd never even made a sandwich. What a pathetic realization to come to right now.

"What are you doing?" My voice was surprisingly steady. I started spreading the mustard on a slice of bread, hoping that was right. I really didn't want to get murdered over a sandwich.

"Just securing my investments."

"What?"

"The world only needs one Cordelia Montgomery. She'll inherit the family fortune in a few days. I'd much rather it be the Cordelia Montgomery that my little brother already has wrapped around his finger."

I swallowed, glancing up from the sandwich fillings. "You came here to kill me?"

Where was Victor? If Julian had kidnapped Del from the hospital to *secure his investment*, Victor must have realized by now that she wasn't there. He had to be on his way back.

"You're the elusive Cordelia Montgomery," Julian mused, "you're a mystery to the whole world. I figured we'd spend some *quality* time together before I shoot you."

I didn't like the way he said '*quality* time' - but at least that did buy me *some* time. It bought Victor time.

"Here." I pushed the plate with the finished sandwich across the counter at him.

"That's not how you serve food, Cordelia." He waved the gun in the direction of the dining table, and my eyes landed on my phone that I must have forgotten there at some point today. If I managed to set the plate down with one hand, and swipe the phone with the other...

I carried the sandwich past Julian, acutely aware of his steps behind me. "Where do you want to sit?"

"Right there is fine."

"Here?" I lowered the plate without turning around. My phone was just a few inches left of me. I just had to take a small step to the side, angle my body in a way that suggested I was waiting for Julian to sit, stretch my fingers a little- Julian swiped the phone off the table.

"Do you think I'm that stupid?"

I squeezed my eyes shut, but the bloody memories welling up weren't any better than the present.

"I asked you a fucking question." Julian yanked at my arm until I faced him. "Do you think I'm that stupid?"

"No, I do-" The phone smacked across my face. Copper taste exploded in my mouth. Before I could fully process that he'd just hit me with my own phone, Julian threw it on the ground and dug his heel into it. The cracked screen collapsed under his shoe.

I hadn't backed up my photos in weeks.

Another pathetic thought.

"Sit down." I let him throw me into the chair across from his, still too stunned to put up much of a fight. He had a duffel on one of the chairs and dug some thin rope from it. If he had placed his duffel there in preparation for this, he must have seen my phone. Maybe he'd even placed it there. He'd wanted me to go for it. He'd wanted a reason to hurt me.

Tears welled up and I tried to blink them away, but Julian tied my ankles to the chair tight enough to cut my skin and that just prompted more tears. He did the same to my wrists, binding them behind the chair.

"I'll go make sure the new Cordelia survives her injuries," Julian hissed. "Don't move."

He left me in the kitchen, and I let out one quick sob, just to get some of the pressure of my chest. Then inhaled deeply and tested my restraints. My toes didn't even touch the ground, and my arms wouldn't bend high enough to cross over the backrest. Ditching the chair wasn't going to work. But I just had to make it across the room.

This house was secure. As long as you didn't invite the gunman in voluntarily, it had the systems in place to keep me safe. So I just had to make it to the security system by the door and hit the silent alarm.

I wiggled my hips and shifted my shoulders to find a way of maneuvering the chair. It took me a moment, but I managed to do it without toppling over. Inch by inch.

Barely made it two feet when Julian walked back into the room, gun in hand. "Are you kidding me?"

"Would it help if I said I was just going to get us something to drink?"

Face like stone, he marched across the room to his bag and pulled out a bottle of wine. He held it up demonstratively.

"That's messed up," I said before I could stop myself. Who brought a bottle of wine to a murder?

It was the wrong reaction. Julian swung and threw the bottle across the room. It shattered against the wall, shards and wine spraying everywhere.

At least it was white wine.

God, I was messed up.

Maybe my violence threshold had just been blown to pieces sixteen years ago, but I should have been freaking out more.

Julian must have thought the same, because he stalked over and grabbed the back of my chair "I told you not to fucking move." He shoved me against the table. The tabletop rammed into chest, wrangling a pained gasp from my lips. And in that split-second of pain, he shoved his gun into my mouth.

I screamed.

I wasn't sure how or if I was even using words. All I knew was panic and adrenaline seizing my body, and I didn't want to die. I didn't want to die. *I didn't want to die.*

Julian tore the metal from mȳ mouth. The cut on my lip started bleeding again, but it barely registered. He grabbed the back of my head and smashed it forward, banging my forehead into the table just enough to stop my screams.

"This would all be a lot less painful if you cooperated," he hissed against my ear.

"Getting shot?" I mumbled, blinking against the throbbing in my temple.

"Maybe not that part. But everything that comes before." He kissed the back of my head and I winced. *Quality time.* I'd rather he shoot me outright than make me find out what exactly he meant by that.

He sank into the chair across from me and placed the gun beside his plate.

As long as he ate and talked, I was safe. Fine. One minute at a time.

"So you'll kill me, Del officially becomes Cordelia, and then what?"

He hummed a wedding tune I'd only ever heard in movies.

"You really think she'll marry Beck after you've killed me? She'd be stupid to say yes."

"She doesn't exactly strike me as very smart to begin with."

Asshole. Del was probably one of the smartest people I knew.

"You're such an idiot," I laughed, trying to lace my voice with as much contempt as I could. Julian just raised his brows while he crossed the kitchen to get himself a knife and a fork. "Even if Delilah marries your brother, *you* won't get access to the Montgomery estate."

"Well, not yet," Julian mumbled and shoveled a piece of sandwich in his mouth. "She'll pop out a child two or three years from now. And then if something were to happen to Cordelia Montgomery, her child would inherit the whole lot. Sure, the inheritance would be tied up in a trust, but who better to oversee the trust than Daddy dearest. You know, women die in childbirth all the time, right?"

I gaped at him. He'd kill Delilah. If he got her to marry Beck, she was a dead woman walking. And for what? My stupid inheritance? Hotels and money? None of that even mattered anymore. "As of Friday morning, 8am, all the assets that were tied up in the Montgomery name will be gone, Beckett. Except for my house and my personal trust, which is probably less than what you take home in a year."

"Gone? What do you mean gone? You couldn't have bankrupted your father's company in six months. You had no access to it while it was legally tied up."

"Oh no, that's the best part. Delilah was going to give a big speech at the White Ball next week. All the money is funneled into the Theresa Montgomery foundation to stop violence against women." I blew my bangs from my face, hopefully flashing the growing bump on my forehead and the drying blood on my lip. "Do you see the irony of this situation?"

"Bullshit. Nobody would be that stupid. You and that girl have been lying to everyone for weeks." He picked up his gun again, nostrils flaring. "This is just another lie, trying to weasel your way out of here, so you can crawl back to your little boytoy and pretend the world doesn't exist."

Boytoy? Victor? Where was Victor?

"Hey!" Del yelled from the backdoor right before throwing a small potted plant across the room. Instead of hitting Julian, it smashed on the floor, adding soil to the shards and wine cocktail.

Backdoor... Had she climbed out of her window?

The two of them exchanged some heated words while I still tried to figure out how Del made it from her bedroom and into the kitchen with a broken arm and god knew what other injuries.

A moment of silence fell. My breath rattled up my throat. "What happened to you?" I asked.

"Car accident." Del swallowed. "What's going on here?"

"Oh, you know. He wants to wine and dine me, rape me, kill me, and make you the only real Cordelia."

"Busy schedule, Julian, huh?"

Del saw the gun coming as much as I'd seen the phone. He whacked it at her head. In her messed-up state, Del stumbled backwards, trying and failing to catch herself on a chair and falling into the drinks cart instead. I yelled something unintelligible, and tried to bend around the side of the table, if only to be a few inches closer to Del.

Fresh blood gushed from the wound on her forehead and if she'd been pale before, she was turning sickly green now. I couldn't do this again. I couldn't have her blood on my hands. But I couldn't even throw my weight sideways enough to move the chair anymore, because Julian had lodged me against the table. I twisted my feet and flexed my shoulders. If I knew how to dislocate my joints to get out of these restraints, I would pull my bones apart, just to stop Julian from hurting her.

"Go back to your room Delilah. Beck will come check on you in the morning. At least we can now all stop pretending."

"Pretending?" She stuttered.

"Oh dear, you really are as blonde as you look, huh?"

I saw Beck behind his brother a moment before the others spotted him, his eyes torn wide as he took in the scene. "Julian, what the fuck?"

The two of them argued. Then all three of them argued. I barely paid attention, my eyes solely on Del. The cut on her forehead didn't stop bleeding. She was barely staying upright. Somehow, she made it across the room to me, grabbing my hands behind the chair. I tightened my fingers around hers as fast as I could. Beck wanted to get her to a hospital. That was good. He could get her out of here. Keep her safe. At least for now. She folded over and threw up at one point, but it wasn't much, mostly bile - and in the grand scheme of things, that seemed like an easy fix.

I didn't click back into the conversation until the name Yelchin dropped.

If Victor wasn't here by now, they had something to do with it. He'd been perfectly safe from his family for five and a half years, and they weren't going to screw that up for him.

"Leave Victor out of this," I hissed. "You want my name? You can have it. I'll marry either one of you right now."

"Too late." Julian shrugged. "His family picked him up right after he got Delilah released from the hospital for me. He really thought he was hiding, huh? They only let him stay here for this long because they knew how valuable of an asset *you* were. It cost me quite a bit to get them to pull him off, but he was just never going to leave your side."

No, no, no. Julian couldn't have just sold him out.

Five and a half years.

He was happy here.

They were going to kill him.

He was supposed to be with me.

"We're leaving," Beck said.

"I'm not going anywhere without Cordelia," Del gasped, "and I'm not going anywhere with you." I squeezed her hand behind my back for reassurance. I mumbled something about going to the hospital with Beck, but it was lost in their back and forth.

"Fuck, Julian, at least get a first aid kit before she loses any more blood."

"Jesus fuck. Always so dramatic. She'll live. You don't need her to be fully functioning to marry her," Julian grunted. She didn't have to be *fully functioning*? What kind of fucked-up did you have to be to think like that?

I barely heard the three muffled *pops*. The bullets thumping into Julian's body were louder than the shots actually being fired.

His body jerked around them, but he silently fell to the ground, no scream, not so much as a grunt. And in the blink of an eye the man who wanted to kill me at the dinner table turned into a dead body on my kitchen floor.

"He sure likes the sound of his own voice."

I liked the sound of *that* voice. Every muscle in my body relaxed. Each taut nerve loosened.

"Victor," I gasped.

"See? This is what happens when you start messing with my family." He stepped through the open backdoor and tossed his gun with the silencer onto the side table before walking towards us. He gave Beck and Del a quick once over as he worked the ties around my wrists. One thumb calmly circled the inside of my palm. "Delilah, you look like shit."

"Thanks," she breathed.

"Let's get you out of here, Blondie," Beck said and tried to grab a hold of her.

She slapped him with more strength than I would have expected from her in this condition. "I told you to stop touching me."

"Cordelia?" Victor asked the second my wrists came free.

"I'm fine," I reassured him, eyes on Del's trembling frame.

"I'll take Del," Victor said and bent down to let Del wrap her arms around him for support, "clean up your mess, Beckett."

CHAPTER THREE

Cordelia

"I'm not sure about this anymore," I sighed.

This didn't look romantic.

The swirly font on the box of pastel macarons was mocking me. I'd meant for it to look Pinterest-worthy, laid out on the bed with some flowers and a handwritten note. Instead, the box was dwarfed by the expanse of the mattress and washed out by the bouquet of colorful dahlias.

I wasn't good at gifts.

I'd never gotten a chance to get good at gifts.

My father had been too rich to need anything, and not senti-mental enough to appreciate the things he couldn't buy himself. So, now I stared at what was meant to be an engagement present, and the plushie on Delilah's bed stared right back, judging me for my choices.

I glanced over my shoulder at Victor, who still held the massive box the flowers had been delivered in. The white and silver packaging was a stark contrast to his ink-covered hands.

He quietly raised his brows as if to ask: *What's wrong?*

I grimaced at my pathetic attempt at gift-giving. I should have just gotten them something useful. A washing machine maybe. Then again, we had a housekeeper, so Del and I weren't even doing our own laundry. Even once she'd move in with Beck, I doubted he handled his own laundry. Plus, he probably had a state-of-the-art washing machine anyway...

Maybe a new laptop, so Del could stop using that thing that made more noise than a jet engine. Then again, that wasn't really a couple's gift.

A dozen other present ideas raced through my mind, alongside all the reasons why they didn't work.

I could have at least added a travel voucher for them to go to Paris, so the macarons would have made more sense. City of love and all that. But Axent, Beck's company, probably ran half a dozen hotels in Paris and he had a private plane. So what would they use a voucher for? Disneyland? I couldn't imagine Beck wrinkling one of his crisp suits on Hyperspace Mountain.

"Do you think Beck would voluntarily ride a rollercoaster?"

"If Del asks," Victor replied without missing a beat, but his eyelids twitched *just so*, and his pupils zeroed in on the macarons. I'd skipped a few thoughts ahead and he was trying to piece them together.

I didn't even bother explaining, because Beck and Del were about to land in Boston after just having spent a week in England. They were hardly going to jet off again just to ride a rollercoaster and meet Cinderella.

"It's good," Victor said after a moment of silence.

I turned around to face him fully, and this time his undivided attention was on me. He gave me a small nod to reiterate his words. Victor didn't talk much unless he needed to. And over the last few years, he needed to less and less, as I understood even this small affirming tilt of his chin, and it eased some of the tension in my chest.

"She won't hate it, right? She won't think I'm a bad friend for just getting her glorified French cookies? She won't think I'm a bad roommate because I just barged into her room?" This stupid tremor in my confidence wasn't new but it had lain dormant for a while. I'd never been good at maintaining any sort of friendship. Even as a little kid. But I also hadn't *wanted* to keep a friendship for over a decade. Now that I did, the worries were back.

"It's good," he repeated.

"They are very good macarons," I said, more to convince myself than him.

"Let's go eat something."

"Good idea."

Eating something was more than just a quick snack. *Eating something* was Victor whipping up cheesy chicken pasta and setting my afternoon meds out on the counter for me. Protein and Adderall. *Eating something* meant feeding my body the chemicals it needed to slow my thoughts and, by extension, ease the anxious ones.

Before I could actually eat something, my computer chimed in the next room. That was my sign that my lunch break was over. I had spent most of it on Del's present. I could technically set my own hours, but I had a meeting to get to.

"I'll have to eat later," I said.

Victor pulled an unimpressed brow at me, but didn't say anything when I sprinted from the kitchen to silence the incessant ringing in my office. Fitzi blinked at me from his spot on the windowsill before turning back around to watch the street. When Del had moved in last year, she had brought the fluffy gray cat with her. More often than not, he followed me around like a shadow when Del was out.

"What's so interesting out there, huh?" I asked as I dropped into my chair. I glanced past his huge body at the gray skies, wet pavements, and the leafless magnolia in front of my house. It usually provided a nice extra bit of privacy. My spine stiffened as a passerby looked up at my windows, even though I was hardly visible from here. Maybe I should look into planting an evergreen out there instead.

My computer started chiming again, ripping me from my tumbling thoughts. I clicked on the scheduled meeting. Monica's face filled my screen, a second later Amani's camera came to life, too. I closed the preview of my own webcam. As much as I was getting better at letting others into my house, physically or digitally, I didn't want the visual reminder.

"Good morning, ladies," Amani sing-sang.

Her chipper voice immediately brought a smile to my lips. "Good afternoon," I brought a window for meeting notes up on the side of the screen, "how's the west coast?"

"The absolute west." She drummed her fingers against her keyboard. "Badum-Tss."

Monica just chuckled and slightly shook her head. Amani was 28 years old, overflowing with confidence and positive energy, and ran our small marketing and comms team. Monica was the opposite. She had been working for various charities, boots-on-the-ground, for almost forty years. If there was a practical problem, she was the one we turned to. As the founder of the Theresa Montgomery foundation, I was responsible for all the executive decisions. There was a much bigger team behind the foundation, but these Friday meetings were just us.

"Define *professional*," I said a few minutes into the meeting after Amani had announced that she needed a professional photograph of me for the website.

"Not taken on someone's phone *and* taken by someone who has some sort of professional experience behind the camera."

I grimaced.

"Do you want me to find you a photographer?" Monica asked,

not voicing what she actually meant. A safe photographer. A discreet photographer. Someone in and out of my house in ten minutes.

I had no doubts that she could find one, or even had a few in her old rolodex, but she wasn't meant to spend her time and resources on assisting me. "No, I'll manage," I said, "thank you."

"I wouldn't ask if it wasn't important. I'm sorry," Amani said, "but people don't trust us enough. At least not the ones we need to reach, the ones who aren't chronically online and don't follow the high society pages. They hear *Montgomery*, and they think of your father. And I'm sorry, but your father sucked. I saw that interview from 2002, where he..."

My attention drifted away from my screen to Victor filling the doorframe to my office, all height and muscle, holding a small tray. He raised his brows as if to ask for permission and I gave it to him with a small nod.

Victor knew exactly how the camera was angled and kept himself safely out of the picture when he placed my lunch on a stack of folders on my desk.

"Thank you," I mouthed.

"Is that Victor? Hi Victor," Amani cooed. She liked to call him my ghost, because she never saw him, and things just appeared out of thin air for me.

"Amani," Victor acknowledged while collecting various mugs off my desk.

"God, I love his strong and manly voice," she sighed, "wait, can he say my name again? I want to record it."

Victor just raised his brows at me and I replied with a shrug. "Up to you."

His shoulders rose and sagged in a silent sigh before he nodded.

"Amani, queue up your voice recorder."

"Oh my god, this is happening. Okay." She fumbled around on her computer, a huge grin splitting her face. "Okay, go."

Victor looked at me, his eyes so focused, my lungs constricted and the air spasmed from my chest.

"Amani," he said, voice dropped to a low rumble.

"Goosebumps!" Amani shrieked from inside my computer.

I didn't break eye contact with Victor though. Something thick hung in the air between us and maybe, just maybe, if I looked at him long enough, it would crystalize. It would turn into a truth. Something we could both acknowledge.

Because another woman had just declared her preference for his voice. Because she liked the way he said her name. Because he had said it again when she'd asked him to.

It was nothing.

A miniscule favor.

Silly.

And yet, I still couldn't force the air back into my lungs.

"If he ever wants to join the team, he could totally do some voice overs for our social media," Amani said on the other side of the screen.

I looked away. And oxygen flooded back into the room when Victor turned his back.

"He has a full-time job," I whispered, voice breathless.

"If we're talking about hiring people, I have some actual requests," Monica finally chimed in, and I had never been more grateful for her hands-on attitude. I okayed whatever new hires she suggested over the rest of the meeting, and probably agreed to a few more requests I than I should have, but my thoughts were swimming away from me.

For once, I doubted even the ADHD meds could have caught them or slowed them down.

Victor had never shown even an ounce of interest in anyone. Amani... He had only ever acknowledged her in my meetings. They hadn't spoken more than three sentences at a time to each other. He couldn't actually be interested in Amani, could he?

It would have been far easier to convince myself that he was just being polite if Victor had ever been polite. Del had waltzed into our lives, and I'd had to constantly remind him to dial down the hostility, even if she eventually grew on him.

Amani *was* pretty. She had light brown skin with warm olive undertones, and her hair was dyed silver gray. She also sported about as many piercings as Victor did tattoos, so that probably meant their tastes matched.

I spent the rest of the afternoon staring at the plate of chicken pasta. I couldn't eat a single bite. A strange kind of nausea nested at the bottom of my ribcage, chewing at my insides, and coating my tongue in a bitter taste. Maybe I was getting sick.

CHAPTER FOUR

VICTOR

Once upon a time I had planned to lay low at Cordelia's place for a few weeks until my chance to get out of the country cleared up. Now, however, my skin was crawling at the thought of leaving even if only for a few hours.

"Are you sure?" I asked for the third time in about fifteen minutes.

"Go," Cordelia rolled her eyes at the snack bowls she was meticulously arranging on the sofa table, "they'll be home soon."

I didn't mind leaving her alone with Delilah. Beckett was the problem. He may have been putting on the 'changed man' act for a few months, but he was still the same calculating son of a bitch who had planned to marry Del-as-Cordelia, and stick Cordelia in a glorified rubber cell in Switzerland for the rest of her life. Leopards didn't change their spots. I was proof of that. May have pretended

25

to be a house cat for a few years, but I'd fallen right back in with the pack of predators.

"The rest of the chicken pasta is in the fridge, and there's soup in the freezer."

"We're ordering bubble waffles," Cordelia said.

"Just in case you crave real food." Between the table-load of sugar in front of her and those dinner plans... How that woman hadn't died from scurvy before I had started cooking for her was beyond me.

She still didn't look up from the snacks, only making a shooing motion in my direction. She hadn't looked me in the eyes all afternoon. Cordelia didn't know where I was off to, but she was getting better at not overthinking it when I wasn't here after dark. Clearly, it still bothered her though.

When I'd taken this job, I'd known it wasn't a regular security position. I'd known I'd move into this house and spend almost every hour of every day here. And with each month that had passed, I'd looked over my shoulder less and less. It had been good. Even when Cordelia had bought the house next door for me to have my own space, I only ever left here after she went to bed, and I was back before she got up.

I may have craved the comfort of disappearing from the world, but Cordelia *needed* her safe haven.

"I'll try to make it quick," I said by way of goodbye, and she just waved me off. For all the ease in her wrist, her shoulders and neck were stiff as stone. She was a shitty liar even if she didn't say anything.

I didn't like leaving her alone. I didn't like leaving her - *period*. I wasn't sure when that had started. Being by her side had become part of me over the years. Cordelia had become part of me. At least when I was with her, I could usually make sure that she was safe.

Tonight, however, leaving her was going to keep her safe.

THE COLD DRIZZLE DID NOTHING TO MAKE THE ORANGE glow of the restaurant's windows look more inviting. I would have gladly stayed on the dark sidewalk across the street all night, getting soaked to the bone. Not that I had that option.

I didn't spare Luka more than a glance when he jogged over from the restaurant with his collar pulled up.

"You're late," he bit out.

"I'm here, aren't I?" I narrowed my eyes at the windows again, but I couldn't spot Petya from here. He'd chosen the same restaurant where we'd discussed my path forward after my injury six years ago. No doubt, he'd also be sitting at the same table in the back. Just to make a point. I'd never *truly* left. I was exactly where I'd been back then.

"You're going to get us killed on your first day. Is that the plan?"

"I'm here," I repeated and crossed the street with him, not ready for more conversation than need be.

I hadn't seen or spoken to my cousin in six years, but he had been the only one who knew I'd hidden with Cordelia. I had trusted him. Last August, it turned out, the rest of my family had been well aware of my whereabouts. *My uncle* had been well aware. He'd just been biding his time until my position with Cordelia would become useful: Once Cordelia's father died and she'd inherit a massive fortune. While Cordelia had decided to put her inheritance into charity, diminishing her usefulness, the fact of the matter remained. My uncle had known where I was, and only Luka could have told him.

It wasn't until we were inside and Luka threw his jacket and scarf over the coat stand, that I got a good look at him. We shared enough features to be mistaken for brothers, light skin, green eyes, sharply angled jaw, brown hair, both trimmed short. But where my tattoos reached up to my chin, his skin was ink-free. He'd collected a few scars though. One through his right brow, and a long jagged one from his ear down his neck. He'd also beefed-up, no longer the spindly 24-year-old he'd been six years ago.

"Come on," he muttered.

Petya sat with his back to the door. Another point made. He could turn his back to me and know that I wouldn't put a bullet through his skull. If Luka wouldn't stop me, the two men standing at the back wall, their guns not even hidden, would.

"Sit down, Vitya. Eat."

Hearing his dark graveled voice, scratched up from years of smoking cigars, should have irked me. I'd gone six years without that voice in my ear. I should have been upset. I should have had some sort of reaction to it.

The fact that I didn't just proved that I had never truly left.

I wordlessly sat down at the round table with Luka, and started cutting into the steak already waiting for me. He was literally handing me a knife sharp enough to kill him with, knowing I wouldn't. We sat there for a few minutes, eating. Fucking family dinner. At some point, a waitress came and sat down a glass of red wine in front of me. I had no doubt that it was old, expensive, and chosen specifically to pair with the meat.

"I'm glad to see you didn't let yourself go on your little sabbatical," Petya said when he reached for his own drink.

I just raised my brows in response. A little sabbatical. As if I was *eat, pray, loving* it up for six years.

"That will make your comeback a lot easier," he said with a bright smile while shoving another piece of rare meat in his mouth.

I'd expected as much.

Comeback.

The word still hammered home everything else tonight was supposed to remind me of. I had never left. There was no way out.

My parents were proof that the only way out of the family was in a body bag.

Comeback.

It was the only reason he'd left me alone for months. The UFC didn't have regular seasons, but when other sports went quiet in spring, things got a lot more heated in the octagon. People who didn't care about MMA suddenly tuned in, desperate to watch *something*. Spring meant big weekend events. It meant cards filled with the best fighters in the world. It meant a *comeback* would be a spectacle.

The NFL had just wrapped up two weeks ago. NHL and NBA would follow over the next two months.

He would want to wait. Start the rumor mill.

May. Possibly June. I had no more than three months to get back into fighting shape.

"Let me be very clear, son," Petya said when I didn't react to his little announcement.

I cut him off. "I'm not your son."

"You're family."

Debatable. Petya was my blood. He wasn't truly family.

"You want me back in the ring," I said, just to show that I knew exactly what he brought me here for.

"I don't *want*. I'm telling you that you will be back in the ring."

"Okay."

"Don't pull that face." He kissed his teeth in disdain.

"I said okay." I wasn't pulling a face. Schooling your features was one of the first lessons you picked up when you had Pyotr Yelchin for an uncle. My eyelids didn't so much as twitch if I didn't want them to.

"You can go in the ring, or I can find a position for you that would require a change to your living arrangements. Is that what you want, son?"

We both knew that wasn't a real question. We both knew it

was phrased perfectly to hide the threat. My living arrangements included Cordelia. They hinged on Cordelia. She was the very reason I sat a few feet from the man who continued ruining my life, holding a knife sharp enough to slit his throat, and I was going to follow his every command like a fucking lapdog. I wouldn't let him take more people from me.

"I said okay," I repeated.

"Good." Petya turned back to his steak. "Now eat."

I ate.

"I'll be your middleman," Luka said outside, after our dinner during which Petya had caught me up on his wife's new interest in dog shows and their three yappy chihuahuas.

"You mean babysitter," I corrected him.

"You know how it works."

"So you're not driving anymore?"

"No," he said and lit a cigarette. He took a deep drag before tapping the side of his neck with the scar. "Can't turn my head far enough anymore."

"Your father knows I won't make it past the year, right? My brain is a ticking time bomb."

"Yeah."

"Fuck." Petya was running his investments into the ground one after another.

He had revolutionized the east coast business. Our side of organized crime had flourished for many years because unlike the Italians, we hadn't closed the ranks to outsiders. That meant tech geniuses, engineers and hackers put us on the global map. The problem with outsiders, however, was that their loyalty could be bought.

So Petya had borrowed an idea from the Italians. He kept things in the family. He just made sure every single one of us had a designated role as soon as we showed any kind of talent.

I'd been seven when he'd realized that I had a mean right hook and took a beating better than the other boys in our family.

Around the same time, Luka rode his tricycle off the roof and into the pool.

So while Luka learned to drive like he was in a Fast & Furious movie, I was put in the ring.

It never hurt to have professional athletes in the family. Trafficking high-profile criminals from country to country was a lot easier if they were part of an international champion's entourage. I'd once traveled with a 5-person-team of drug lords posing as my massage therapist, my social media manager, my personal chef, my trainer and manager. - The upper hand in the gambling halls was a nice bonus.

"Care to tell me why I need to make a comeback?" I asked. "Smuggling something? Someone?"

"I don't know," Luka said.

"I can't tell if you're lying to me anymore."

Luka huffed out a laugh. "You've never been able to tell. I just let you think so because we're brothers."

"No, we're not," I said and left him outside the restaurant.

IT WOULD HAVE BEEN COMPLETELY REASONABLE TO GO to my place after that dinner. I could have taken a shower to wash the steak house stench off and hit the bed. I would wait until breakfast to calmly talk Cordelia through what my uncle's presence in my life meant for her.

I wasn't reasonable when it came to Cordelia.

Three locks and one electronic pass code let me inside her house, which was way too quiet and way too dark. Blue light was flickering from the TV room but there was no excited chatter, which would have indicated Delilah being with Cordelia - and there was no noise upstairs, which would have indicated Delilah and Beckett having gone to bed.

The meeting with my uncle had my nerves on high alert, and I quieted my steps as I walked down the hallway to check the other rooms for signs of life. By the time I made it to the TV room, I was mentally prepared for the worst. Instead, Cordelia lay on her back on the sofa, swiping on her phone with one hand, while the other was deep in a bowl of gummy bears. Some nature documentary was running in the background. She tended to listen, not watch.

The tension drained from my shoulders, and I sighed.

"What are you doing?" I asked.

She wasn't surprised by my sudden appearance, merely propping herself up on her elbows. "I was waiting for you, silly." If the empty bottle of rosé on the table hadn't given her away, the lilt in her words would have.

"Did you drink that by yourself?" I asked, narrowing my eyes at the empty wine glass.

"Yeah," she breathed and shot off the sofa, rearranging her snack bowls to hide the mostly empty gummy bear one, "Del called. They went straight to Beck's because Brody's sick. She didn't want to stay with her friend."

Whenever Brody's name came up, my stomach curled with guilt. I'd shot the man that had hurt Cordelia and threatened her life. Julian Beckett. Beck's brother. Brody's father. I would shoot him a hundred times over to keep Cordelia safe without feeling guilty, but I had turned that girl into an orphan, leaving her in the care of her uncle. That came with its own kind of guilt, and it hit too close to home.

After tonight, this was just another reminder that my actions would always take a toll on Cordelia. If Brody still had a father, Cordelia wouldn't have been alone tonight.

Sure, it was only a matter of time before Delilah officially moved in with her fiancé, but tonight... Tonight, she would have been here if it hadn't been for my actions.

"This goes in the kitchen," Cordelia mumbled, swinging the

empty bottle and glass around. Her lean body was swaying dangerously.

"Here." I reached for it before she'd fall and hurt herself.

"I need to sit down," she announced the second I'd taken the things from her, and belly-flopped onto the sofa.

Alright. Any discussion about my uncle's plans for me was tabled for tonight. I set down the bottle and glass, and walked around the sofa to kneel down in front of the 5'10" blonde mess that had gone all limp. "Feel sick?" I plucked some of the platinum strands from her face. "Need to throw up?"

"Nope," she sighed in my face. Her breath was sugary sweet from the rosé. "Just tired. Did you know gray wolves mate for life?"

"I didn't."

"It was on TV." One of her arms shot out to point at the flat screen, and I ducked to avoid being punched in the face. "They have six babies every year though."

"That sounds exhausting," I said. I'd figured out a long time ago that it was easier to jump on Cordelia's train of thought rather than trying to keep her attention on the conversation you thought you were having.

"Right?" She pulled her arm back but instead of tucking it back against her side, she wrapped her hand around my shoulder. "Bed?"

"Sure."

"Not together," she quickly shot out, "alone. You have your own bed."

"I got that." I didn't make much of the comment. If I had to guess, she got there from thinking about gray wolves making wolf babies. Instead, I focused on getting her to her feet, steadying her with both hands on her waist.

"Okay." She stretched out both arms for balance as if the living room floor was a tightrope. She still wobbled.

"Cordelia?" I asked. One word and I'd carry her upstairs. This was hardly the first time I'd seen her drunk, and it wouldn't have been the first time I'd have to carry her.

"I can do it." For the first time all afternoon, her eyes snapped up to meet mine. Her glacial gaze suddenly focused on me with enough clarity to freeze me in place. "I can do whatever I want. I'm in total and full control." She wrapped her arms around my neck and before I was able to process her actions, she pressed her lips against mine.

For a short moment, my body reacted of its own accord. I bent to her, her sweet taste and soft mouth clouding all judgment. My hands tightened around her waist, fingertips digging into her curves. I pulled her closer until her body was flush with mine and her warmth seeped into me. My tongue met hers. Every muscle that had been wrought tight for the last few hours, every alert nerve, eased into the kiss where the only thing that mattered was *more*. *More* of her taste, *more* of her warmth, *more* of her body. I was desperate for *more* and she gave it.

She let out a low moan and my momentary illusion shattered.

This was Cordelia.

Cordelia.

I tilted my chin down, breaking the kiss. I left it down even when her small whimper of protest tugged at my instincts to give her what she craved.

"You're drunk," I breathed and shook my head. Despite my words, I was unable to ease my grasp, to put any distance between us. I knew how wrong it was, but I *had* her.

"I want to." Her arms tightened around my neck as she pulled herself up. She kissed me again, but this time I remained still. Her hungry mouth crashed over my tightened lips. It was the only rejection I could muster up. I would have liked nothing more than to grab fistfuls of her golden hair and kiss her until those pouty lips were red and swollen.

"Oh." Cordelia fell back, rocking on her heels. As she did, my hands finally eased, only able to let go when it was her decision. Cordelia's lids fluttered rapidly as tears sprung up.

"Let's get you to bed." I swallowed around the knot in my throat.

"I can do it." She twisted away from me and stumbled around the sofa. Her steps were clumsy and she steadied herself by the furniture she passed.

"Cordelia, wait." I stepped towards her, but when I did, she immediately stepped backwards and her body swayed enough to almost tip. So I stayed put and waited for her to catch herself against the console table.

"Good night," she gasped, breath rattling.

This was wrong. I was supposed to help her and get her upstairs safely.

I wasn't the one she pulled away from.

I wasn't the one she kissed. At least I hadn't been in years.

God help me, because a few seconds of her mouth on mine and Cordelia Montgomery had obliterated six years of keeping a sensible distance. Back then, it had been easy to revert to sensible. I'd barely known her. Now I sometimes understood her thoughts better than my own, chopped vegetables small enough to hide them from her, could draw the exact shape of the birthmark on her left shoulder, and I just wanted to keep kissing her.

CHAPTER FIVE

Cordelia

I was hiding under my blanket. Couldn't face the consequences of my own actions if I just stayed here, right? Fitzi had curled his fluffy warm body against me, and I selfishly told myself that moving would just wake and upset him. I was perfectly justified in hiding for however long he wanted to nap.

I'd started googling how to act after kissing someone you shouldn't have kissed, but the results had been bordering on extremely creepy, so I'd switched to adding cat toys to my ever-growing shopping basket. Couldn't face Victor if I just spent the day online shopping.

My coward's plan was diminished by a knock on my bedroom door.

"Breakfast."

Nope. That very much was Victor. Who I shouldn't have

drunkenly kissed. The handle clicked, but the door remained locked. I inwardly thanked my drunk self for being that proactive.

"Cordelia?"

"One second," I squeaked and pushed my covers off. I didn't even know what I looked like. I'd just fallen into bed with half my clothes on, not bothering with makeup remover. It shouldn't have mattered because Victor had seen it all. The good, the bad, the ugliest. But it mattered because I'd kissed him. And then I'd kissed him again after he'd pulled back. I'd drunkenly thought he'd been kissing me back. That he'd liked it. But he'd set clear boundaries and I'd blown through them. I was so, so stupid.

I grabbed my pillow, pressed it over my face and groaned into it, unable to contain my frustration.

"Are you alright?" His voice was muffled by door and down feathers.

I tossed the pillow aside and grabbed my dressing gown from my bedpost to cover my state of half-dress. Victor waited outside the door, holding a tray with a breakfast waffle and painkillers.

Still being considerate after I had been the most inconsiderate mess last night.

"You didn't have to bring that upstairs," I croaked and opened the door a little wider.

His eyes roamed over my body and I tugged on the ends of my belt, just to double-check the robe was closed tight. He wordlessly placed the tray on my vanity table, his eyes never leaving me. I knew what he was doing. He always scanned me head-to-toe like I was hiding injuries from him. But for once, that felt like too much attention, when I just wanted to crawl back under the covers.

"When did you get home last night?" I asked, the question over my lips before I thought it through.

His brows jumped up as if to say *'Is that how you want to play it?'*

We stared at each other for a long moment before I finally lifted my shoulders, too much of a chicken to speak.

"Around eleven," he said.

"Is everything... did you... good night?" Queen of word vomit. Right here. *Hand me a crown and call me Your Majesty.* I wasn't even sure what I was asking. I'd messed up so much.

After that dumb call with Amani, I hadn't even been able to look at Victor, too scared of seeing a spring in his step or a lovey-dovey smile on his lips. And when he'd told me he'd be out all night, I had been too scared to ask. What if he had a date? What if, through some weird roundabout way, he and Amani had actually connected and had scheduled a Facetime date? I couldn't actually picture Victor on a Facetime date, but my brain had convinced me that he was pulling away for someone else. And then he had *physically* pulled away when I'd thrown myself at him.

"Cordelia?"

"Hmm? Sorry." I blinked and shook my head. Last night's alcohol didn't help with the racing thoughts.

"I said, it will be alright."

"Alright?" My chest expanded a little more in the hope that he was saying what I *thought* he was saying, but I couldn't force a smile.

"Alright," Victor confirmed.

Despite that reassurance, I was as good as useless that day. I tried to distract myself by researching photographers in Boston who could handle discreet jobs. Which led down a rabbit hole of boudoir photography, then maternity photo shoots, and finally wedding pictures - at which point I shut my computer down because there was too much kissing on my screen.

I spent about an hour staring out my office window, because I couldn't bring myself to leave the room. Victor was out there. As long as my office door remained shut, he stayed outside. At least Fitzwilliam was still glued to my side, curling up in my lap while I counted the steps outside every town house I could see from here. It wasn't a good distraction, but it kept me busy until a familiar car pulled up on the street.

I shot out of my chair and waited behind my office door until I heard her shuffling inside.

Once I was sure Del was within reach, I yanked the office door open. She jumped and stared at me with wide eyes. "What the hell?"

I just grabbed her and pulled her inside. Fast enough for her bag to drop to the floor.

"Sorry," I hissed and shut the door, flattening my back against it just to be safe.

"What's happening?" Del blinked, turning in a circle, eyes roaming over the room like an actual threat might jump out from the shadows. She was short and dainty, but she'd been going to the gym more, and her stance looked somewhat ready to kick a wannabe-intruder's ass. Or at least try.

"Sorry," I said again, "but I had to catch you. I need to talk to someone."

"Oh. I'm not staying. I didn't even properly park the car. I'm just grabbing some clothes."

Right. I inhaled, and mentally recounted everything that had been going on for her. Engagement trip to London, followed by taking care of a sick teenager. "How is Brody?"

"Better, but not by much. My last pair of clean pants was in the projectile vomit zone, so..." She gestured vaguely at her legs, covered by a pair of very loose, very green training pants that bunched around her ankles. Probably Brody's if I had to guess. She also wore a wrinkled T-shirt and had fumbled her warm blonde hair into a stubby ponytail. She really didn't look like she meant to leave the house today.

I had to be an even bigger mess than I'd thought, because I egotistically asked: "Do you have like five minutes?"

My face must have betrayed me, because Del's brows furrowed and she sank into one of the armchairs by the window. Fitzwilliam hissed at her for coming too close to his windowsill spot, but she just crinkled her nose at her cat before turning back to me. "What's wrong?"

"Everything." My knees suddenly felt too spongy to support my weight, my spine too brittle to keep me upright, and I let myself slide down against the door. "I kissed Victor."

"I know."

"You know?" I wrought my hands in front of me, then shook them out, then ran them through my hair.

"You know that I know. We talked about this."

"No, not six years ago," I whined, "last night."

"Oh. Wow." Del's eyes widened. "Based on your tone, I'm assuming it wasn't good."

It was good. Oh god, that first kiss. I was struggling not to mentally replay it again and again. When his fingers dug into my waist and his lips collided with mine and his tongue swept past my teeth. But he pulled away. The second kiss was the catastrophe. "I pretended it didn't happen."

"You jumped ahead. Context please."

"Right, so, I was a little tipsy. I kissed him. And the first kiss was great, I think. But then he got all serious and told me I was drunk, and when I tried to kiss him again, he was stiff as a statue and told me to go to bed."

"Did you only kiss him because you were drunk?" She narrowed her eyes. "Tabitha gets really horny when she's drunk."

"Yes, I did, but not like that. Not in a silly drunk hookup way." I brushed my hair forward until it hid my face, and when that wasn't enough, I folded my hands over my eyes and wished I could crawl back into bed. "It's so complicated. We can't even... I mean, he's my... and I'm his... and after everything..." I struggled to find the words to describe the knot of emotions in my chest.

I heard some rustling and quiet steps on the floorboards before I felt Del lowering herself next to me. Her thigh pressed against mine. "Why did you kiss him?" she asked quietly.

"It's like the wine just dissolved my better judgment," I mumbled, "and I just did what I want to do when I'm sober."

There it was. The stupid little truth. Out in the open.

I wanted to kiss Victor.

The reason I felt sick when he said Amani's name in that low, spine-tingling way. The reason I couldn't look him in the eye when I thought he might have a date.

"I get that. Alcohol does momentarily help with my social anxiety," Del just said without acknowledging how big and stupid and impossible the idea of kissing Victor was.

"And this morning, I pretended like I didn't remember."

"Did he actually buy that? Victor's usually not that easily fooled."

"Oh, he definitely didn't, but he went with it."

"I see." She hummed.

"I'm so stupid."

"Hey, you are one of the smartest people I know." Delilah delicately plucked my hands away from my face and fumbled with my hair to separate long strands from bangs. "You just did something a little stupid."

"Maybe he has a girlfriend."

"I think we'd know if he had a girlfriend," she scoffed, "he spends most of his time five feet away from you."

"It could be a long-term, long-distance, low-commitment casual kind of girlfriend."

"Cordelia," Del sighed, "I know this is the pot calling the kettle black, but spiraling isn't going to help in any way. You actually have to talk to Victor. Have a healthy conversation."

"I can't. What if he leaves? What if he quits? The second kiss... He clearly didn't want that second kiss. And, on top of that, I'm his employer. Oh gosh, I didn't even think of that up until now. I'm his actual employer, Del."

"You two kissed before, right? He didn't leave then."

"That was different."

"Why?"

"He was *meant* to leave then. He wasn't meant to be permanent."

Del's phone buzzed in her pocket and she leaned back, quickly declined the call, then looked at me again. I'd still caught Beck's caller ID on the screen. She was here instead of caring for her future step-daughter... step-niece... step-Brody. First I made sure to destroy my relationship with Victor, and now I was so self-centered, I'd be pushing Del away, too. "Look-" she said.

"You should go. I'm keeping you."

"Cordelia, listen to me," Del narrowed her eyes at the ceiling while rubbing her thumb over the back of her hand, clearly about to break some very uncomfortable truth to me, "as someone who has been subjected to unwanted physical advances by their boss, I think you need to talk. There's a chance Victor truly didn't want anything to happen. If that's the case, you need to apologize. You can't pretend the power imbalance away. You are literally the reason he has a roof over his head." She sighed. " Knowing your history, however, I think he meant exactly what he said. You were drunk. He might feel like he would have taken advantage of you if he had acted on the kiss."

"Can't I just send him an apology gift basket?"

She leveled me with a cold glare. "Are you serious?"

"Maybe." Not really. I still sucked at presents. Del hadn't even gotten to her pathetic macarons yet. And the flowers had probably wilted overnight.

"Do you need me to stay? I'm not sure whether this is the kind of situation where I should stay and comfort you - or tell you to just go talk to Victor."

"It's fine. You don't have to stay."

"Are you sure?"

"Yes." I shuffled away from the doorway but stayed rooted to the floor, leaning against my desk instead. "One last question."

"Yes?" Del tucked and pulled her too-large pants into place as she got off the floor.

"When you marry Beck, does that make you Brody's step-mother?"

"Uuh." Del blinked, not quite as used to my skipping thoughts as Victor was. "No, not really. Beck will never replace her dad. We're just her guardians, I guess. The people responsible for her well-being."

"Okay. Sorry for keeping you. Go." I waved her off.

"I'm sorry that I can't stay. I'll call you later, okay?"

The second she was through the door, I pulled a strand of hair to my chest, wrapping it around my fingers. If Beck wasn't taking his brother's place, and Del wasn't Brody's step-mother, that meant my actions had turned the girl into an orphan.

I had been the one encouraging Del to connect with Beck when she'd been working as my body double. I had been the one who opened the door for his brother Julian. I had been the one too stupid to realize his intentions, too weak to fight back, too absorbed in myself to realize that Victor may have done his job by shooting Julian, but he'd also cost a teenage girl her family.

Like I hadn't gone through the exact same thing.

I was ruining lives left, right and center.

CHAPTER SIX

Cordelia

THE REST OF THE WEEKEND PASSED IN A BLUR, AND I thankfully barely saw Victor. I avoided the kitchen when I knew he was making food, and our entire conversation on Sunday consisted of two texts:

VICTOR • 08:42AM

Basement

Translation: *If I needed him, he was downstairs, either in the gym or the pool.*

CORDELIA • 08:45AM

Winter Garden

Translation: *I decided to put on one nature documentary after another to keep my thoughts far, far away from the fact that I kissed you. I'll be repotting my plants for the rest of the weekend to keep my hands busy. Please don't interrupt me. I would die of shame if you so much as looked at me.*

I wasn't quite sure he got the entire meaning behind my two words, but he didn't seek me out either.

THEN ON MONDAY MORNING, I WOKE UP TO A TEXT message that both relieved some of the pressure on my chest, while it simultaneously restored Friday's sour dread in the pit of my stomach. Was that jealousy?

VICTOR • 07:29AM

Errands. Smoothies in fridge. Back for dinner.

Maybe *Errands* was the name of his long-term, long-distance, low-commitment casual girlfriend.

Sitting on my office floor with a banana chocolate smoothie, I stared at the little blue button on my laptop screen. I just had to click that and I'd know exactly where Victor was running errands. Technically, he was on the clock, so it was well within my right. But it was a huge infringement of privacy. I'd already kissed him against his will. I couldn't turn into a full obsessed stalker now.

Amani had pinged me about the photograph for the website, and a wave of acid had swept up my insides at her gorgeous smiling profile picture. So instead of looking for a photographer, I had brought up the app that let me track Victor's phone.

This was truly a new level of pathetic.

I was obsessing over nothing.

Realistically, I knew that.

Didn't stop the images from forming in my head. Of Victor's large hands wrapping around Amani's waist like they had around mine. Of the metal in her pierced lip pressing into his mouth...

Still glaring at the blue 'track now' button, I grabbed my phone and dialed a number I had saved but never actually used

45

before. Tabitha, one of Del's best friends, picked up after a few rings.

"Cordelia?" she asked, sounding about as confused as I felt. Her short dark hair was wet and slicked away from her glistening face. If her bare shoulders and lack of visible fabric were any indication, Tabitha was currently naked.

"I'm sorry, I didn't know who else to call."

"Are you okay? Is it Del?" She asked while throwing a towel over her shoulder.

"No, everything is fine," I quickly shot out.

Of course she thought that I'd only call her because of Del. We'd never even been alone in the same room without Del or their other best friend, Defne. As much as I loved Del, it was always Tabitha who regaled us with tales of her romantic and sexual adventures. It was Tabitha who might have some sort of wisdom to share with me. Because if I knew anyone who had ever kissed someone they shouldn't have been kissing, it would be her. And I'd never been good at learning from theory. I needed tutorials with real life examples.

"I need to talk to *you*, actually."

"If this is about the bachelorette party, I already told her I wouldn't plan that. Way too much responsibility."

"Is this a bad time?" I asked when I clearly spotted someone else behind her shoulder. Even if the background was blurry, that someone else was also very naked.

"No, just got out of the shower. It's fine."

Part of me wished she had told me to call back later. I could have so easily chickened out of that. "You've kissed people before, right?"

"Uh," a grin spread over her lips, "yeah. Plenty."

"Ever kissed anyone who actually had a girlfriend?"

"Are you asking if I've ever had an affair with someone in a relationship?" Her face disappeared from the screen, replaced by the view of a ceiling fan. "Keep talking, just getting dressed."

Not having to look her in the face made the next words a lot easier: "If you kissed someone, and he had a girlfriend, how would you know?"

Someone chuckled in the background. A *manly* chuckle. As if this phone call wasn't humiliating enough. At least Tabitha barked "Get the fuck out!" at him, before returning to the screen, now wearing a turtleneck. "Well, if he's a stand-up guy, he'd tell me something along the lines of '*This can't happen. I actually have a girlfriend.*' but if he's a dick, you won't know until you're sixty-nining on his couch and his girlfriend walks in because she got off work early."

"That's very specific."

"Real life example, but you get the gist." She raised her brows at me. "Care to tell me who you've been kissing, Cordy?"

"Cordy?"

"Kissing. Who."

I told her everything that happened Friday night. At least this time, it came out a lot more coherently than when I'd told Del. I'd replayed the whole situation in my head so much, the words tumbled from my tongue.

I also told her everything Del had said, and how I had ignored her advice and actually hadn't talked to Victor at all.

"I love Del, but take her words with a grain of salt."

"Why?"

"Because she's careful, and a bit of an overthinker." Tabitha walked to the bathroom with her phone and propped it up at eye level, before squeezing some lotion into her hands and rubbing it into her face. "I've googled your boy, Victor, when Del moved in with you guys. He was a pro athlete before he started working for you, right?"

"Yes." No need to mention to her that he'd only been fighting in the UFC for his uncle.

"In my experience, pro athletes have no trouble getting their dicks wet. He's probably kissed more girls than he even remembers. If I had to guess, he's not actually bothered by the kiss." She started patting some other oil or serum into her skin, but looked at her camera - and at me - as she continued. "If you drunkenly kissed me, I genuinely wouldn't care the next morning. People kiss all the time. I think I kissed like three guys this weekend alone."

"So you don't think he has a girlfriend?"

"No," she chuckled, "I think the more important question is whether you want to be his girlfriend."

"I..." My voice died in my throat as I tried to come up with a reply.

I didn't want to be his girlfriend, and I didn't want him to be my boyfriend. Those terms felt way too silly. They sounded like movie dates and cooking classes and relationship milestones.

I may not have gone on a single date in my entire life, but the idea of going on one with Victor seemed ridiculous. So he'd cook dinner, just like always, but now it was supposed to be romantic? What? Light a candle to set the mood?

It wasn't like he could take me out to a nice restaurant, or on a sunset walk.

Regardless of my ability to leave the house, even those dates sounded like they were meant for others. We basically already shared a life.

When it came to Victor, I didn't want evenings that ended in a kiss. I didn't want to make a fuss over a three-month-anniversary. I didn't want to be *Instagram official*.

I just wanted him. All of him. All the moments I hadn't gotten yet. I wanted to wake up in the morning and see him next to me instead of having to walk downstairs. Hold his hand instead of his gaze. Run my fingers through his hair when he was being overprotective. Kiss him.

Gosh darn it, I wanted to kiss him.

"Cordelia? Still there?" Tabitha's voice snapped me from my thoughts.

"Yeah, sorry." I shook my head to clear it. "Just thinking about your question."

"Do you want to *date* Victor?"

"No," I said, "I want more than that. I want everything."

VICTOR

"Here," Luka threw a zipped nylon bag in my lap as we passed the gate.

Instead of checking the contents, I glanced out the window as we got behind the walls and rolled up the curved driveway. Petya's estate looked exactly like it had six years ago. Just another bland mansion on a street of colorless mansions. The others might have had a tennis or basketball court in the back, but Petya's estate had both. The others had garages for four cars, Petya had one for six. And of course, his pool was the biggest on the block.

If you looked up the definition of the whole golden cage thing, this place would show up in the search results. All the luxuries you could want, the staff to wipe up your mess, and the lavish parties you'd see on TV. Just no way out. I'd grown up here with my cousins. My parents had lived here until the day they tried to make a run for it.

Luka and I used to talk about leaving.

"Home sweet home," I muttered.

"Sorry to break it to you, but Irina has raided your closet after she burned her dresses and declared she wasn't playing dress-up anymore."

"Irina?"

"She's around here somewhere."

"Not in college?" Luka's youngest sister had been a pimply teenager when I'd left, but last I'd been aware of, she was meant to study abroad.

"No. Quit stalling," he nodded at the bag.

I sighed and unzipped the damn thing. It held a phone, a key badge on a black lanyard, and an unloaded gun. I pocketed the phone and threw on the lanyard. Then I took the gun out, passed it from hand to hand, turned and twisted it, before dropping it back in the bag. With my fingerprints all over it, it was an easy insurance policy.

"Thought you'd make me beg," Luka chuckled.

"I'm not stupid enough to think I have a choice in any of this," I replied and got out of the car.

Petya didn't need a would-be murder weapon with my prints on it. He already had the perfect insurance policy. She was tall, blonde, whip-smart and sometimes too kind for her own good.

"Your key will get you through the gate," Luka explained, distracting me before my thoughts could turn back to the five minutes that had been replaying on my mind since Friday, "and through most doors inside. Every room automatically locks now, so keep that damn thing on you or you'll get locked in the kitchen or something."

I acknowledged his explanations with silence, while he held his own pass against a scanner by the door, then lowered his head to the scanner.

"All doors *into* the house have face scan, too," he said, "we'll just grab that off your phone once it's set up."

Petya had to be pulling big shit if he'd beefed up his security to automatic face scans. I'd never been much interested in the business, but at least this meant I wouldn't have to memorize daily changing key codes anymore.

"Yury has agreed to come back to train you."

"Did he? Did he *agree*?" I couldn't help the sarcasm dripping through.

Luka shot me an exasperated look over his shoulder that almost startled me. He used to be amused by my sarcasm, while his humor had just been outright dark. That was the thing about growing up in a place like this. You had to take its power. If you couldn't make fun of the dark, it would kill you sooner or later.

We passed the white marble entryway with its large staircase, and took the hallway to the living room at the back of the house. Luka did have to scan his pass at every goddamn door, each one of them snapping shut behind us.

For a split second I considered bringing the mechanism up to Cordelia, but immediately thought better of it. She would feel safer for about twenty minutes before going to grab something from the kitchen and locking herself in because she'd left the key on her desk. As forgetful as she was sometimes, I knew she still remembered kissing me. She was a horrible actress and an even worse liar. Forgetting her key or her phone was one thing, but forgetting the way her teeth had skimmed over my bottom lip?

"We went with the last measurements we had on file," Luka pointed at the two bags on the sofa. One was a brand new gym bag, thick fabric strained by its contents. The other was my old familiar fight night bag. The UFC logo was scratched up and the right handle was fraying around the edges.

If they were gunning for any sentimental reaction, they had misjudged me. At fights, they threw plenty of new branded bags, caps and jerseys at you. The only reason I'd kept that battered thing was because my uncle hated it. He had a good poker face and never reacted to the bag, but his need to always have the biggest, best and shiniest toys wasn't a secret.

Just ask whatever twenty-something girl he had currently wifed.

I dropped onto the sofa next to the bags and raised my brows at Luka, still not deeming him worthy of actual conversation.

"Let's get started," he sighed. Luka had a checklist prepared, and we spent the day going through it.

Not talking to Luka would have been stranger if I didn't have that small voice in the back of my head, reminding me that he'd sold me out. He was the reason Cordelia was in danger. Whatever loyalty I might have felt towards him six years ago had gone cold.

So I let him poke and prod and measure me.

I signed whatever papers he laid out.

I went through all the motions of the day like a cheap hooker who didn't get paid enough to fake it.

"Oh man," a young, clear voice interrupted us halfway through setting up the training schedule on my new phone, "hate to see you *here*, Vitya, but it's *good* to see you."

I raised my brows at the young woman standing in the door-way, still clutching the door handle. She was in her early twenties, athletic enough to be of some use, but not muscular enough to be part of the security detail on the grounds. Even if she'd grown a few inches, and her face had slimmed down, the mane of brown corkscrew curls gave her away. They'd grown from her shoulders to her waist over the last few years.

"Irina, not now," Luka groaned in the exact same tone I'd heard a million times over.

For the first time that day, my stomach flipped.

"Shut up, dumbass," Irina yapped back. Just like always. Her cheeks puffed up, and her eyes narrowed. For a moment, we were dumb kids bickering over who got the remote.

Irina stepped forward and the memory shattered. She was carrying. Irina had a gun.

I stayed quiet, tilting my chin, waiting for her to get closer. She opened her arms, and I got up and hugged her, because when someone with a gun asked for a hug, you didn't say no. Her arms wrapped around me but her head barely grazed my chin. Still tiny. Tiny Irina was carrying a gun.

It made no sense, and all the sense in the world.

"You put on weight," she mused, patting my sides. It wasn't meant as an insult. My body had always been up for discussion in this house.

"You carry a gun," I replied.

"Weird how things change, huh?"

"Not always for the better it seems."

She shrugged and pulled away from me to look over the paperwork on the table. "So you really are back?"

"Weird how things stay the same, huh?"

Luka slid some of the papers out of reach from Irina. "If you two are quite done with your reunion..."

"I'm not done actually." Irina rolled her eyes and angled herself between Luka and me, demonstratively looking only at me.

"So, you're not in school. What are you doing these days?" I asked, willing to see how much Luka would let us push him around.

"Oh, you know..."

"Irina, we have a lot of stuff to get through today," he grumbled.

"Luka chill the fuck out," she hissed over her shoulder.

"I don't know, actually," I said, completely ignoring Luka. "What are we all doing? We work for the family."

The fact that she didn't specify what exactly she was doing for her father told me more than if she had made up some innocent busywork. With Luka off the wheel, Petya was drawing his kids into his inner circle.

"Not all of us," I replied in a dry tone, as if I wasn't fishing for information, "I heard Nat was getting married."

Irina rolled her eyes at me. "Not for love, for the family."

For the family. Three words that cracked through me like a lightning bolt. Fuck composure. Fuck playing things cool. I shot a dark look at Luka, who didn't meet my eyes. He suddenly seemed very interested in stacking the paperwork into one neat pile.

"Are you serious?" I asked.

"You don't get to come back and judge us." His voice was so calm and collected, my hands automatically balled to fists by my sides. If Irina hadn't stood between us, he would have caught one in the face.

"I can't believe you're letting him do this to her." An arranged fucking marriage. Petya had joked about it a couple of times, and we'd always brushed it off. It was one thing to train us to perform like circus animals, but now he was marrying off his daughter like some fucking prize mare. "She's your sister."

"Go touch grass, Victor. I didn't *let* him do anything. He's controlling all of us. You included."

Irina turned slightly, just enough to be out of range if fists did start flying.

I stayed still.

"Do you really think I could've stopped him?" Luka challenged with his chin tilted high. "Nat is pretty, but she has two left hands and dropped out of school before she could learn to code as much as a website. This is as good as it was ever going to get for her. I made sure the guy's not triple her age. I made sure she's not marrying a fucking sadist."

"Shit," I gritted out through clenched teeth.

"He's okay," Irina whispered. She wrapped her arms around her middle and dropped back against the table, deflating. "He's in politics, but too conservative to be openly gay. Nat will have a nice house, get the dog she always wanted, and for what it's worth, he's never going to lay a hand on her."

"It's the best I could do for her," Luka added.

I should be staying out of this. I only came here to do exactly as I was told, for however long they needed me. I only had to follow orders to keep Cordelia safe. I couldn't get mixed up in any of their family issues, even if the idea of Nat marrying a dirty politician felt like a bare-knuckle punch to my spine.

Luka, Irina and Natalia all had a future they could fight for, and they all acted like their lives were already forfeit. Maybe they were. Wasn't I the textbook example of being unable to outrun this family? Worse, not only did I come back, I'd come back with something to lose. It wasn't just my life on the line if I tried to run this time.

I smoothed my hand down my face and allowed myself two breaths to put everything I'd heard over the last few minutes into an airtight container, and move it to the very back of my mind.

I had to do the same thing I had done six years ago and trust that if they wanted to get out, they would find a way for themselves.

I had no aspirations to be anyone's savior.

This was no different than stepping into the octagon. Eyes on the fight. Head in the ring. It only took one distraction and you were lying on the mat, bleeding.

"Fine," I finally muttered, and turned to Luka, "what's next on the list?"

CHAPTER SEVEN

Cordelia

VICTOR · 08:01PM

Dinner

CORDELIA · 08:03PM

I'll eat later. Need to finish this presentation.

VICTOR · 08:03PM

Liar.

CORDELIA · 08:09PM

You can go home. I'll be working all night.

VICTOR · 08:10PM

Stop avoiding me.

I GLANCED AT THE THREE LITTLE WORDS ON MY PHONE that called me out on my bullshit. The problem with kissing your bodyguard, it seemed, was that he knew your every move better than you did yourself.

Even if he couldn't see me, I stuck my tongue out at my closed office door. He should have known that I also didn't take well to being ordered around.

CORDELIA · 08:12PM

No.

VICTOR · 08:13PM

I will drag you into the kitchen and force feed you. You haven't eaten all day.

My stomach churned at the reminder, gnawing at itself. This was exactly why Victor had shown up with the smoothie maker a few weeks after I'd hired him. I just forgot that I was hungry. I usually didn't realize that I should eat until my insides were about to consume themselves. By the time those cramps hit, I'd just scarf down whatever I could get my hands on.

Smoothies were a somewhat healthy alternative to chocolate, crackers and cheese.

CORDELIA · 08:14PM

Not hungry.

VICTOR · 08:14PM

Liar.

VICTOR

THIS WOMAN WAS GOING TO BE THE DEATH OF ME.

I'd walked away unscathed from a drug cartel shooting at 21, and Cordelia Montgomery would be the one to put me in the grave over a goddamn baked potato.

When ten minutes passed without another text from her, I stalked to the front door, opened it, slammed it shut, and waited in the hallway.

Five seconds, then her desk chair rattled over the floorboards. Another five before her office door opened. That demonic cat shot out and up the stairs first, then a head of messy blonde hair followed. Seemed like she'd been fidgeting with her hair a lot today. She bent around the doorframe to look down the hall towards the kitchen.

Not avoiding me - my ass.

When she finally turned the other direction and spotted me, her whole body twitched.

"Crackers," she hissed, clutching her hand to her chest.

Her ability to avoid swearing, even when startled, still kept me on my toes. *Crackers* was new.

"Your food is getting cold." I wasn't going to give her the chance to disappear again. Not when she was starving herself because of me. Without waiting for her reply, I wrapped my arm around her waist and hauled her into the hallway.

"Victor," she screeched, slapping my arm.

Instead of relenting to her struggles, I just lifted her up. Despite her height, and those long smooth legs, Cordelia was still a few inches shorter than me. She kicked her feet and let out a yelp, but she wasn't getting a choice in this. Sometimes keeping

Cordelia alive just meant reminding her of her basic physical needs, like food and water.

By the time I set her down in the kitchen, her face had gone bright red, and her chest was rising and falling fast. Lips trembling, she tugged her ruffly pink sweater back into place. Her storm blue eyes bored into mine, wordless anger simmering beneath the surface. All riled up and with her hair a mess, she almost looked like she'd just gotten laid.

The thought echoed through my skull.

Fuck.

That was *not* the right direction.

I tore my gaze away from hers and forced myself to focus on my hands when I got the potatoes out of the oven. It was just that kiss messing with my head. Nothing more. It had been three days and I swore I could still taste her sweet mouth on my tongue. God, I wanted more of it.

"Talk," I barked, maybe a bit too gruff, but I needed her to fix my brain. Say something smart and pure and seemingly random, so she could return to being *just* Cordelia.

"How do you feel about going to the movies? Like, popcorn, movie theater, as an activity, what's your opinion?"

Perfect. Yes. Random question.

"I don't know. Never been," I replied, plating our food.

"You've never been?"

"I don't really watch things."

She huffed, clearly not finding the answer she was looking for. "What about taking walks?" she asked and followed me to the dinner table.

This was good. Random conversation. Dinner as always, sitting across from Cordelia. I set down her plate, with nothing but potato and sour cream, and mine with some vegetables stuffed into the potato. "Walk where?" I asked.

"No destination. Just taking walks."

"Why?"

"I don't know. People take walks, right? Sunset walks, beach walks. It's a thing."

"Can't I just go for a run instead? At least I'll be getting something out of it."

"I'm assuming people do find some sort of fulfillment in taking a stroll down the shore for an hour."

I shrugged and shook my head. If I'd ever taken a walk, I couldn't remember it. I'd definitely never taken a sunset beach stroll. "Never tried it."

"Dinner at a restaurant?"

I blinked. "You're listing *outside* activities." Not outside as in *nature*, outside as in *not-in-this-house*. Activities Cordelia couldn't take part in. We'd ventured *outside* only a few times over the last years, usually for medical reasons.

"I'm just wondering where you could have been all day." She stabbed her fork into her food.

"Stop lying to me."

"I'm not."

"You think I was having dinner at a restaurant?" I pointedly stabbed my own potato.

"Where were you?"

"Do you want me to lie, too? Or do you want the truth?"

She swallowed, her throat bobbing, and for one flashing moment, I wanted to run my tongue up her neck and hear her whimper. My fork clattered to my plate. I had to get a fucking grip on myself.

"Lie," Cordelia whispered.

I needed a safe topic. Something nice. Positive.

"I was out shopping for your birthday present."

She snorted and shook her head. "That's a terrible lie. But thanks for the tea cup in advance."

I pushed my food aside and leaned forward. "Thirty is a big one. You might just get a whole tea set."

"Oh *golly gosh*, exactly what I always wanted."

"Don't pretend like you don't have at least three eBay tabs open on your phone right now."

"I do not."

"Fine, show me your phone." I held out my hand.

Her gaze flicked from my palm to her pocket, while she actually considered handing over her phone. In that moment, something shifted in her face. Without looking up, she mumbled, "Now tell me the truth."

"I have to work for my uncle for a couple of months," I replied without missing a beat.

Her entire body went rigid. It looked like she wasn't even breathing. Maybe she'd convinced herself that I was off the hook. There was the very real possibility that she'd forgotten, over the last few months, that my uncle no longer deemed my employment here useful enough to leave me alone. Without her inheritance Cordelia was still rich, but thankfully not rich enough to be useful. Her *usefulness* wasn't something she worried about every hour of every day. That's what I was here for.

"I won't let him anywhere near you," I added when her silence became eerie.

"I'm not worried about my safety," she said, life flooding back into her limbs. Her spine straightened. Her shoulders rolled back. She leveled me with a hard, confident look. It was the same one she had when she was negotiating, talking to her legal team, and going to the mattresses for her foundation. "Are you involved in anything dangerous?"

I weighed my head from side to side to make the lie more believable. "No, not really."

"Can you tell me what it is?"

"No." Not that Petya would mind. It wasn't going to be a secret for long anyway. Maybe telling Cordelia the truth would have been fair, but it also would have added to her worries. I couldn't do that to her.

She knew that I had gotten out of the ring after one too many concussions prompted a CTE scan that showed just how fucked my brain really was.

She knew that I was one ill-placed hit to the head away from irreparable damage.

Telling her the truth would do her no good.

"Victor," she sighed and pulled some hair in front of her chest, threading a strand through her fingers, "I kissed you. I practically threw myself at you."

Thank god for Cordelia's fast brain. The kiss. I would much rather talk about the kiss than about my uncle. "You were drunk."

"That's no excuse for my behavior."

"It happens." It had happened before. Almost exactly six years ago. Less drunk. Less her fault. I'd kissed her then, and she'd been the one to stop it. After a minute or two. Back then, I'd had no intention of staying. Now, that was the only thing I wanted, and if she needed to pretend the kiss didn't happen, it didn't happen. If she regretted the kiss, we'd just move on. If she'd actually *meant* to kiss me... I stopped the thought before it could fully form.

"If you want to speak to a lawyer, or a therapist, or both-"

I fell back in my chair like she'd slapped me.

"I mean because I'm your boss. It's well within reason."

"Bullshit," I said.

"Does that mean we're alright?"

"We're alright, Cordelia." *Moving on* it was.

The only reason I might need a fucking therapist was that I watched her fingers twirl through her hair, and I suddenly saw myself wrapping her ponytail around my fist and yanking her head back while I stood behind her - and neither of us was wearing clothes in that scenario.

"Speaking of my birthday. Before. With the tea cups."

I nodded. Birthday. Safe topic. Nice. Positive. Fully clothed.

"I'd like to invite some people for my birthday, have a proper cake and party. Del, obviously, and Beck. Tabitha and Defne."

"Sure?" The girls had all been over, and Beck had stayed with Delilah a few times, but Cordelia had never dealt with all of them here at the same time.

"Maybe we can do a test run. Without the people."

"Let me figure out my uncle's schedule for me before you start planning."

She bit her lip. "I might change my mind."

"That's okay."

We finished eating and Cordelia told me about work and about her weekend, about repotting plants and about the loneliest whale in the world, whose whale sounds traveled at a different frequency, so he wasn't able to find or communicate with other whales.

She pulled her phone out and hovered in the doorway while I loaded the dishwasher. "Victor?"

"Hm?"

"Not a tea set. A musical teapot. They used to make them in the fifties, with little music boxes in the bottom, playing *Tea for Two*. That's what I want for my birthday. Musical teapot. Tea for Two."

"Alright." I nodded and earned myself a big beaming smile that eradicated the last shreds of tension from the past few days. Cordelia twirled around, and basically skipped down the hall and up the stairs.

If that was her reaction, I really had to figure out where to get her a music box teapot.

Six years ago, I'd turned my nose up at Cordelia's pink patchwork home. Having grown up under Petya's roof, I was used to everything having to be expensive or state-of-the-art. Cordelia, on the other hand, didn't care whether she was collecting kitsch or rare antiques. Anything was fair game, as long as it fit her pastel pink, rococo-inspired, cotton candy dream house.

She liked what she liked, and she didn't care what value other people placed on an item. Or a person. It had taken me way too long to admit that this didn't make her silly and naive. It meant she had more integrity in her pinky than most people had in their entire body.

CHAPTER EIGHT

Cordelia

THE PEN CAP CRACKED AND THE LITTLE CLIP FLEW through the air. I lost sight of it before it could land.

"That's bullsticks," I muttered, eyes back on the graph on screen.

"Come again?" Amani fumbled with her headphones.

"It's absurd," I said, finding a better word to express my feelings. "We're *helping* people."

"We're mostly helping *women*," Amani corrected, "leaving husbands, getting abortions, going to court."

"Because they were being abused!"

"Yeah, I know that. It's politics, not common sense."

Amani's words threatened to trigger a spiral in the wrong direction, so I dug my fingernails into my cheeks and forced my eyes to stay on the graphs. The number of people accessing the services we offered at our Florida center had dropped steeply. Mostly thanks to a bunch of protesters gathering in the parking lot every day. Hiring security guards had plateaued the drop-off, but people were still too scared to walk past an angry mob.

These women were supposed to feel safe with us.

It took many of them all their strength to even get in touch with us, especially those who had to do so secretly. Some of them never went back home once they walked through our doors.

I couldn't let a handful of assholes threaten the safety we were meant to offer.

"What can I do?" I asked because there was a reason it was Amani, not Monica, on this call. Monica would ask for assets like more security, or safety fences.

"Where do you see yourself in ten years?"

"What?"

"If you wanted to launch a political career, drive change on a much larger scale, this would be your opportunity to build a platform."

"That's-" *Absurd* didn't even begin to cover it. How on earth was I supposed to go into politics? Even city officials were required to attend public events. I was driving change on my own terms. The Theresa Montgomery foundation was already so much bigger than I'd allowed myself to imagine just a few years ago. I wanted to have at least one facility in every state by the end of next year.

"I say this with all the respect you deserve," Amani continued when I struggled to find the words, "you're a rich white woman with name recognition, pretty privilege, and - to put it bluntly - a tragic origin story. If you wanted to go into politics, you could. I'd whip you up a campaign in 48 hours."

"That's-" This time, I swallowed the *absurd*. Maybe it wasn't. I couldn't think ten years ahead though. Not when, at this very moment, a survivor of human trafficking might not feel safe enough in our parking lot to access the help she needed. "What are my options?"

We spent the rest of the day going over different strategies to deal with the situation. There was no use in fighting this kind of crowd, which meant we had to make ourselves as visible and as accessible and as welcoming as possible. The visibility part was mostly going to be on me. I wasn't about to campaign for senate, but my quick photograph for the website had just turned into a video campaign. Which meant more than one stranger in my house for more than thirty minutes.

As soon as the little *swoop* sound indicated that Amani had ended the call, Victor stepped into the doorway. My eyes trailed on their own accord. He'd swapped his usual button-down shirts and suit pants for more casual clothes the last few days as he spent more time downstairs in the gym, or outside. The black henley shirt was rolled up to his elbows, exposing all the deep black ink of his toned forearms. My tongue turned to stone as my brain reminded me how it felt to have that arm wrapped around my waist. I'd liked his hands on my waist when he'd kissed me, but when he'd carried me into the kitchen, those arm muscles had pressed so deep into my flesh, my inner organs still sported that imprint.

Victor cleared his throat. He leaned there, brows raised, waiting.

He treated me no differently than before the kiss. I was struggling to do the same.

How could I go from admitting to Tabitha that I wanted a whole life with Victor to just... cohabitating?

"You know, eavesdropping is very impolite," I said and offered him a sweet smile.

"You can't invite random people in when I'm not here."

"I can't?" I raised my brows at his gruff tone.

"Cordelia," he warned, a hint of exasperation in those four syllables.

"You don't get to tell me what to do."

"I'm trying to keep you safe."

"You can run all the background checks you want on them. You can install security cameras all over the house. You can keep me safe without making decisions for me."

He worked his jaw, shook his head, and stalked off down the hallway. The basement door banged shut just a moment later.

That was definitely not the way to his heart.

> CORDELIA • 03:53PM
>
> Follow-up question.

TABITHA • 03:58PM

one sec

My thumb hovered over my screen, ready to accept an incoming call. Instead, a new notification popped up.

• FRAP SLUTS •

Cordy was added to the chat.

TABITHA • 03:59PM

better

DEFNE • 04:00PM

Cordy as in Cordelia??

> CORDELIA • 04:00PM
>
> What's happening?
>
> CORDELIA • 04:00PM
>
> Yes, this is Cordelia.

DEL • 04:01PM

Hi! 🖤 I just got in the car. I'll be home in a bit.

TABITHA · 04:02PM

decided to make Cordy an honorary frap slut because she has a ladyboner for her manservant and the situation requires a council session

DEFNE · 04:03PM

OMG Cordelia and Victor? YES.

I SUCKED IN A BREATH LOUD ENOUGH TO FREEZE AND stare at the open door - just in case Victor would come running to check on me. But everything remained quiet. I dragged my eyes back to my phone screen. Defne's message was so short and so simple, and yet I wasn't sure I'd ever seen it spelled out like that.

Cordelia and Victor.

I suddenly got the urge to trace those three words in my notebook until the pen tore the pages. Typing them out was almost as good.

CORDELIA · 04:06PM

Yes. Cordelia and Victor.

DEFNE · 04:06PM

I love that for you!

TABITHA · 04:07PM

Cordy you had a Q

CORDELIA · 04:09PM

I would like it to be Cordelia and Victor...

CORDELIA · 04:09PM

But how?

DEFNE · 04:10PM

Wdym?

CORDELIA · 04:11PM

I know more about propagating succulents than I know about romance... and propagating succulents really isn't that hard.

TABITHA · 04:12PM

I don't know romance but I know how to get laid

DEFNE · 04:13PM

I can be there in 20.

TABITHA · 04:13PM

perf

DEL · 04:15PM

I'm bringing coffee 🖤

THE GROUP CHAT WENT QUIET. I SHOULD HAVE GOTTEN up to figure out what snacks I could offer them to go with the coffee, or to tell Victor they were coming over, or to put on fresh clothes because I was fairly certain Amani had made me sweat through mine, or possibly all three. I tried to decide which would come first, and by the time I blinked, the clock on my phone showed that fifteen minutes had passed. I just managed to shut off my computer and get up when the security system at the door chimed.

Del shuffled through the door, looking like a pack mule with her oversized down coat, her heavy backpack hanging off her shoulders, and a paper tray of four huge frappuccinos balanced in front of her.

"Let me get that," I said and grabbed the coffee from her.

"Thank you." She smiled. Her cheeks and nose were bright red from the cold. "I'm so ready for spring."

"Me too." Not that I had much exposure to the cold, but

spring meant planting flowers and watching my backyard come back alive, and soaking up sun in the winter garden.

"Where's Victor?" Del asked while she hung up her jacket, bending her neck to search for him behind me.

"Basement."

"Again?"

"It takes a lot of hard work to stay in shape." I hadn't told her about Victor's uncle yet. Not only because I didn't know how dangerous it might be, for her or for Victor, to share - but because I'd put her through more than enough drama for one lifetime.

"Or to work off sexual frustration."

"Excuse me?"

Her smile dripped with false innocence. "Tab is probably better at explaining that one."

"The walls of this house are not as sound-proof as you might think," I replied, "it sounds like you know exactly what you're talking about." Beck didn't stay over much, considering they had his teenage niece to look after, but when he did, they weren't very good at being discreet.

She just laughed and grabbed the coffee from me, breezing towards the TV room.

Tabitha filed in a few minutes later, unceremoniously shoving a box of pink-glazed donuts at me to strip off around five layers of jackets until she was wearing nothing but leggings and a long-sleeve crop top. Most of her clothes had brand logos on them. Some of them were even personalized with her name or social media handle. I'd watched some of her videos online, but yoga just wasn't for me. When I worked out, I had to keep my body busy enough not to get bored.

Defne arrived in a bright red teddy coat and matching beret. It should have made her look like a cartoon character, but her perfectly coiffed long black hair, spotless tan olive skin, and big brown eyes just made her look like she'd popped off the pages of a fashion magazine.

"I brought drinks, in case you need some liquid courage to talk this through," she said, holding up a tote bag that rattled with the promise of glass bottles, "I'm obsessed with pomegranate lemon raki right now. It's a bit bitter though. I also have plain bubbly, and some bright pink vodka thing that I only bought because I know you like pink."

It didn't click until then that Tabitha might have chosen the donuts based on their color, too. My insides seized, and I suppressed a strange hiccup.

"Thank you," I said through a suddenly clogged throat.

"Let's do this."

We closed the door to the TV room and they told me to text Victor that he wasn't allowed to come in because Defne needed girl time. I left out that last part in my actual text. I didn't need to lie to him. He reacted with a thumbs up within seconds.

"So what are we talking about here?" Defne asked. She was simultaneously slurping her chocolate frap and pouring pomegranate, lemon juice and raki into a crystal tumbler.

I glanced over at Delilah for help but she just nodded encouragingly.

Guess I was really doing this. Somehow. Maybe.

I took a deep breath, and then relayed everything that had happened the night I'd gotten drunk - and everything since. "...and now Del thinks he's working out so much because he's frustrated."

"Sexually frustrated," she corrected.

"Sounds about right," Tabitha said while Defne nodded her agreement.

"But there's no precedent... he's never..." I tried to find the right words, the thought barely even solid in my mind, because I'd figured he was working out to keep up with whatever his uncle had him doing.

"He's never dated anyone?" Tabitha asked.

"I'm sure he's dated someone at some point," I replied.

"Since he started working for you," Defne added.

"Oh, no, I don't think so." I swapped my hazelnut double espresso frap for one of the pink premade drinks Defne had brought. Discussing a single kiss was one thing. Theorizing about Victor's whole love life... that required alcohol. "Definitely not the first three years, when he had Del's room. He technically lives next door now. I don't really know what he does over there."

I'd bought him that house because it had seemed like a good idea at the time. Give him some personal space while keeping him nearby. I'd only ever been there a few times, but it never looked like he had changed anything about the place since the day I'd viewed it with the realtor. There definitely hadn't been any couple pictures on the walls or side tables.

"So what you're saying is that this man has possibly been celibate for at least six years? And then you tackled him with those tits pressed up against him?" Tabitha whistled. "Yeah, he's about to explode."

"What do my t- What does my chest have to do with anything?"

"Can you not say *tits*?" Tabitha grinned.

My neck started to burn with the onset of a blush, but before I had to defend my word choices, Defne cleared her throat. "Take our tiny Delilah here as an example," she framed Del's face with her hands as if pointing at a graph for a presentation, "Del was never much bothered with sex. She dated for companionship, not to get laid."

"You say that like it's a bad thing," Del grumbled.

"That meant Del could go a very long time without having sex and never miss it," Defne continued unfazed, "but now that she's figured out how to get off, if Beck is out of town for more than two days, she's suddenly whining in the group chat about how much she misses his dick."

"Hey! I do not!" Del slapped Defne's hands away.

"You do. You just use different words," Tabitha agreed, "and you get worse when you're ovulating."

"Excuse me?"

"The point is," Defne heaved a sigh and trained her warm brown eyes on me, "you got physical with him and it's not that easy to forget how good that feels. And you have great tits. That's also the point. Are they real?"

"Real?" I blinked.

"Implants?"

"Oh, no, they're real."

Del waved her hands through the air. "Guys, stop distracting her." She plucked the cocktail from Defne's hands, before focussing back on me. "What they're trying to say is that Victor might have an equally hard time moving on from the kiss as you do."

"I still don't understand what my chest has to do with his workouts."

"Cordy," Tabitha straightened up, eyes unfocused and brows furrowed, "sorry to bring this up, and I promise this isn't me distracting you, but how long since your mom died?"

"You can say that she was murdered," I replied, because people always shied away from the word as if it was shameful, "she didn't just *die* from old age or illness or anything. And it's been almost 17 years."

"Right," she nodded, "and you've been staying at home ever since she was murdered, right?"

"Yes," I said. As much as I was open about my mother's murder, the effects it had on me were still harder to talk about. Especially because, over the years, I'd heard about every quick fix in the book for PTSD-related agoraphobia. Meditation. Short walks to the mailbox and back. Electromagnetic waves, crystals, hypnosis...

"In seventeen years, you've never dated anyone? Even just online?"

"No."

"Oooh," Defne let out under her breath.

Tabitha's eyes cleared up when she blinked at me, coming to the only logical conclusion there was: "You're a virgin."

"Yes."

A beat of silence passed as we all sat with that confirmation. Del was the one to break it first. "Are you even interested in sex?" she asked. "Because plenty of people aren't. That's totally normal."

"Yeah," I shrugged, "and I don't feel weird about never having slept with anyone. I'm not a virgin by choice, but by circumstance. I'm very careful about who I spend my time with. That limits my options."

"The circumstances suck, but I'm glad that you never felt pressured to have sex," Del nodded, "you're doing this at your own pace."

"For what it's worth," Defne said, "I'm really glad that I waited until I was with someone who made me feel comfortable and safe and cherished."

"Well, to get us back to the topic of your great tits," Tabitha cleared her throat, "you might be thinking about the kiss. He's probably thinking about railing you six ways to Sunday after getting a preview of what your tits feel like."

"He's not like that," I said.

Del snorted and avoided my eyes.

"I promise you, he's thought about it," Tabitha said.

"Del?" I asked.

She lifted her shoulders and grimaced, staring down at the rest of the whipped cream in her cup. "I *don't* think he would tell you. I *do* think that if you are ready for something complicated, you have a chance of making things work this time."

"This time?" Defne and Tabitha asked almost simultaneously.

"We've kissed before," I replied, "once."

"Oh my god, really?" Defne gasped, while Tabitha asked: "When was that?"

"Six years ago."

"Six *years* ago?" Defne balked. She was the youngest of us. She had turned 25 in early January, which meant six years were basically a quarter of her life. Six years ago, she would have been a teenager.

"We need more details," Tabitha said.

"I've been so curious about this," Del pulled her legs up and propped her chin on her knees, "you never told me about that kiss."

"You never asked." I blinked. If she had asked, I would have told her. It wasn't a big secret.

My gaze moved over their patient, encouraging smiles, and my chest flooded with warmth. Maybe she'd never asked because you were supposed to volunteer this kind of information amongst girls. I vaguely remembered my early middle school days, giggling with my friends around the lunch table and falling silent only when a cute boy walked past.

I hadn't had *friends* in a long time.

"Okay, Cordelia," Delilah smiled, "what happened six years ago?"

CHAPTER NINE

VICTOR

SIX YEARS AGO

"THERE YOU ARE!" CORDELIA ROUNDED THE CORNER TO the kitchen and grimaced at the salad I was preparing. How that woman could survive on ice cream and Nutella alone, while maintaining a perfect hourglass figure, was beyond me. Well, not quite, she put in a lot of time swimming laps.

"Looking for me?"

"Can you give me a ride?"

"A ride?" My brows jumped up. She hadn't left the house once since I started here. It had been almost seven weeks - and in only two days I'd be out of this eyesore of a Barbie house.

"You have a driver's license, right? I don't remember if we covered this in your interview."

"Sure. Right now?"

"Yes, please."

"Where are we going?"

"The doctor's office."

"Oh." I glanced at the oven clock. It was past 8pm. That was probably the best time to have a doctor's appointment if you wanted to avoid people. "Two minutes." I wiped my hands off on a dish towel and started clearing the counter.

"Could you hurry?"

"Next time, just give me a heads-up and I'll be ready for your appointments," I said. There wasn't going to be a next time, but hell, the next guy could thank me for teaching her a bit of common courtesy.

"I know. I'm sorry. It's kind of last minute."

The tremor in her voice made my head snap up. Cordelia didn't stutter. She may talk a mile a minute or start the same sentence five times without noticing, but she never wobbled. "What's wrong?"

"Nothing."

"You're a really shitty liar. Anyone ever tell you that?"

"Car. Now. Please."

"Tell me what's wrong." I wasn't asking anymore.

"I need a doctor and you won't drive me. That's what's wrong." She wrapped her arms around her middle, the neckline of her sweater slipping to reveal just a hint of delicate pink lace underneath. For the first time in seven weeks, I didn't mind that goddamn color.

"I can administer first aid." I dragged my eyes away from her bra and scanned the rest of her, trying to find a flaw and coming up short.

"Goodness, Victor, I need an OBGYN." She pointedly looked down at her hips. "Can we please go now?"

"Shit. Yes. Shit, sorry." That was definitely something a doctor had to take care of. I left the salad and vegetables out and followed her to the garage. Her car was a sensible city limousine, and my first thought was that it wasn't pink - my second one, that of course it wouldn't be pink. Once outside, Cordelia wouldn't want to be seen.

She wordlessly got in the backseat and buckled in, and I was already halfway in the driver's seat when I realized she wasn't closing her own door. Who knew if she had ever opened her own door before tonight? Any other time, I would have rolled my eyes at how spoiled that made her. Instead, I just shut her door, tapped it twice, then got in my own seat.

The car took a moment to splutter to life, but at least the battery wasn't dead.

"You can't leave a car collecting dust like that," I said while she brought up the GPS on her phone, "you need to drive it every once in a while or it won't start."

"You can use it whenever you want. I don't drive."

That wasn't the point. The fucking point was that next time, she wouldn't be getting to the doctor if she didn't stay on top of the car's maintenance. Neither her old security guy nor Cordelia had even mentioned the car to me, or I could have looked after it. I'd have to write a whole fucking handbook for the next guy.

"Tell me what's wrong," I repeated my words from the kitchen, finding her face in the rearview mirror. She had her eyes closed, but the tension was written all over her face.

"No," she breathed.

I kept one eye on the road, one eye on her. Maybe it was the street lights at night, but she looked paler. The fuck was I supposed to tell the doctor if she fainted?

"Are you in pain?"

"Can you please shut up and drive," she snapped, "you're making me insane."

Damn. This was the first time she'd raised her voice at me. And she'd told me to *shut up*, not to be quiet, or to stop talking, or any other polite phrase she could have used to cotton-wrap her intentions.

So I shut up, and I drove her to the women's health clinic she'd chosen.

Inside, Cordelia handled the talking and the paperwork, and if I hadn't spent the last seven weeks with her, I wouldn't have picked up on all the nervous fidgeting. Her hands were constantly moving, but it was slow and almost deliberate. A tug to her sleeve. A brush through her hair. A wipe down her shirt.

Each hallway they took us down, every waiting area we passed, I did a quick scan. The people, the cameras, the exits. Then my eyes went back to Cordelia. Until she was eventually led into an exam room, where I was about to follow until she leveled me with a glare that would have felled a weaker man.

Fine.

I tried to sit in the waiting area opposite, but my feet wouldn't stay still. Eventually, I just started pacing up and down, my eyes trained on that damn closed door.

"You need to relax dude. First kid?" Some bald guy with a huge grin piped up from one of the cheap plastic seats.

"What?"

"First time father?"

"Sure," I grit out before I turned back to the door. He said something else, but I tuned him out. I hadn't made use of that particular skill in a while, but you needed it in the octagon. When you were fighting, you couldn't focus on anything but your opponent. Right now, that meant focussing on the door that kept me away from Cordelia.

After forty-seven minutes, that door finally opened back up, and Cordelia stepped outside. I automatically did another sweep of her, not finding any new wounds or cuts or bandages, or god knew what the hell I was looking for. Her hands were balled into tight fists around the ends of her sleeves, and her shoulders were shaking.

Shit.

That had to be bad news.

"What do you need?" I asked, stepping up and wrapping one arm around her back before she'd keel over. Where was that fucking doctor?

"Take me home please."

I swallowed the urge to question that decision. "Of course."

I opened and closed the car door for her this time, but by the time I got into the driver's seat, she'd not moved a single digit, just sitting and staring and trembling. This seemed like something those doctors with their fancy medical degrees should have been taking care of.

"You need to-" I cut myself off. She didn't look like she *needed* to do anything. I twisted around, kneeling in my seat to lean over the center console. It was a bit of a stretch, but I managed to grab the seat belt and buckle her in. She didn't even react when I fumbled with her hair to free it from the seat belt across her chest. "Want to try a different clinic? Get a second opinion?"

She shook her head. "I'll be fine medically," she stuttered, "this is a panic attack."

"You're having a panic attack right now?"

"Yes." She closed her eyes again, and I could watch her trying to slow her breathing, trying to get a control over her trembling limbs, but it would only work for a short moment before the tremor was back.

"What can I do?"

"Home."

"Okay."

It was a wonder I got us home in one piece. My attention wasn't on the streets, but on the girl in my rearview mirror. The further we got from the clinic, the less she stirred. By the time we pulled into the garage, her lips were the only thing still quivering.

I got her out of the car and into the house, but she halted by the stairs before I could ask her if she needed me to carry her up.

"You're going to leave, aren't you?"

Maybe Cordelia was more observant than I gave her credit for. I didn't reply. I didn't want to tell her and make her night even worse.

"Two weeks?" she asked.

I didn't reply.

"One week?"

I didn't reply.

"I see."

"It's nothing personal, Cordelia," I said as if that could somehow fix anything.

"I need to sit." She glanced around, her hands hovering in the air but finding nothing but me within immediate reach. "Not because of this. I'm not mad at you. I just need to sit down."

"Here." I grasped one of her hands, her fingers icy and slim in my palm. Deciding against carrying her upstairs, I slung my other arm around her middle and led her into the living room instead.

"Fuck," she moaned as I lowered her onto the sofa.

I choked on my laugh and turned my face into my shoulder. She still caught it.

"What?" She raised her brows at me but didn't let go of my hand, keeping me bent over the sofa for her.

"You don't curse."

"I'm in fucking pain and you're fucking leaving. Fuck is the only appropriate word." Her grip on my hand tightened with every word, the anger and frustration tinting her cheeks bright red. Her fingertips dug into my skin, and her eyes stayed on mine unrelenting. The unspoken challenge filled the air between us. She was waiting for me to lie, to placate her, to tell her everything was going to be just peachy.

My nerves crackled. Each fiber of my body was trained to respond to confrontation with physical violence.

Automatically, my gaze swept over her for the third time that night to find a weakness. It caught on the spot where her sweater had dropped off her shoulder again, where her chest was rising fast against the thin lace edge of her pink bra.

My instincts took over, my body springing into action, my hand tightening around her fingers, my weight launching forward. Before I could contemplate my actions, my mouth was on hers. And when she let out a surprised whimper that burrowed down to the base of my spine, every last thought escaped me.

Cordelia opened up for me without hesitation when my tongue swept her bottom lip. God, she tasted like sugar and cream and I couldn't get enough of it. My kiss turned hungry. I leaned into her, a knee between hers, and had to steady myself on the back of the sofa to stop from toppling over.

She hooked her free hand into my collar, pulling at me, whimpering every chance she had to take a breath.

Those small sounds did something to me. My pulse spiked at every single one of them, and the second my mouth closed over hers again, I kissed her with enough force to bruise those perfect pink lips.

On the next whimper, I'd leave her mouth, I'd kiss my way down her neck to that small triangle of lace.

Except, when I came up for air, lungs desperate for reprieve, Cordelia's hand around my collar tightened. She pushed me back, and instead of a needy little whimper, I got a breathy *"I can't."*

"Shit," I hissed as my peripheral vision cleared, and suddenly there was more to the world than Cordelia's lips.

"Oh fudge." She grimaced and pressed her hand over her stomach. "Cramp."

"Right." I fell back, crouching down in front of the sofa. I had to be seriously fucked-up to jump her when she'd been getting treated at the hospital half an hour ago. "Sorry."

"It's a burst ovarian cyst. It'll take a little while to heal," she said apologetically, as if I was about to get mad at her for not getting any action tonight. That was the least of my concerns.

"Isn't that serious? Shouldn't you have stayed in the hospital?"

"It looks okay. If I get worse, develop a fever or anything over the next few days, I'll need surgery. For now, I just have to get through this pain." She adjusted her position, grimacing, and I reached over her lap to help rearrange one of the pillows.

"I'll postpone my flight."

"Don't." She sighed and sagged into the cushion.

"You're alone." The words weren't meant to sound insulting. There hadn't been a single visitor in last seven weeks if you didn't count the housekeeper or her therapist. I'd heard her on the phone with her father twice, and both phone calls had ended within a minute. Cordelia was alone in the most basic sense of the word.

She rolled her eyes at me. "I have a phone. I can dial 911 if it gets worse."

"You hired me to keep you safe. Let me do my job."

"I thought you were quitting." The edge in her voice was the same challenging one from before, but she was slowly melting into the sofa, no tension left in her muscles.

"Consider this my two weeks' notice," I said.

"Okay," she sighed, the rest of the fight deflating even from her voice. "Could you please help me get upstairs?"

"Of course." I'd have to figure out how to tell Luka tomorrow. We were in more of a one-way conversation these days, with him dropping off updates and my papers in the mailbox. For now, I slid one arm around Cordelia's waist and one around the back of her knees and got her off the sofa. Her arms folded around my neck, and her head immediately dropped to my shoulder. That girl was done for tonight.

"Victor," she mumbled halfway up the stairs.

"Yes?"

"Could we never mention the kiss again? Would that be alright?"

"Yes," I agreed, "that's alright, Cordelia."

CHAPTER TEN

Cordelia

I SHOT UP IN BED. SWEAT COATED MY SKIN AND I GASPED for air. My chest didn't expand enough. I couldn't breathe. *A gloved hand pressed over my mouth.* Not real. I shook my head. I shook the image off. Shook off the scent of leather gloves. Nobody was here. The sheets tangled around me as I twisted, desperate for the glow of the star-shaped night light across the room. There it was. A small, blue shimmer against dark walls that eased the pressure behind my ribs.

I was at home. I was in my room.

"Grab the girl, Nick."

My head snapped to my right but the shadows were still.

Not real.

It took me three tries to switch on my bedside lamp, my fingers trembling too much to grasp the switch. The lit-up room was empty, because of course it was. Nobody lurked in the corner to jump me. Nobody tried to drag me into a van while my mother bled out on the ground.

Fitzwilliam stretched on the windowsill and jumped onto the bed with surprising agility for such a huge cat. He curled into my lap, purring.

"Thank you," I whispered, sinking both hands into his warm fur, letting his rumbling body ease my pulse.

I blew out a breath and glanced around my room again.

Oil painting on my wall. Real.

Potted plants taking over the window. Real.

Mountain of unopened boxes containing cat toys. Real.

One more deep breath before I rolled my shoulders back and climbed out of bed. There was a strange routine to the night terrors. Despite the adrenaline pumping through my veins and my brain trying to convince me that I was about to get kidnapped, I was used to everything that followed once the lights came on. Sleep was out of the picture for tonight.

I grabbed my phone from its docket and sent Victor a pink flower emoji. There were dozens of them in our chat history, usually sent sometime between 3am and 5am. It was the easiest way to let him know I was up without actually putting into words why.

The first time I'd woken him with my screams, he'd stormed into my room, ready to cut someone down.

Last year, when Del first moved in, he'd stayed in the guest room for a few weeks - and when my screams woke Del, he was there to stop her from turning it into a big deal.

Nowadays, both of them had as much of a routine as me.

I slipped on my dressing gown, dropped my phone into the pocket, and washed up. My hair was a tousled mess, but I managed to pin it into a braided bun that wouldn't require me to take a shower right now. Stripping naked and voluntarily standing in a tiny cubicle from which I couldn't see the rest of the room? No, thanks.

By the time I looked somewhat presentable and made it downstairs, Victor stood in the kitchen, filling a cereal bowl with diced fruit. His hair was just getting long enough to stand off at all angles, which was odd for someone who usually kept it meticulously trimmed short. But my attention was actually caught by the tight stretch of his black t-shirt and gray sweatpants, my stomach flipping upside-down in response. That had to be a lot of sexual frustration he was working off, if those bulging muscles were the result. He'd always stayed fit, but this was new. And I didn't hate it.

I was being awkward. Clenching and unclenching my fists, I forced myself to stop staring.

"Hi," I said, voice croaky from either sleeping or screaming.

"Morning." His eyes roamed up and down my body. Unlike me, who had been ogling, he was just doing what he always did: Checking if I was alright. Pleased with the result, he slid the bowl over the counter.

I grimaced at the heap of vitamins in front of me.

My routine usually included something with way more sugar and cream. He'd been faster this time.

When I didn't pick up the fork, he let out a sigh and rummaged through the cabinets, bringing back a box of chocolate chips. He set it on the counter with enough force to let me know exactly what he was thinking about my choices.

"Thank you." I smiled and emptied half the box over my fruit.

Victor wordlessly took the seat next to me at the counter. He cut pieces off an apple, bringing them to his mouth with the knife still in hand. The backs of both his hands were inked with black roses, but on his left hand, each finger also sported a different kind of dagger. Holding a knife in those fingers should have looked menacing. Not so much when he was slicing into a bright red Pink Lady.

"You're staring," he noted without looking at me.

"You eat apples weird," I said, because it seemed better than admitting I was staring at his fingers.

He hummed and cut a perfect crescent slice off, holding it out for me, wedged between the blade and his thumb.

I took it and watched him go back to slicing random bits off the fruit for himself, his long fingers so precise in how he turned it over in his hands, going round and round. The muscles in his forearms flexed with each cut, and I forgot to chew the apple in my mouth.

If you are ready for something complicated. Del's words from the other night came flooding back. I'd been busy enough with the preparation for the video campaign not to dwell on them, but something about the way Victor handled that apple... Was I ready for something complicated?

"Is it Whitaker?" Victor asked.

"What?" For once, I was trying to grasp the conversation he was having in his head without me.

"Are you on edge because Silas Whitaker's coming over?"

"Oh. Maybe." It wasn't like the nightmares were always triggered by something happening, but in this case, that would actually make sense. Silas was the videographer I'd contacted for the campaign, and we were around ten hours and 32 minutes away from him standing on my doorstep. Okay, so maybe that was on my mind. "It'll be fine," I said, not sure whether I was reassuring him or myself.

"I'll make it back in time."

"I know." I dug around in my bowl until my spoon was loaded with nothing but raspberries and chocolate. "Do you want to tell me what's on your agenda today?"

"Yes," his mouth set in a stern line, "but it's probably better if I don't."

Complicated didn't even begin to cover it.

"I wish you would," I breathed, "I keep worrying about what

you're doing when you're not here. Who you're with and if you're being careful."

"Cordelia." His hand moved across the counter, but with the knife still held steady, only his pinky stretched for my wrist. It was the smallest touch, meant to comfort me, but it sent an electric spark zapping up my arm instead. "I promise you that I'm safe. Right now, Petya is just yanking my leash."

"Right now? What about later?" His touch immediately forgotten, the implication of his words raced through my mind, a dozen different scenarios playing out. Shots being fired, either by criminals or the police. The police wouldn't know that Victor was good. They would shoot him without hesitation if he was caught in some raid.

He didn't reply, which just confirmed my suspicions.

"I refuse to pick any more coffins. Two is more than enough."

His eyes narrowed, but he followed my jumping thoughts. "I promise not to die."

"How can you promise that? You don't know that."

He calmly placed the knife aside and turned to me. Before I could swivel around myself, his hand was on the seat of my chair, and he turned it until I came face-to-face with him.

"It's simple, zhizn' moya," he grew still, the rumble of his Russian hanging in the few inches of air between us like a film of smoke that made it harder to breathe, "ya otkazyvayus' pokinut' etot mir ran'she tebya."

"What does that mean?"

"I refuse to."

"You can't refuse death." My hands itched to reach for my hair, but it was all braided away. Refusing to die was not a good enough plan. It wouldn't stop his uncle from putting him in danger.

"Death can try to take me away from you, but I will be the one left standing." Victor's forest green eyes bore into mine. I wasn't sure I could have looked away if I tried. And for a moment, caught by his attention, every cell in my body stilled.

He would be the one left standing. Real.

I nodded.

CORDELIA • 2:05PM

Are you going to make it on time?

CORDELIA • 2:11PM

Please tell me you're on your way.

CORDELIA • 2:13PM

Please.

CORDELIA • 2:19PM

Victor?

CORDELIA • 2:24PM

I swear to god, if you're not here in the next five minutes, I'm revoking your gym rights.

CORDELIA • 2:24PM

I will never play chess with you again.

CORDELIA • 2:25PM

Say goodbye to your protein bars.

CORDELIA • 2:28PM

Please tell me you're okay.

"Come on in." I stepped aside to let Silas pass by. My eyes lingered on the street just a moment longer, but Victor's car wasn't coincidentally just pulling up.

I led my guest to the office, but I left the door open just in case.

That was all the nerves I would allow considering the stranger in my house.

Silas Whitaker strolled into the room like he'd been there a thousand times before. He draped his brown wool coat over the back of one of the chairs and took a seat, not waiting for me to direct him, not even looking around to take in his surroundings.

"Can I offer you something to drink?" I asked. *Please don't let him ask for coffee.* I had no idea how to operate that contraption in the kitchen.

"Thank you, I'm good."

"Let me know if you change your mind."

Silas' dark brown curls were disheveled to just the right degree of carelessness, his goatee was precisely cut into a devil-may-care kind of shape, and his skin was just tan enough to let you know he hadn't spent all winter in the country. And that didn't even touch on the perfectly starched shirt collar popped out over the vintage knit sweater.

And in all his perfect calculation, he waited for me to take my seat before speaking again: "Cordelia, can I just say that I'm honored to meet you? Thank you for getting in touch."

"Honored?" I asked.

"I know the sharks have been circling for months. Everyone's desperate to get an exclusive sit-down. You're a hard woman to get a hold of."

"I'm a very private person."

"Of course," he leaned forward on his knees, putting on a toothpaste commercial-worthy smile, "that's what we should focus on, too. You as a person. I'm not here to rehash the same headlines from years ago."

I blinked at the man in front of me. Too perfectly imperfect. Too focused on saying the right thing. "You're different from what I imagined," I said because I was getting the distinct feeling that I was wasting my time. "I wanted to meet with you based on the piece you did in Tanzania."

"Tanzania?" His mask slipped. Silas' brows furrowed and his easy smile dropped. "That was ten years ago."

"Yes. I have since donated a considerable amount to the organizations you accompanied on that trip. I keep in touch with one or two of them. They've been making great progress against the poachers in the south."

He fell back in the chair. The confusion on his face highlighted the little lines around his eyes. He was only a few years older than me, but he'd traveled enough for the sun to mark his skin. "Tanzania?" he asked again.

"If you're willing to treat the Theresa Montgomery foundation with as much care and respect, I'd love to hire you for our video campaign. I'd need three short videos and one longer one, around fifteen minutes. We have to show people that we exist, how we can help them, and that they're safe with us."

The job prospect seemed to get through to him. Interest piqued, the confusion made way for what I assumed was his business face. "I would like to propose a deal."

"Pitch me," I replied, unfazed.

"I'll do your campaign. I can make your foundation look like it was blessed by Mother Teresa herself." He nodded. "But afterwards, I want to shadow you. I don't care if it takes a month, six months, or a year. I would like to really spend time with you, see everything you have accomplished and will accomplish. I won't lie, we will have to talk about your family. Because that's where it all started and that's what has already grabbed people's attention. However, I'd prefer to keep that part to a bare minimum. You're the story, not your parents."

"I'm not a story," I said, shaking my head. Amani had called my past a tragic origin story. Now even my present and future were supposed to be turned into a *story*?

"Take a few days to think about it."

"Think about what? You wanting to follow me around for a

year? I don't do much. I sit in this office and type on my computer all day."

"Why don't you let me be the judge of what's interesting. It's my series."

"Oh, it's a series now?"

"Would you prefer a thirty-minute interview with the same boring questions you've heard a dozen times already and have mostly declined to answer?"

"I'm flattered, Silas, but I don't think this will work. I'm trying to drum up PR for a charitable foundation, not get a Netflix special."

"Again, you don't have to worry about that. Let me shadow you for a week. That's all. Just to show you what it would be like, what I can do if you give me that time."

"You want to audition to make a reality show about me?" That's all his production company had been spewing out the last three years. Reality shows. I'd hoped the man who had sparked my fascination with nature documentaries still existed, but maybe I'd been wrong.

"It's a docu series. About you, about the Montgomery fortune, about the Theresa Montgomery foundation, all the people working behind the scenes, and the many women bene-fiting from it."

"What would shadowing me look like?"

"I'll come over with my team-"

"No," I cut him off, "no, that's..." My breathing shallowed at the thought of a whole group of camera men and sound guys trampling around my house. Going into all my rooms. I wouldn't be able to keep all of them on my radar at all times. And if Victor followed one stray around, then I would be alone with the rest of them. Except Victor wasn't even here now. He was already leaving me alone with this total stranger who was nothing like what I'd expected.

"No team," I said, voice short, "not in here."

"I'd come over with my team for one day to set up the lights and microphones. That's all. You don't even have to be here for that."

"Thank you. I will think about it." I got out of my chair and pointed a very direct arm at the door, wishing it wouldn't betray me by trembling like a leaf in a breeze.

"Cordelia-"

"Silas, please leave, or it's an automatic *no* from me."

At least he had the good sense to take me by my word and take his jacket. "It was a pleasure meeting you, Cordelia."

"I wish I could say the same, but then I don't take pleasure in meeting *anyone*."

He chuckled and was still smiling when I directed him out the front door, not taking my eyes off him until he was down on the sidewalk. Once I'd shut the door and turned the lock, I crumpled to the floor. Whatever will had kept me upright dissipated. This wasn't how it was supposed to go. He wasn't supposed to be *that*. And I wasn't supposed to be alone.

I wasn't supposed to be alone.

I pressed the heels of my hands into my eyes to stop the images from flickering up. Just as one stupidly predictable shape burnt through the lights behind my closed lids, the house alarm beeped. I had to scramble backwards to avoid being crushed by the door swinging open.

"Fuck," Victor breathed before he'd even fully stepped inside.

His shoes were wet. Rain. Just rain. Not-

"Cordelia?"

"Hm?" My head snapped up, and immediately swiveled back down because he was crouching in front of me.

"Come on." Victor shrugged out of his wet jacket and left it on the floor before his arms closed around me and he pulled me to my feet. He shuffled us into the sitting room. The sofa was much softer than the floor, and warmer too. Victor's fingers gently tugged my chin from side to side, before picking up my arms by the wrists, eyes scanning every inch from shoulder to pinky. This inspection was much more thorough than his usual once-over, and I didn't have the strength to protest, or to even form the words to tell him I wasn't hurt.

"I'm sorry," he sighed, when he was happy with the state of my body, sitting on the coffee table with my feet in his lap.

"I- I-" The sentence died on my lips, a hiccup breaking through. The tight feeling in my chest was spreading, stifling my nerves and filling my ears with a dull rushing sound.

"I know. I'm sorry, Cordelia." His thumbs circled over my ankles. "I fucked up."

My mouth opened but no sound came out. I hated this. At the same time that my body was going into complete frozen panic, I knew how absolutely silly I was being, how stupid it was to freak out over someone visiting my house.

"It's alright. I've got you." Victor shifted onto the sofa next to me and tucked me against his side. A strong, earthy smell clung to his skin and I tried to let each inhale ground me. His chin folded over my head as he kept repeating the same phrase over and over again: "It's alright. It's alright. It's alright." He held me through my muscles shaking and my breath stuttering and quiet tears rolling down my cheeks, and he still held me when every last shred of energy was spent, and I sagged against him.

"It's alright," he still whispered when the exhaustion took me under.

CHAPTER ELEVEN

VICTOR

"Again!" Yury yelled like the relentless motherfucker he was.

My stamina had been shot to pieces over the last few years, but I had something to fight today. It was hard to get tired of punching Yury when he was the reason I hadn't made it home to Cordelia in time for her meeting. He was the one who had gone off-schedule. I hadn't even showered, just sprinted off, and I'd still been too fucking late. Each hit I landed was for the girl I'd scooped off the cold ground. The same one who had reassured me with a smile today that it was okay for me to leave her again.

I made it twice as long as last time, before the old man gave me the sign to wrap it up. I threw one more punch to his gut for the sick pleasure of hearing him grunt. Could have gone a few more rounds without getting sick of that sound.

"What was that about?" Luka asked when I walked out of the shower.

Petya had built an entire extension behind the house twenty years ago, just for me to train without anyone spying on my moves. Luka was leaning against a treadmill, barely looking up from his phone.

"What?" I asked, still keeping my communications with him to a minimum.

"I know how you fight when you're angry. It's sloppy."

"Do it better then."

"Hey, I'm not criticizing you," he shrugged, "that's Yury's job."

Except we were focused on endurance, so Yury had no reason to rip into me for my moves lacking precision. "What do you want?"

"Fetching you for an audience with his eminence," Luka pocketed his phone and fell into step beside me.

Since I had no choice, I just followed his directions. I knew what would happen if I refused a meeting with the great Piotr Yelchin and just walked out the front door. When I'd pulled that shit at 19, because I was chasing some college girl, Petya's men had showed up on her doorstep. They had given me a bloody lip and a black eye, and had dragged both me and the girl to the dinner table without giving us the chance to get dressed. She'd sat there barefoot, in her jeans and black bra, me in my boxers next to her, and we had to eat and make conversation like nothing was wrong.

Needless to say I'd never heard from her again.

Luka led us upstairs to Petya's office. He knocked twice and waited for his father to call him in before he scanned his key against the scanner.

My uncle sat behind the sleek desk in a colorless room. Everything in here was gleaming and polished to a sterile degree of white. Like walking into a sick version of heaven, but you were greeted by the devil in a Brooks Brothers suit.

"Come, sit, Vitya." My uncle waved me forward. Luka stayed near the door, but I wordlessly followed command. "You've never been much of a talker, but you have gone quiet. Don't tell me that blonde shrew has muzzled you."

He wouldn't get a rise out of me by going for Cordelia. I knew better than to give him that ammunition. I raised my brows.

"She cut out the tongues of all her little servant boys?" he taunted.

I shrugged.

"Yury tells me you're making progress," he said after a moment of silence passed.

"Yes," I confirmed.

"Good, good." He hummed before reaching into his jacket. My pulse skipped a single beat, preparing for the sight of a gun. Instead, Petya produced a thick cardstock envelope with my name lettered in gold foil. "I expect you to clear your schedule for Natalia's wedding next week. It would be a shame to miss such a momentous family event."

"I never agreed to quality time."

"Consider it the unofficial announcement of your comeback. Your return will be a welcome sight to many. Possibly even some sponsors."

"What sponsors?"

"Friends in the import-export business." The sly grin on his lips spoke volumes of how little he trusted me. A few years ago, he would have openly boasted about how easy it was to get Russian hookers into the country through surrogacy schemes, or how he was tripling his business by cutting coke with horse tranquilizer. *Import-export* was as detailed an account as I would get from him now.

"Fine." I held my hand out.

"You will not ruin Natalia's wedding day with this attitude, son."

Still wasn't his son. "I'll smile."

"Good. And get a goddamn haircut." He harrumphed in a way that let me know I was dismissed.

"Petya," I rose from my chair and leveled my uncle with a look that might just cost me later, "tell Yury that if he changes my schedule again, I'll make sure we'll need to find a new trainer soon."

Against all odds, Petya bellowed out a laugh. "Good to see the little shrew only got your tongue, not your balls, Vitya."

Pocketing the damn wedding invitation, I beelined for the door. Luka was there to open it with his key fob before I could even think about fumbling mine from my pocket.

"Do you have an actual fucking death wish, asshole?" Luka breathed as we jogged down the stairs.

"It's a game."

The second we stepped outside, his lighter flashed and he had a cigarette dangling from the corner of his mouth. "One that you're not going to win."

"Depends on your definition of winning." Mine had certainly changed.

"What's your definition of winning then?" Luka scoffed.

The dealings of our family had always hung over our heads like thick, black clouds. You either found your umbrella before the worst of the rain could hit you, and you made the best out of your wet shoes, or you tried to outrun the rain. Unlike Luka, I was now focused on the third option: Holding my umbrella over Cordelia's head.

"I'll tell you when I'm sure you're not a snitch."

"Victor-"

"Places to be," I said instead of letting him speak and got in my car.

"Hey, hold up!" Irina shouted down the driveway before I could shut my door. She barreled towards me, curls bouncing. "Give me a ride." It was neither a question, nor did she wait for me to reply as she plopped into the passenger seat.

Luka just threw his hands up and went back inside. Guess that meant I was giving Irina a ride.

"Why are you in my car?" I asked when we passed the front gate of Petya's estate without anyone stopping us to drag my little cousin back.

"Because Dad tracks mine."

"I'm pretty sure he's put a tracker on this one, too."

"Sure, but I can just get out at a random red light and then walk or grab a cab. He won't even know where I got out of your car."

"He's probably tracking your phone."

"I wasn't born yesterday, Vitya. I left it at home and I'm only using cash, so he can't track my cards."

I glanced over at the young woman clamoring for some freedom, dark makeup around her eyes, clad in a pair of low jeans and a crop top under her jacket.

"Date?" I asked.

"Yeah," she breathed, looking out the window.

I wondered if Irina knew about my parents. Did she know that her father had killed his own sister - my mother - for this kind of shit? My parents had wanted their freedom. They had tried to make a run for it when I was seventeen and was already being trained by Yury to join the family business. I came back from a fight in Vegas and suddenly had ashes for parents.

"Do you have a pen?" I asked.

"Around here somewhere." Irina opened her purse and started rummaging around in it. "Why?"

"I'll give you my number in case you need a ride home tonight."

She hesitated for a moment before writing my number on an old gum wrapper. "Thanks."

"Stay out of trouble, okay?"

"Please," Irina rolled her eyes at me with a grin, "I bring the trouble."

She hopped out of the car at a street light near the city center, and pulled up her jacket's hood against the drizzle. Maybe I had to reevaluate my definition of winning against my uncle. Maybe I had to find a way to get Irina under the safe umbrella, too, before her father could snuff out her desire for freedom.

WHILE I DIDN'T LIKE LEAVING CORDELIA ALONE LONGER than needed, I'd been able to give her a heads-up today. I had one more errand to run.

Despite offering to pay for his time, the scraggly old shop-keeper had refused my request for an after-hours appointment, when Cordelia would have been asleep. I could have thrown my name around. Most shop owners in Boston were either in our pocket or the Italians', but I didn't need some Patriarca bastard coming after me, trying to make a name for himself at an antiquities shop.

The golden bell above the door startled the tiny man with thick glasses behind the counter. Apparently he didn't get a lot of visitors. Not surprising. His website looked like it had been built in the 90s, but at least his phone number had been accurate.

"Hello there," he croaked, "is there anything I can help you with, sir?"

"Here for the teapot," I said, refusing pleasantries.

"Right, right. Of course." He tapped a bony finger against his temple as if he needed to jumpstart his brain.

The shop was tiny and it was stuffed to the ceiling with clutter and dust. I was sure Cordelia would have a field day rummaging through every cabinet, finding trinkets and hair clips and tea spoons. I'd always been fascinated with history, if only because of Petya's obsession with everything modern, but I didn't need to own some dusty musket to appreciate its perseverance over time.

"Here it is." The shop owner resurfaced behind an old chest of drawers and set the white porcelain teapot out on the counter. It was shaped like an onion, decorated with swirls of gold and flowers in various shades of pink. It was as gaudy as it could get without actually being pink. She'd love it.

"Music?"

"Yes, right in the bottom here." He turned the pot over to twist the music box handle round and round. "It goes without saying that you shouldn't soak it in water or put it in the dishwasher."

"Sure." I waited for the tune to play. Tea for two. Doris Day had crooned the song for me dozens of times as I had memorized the melody, so I'd be able to recognize it.

The teapot did start playing the correct melody, but it was distorted. Almost like it was playing underwater.

"It's too slow," I said.

"Oh yes, these music boxes get a little pesky with age. Of course, being built into dishware doesn't help, does it? Who bothers to do maintenance on their teapots?"

He was talking too much for a straightforward transaction. "Can you fix it?"

"Well, yes, but..."

"I don't care if it costs extra."

"Hmm." He scratched his chin and narrowed his eyes at me. "It will take me a few days. Longer if I need to install a new spring."

"I'll pay half now, half when it's fixed, plus the repair cost."

He stopped talking as much when I tossed the bills on the counter. "Of course. I will give you a call when it's ready."

That was Cordelia's present sorted. Next on the list was making sure that yesterday's incident with that video guy hadn't changed her actual birthday plans. She'd been making strides with having people in the house, and I was not going to be the reason she regretted it.

CHAPTER TWELVE

Cordelia

"What did you do?" My house had exploded. Or at least the furniture had. Not literally. It just looked like one of my midnight urges to rearrange the living room, only to run out of steam at 1am when everything was peak messy.

Except, I had spent all day in my office, perfectly sealed off. I had spent the entire rest of the week there, wonderfully alone with my work, ignoring every ping I got from Amani about the video campaign. So, unless I was suffering some strange form of amnesia, the chairs in the hallway weren't my fault. Victor, however, stood on the armchair in the living room, arms crossed in front of the chest.

"The floor is lava."

"Excuse me?"

"The floor is lava!" He pointed at the haphazard furniture. "Get on the damn chair, Cordelia."

"Don't yell at me," I shrieked at this loud tone, but I still climbed onto the chair.

"The game is simple."

"Game?" I laughed and raised my brows at Victor across the expanse of the hallway and the living room, nothing but air between us.

"You said no more chess."

"We can play chess if you want."

"The game is simple," he started again, because apparently our weekly chess match had just turned into a round of *the floor is lava,* "you just have to complete three stations to get to the ice cream. You are only allowed to step down when you reach each station. If your feet touch the ground on your way, you lose an ice cream topping."

Dangling ice cream in front of me was cruel. He knew I'd play for a bowl of rocky road with gummy bears, sprinkles and whipped cream.

I opened and closed my mouth, unsure of what to say, but my eyes were already roaming the hallway, trying to figure out where else I could step. The small bench that usually stood next to the coat rack was conveniently placed five feet away from me, taking me closer to the living room, where more chairs cluttered the room and the sofa had been turned 90 degrees. He'd been busy.

"Okay. Fine. What are the stations?"

Victor pointed at the drinks cart from the kitchen that had conveniently found its way to the corner of the sitting room. "The cocktail bar. Make up your own drink with at least three ingredients and it has to taste good."

"I can do that."

"The craft station, where you have to make something useful. Can't just be a picture." He pointed past me and I glanced at the far end of the hallway, where he'd set out a ton of DIY stuff.

"Then why's there a canvas?" I asked, narrowing my eyes at the old frame that I probably bought ten years ago or so.

"I don't know. You have too much art and crafts stuff. I just grabbed a few things from the basement."

"You can't just grab *a few things*. It's sorted by project. You have the jewelry making box, the soap making equipment, embroid- I mean, you can't replace the wick for scented candles with glittery embroidery yarn."

"You'll figure something out." A small smirk played over his lips, and my stomach flipped. I was going to play a dozen rounds of this game for the chance of seeing that again.

"What's the third station?" I asked, suddenly breathless.

"TV room karaoke."

"Nope. You lost me."

"One drink, one trinket, one song, and the ice cream is yours."

"Or I just get off the chair, walk to the kitchen and get myself some ice cream."

"It's not in the kitchen. It's in a cooler, which I have hidden somewhere in this house. You complete each station, and you get a clue."

"Fine," I blew out a long breath, "I'll play, but you have to tell me why."

"Because you need to have some fun."

"I don't..."

"Come on, Cordelia. The cooler won't keep the ice cream frozen all night."

"Okay, okay, I'm coming. Jeez, you're bossy." I grabbed the back of my chair for support and took a large step onto the bench. Beyond that, nothing was within immediate stepping distance. "How am I supposed to get anywhere from here?"

Victor jumped from the armchair to the sofa and waved for me to join him. "Jump. I'll catch you." I hesitated, jumped, almost slipped off the sofa's arm rest but Victor's hands were around my middle before my balance could tilt. "See?"

"Thanks," my breath stuttered in my lungs as I gazed up into his stark green eyes. There it was again, that voice in the back of my head that told me to kiss him. To just go for it. That being this close to him was right. I cleared my throat but Victor didn't let go of me. "Usually, I'm the one with the silly ideas, and you tell me not to turn the entire house into a blanket fort, not to fill the pool with bubbles..." *Not to hire a body double to take my place.*

"Desperate times." His thumb drew the slowest of circles over my back, pulling a deep shiver from my chest that rattled down to my tailbone.

"I'm in desperate need of fun?" I felt my tongue move, but the voice sounded throaty and foreign in the space between us.

He tilted his head in a curt nod that brought out the small cleft in his chin. Goodness, I wanted to run my tongue through-*nope*. I cleared my throat and shuffled back on the sofa.

After consulting Del, Tabitha and Defne for many hours and over many texts, I had come up with the simplest of plans: Wait until Victor made a move. I'd kissed him, so the ball had to be in his court, right? So he could kiss me, or ask me out, or do whatever it was people did to romantically pursue someone.

He could even serenade me. Karaoke was on the docket tonight, right?

Or stand in the backyard and yell up at my balcony like Romeo. Except I didn't have a balcony, just a window. And it was freezing outside.

"Drinks?" Victor asked, snapping me back to the present.

"Yes."

The next few minutes consisted of me trying to jump between a footrest and the sofa table, which were entirely spaced too far apart. After my first few almost-jumps, Victor started yelling at me in Russian, and I yelled back that I was not risking my rainbow sprinkles in the first round.

When I did make the jump, I collapsed onto the sofa table in giggles, completely out of breath. But I'd done it. Victor followed with two long strides. Completely unfair advantage with his longer legs. He stood over me, shaking his head.

"Impossible girl," he huffed with just a hint of another smirk before helping me up.

My chosen cocktail consisted of mango and passionfruit juice, coconut water and two shots of rum. Victor deemed it good enough and paused the game just to get some ice cubes from the kitchen.

My first clue towards the ice cream was 'nice view' which didn't exactly help, because every room at the back of the house overlooked the backyard and the Charles river just behind it.

"What do you want me to make you?" I asked halfway to the craft station. The rum buzzed through my limbs just enough to make launching myself through the air a little easier. At least for me. Probably also thanks to the last shreds of my meds still coursing through my system. Those had the rum pumping through my veins at a hundred miles per hour.

"I can't tell you. You have to come up with the idea."

"Why?"

"It's part of the fun."

I crinkled my nose at him while balancing with both feet on a bar stool from the kitchen. I had to lower myself onto it before I'd be able to step onto the next chair, so my voice came out like a grunt when I said: "I don't know why you think I'm not having fun. I'm having loads of fun. All the time."

"You're the worst liar I've ever met," he replied dryly.

"Enlighten me then," I huffed, clinging to the stool while the tippiest tips of my toes stretched for the next chair's backrest, just to turn it a bit.

"You've been holding back since last year, since I killed Julian Beckett in your kitchen."

My hands slipped. The stool capsized. My toes were still

caught on the next chair's backrest, when my world tilted sideways and I crashed to the floor. A sharp bolt shot up my tailbone. Then the stupid stool smashed into my shoulder before clattering to the floor, leaving a dull pain in its wake that promised a humongous bruise. "Ow." I grunted.

Victor's hands were on me before I could fully process the fall. He pressed his fingertips into my wrists and my knuckles, checking for broken bones, when my ass had really taken the brunt of it. "Alright?" he asked, no time for the whole sentence.

"Alright," I replied, letting my hands go limp in his, soaking up the warmth of every touch. "And my feet technically didn't touch the ground."

"Hmm?"

I nodded at the one foot still on the chair, and my other slung over my lap. "My feet don't touch the ground. I don't lose any ice cream toppings."

He laughed. An actual Victor laugh. I had heard that sound only a handful of times over the years, and it was the best thing in the world. Completely husky, rumbling from his chest like a rockslide. "You're right."

"I might need help getting up though. Is that allowed?"

"Of course."

"Thanks," I said but when his arm came around my shoulder, pain flared back up and I shrank away with a hiss.

"You're not alright."

"It'll bruise. It's fine."

"Get up. I'll have a look at it."

"I'm not getting up. My feet will not touch the ground."

"I'm not playing, Cordelia."

"Well, I am. For glory. Until the bitter end." I stuck my tongue out at him. He could watch me have some fun. I would not give up my rainbow sprinkles over a technicality.

"Fucking hell," he breathed and grabbed my foot off my lap. In a singular swift move, Victor lowered himself with his back to me, and wrapped both my legs around his middle. "Good arm," he commanded and I gave it to him. He hooked it around his neck at a precise angle, then shot off the ground.

I let out a banshee-worthy squeal. Undeterred, Victor's steel grip closed around my crossed ankles, and my elbow, locking me onto his back.

Piggyback ride.

The term swam somewhere in the back of my brain among other words I hadn't had use for in almost 20 years.

Only that my idea of a piggyback ride and this didn't correlate. Not when my skirt pushed up against my hips. Not when my thighs choked his hips until his belt loops would leave lasting grooves. Not when my nose pressed into his shoulder and his earthy scent coated my nerves like syrup.

"Here you go."

The ride was over before it had even started as he lowered me to the blanket that marked the craft station. I quickly tugged my skirt back into place, heat blooming on my cheeks. I was such a lost cause.

"You craft, I check your shoulder," he ordered.

"Yeah, that sounds like fun," I muttered.

"Just run with your ideas."

I picked up a square piece of leather from when I was convinced I should bind my own notebooks. "Victor," I sighed.

"Have fun," he ordered and crouched behind me.

"Gosh, you're annoying."

He didn't react to my insult. Or if he did, I completely blacked out, because his hands were in my hair. He gathered it all together in the back, his warm knuckles brushing over the delicate skin of my neck. My spine stiffened at the touch. It was so careful, so slow, so *new*. Victor had touched me a number of times, but not like this. He draped my hair over my good shoulder, giving way for his breath to feather out over my skin.

"Where?" he asked, voice dropped to a husky whisper against my neck.

I reached around, trying to show him where the stool had hit me.

"Tell me if I hurt you."

I nodded, voice lost in the depth of my body, every cell zeroing in on where his fingertips pushed in under the neckline of my shirt. They scooped up the elastic strap of my bra, too. My shoulder came free, the fabric of my clothes barely touching my throbbing skin.

"It got you good." A single digit traced the heated outline of where the bruise was forming. "Lift your arm for me."

My brain switched to autopilot as I moved my arm in each direction he advised - and I pathetically soaked up every single touch he afforded me. "Let me get you some ice."

"It's fine," I breathed.

"I'm sorry." I almost didn't hear the words, quietly uttered into the crook of my neck.

"For what?"

"Letting Julian get to you."

"You didn't- what are you- why would-" I shook my head against the onslaught of crisscrossing thoughts. "I let him walk through the front door. That's on me."

"I should have been here."

"I asked you to look after Del. You did exactly what you were supposed to."

"I shouldn't have let Julian blackmail me into getting Del released from the hospital."

"Are you serious?" I twisted around to glare at him over my bare shoulder. "No. You do not get to come into *my* house and feel guilty for being on the shitty end of someone's blackmail schemes. What the actual fuck, Victor?"

"Fuck?" He worked his jaw, my use of a few swear words apparently hitting home. "No, that's not-"

"You did everything he asked as soon as he asked. My life would be very different if my father had done the same seventeen years ago. I wouldn't have sat in that room for days, wishing they'd just get it over with and kill me like they'd killed my mother. You do not get to feel sorry for *doing the right thing* instead of trying to outplay someone with a gun."

"He didn't let you go. I did what he wanted, he still didn't let you go, and he got my family involved."

"That's not on you."

"I should have-"

"Shut up," I bristled, "I took the risks. I came up with the idea to hire Delilah. I encouraged her to date Beck. Those things are on me. You went along with every single stupid idea. It's not your fault that things spiraled out of control. Six years ago, you asked me to hire you so you could hide from your family, and I put that in jeopardy. So yes, I'm being more careful. Maybe I am holding back. Because I'm trying to calculate for bad things happening, not just to me, but to the people I care about."

"Hmm."

"What?"

"Not the fun night I hoped for."

I snorted. "Here, give me two minutes." I turned back to the piece of leather now completely crumpled in my fist. I smoothed it out before cutting it into shape. One golden eyelet and a key ring later, I had crafted a smiley face keychain. "Proof of having fun."

He wordlessly took his key from his pocket and worked the keychain onto it.

"You can't plan for every asshole coming for your throat," he said, laying a careful touch to my shoulder, "you can have the best defense in the world, but someone's going to land a punch, and you have to roll with it or you'll get knocked out."

"Is that MMA wisdom?"

"Yes, and you know what else is?"

"What?"

"Defense doesn't win a fight."

"Easier said than done."

"Up you go, let's put some ice on that before it swells up."

"Karaoke?" I asked.

"Next time."

He had the ice cream cooler stored in the winter garden, where he directed me onto the soft cerise chaise lounge and wedged a cold pack between my shoulder and the backrest.

Despite not completing his obstacle course, I got my ice cream with all the toppings. Victor sat down next to me with a single scoop of mint chocolate chip. That just looked like a sad excuse for ice cream compared to the mountain in my bowl - but back when he'd first come to work for me, he wouldn't even touch ice cream. He'd eat an apple, or a carrot. A carrot?! While I was shoveling down pure sugar. So I had swallowed every mean comment about his choice of ice cream flavor when he'd finally given in, even if it was pure toothpaste.

Victor was leaning back on the chaise, eyes on the backyard. The light from the winter garden illuminated a few feet of grass already frosting over with the onset of night, but the rest was complete darkness. Without much to see out there, I allowed my gaze to linger on Victor.

He'd been growing out his buzzcut, but even the soft hazelnut swoop over his forehead didn't soften his features. His face was all sharp slopes. The steep cut of his forehead and nose reminded me of a mountain ridge slicing a line between sky and earth.

Defense doesn't win a fight.

"I wasn't holding back when I kissed you."

If he was surprised by my words, he didn't show it. "No, but you were drunk," he said, not sparing me a glance.

"So taking risks only counts when I'm sober?"

His eyes narrowed but he didn't reply, waiting where I was going with this.

"I'm as good as sober now. Between falling off the chair and this ice cream, I can barely feel the rum." I bit the inside of my cheek. "So in the name of not holding back and having fun... I still like the idea of kissing you."

A moment of silence swelled between us as he flexed his jaw and stared up through the glass roof to the starless sky, where a single airplane was passing by. "I don't think that's a good idea."

Oh.

Oh.

My insides twisted into a painful knot, ice cream dangerously close to making a reappearance. "Okay." I blinked against the rapid onset of tears. "I'm sorry. I thought... I guess I thought wrong. Sorry." I grabbed my dishes and scrambled to my feet. The ice pack dropped to the ground behind me.

"Cordelia."

"Please, don't say anything right now."

He followed me to the kitchen. Wordlessly putting his bowl in the sink after me, hovering as I gripped the countertop to steady my shaking hands. I couldn't even look at him, but I felt him next to me. The warmth radiating off his body and seeping through my skin. His stupid earthy aftershave tickling my nose. I wanted to tell him to leave. At the same time, I wanted to crawl into him and feel that warmth skin-on-skin.

"Ty razbudila vo mne davno zabytoye."

The rumble in his words chased a warm shiver down my spine but I still couldn't look up for fear of the pity I would find there. "What does that mean?"

"I have yet to say *no* to any of your ideas."

My head snapped up. "What are you saying?"

Eyes locked, we stood frozen. The silence in the kitchen was only broken by the clock on the wall. *Tick, tick, tick.* I needed him to say it. If he meant what I suspected, if he wouldn't deny me the idea of kissing him, I needed him to say it. *Tick, tick, tick.*

Victor's chest rose and fell in a deep but silent sigh.

Tick, tick, tick.

"We shouldn't do this until I've figured out my family shit."

"Okay."

"I shouldn't drag you deeper into my mess. I should probably stay far away. That would be the safest option for you. I should leave and let you fix the world with your foundation."

"Oh."

Victor's gaze dropped to my lips.

All the things he should or should not do crackled in the air between us.

I'd known from the day I met him who his family was. I'd known that I'd potentially put myself in danger by hiring him. I hadn't known that he still worried about that, at least not in relation to *us*.

Tick, tick, tick.

"What do you *want* to do?" I asked.

Victor didn't move a muscle, but I could see his thoughts racing behind those bottomless eyes.

Tick, tick, tick.

"Fuck it." He obliterated the last few inches of distance between us. His hands wrapped around my waist and my neck. Every move was a contradiction. He pulled me against him, but pushed me back into the counter. His hands caged me in with no room to budge, but his touch was featherlight. Whatever internal turmoil directed his hands, however, had no control over his mouth, because when Victor kissed me, *he kissed me*. No hesitation, no nipping. His kiss was a fist, stealing your breath and rattling your bones. My knees wobbled and I grabbed onto him, nails burrowing into his shoulders and hair, desperate to keep myself from being knocked out by that kiss.

His teeth sank into my lips, and I whimpered at the sharp burst of pain. Before the sound had even died in my throat, Victor's hands circled my middle and in a split-second, I was on the counter with him between my knees. And then his hands were everywhere. On my thighs, in my hair, roaming my sides and cupping my face, leaving burning hot trails on my skin without ever digging in. And with all the destruction he laid on me, all I could think was *more*.

I tugged at his shirt. I clawed at his neck. I pulled his hair. Desperate for *more*.

Instead of giving me what I craved, Victor jerked out of the kiss.

I gasped, cool air rushing into my chest.

"Cordelia." Victor's voice had gone low and husky and my name had never sounded better.

"More," I whispered, closing the distance between our lips again.

His hand folded around my jaw. Hard. No contradiction left in his touch as he pushed me back. "Zhizn' moya, you don't need to ask for more. You can have all of me. In due time. The first time I fuck you won't be on the kitchen counter."

His words sparked a heat low in my stomach, and yet they washed over me like an icy shower. My hands dropped to my sides. Was that where this would have headed? He would have... He thought I wanted...

All at once, the entirety of who I was crashed into me, because I would never, not once, have a normal experience. Everything was wrong. I was wrong. Victor thought I wanted to have sex with him right here, because he was a normal 34-year-old man who just so happened to work long hours in this house. He'd probably dated plenty. Kissed plenty. Slept with- and I didn't. I wasn't. I was still the same girl who was meant to go to a school dance with Clark Anderson in 9th grade and never actually made it there, because I'd been locked up, and hungry and scared, and my mom had taken me dress shopping and instead I ended up with her blood all over me. They took my jacket but not my shoes. The shoes. It always came down to the shoes. The dark red splotches on white sneakers etched into my brain. When other people closed their eyes, they saw colors and stars, and I saw the exact same pattern of blood stains over and over and over again. A fucked up Rorschach test with only one singular answer.

Something cold and smooth hit my lips, and I blinked.

"Drink," Victor said, tilting the glass of water for me.

I stared up in his vibrant green eyes, as I swallowed, as I let him pour cold water down my throat while my own limbs were lost to my nervous system. I couldn't have moved them if I wanted to.

"What triggered it?" he asked and set the glass down on the counter. His thumb brushed over my lip, catching a stray droplet. "Did I grab your chin too hard?"

"No," my voice came out hoarse, "you did nothing wrong."

"Something I said?"

I shook my head, my gaze dropping to my knees still framing his hips. "I just got overwhelmed for a moment. I liked the kiss. But when we stopped, and I thought about all the other things we could do, my thoughts were going a million miles an hour." I sighed. "The solution is obviously that you can never stop kissing me."

In response he laid a soft kiss to my cheek, and lifted me off the counter in the same breath.

Not the kissing I'd had in mind. I wanted this to be more than a one off make-out session that we might repeat in six years. "I can't wait until I'm 35."

His eyelids twitched in that way they did when he tried to catch my train of thought. I just opened my mouth to explain when his lips closed over mine again. Slow, this time. Deliberate. Just enough for my breath to stutter and the hairs on my arms to stand up. "We will do this. Properly. You have to give me some time to figure things out with my family, but I promise, it won't be another six years. But Cordelia?"

"Yes?"

"I know you. I want you. *When* we do this, I'll be all in. I'm not doing casual with you. We're not going slow."

My ribcage suddenly felt too small for the big, bright, fluttering feeling in my chest, and the only way I could let it out was by smiling. Smiling so wide, my cheeks hurt in an instant.

I could give him time. He could have all the time in the world if, at the end, we could have more of this.

"Alright," I whispered, nodding with my nose brushing against his.

"Alright," Victor said.

CHAPTER THIRTEEN

VICTOR

WELL... FUCK.

How the hell was I supposed to go on after kissing Cordelia Montgomery?

Nothing about the two kisses we had shared before compared to the one from last night. Last night, she had kissed me like she meant it.

The feeling of her thighs clamped around my hips had been haunting me for the last twelve hours. That raspy plea for *more* replayed on loop in my brain. Cordelia Montgomery had completely eradicated my ability to think straight.

I'd eyed the gym equipment for two seconds before I figured that I'd end up crushed by weights because my mind was adamantly focused on how careful her tongue had explored mine.

Swimming was easy. My head underwater, my arms and legs moving on their own, I allowed myself to stay in the memory.

At least until I spotted a bright pink spot on the side of the pool.

I stilled halfway down the lane and wiped the water from my eyes.

Cordelia tilted her head, hands gathering all her smooth hair on one side as she regarded me. She was actually trying to kill me. I couldn't think of a single other reason why she would stand there in sequined little shorts that revealed every inch of skin from her thigh crease to her ankles.

"Are you avoiding me?"

I shook my head.

"You missed breakfast." She lowered herself to the floor, letting her legs drop over the edge of the pool.

"Last time we kissed, you stopped eating. You couldn't be in the kitchen at the same time as me. You have to eat."

"Okay but last time I was embarrassed. I'm not embarrassed about last night."

"I'll be there for dinner," I said and swam up to her, my hands gripping the pool's edge on either side of her knees. "How's your shoulder?"

"Good. It's fine." She was still twirling her hair around her fingers, clearly trying to sort through her thoughts. "Are you sexually frustrated?"

I raised my brows, somehow doubting this was her way of flirting with me.

"Do you spend this much time working out because it's some sort of physical release?"

"No." I'd have to tell her the truth soon. Keeping it from her felt like keeping her in a separate and safe space though, so I stayed vague with my answer. "It's best to be in good shape when working for my uncle."

"I knew it," she muttered as if she'd just won an argument.

"Are *you* sexually frustrated? Is that why you kissed me?"

"No. I kissed you because I want you. Not in an *I want you - I need you - oh my god* - kind of way. I mean, maybe that too at some point. I just want you in my life, for the rest of my life preferably."

"I never considered any other future." I let my hands slide up her warm legs, leaving watery trails from her knees up her thighs. Her eyes fluttered shut and her lips parted when my thumbs dipped to the inside of her thighs. Fuck, I wanted to tease all these tiny reactions from her one by one. "Driver. Bodyguard. Husband. However you want me, Cordelia, I'm yours until the day they put me six feet under."

"I need you to stop touching me." A deep breath rattled through her lungs and her eyes flew open. A storm raged in her blue irises. "Please."

Without another word, I let my hands fall back to the edge of the pool. Cordelia squirmed and pressed her legs together.

"I can give you time," she pressed the words through tight lips, "I can wait for you to make sure your family won't bother us. Just don't make this harder for me by reminding me what I can't have yet. Please."

"I'm sorry." The anguish in her voice was a punch to the gut. I never wanted to be the cause of her pain.

"Yeah." She reached out but her hand froze halfway to my face. It took every drop of willpower in me, not to lean into her. After a moment's hesitation, she got to her feet. "Can you be home for a whole day next week?"

"Of course," I said. I'd deal with whatever Petya would want in exchange. Cordelia remained my first priority.

"Just let me know when's good for you. Silas Whitaker needs to come over to set up a few things for filming, and I don't want to be in the house when he does."

"Whitaker?"

She rolled her shoulders back and nodded. "Not holding myself back. I'm taking a risk."

"Good."

"Do you want me to save you some cake?"

"Cake?" For once, I couldn't quite fathom the five thoughts she jumped ahead.

"We're taste testing wedding cake options. Sorry, I should have told you. Del, Tabitha and Defne are all here." She pointed at the ceiling as if all that separated us from her friends were a few inches of concrete.

"You can tell them that you're saving it for me and eat it for breakfast tomorrow."

"Perfect." Cordelia beamed, her whole body doing a delighted little jiggle. Thank god for the pool distorting my body. The sight of those thighs shaking sent a wave of heat straight to my hips. No need to give Cordelia another reminder of things we wouldn't act on. Yet.

"Put some clothes on before you come upstairs," she said, "all of that is way too distracting." She waved in my general direction, her finger twirling to indicate - what? My tattoos? My biceps?

Either way, it was a badge of honor to know I was affecting her, too.

"Sure," I said and watched her thighs as she sauntered off with an extra kick in her step. That kick probably had everything to do with the outlook of cake for breakfast, and nothing to do with me.

CHAPTER FOURTEEN

Cordelia

VICTOR'S HOUSE WAS THE MIRROR VERSION OF MINE. My stairwell started on the right side of the entrance, his on the left side. My kitchen was at the back of my house to the left, his was on the right. The mirror dimension also bled into the colors. Everything that was bright and happy and beautiful in my house was... just there.

"We bought this place like this, right?" I asked, as I followed Victor to his dining table, where he'd set up a work station for me. It spoke volumes that everything he had brought over - my laptop, a fluffy pink throw blanket, my glittery tumbler, and my holographic notepad - were the only things standing out in this showroom of a house. "Did you never add personal belongings?"

"I have a punching bag. Some books." He shrugged and pulled

the chair out for me. He'd even added one of the furry cushions from my office.

"That's it?"

He shrugged. "Never here long enough to put in the effort."

"Do I make you work too much?" I asked, itching to pull my hair in front of my chest. Unfortunately for my nervous hands, I had taken the precaution of braiding it into a crown today. Silas Whitaker and his men were currently installing lights in my house, and filming B-roll footage. I'd barely slept all night, and if my hair was within reach, I had a feeling I'd end up with the worst knots. "Do you need more time off?"

"No."

"If you want more time at your own place, we can figure something out."

"Cordelia?" Victor dropped into the chair across from me and folded his arms on the table. I tried very hard - and failed - not to stare at the way his white dress shirt stretched over his biceps.

"Hmm?"

"Most of my things are at your place."

"Really?" That got my attention enough to glance up.

"I started adding things a few years ago. I'm still waiting for you to notice."

"You didn't. Like what?"

"I've replaced all your gym equipment."

"You're the only one who uses most of those machines anyway." I shrugged. I might jump on the treadmill for a bit every now and again, but that was it.

"I bought almost every cooking utensil."

"Well, I don't really use those either."

"The sofa in the winter garden."

"The chaise lounge? It's pink."

"Yes."

"No, but that's- I got that a few years- I mean-" I furrowed my brows because I loved that chaise. I'd never even seen him sit on it until the night we played the floor is lava. "When it showed up, I just thought I'd forgotten that I bought it at an online auction or something." That had happened a few times. Squirrel brain got obsessed with hoarding, and by the time the delivery came, I'd forgotten all about my impulse buys. In some ways, it was like giving myself little surprise gifts.

"I have the receipt if you want proof."

"No, I believe you." I sighed. "Anything else?"

"The kitchen radio. Every single white towel because you only owned pink ones when I moved in. Bathroom stuff I keep downstairs. The chess board. Plants. I keep buying plants. I put them everywhere."

I slapped my hand on the table. "I noticed the plants."

"Oh, you did?" He raised a single brow, challenging me.

"Not at first. Then, for a moment, I was sure that *my* plants were secretly multiplying by themselves. The big fiddle leaf fig gave it away though."

"You never said anything."

"You were never there when I found them. I'd make a mental note to mention it to you, forget about it by the next time I saw you, and only remember a few days later. And then it felt awkward to bring it up because of how much time had passed." I glanced around his very plant-less kitchen. "They're mine though. You can't have them back. They've befriended all of my other plants."

"They're all yours," he chuckled.

"I can give you a Pothos if you want some greenery in here," I stood and walked over to where he had plenty of space on his kitchen shelves between a few dusty bowls and wine glasses. "They just keep growing and growing and growing, and this would be a great spot."

"I'm good," he replied from right behind me. I jumped a little, looking over my shoulder. So sneaky.

Too bad about the Pothos though. His kitchen got more light than mine because he didn't have a winter garden attached to it. Instead, a glass door led right to the backyard. Which was separated from mine by a white fence with a little gate in it. If we got rid of that fence, our combined backyards would actually make a great space. If we planted proper hedges around it, I could see myself out there by myself more often, soaking up the sun. I wouldn't have to rely on Victor to stay with me. I could put some lounge chairs out. Maybe next to a little pond. There would definitely be enough space for a pond with some fish. I'd have to look up what kind of pond fish could survive winter in Boston. I was fairly certain I'd seen something about Koi fish being almost indestructible.

"Do you like fish?"

"To eat or to feed?"

I rolled my eyes at him. "To look at."

"Not a fan of fish tanks. Depressing glass boxes."

"We could put a pond out there." I tapped my nail against the glass door.

"Sure. We can rip out the fence."

"Exactly." I whirled around to smile at him. He didn't even need an explanation. He just got what I meant. "We might have to apply for a permit to consolidate both properties. I think that would require them to be owned by the same person though. We did something like that with the foundation, but then again, that wasn't residential property. If it isn't possible to consolidate both properties, we might still be able to legally separate the backyards from the houses and just combine those as a third estate." I stopped rambling when I noticed the little tick in his jaw. "What?"

"You."

"Me?"

"I've been fascinated by you since the first day we met, Cordelia."

My scalp tingled because that compliment hit too close to what I'd heard countless times throughout my life. ADHD girls were manic pixie dream girls right up until that fascination wore off. "You're just getting swept up by the excitement because I'm about to have a new hyperfixation."

"No," he shook his head, "don't get me wrong. The excitement is fun. I love seeing you get excited about glass beads or porcelain dolls or fish ponds. It's part of you just like the inevitable crash when your interest fades. Regardless of that, you *make* things. Again, and again. You learn and you grow, and you *create*. Beautiful things and good places. You put so much good into the world, Cordelia."

"You're exaggerating." I pulled my arms around myself, suddenly feeling like all my flaws were on full display. "Fair enough about the foundation, because we really are trying to make the world a little bit better, but I can't take full credit for that."

"Hmm." His eyes narrowed. "No."

"No?" I laughed. "You can't just say no."

"No, I'm not exaggerating."

"Victor." I rolled my eyes at him. "I was talking about a koi pond. You're making a bigger deal out of it than it is."

He shrugged. "Just you wait."

"Wait for what exactly?"

"You're going to change the world, Cordelia Montgomery, and it's going to be an honor to be there and watch you." He reached out and unfurled my arms, gentle fingers leaving warm ghost touches on my skin.

"In that vision of yours, what do you do? Just watch? I mean..." I inhaled shakily, dreading all the possible answers to my question. For whatever it was worth, our roles had changed. There was no way we could go back to pretending he was just my employee. "You won't have to hide from your uncle anymore once this job is done, right? You can find something that excites you, build something for yourself. You don't have to stay inside with me anymore."

"No." He grimaced, face turning stony. "I'm done. I've had enough excitement for three lifetimes. I want a quiet life. I want a home. I don't need more than that."

"So you'll watch me?"

"I'll watch you."

CHAPTER FIFTEEN

VICTOR

IN EXCHANGE FOR GETTING A WHOLE DAY WITH Cordelia, I would have to be in my cousin's wedding party. Which meant I would be leaving around an hour earlier than I would have otherwise, and staying longer, too. Which wasn't a horrible trade, but I always hated leaving Cordelia alone. Moreover, I hated leaving her alone with Silas Whitaker's equipment all over the house.

It had nothing to do with Whitaker. He'd been in the house the last two afternoons, and Cordelia seemed fine. They had moved from the kitchen to the living room, and he filmed while asking her about the foundation. I'd done my fair share of press rooms to recognize the pattern of increasingly personal questions to catch the most emotional soundbites. Cordelia, however, had a perfect answer every time. She'd been binge-watching media training tutorials on YouTube, and it was paying off.

But Cordelia didn't even like seeing her own webcam view during calls. Her shoulders stiffened the exact same way whenever she passed a tripod or a studio light. I hated leaving her alone when her own house had lost its comfort.

The day before the wedding, I was home early enough to watch them film a segment about the self-defense classes her foundation offered in partnership with August Beckett's gym chain. Another good thing she had created. Beckett had come crawling to apologize last fall. Instead of pressing charges because he had conspired with his brother to get her fortune, Cordelia had bartered for free classes - not for herself, but every beneficiary of her foundation.

And she downplayed it for Whitaker's camera. Never in it for the glory.

I had half a mind to grab that lens and tell the world exactly how selfless this woman was. Instead I waited until they took a break from filming.

"Come here for a second," I pulled her into the bathroom and maneuvered her around, so she stood with her back to me. The mic pack was fastened to the inside of her sequined pencil skirt, and I forced my thoughts to stay on task as I reached past her zipper to flip the switch. The little green light died, indicating that we had some privacy.

"I feel a little manhandled, not going to lie."

"Trust me, you'll know when I'm manhandling you, zhizn' moya." The words were out faster than I could think them through. I had to blame it on the close proximity, and her sugary sweet scent clouding my senses.

"Why are we hiding?" she asked without reacting to my words.

"I have to attend my cousin's wedding tomorrow."

"Oh. Okay."

"Here, take this." I pulled a small slip of paper from my pocket. The yellow Post-It held no information besides a phone number. Hopefully inconspicuous enough for nobody else to pick it up - but I had used one of the glittering gel pens from Cordelia's craft boxes in the basement, so it should be specific enough for her to remember what it was among the mountains of paper on her desk. "It's my cousin Luka's number. You trust him only as far as you can throw him. Don't volunteer any information. This is just for emergencies."

"What kind of emergencies?"

I flexed my jaw, trying to decide how much I could tell her. My absence was already making her uncomfortable, and I didn't want to make it worse. There was a reason I hadn't told her about fighting yet. If she knew that I was putting my health at risk, she'd spiral. I couldn't tell her, and I couldn't stop, because nobody walked away from Piotr.

When I didn't reply right away, Cordelia kept pressing: "Victor, what kind of emergencies?"

"It's a family event. A lot of criminals in one place at the same time."

"Do you think there could be a raid?"

"No, but you never know who thinks they have something to prove in front of the boss."

"Okay." She breathed deeply and folded the note up, slipping it into her blouse's pocket. "Are you bringing a date?"

"I tell you that I'm going to a Russian mob wedding and you're worried about my plus one?"

She crinkled her nose at me. "Well, I have priorities. If you put yourself in any danger, I will kill you myself. Case closed. If you bring some random Tinder girl in a polyester dress as your date..."

"It's a silk dress."

"Victor!" Her cheeks turned bright red. Cordelia was actually jealous of some nonexistent girl she'd made up in her mind.

"Why the fuck would I bring a date?"

She pulled her shoulders up. Her neck was beginning to look like a modern painting, splotched in pink embarrassment. For once, she didn't say anything.

"Cordelia?" I folded my hands around her flushed cheeks and guided her face up to look at me.

"What?" she spat the word like a petulant toddler.

"There's no one else. You're it. End of story."

"Except I'm not, am I?"

"Patience," I leaned in, overpowered by the urge to keep touching her, hold her, lay my lips to her skin - and stopped myself when she squeezed her eyes shut. Right. She'd asked me not to touch her. My hands dropped to my sides.

"Patience isn't my strong suit."

"I'm sorry."

"Yeah, me too," she huffed and switched her microphone back on before slipping out of the bathroom. "Please don't die."

"I'll do my best."

THE NEXT DAY I LEFT EVEN EARLIER THAN I WANTED, just to pick up Cordelia's birthday present across town. That damn teapot better brighten her mood. I didn't even care that it cost me half a fortune, as long as it would make her feel better.

The old man in the antiques shop played me the repaired music box, then wrapped the thing in layers of tissue paper before boxing it up.

Maybe I should have picked up a quick wedding present for Nat, too, but I really didn't give a fuck about this scam wedding. I'd put on a suit. That was all the effort my uncle deserved.

"There you are." Irina caught me off outside the church. "You have been promoted to best man."

"Why? I don't even know the groom."

"Why does my father want anything?"

"To show-off," I grunted.

"Prize steed, Vitya." She clapped her hand over my shoulder and directed me through the side door to the back of the church. Luka was already in the little backroom, grinning from ear to ear as he handed his flask to a blonde guy in a gray suit, who I assumed was the groom. There also was a gangly kid, wearing black, who looked like a younger version of the groom. He probably wasn't quite old enough to drink yet, scrolling his phone instead.

Irina left me with another pat on the back.

"Victor!" Luka bellowed, cheeks red, clearly deep into that flask. "Come here, meet Nat's husband-to-be, her betrothed, the future father of her children."

This was going to be a long day.

Luka threw his arm around my neck and pulled me into their circle. The alcohol stench on his breath was strong enough to choke a man. "Daniel, my cousin Victor. Victor, the newest member of our family, Dan the Man."

Dan the Man gave Luka a short once-over before he pocketed that flask inside his jacket. Good call. "It's good to meet you, Victor. Luka said you're working together? Do you run the car dealership with him?"

Ah, so that's what Luka was up to these days. Couldn't drive them anymore, so he'd gone into trading them. Made sense. Probably made enough money to satisfy his father.

"No, I'm in sports," I said.

"I'm basically his manager these days." Luka patted my chest.

"What sports, if you don't mind me asking?" Daniel was soft-spoken but he oozed the confidence of every politician alive. Chin high, charming smile, just enough of a crinkle around his eyes to make him look trustworthy.

He was marrying into my family though, so anyone would be stupid to trust him.

"MMA."

"He's taught me badass punches, Danny Boy. So don't even think about touching my sister, got it?" Luka swung a fist around without precision and Danny Boy just so managed to duck.

"For fuck's sake," I huffed, "let's get you some coffee before you give anyone a black eye."

"Thank you," Dan whispered and nodded to me. He probably hadn't gotten a say in his choice of groomsmen beyond his brother.

I dropped Luka into one of the chairs by the small refreshments table and filled a coffee cup from the thermos. "What the fuck's gotten into you?"

"Natalia is getting married to Dan the Man today!" He flung his arms out, spilling coffee all over his hand and the tablecloth, thankfully sparing his suit. "Weddings are fun. Weddings are supposed to be fun. I'm not the party pooper, *you* are."

"Let's save the fun for after the ceremony, Luka."

"My sister is marrying Daniel because I set them up." He pointed at the groom who nervously tapped his hand against his chin while watching us. "Daniel's gay. He doesn't even like her *like that*."

"Yeah, I know." I pushed the hand with his cup against his lips. "Let's keep that between us."

"Fine," he grumbled into his coffee.

I forced him to down three of the cheap crumbly church cookies between gulps of coffee. By the time the second cup was empty, he seemed at least lucid enough to stand by the altar for 45 minutes without causing a scene.

"And I thought it was the groom's job to have a meltdown," Daniel mumbled as we filed out the door.

"Don't you fucking dare," I hissed, "just fucking smile and nod and say *I do*."

The ceremony went down without a hitch. People stared holes

into my suit for a few minutes, but I didn't give them the satisfaction of reacting to their surprise of seeing me here. Once those church doors opened and the bride walked in, I was forgotten anyway. Natalia was dolled up to the nines, glossy brown curls, a thick layer of makeup, and a dress the size of a tent. She shot me a tight smile when she spotted me before her eyes returned to her new husband.

I managed to avoid people right after the ceremony, staying on the sidelines until it was time to head to Petya's for the reception. The house had been crawling with vendors for days. It was the perfect opportunity for my uncle to show off. Irina had told me that the wedding cake was apparently covered in edible gold and decorated with diamonds.

I just parked my car on the side of the driveway and walked a few steps to find enough signal to call Cordelia, when the ear-piercing screech of tires stopped me. I whirled around in time to see a bright yellow Lamborghini slam into my car. Only a few meters from where I'd been standing seconds before.

My car folded in on itself, crushed between the side of the house and Luka's car.

What the actual fuck?

People were yelling and running, and I started for Luka's car - but then his door swung open. He stepped out, completely unbothered, laughing his ass off while clutching that damn flask to his chest.

"Are you fucking kidding me?"

Luka still laughed, wiping tears from his eyes as he spotted me. "It's not," he gasped through his laughter, "it's not that bad."

"You totaled my car."

He slammed his car door shut and waved the flask towards my fuming car. "It's not your car, is it? You let your girlfriend pay for everything."

"Fuck!" I swung myself over the crumpled hood of his

Lamborghini, scrambling to get to the trunk. Because the car *was* Cordelia's. And so was the teapot in the back.

"It's not even a nice car. I can get you a better one."

"Keep your stolen scrap metal," I grunted, trying to stem the trunk open. The car frame was so bent out of shape, the handle didn't even budge.

"What? Now you won't even accept an apology car?"

I ignored him. I wasn't going to argue with his drunk ass - and I wasn't going to accept a stolen car, only to risk being pulled over with Cordelia in the back. The trunk didn't give, so I jerked open the back door and climbed onto the backseat. It was covered in glass from the broken windows. Luka had managed to do a fucking number on this thing.

I tipped one of the backrests forward, giving me an opening to the trunk.

"Shit. Get out of there, bro." Luka's hand wrapped around my ankle, and I kicked back hard and fast, connecting with the soft tissue of his stomach. He groaned and his grip on my leg disappeared.

The cardboard box was half-flattened. There was no way the teapot had survived that. Fuck. I still hugged it tightly as I scrambled out of the car.

Luka sat in the dirt next to it.

I put some distance between me, the car, and my cousin, then set the box down on the ground and carefully opened it - as if one wrong move could shatter the teapot more.

Half the porcelain was still intact, clinging to its round shape - the other half had been decimated to shards. While I could have still glued those pieces together, the small music contraption at the bottom was folded up like the car itself, small cogs and springs poking out the sides of the warped metal.

"What's that?" Luka laid a hand on my shoulder and leaned over me.

"Take your hands off me," I grunted and shook him off.

"Bro, I just wanna see what you're making such a fuss about."

His hand was back on my shoulder, and this time, he didn't get a warning. I grabbed him by the collar and I hauled him over me.

Luka landed in the gravel with a loud *oomph*.

And it wasn't enough.

Fucking Luka.

Fucking Luka being fucking careless.

"You. Told. Him." Each word landed a crunching punch. I punched him until his face turned bloody. "You were supposed to be on my side, *bro*."

"Get off him! Stop! Victor!" Daniel grabbed my arm, then ate his own words when I punched him hard enough for blood to spray from his mouth.

Someone else tried to hold me down, and at that point, the faces blurred together. Two men were on the ground next to Luka and Daniel before the unmistakable click of a gun froze my muscles.

"Go home, Vitya."

Irina pointed her gun at me. Not at my head, but at my gut - much more painful - much slower death.

"Can't. In case you didn't notice, I don't have a car."

She tossed a key at me and I caught it mid-air. A silver Mercedes star winked at me from my palm.

"It's the dark blue GLS in the driveway. Don't worry, it's not stolen. I won it in a bet."

I spat on the ground, a hint of blood coming out. One of these guys must have landed a punch, but I didn't know which one. I just looked at the bloody pulp that was my cousin. "He owes me more than a car."

My eyes found uncle Petya standing on the edge of the gawking crowd, a huge shit-eating grin on his face. He didn't give a fuck about his unconscious son, or his bleeding son-in-law. I'd given him the exact show he'd wanted.

Prize steed.

Comeback officially announced.

I stepped around Irina and shouldered my way through the people, only stopping before Natalia, who looked about as unimpressed as if I'd just knocked out her accountant, not her new husband.

"Congratulations," I grit out, "I hope it's worth it."

CHAPTER SIXTEEN

Cordelia

"One last question and then we'll wrap all of this up." Silas clicked around on his camera.

"Complete wrap?" We'd been doing this for a week and the gleam of the black lens didn't send my pulse racing anymore. Mostly thanks to Silas. I may have judged him unfairly before.

Yes, he was completely calculated. In some ways, he seemed like my exact opposite. Everything he did had purpose, including his appearance. He presented this image of someone who looked just careless enough for people to trust him, but he was a control freak. Me, on the other hand? I tried to make people believe I was in control, when I felt like Alice tumbling down the rabbit hole more often than not.

Once I figured that out about Silas, I knew how to work with him.

"Yes, very last question," he confirmed with an encouraging smile. That smile told me that he wasn't about to ask about the business side of the foundation. That was his *I need a candid answer* smile. "The foundation was named after your late mother. Can you tell us something about her life? Is there a memory you're particularly fond of?"

"I'm fond of every memory I have of my mother. I wish I had the chance to create more with her." My fingers itched to dig into my cheeks to keep me focused, to stop spiraling down a ramble of memories. I'd anticipated a question like this though, so I smiled and gave him the answer I'd prepared:

"My mom was an artist. She painted. Every painting you see in this house is one of hers. Every Saturday, she would take me to her studio and we'd paint together. For an hour or two, she'd show me her big coffee table books full of masterpieces, talk to me about light and composition and color, and every week without fail, she said 'Now forget everything I just told you and have fun making something. It just has to be yours.' - god, I sucked. I went through a few months when I just dumped so much glitter onto the wet paint, you couldn't even see the colors underneath. But we had so much fun. She went along with every crazy idea. I mean, she kept restocking the glitter. And she never said a bad word about my paintings. She just asked me if I enjoyed making them." My voice cracked. All the interview prep in the world couldn't stop the pain. "Sorry."

"Thank you for sharing that, Cordelia."

I shut my eyes to refocus, but her blood stain waited for me behind closed lids. Bright red soaking into white canvas. My breath rattled in my lungs as I pushed out of my chair. "I need a minute."

"Of course."

I unclipped the microphone from my collar and handed it to Silas as I slipped past him and out into the hallway.

"Come here." A hand wrapped around my wrist and I was pulled to the side, coming face-to-face with Victor's collar.

"I just need a minute please," I repeated the same futile words, throat burning as I stared at the ink on his neck.

"Take all the time you need. You're alright." He pulled me against his chest and folded up my arms between our bodies. Once I was positioned, Victor wrapped me in a tight embrace. His muscles flexed and locked around me. His large hand splayed over the back of my head, keeping my face buried against his shoulder. A quiet voice in the back of my mind reminded me that we weren't supposed to be touching like this, but then everything stilled - even that voice. Even the constant buzzing in my bones. Victor held me together when my body was on the verge of coming apart.

"Thank you," I mumbled after a while. Could have been seconds. Could have been hours. Victor loosened his grasp without further prompting and I blinked up at his concerned gaze, the green of his eyes as dark as pine. "I need to wrap things up with Silas."

"Here," he smoothed his thumbs along my cheeks, and carefully swiped a curve under my eyes, "better."

"I just-" I exhaled shakily, my words not quite back yet.

"You've got this." It sounded more like a fact than encouragement when Victor said it. Indisputable truth. *I got this.*

"Alright." I nodded and fell a step back. Every cell in my body shivered, yearning to go back to his warmth.

Victor opened his mouth as if to say something, but he eventually just nodded at my office door.

I got this. *I got this.*

"Do you have everything you need?" I asked Silas when I walked back into the room, not even giving him the chance to voice his sympathies. If he could put on a facade for work, so could I.

"Yes. I'll get my equipment and get out of your hair."

"Can you email me the next steps, just so I have them in writing? And how long do you think you'll need to edit?"

"I'll have the campaign videos over to you in a few days. The rough cut of the other material is going to take a little longer."

"I'm going to need exact time frames, Silas." Otherwise I would enter an unending waiting mode during which nothing would get done.

"Sure," Silas nodded, "you'll have the campaign videos by Friday. My video in about two weeks."

"Perfect."

"I'm leaving this, in case you think of anything you want to add to the video." He placed a small handheld camera on my desk. "Even if it's just a voice-over."

"I don't think that's necessary." I narrowed my eyes at the small device.

"Unrelated to whether or not you decide to go forward with the series, it was a pleasure to get to know you. You're a very impressive person."

"Thank you. I wish I didn't have to be."

"What do you mean?"

"We live in a messed-up world that is so hard to improve that it's impressive when a rich white woman tries to do it on a fairly minuscule scale."

"That would be a good soundbite. You should record that." He winked and pointed at the small camera again.

That was so not happening.

I couldn't wait to get him and all his cameras and lights out of the house.

CHAPTER SEVENTEEN

Cordelia

THIRTY.

Three. Zero.

My chest tightened at the sight of my age spelled out like that. I'd made it to thirty. I'd heard so many stupid jokes about turning thirty, mostly on TV. None of these idiots grasped how precious this number was. There had been an incredibly hard time in my life when I hadn't been sure I'd even make it to twenty. Thirty was even better. Heck, I couldn't wait for forty.

The pink candles started blurring and I quickly blinked against the tears gathering in my eyes.

"Thank you," I said and smiled at Del, who had shown up with the flower-shaped cake.

"Of course." She tapped Beck's hand wrapped around her middle, and he let her go on command, only for her to curl her arms around me. "Happy Birthday! I'm so lucky to have you in my life."

"Likewise," I mumbled against the crown of her head with my arms tight around her shoulders. Even if Del spent more and more time at Beck's, she was, in many ways, the little sister I never had. Not only because my dresses kept mysteriously disappearing from my closet.

"You should blow out the candles," she said and loosened her grasp. Beck's arms were around her waist again before she had even properly stepped back, and I couldn't help but grin. That man was dark hair, cold eyes, muscles and confidence, all stirred up and poured into a suit, but god forbid he wasn't touching Del. Even when she was just out of reach, you'd find his finger hooked into her belt loop. Couldn't fault him for holding on when he'd almost lost her last year.

"Do you know what you're going to wish for?" Defne asked, hands clasped under her chin.

"I do," my eyes skipped to Victor for just a heartbeat, meeting his direct gaze, before I forced them back to Defne, "good weather for Del's wedding."

That got a few chuckles before I leaned over the kitchen table and blew out the candles, wishing for the one thing I actually wanted. *Cordelia and Victor.*

People found their seats around the table and I handed out cake to everyone, except Tabitha who was trying to combat her constant stomach issues by cutting out sugar. And I sprayed a mountain of whipped cream on my cake, and everyone talked about cake flavors and about summer weddings and about the flower-shaped napkins, and it was good. Having people in my space was good.

"I'm not saying you bought the cake for that reason. I'm just saying, it's a very light pink, and there's probably smarter ways to cut it," Tabitha argued, waving her hands at the cake. With half of it gone, the two and a half remaining petals did look a little suggestive, but Del was insisting that she didn't see *it*.

"If you say so," Del sighed.

Defne leaned over to Tabitha and fake-whispered: "Maybe Beck's is horribly deformed and that's why she can't see it."

Beck's brows jumped up, his drink halfway to his lips, his other hand resting on the back of Del's neck. "I'm choosing not to dignify that with a response."

"How's this?" I asked and leaned forward, cutting off the half-petal and loading it onto my plate. I could do a third slice of cake.

"Well, now it's just balls," Tabitha huffed.

"Oh, yeah, I can see that," Del said.

All four of us broke out in laughter, while Beck grinned and pulled Del over to kiss her. I looked away from their affectionate moment, to find Victor already focused on me. I tilted my head in a silent question to see how he was coping with having people over, and he responded with a small smile and nod.

"I need something stronger to deal with this lovey-dovey crap," Tabitha announced and jumped up to go for the drink cart.

"Speaking of lovey-dovey crap," Delilah leaned back in her chair and bit her lip, "there's something I've been meaning to ask you."

"Me?" I asked.

"Yeah," she nodded, "how would you feel about hosting our wedding in your backyard?"

The images came faster than I could process them. A wedding arch, chairs, Del in a white dress, people wearing pretty clothes, people filling the chairs, people shuffling through my house, Del throwing her bouquet at a group of young women, children running around and tossing flowers-

"I don't think that's a good idea," Victor said, cutting off the film in my thoughts.

I sucked in a deep breath and nodded. "He's probably right."

"Before you make a final decision," Del smiled and cut a quick reassuring glance at her fiancé, "it would just be the six of us here already, my mom and grandma on my side, and Isaac and Brody on Beck's side."

"That's it?" I asked. "Ten people?"

"Yes, well, eleven. Someone needs to officiate," Del pulled her shoulders up, "I'd rather have *you* at my wedding than two hundred people who don't mean half as much to me. If this would make it possible for you to attend, I'd love it."

"Oh, you don't have to do that for me." I blinked against the tears shooting into my eyes. I couldn't let her make that kind of sacrifice. "You should have the wedding you've always wanted, regardless of whether I can be there."

"I'm already compromising on not marrying an English lord." She grinned.

"I'd buy you a country estate in England right now if you'd let me," Beck replied in a tone that implied they may have had a similar conversation before.

"Right now? You have a guy on speed dial?"

"I have a guy."

"Besides," I said, re-entering the conversation, "we're planning to remodel the backyard. Get rid of the fence and install a small pond."

"Perfect," Del beamed, "I've always *wanted* white ducks at my wedding instead of doves."

"Are you actually serious about this?"

"Yes."

"What about you?" I swung my attention around to her fiancé. "Surely you planned on a big wedding with a band and a caterer and more guests than your best friend and your niece."

Tabitha wordlessly put drinks in front of everyone, and I made the mistake of downing mine without looking. The tequila burned down my throat and Tabitha let out a loud cackle. "I was going to cut up a lime to go with that."

"Think about it, Cordelia," Del said, clasping Beck's hand in her lap, "we've talked it through, all the *if*s and *but*s. We just need to know if you'd be comfortable with us having the wedding here."

"I'll sleep on it," I promised.

VICTOR

"I HAVE TO TAKE THIS." I PUSHED AWAY FROM THE table, phone in hand, and slid my half-eaten piece of birthday cake over to Cordelia. She barely looked up, too deep into some made-up game that involved a deck of Uno cards, three dice and Defne's Tamagotchi. I had somehow lost in the first round when I chose to eat a green jelly bean over a yellow one - but Cordelia seemed completely in her element.

Which made it even harder to get up and leave her. Her enjoying the company of others was new, and it was captivating.

"Keep it short," I told Luka, once I made it to the winter garden and slid the glass door shut behind me.

"Thanks, I'm doing great. My face no longer looks like a horse trampled around on it. Apology accepted." Sarcasm dripped from his every word.

"I'm not apologizing."

"Of course not," Luka scoffed. "You're on the card in two weeks, Atlantic City."

I wasn't sure what a stroke felt like, but the sudden sharp burst in my temple had to come close. "It's too soon. I haven't even taken the drug tests yet." The words sounded hollow even to my own ears. As if Piotr Yelchin needed to follow some official anti-doping rulebook. He'd grease the right hands and suddenly official records showed that I was clean.

"You're fighting Chapman."

I didn't give a flying fuck who I'd have to fight. I sat down on the small pink sofa and rubbed the bridge of my nose. "Main event?"

"No."

"Main card?" I asked.

"Yeah."

"Fuck. Fine." Could have kept it a secret a little longer if they had pushed me into the opening rounds, which didn't even get TV coverage. Being part of the main fights meant my name was going to be out there again. I glanced through the glass door at the group of girls yelling at each other over the glittering Tamagotchi, Cordelia waving an Uno Reverse card through the air. I dragged myself away and dropped onto the plush lounge chair instead. "When's the announcement going up?"

"Tomorrow." Luka heaved a sigh on the other line as if he was the one about to get in the octagon. "My father expects you to win this one."

"I figured." There could be weeks if not months between fights. Winning this one would open the doors to much bigger events later this year. Those were likely the events Petya was actually interested in.

"He was pushing for Vegas in four weeks, for no other reason than showing off. I figured AC is easier. I'll drive you back right after the fight. You'll be home for breakfast."

"Why?"

"Because I do owe you more than a car."

With those words the line went dead. At least he'd finally confirmed what I'd known for months. Fucking snitch. Not that it mattered much anymore.

I stared at the black phone screen, as if it would give me

instructions on how the hell I was supposed to break the news to Cordelia, but my reflection only blinked back at me.

"There you are." Cordelia slipped through the sliding door and shut it behind her, only to lean back against it and offer me a smile. She was wearing a ridiculously puffy and dangerously short dress that made her look like a marshmallow with long, smooth legs. Forget about the marshmallow part, I wanted those long legs wrapped around my hips again. "I had a pair of fives and then the Tamagotchi didn't eat the salad."

I wasn't entirely sure what that meant, but from her tone, I guessed that she was out of the game. "I'm sorry."

"Oh, well, it's fine," she sighed and walked over, each step quieted by her slouchy fuzzy socks that somehow didn't take away from the fact that I wanted those ankles crossed behind my back. "What are you doing?"

"Do you want me to lie?" I blinked up at her.

"Yeah," she nodded, standing in front of me with that stupidly short dress taunting my line of sight, "you can tell me the truth tomorrow."

"I actually got you a musical teapot but I broke it, so I was searching for another one." I hadn't even told her about her new car, or why the old one was gone. But I'd noticed the small quiver in her brow when I'd given her a birthday present too small to contain a teapot. "I'm sorry."

"Thank you, but then you really shouldn't have gotten me the teacup," she said, delicate fingers wrapping around my shoulder, "you could have just told me about the teapot. Maybe I could have fixed it. I'm great with superglue, you know."

"Yeah, I'm not cutting your hair again next time you experiment with superglue," I said, way too aware of her thumb circling over my collarbone.

"Hey, I still think bangs suit me." She grinned and tossed her hair from side to side - and that was enough to bring back the mental image of wrapping it around my fist and exposing her throat.

For fuck's sake.

That Tequila was really messing with me. Paired with her gentle touch. And the tiny dress didn't help either. I'd always fucking loved those legs. They'd been one of the first things I'd noticed about her. But now that I'd stood between them with her mouth on mine, it was becoming harder to stifle all the intrusive thoughts I previously would have considered inappropriate.

"Sit down," I huffed and closed my eyes because I clearly couldn't be trusted around the sight of her thighs anymore.

"Excuse me?"

"Sit the fuck down, Cordelia."

"Are you giving orders now, Mr. Yelchin?"

"Do you want me to?" Shit. My voice dropped way too low for that question not to be loaded with a dozen more meanings.

"Yes," she replied without missing a beat, "tell me what you want me to do."

Fuuuck.

My eyes flew up to meet hers. She was regarding me through lowered lashes, her storm blue eyes completely focused on me, soft lips parted in anticipation. The things I could do to those lips.

"I want you to," *go back inside, go to bed, put on some pants,* "sit down." The words were the same, but I wrapped my hand around her wrist, locking her touch against me, and I leaned back, opening the expanse of my lap for her.

Cordelia shot a quick look over her shoulder but even though we were in a glass box, we were as invisible to the others as if the walls were solid. They were still deep in that game. Satisfied with that, Cordelia turned to me again, her nails digging into my shirt as she sank onto my lap. Her lips trembled with each breath, but as pretty as they were, my eyes immediately fell to her legs framing my hips. That tiny dress rode up. A peek of silky white fabric had heat shooting through my bloodstream.

She was going to be the death of me, and I didn't even care. Let me drown in her. Let her burn me alive. I would suffocate for just one touch. I wanted her as close as I could get her. And tomorrow I could blame the alcohol for not caring about the consequences tonight.

"Are you okay?" I asked, clenching and unclenching my hands around nothing but air, when her waist was right there, dipping in like the perfect handle. I should have gotten a damn award for my self-restraint.

"Can you scoot back a little?"

I pushed myself back on the sofa, and with that, her hips tilted around my thighs, dress fully riding up to expose her very flimsy underwear, ass cheeks pressing against my legs, and she- she let out a fucking whimper as she shifted against me.

"How drunk are you?" I asked.

"I had a small sip of champagne, three pieces of cake, one shot of Tequila, and then the rest of your cake. I'm *very* sober unless you count a sugar high." She traced the slope of my cheek with her thumb, as she searched my eyes. "What about you?"

"Sober enough to know this is a bad idea," I replied.

"Do you want to stop?"

"No," I said and finally let my hands sink to her legs. God, I loved how soft her skin was. She shivered and let out another whimper when my fingertips brushed against the silky edge of her panties. "I want to hear all the sounds you make with that pretty little mouth."

"Victor," she breathed.

"Touch yourself, zhizn' moya."

"Usually, I'd-"

"That was an order."

She shot one last look back at the party inside before she pulled her hand from my face and dipped it between her legs. She rubbed over her panties, but didn't let out another sound until she tipped her hips back and forth, grinding against me. My cock jerked in my pants but at least she wasn't grinding over it, or this would have gotten real painful, real fast.

"You can do better than that," I said, "show me how you get yourself off."

A determined look furrowed her brows but instead of slipping her fingers into her underwear, like I'd expected, she grabbed the backrest behind me for leverage. She wiggled her hips before she started sliding back and forth, cheeks glowing red as she huffed out hot air. Fuck, even through the satin, I could see how her lips had parted around the curve of my leg. She was grinding her clit against me. And her panties were beginning to bloom darker.

My voice rumbled low from my chest: "You're making such a mess with that wet pussy, zhizn' moya."

"This feels- It feels so- good." Her words dissolved into a soft moan when I grabbed hold of her hip bones and pulled her harder against me.

She was fucking glowing. Her cheeks were pink and her eyes were glossy and her hair swayed, and she looked like a goddamn angel, outlined by the glow from inside.

"Go faster," I commanded and she followed suit, head dropping back. I sank my mouth against her long tender neck, nibbling and kissing, consuming the sweet taste of her skin. Meanwhile my hands worked to meet her pace, to help her get the leverage she needed.

Her moans grew louder and I stifled them with my lips on hers. Didn't need an audience for this. No, this angel was all mine.

Cordelia was gasping against my mouth as she fell apart, legs jerking, fingers grasping at my shoulders to keep herself upright. Finally she slumped forward with a hitched little sound that would stay etched into my memory for the rest of my life.

My arms closed around her back and it took me a moment to register the wet warmth sinking through the thick fabric of my jeans. Cordelia was still trembling, catching her breath, but her panties were soaked and a matching large dark spot bloomed on my jeans.

"I'm sorry," she mumbled, "that happens sometimes, but it's perfectly normal."

I couldn't stop the thundering groan as I puzzled out what she meant. As if my self-restraint wasn't stretched taut enough. How did I even file away the knowledge that Cordelia was a squirter? That grinding against my leg had made her come hard enough for that? I shifted under her, my jeans suddenly way, way too tight.

"It's not what you think it is," she rushed the words out, completely misreading my reaction, and I tightened my arms around her to stop her from getting up.

"I know what it is," I pressed a kiss to her temple, "and it's so fucking hot, I'm trying very hard not to bend you over and fuck you right here just to see if I can make you squirt again."

Her spine stiffened. Shit. Fucking Tequila and my loose tongue. "Victor..."

"Yes?" I loosened my grasp on her and she leaned back, glassy eyes finding mine, skin flushed and glowing. So goddamn perfect.

"I'm still," she was interrupted by a loud cheer inside and she turned to see Tabitha standing on the table, making it rain Uno cards, "hungry. I'm going to go back inside."

I had a feeling that wasn't what she'd meant to say but I had already fucked up enough, so I let her unfurl herself from my lap. She wiggled her dress back down until it hid her soaked panties, but her eyes caught on my jeans.

"Don't worry," I said, "go get yourself some more cake. I've got a change of clothes downstairs."

"Alright," she whispered, shoulders too clenched to mean it.

That's not how she was supposed to use that word. Our word. She wasn't supposed to lie to me like that. And she wasn't supposed to lie like that after how beautifully she'd just come apart in my lap.

I got up and crossed the distance to her, cupping her soft face in both hands and forcing her to look at me. I'd meant it when I'd said that I was going to go along with all of her ideas. She was creative and bright and passionate, and more often than not, she started second-guessing those impulsive ideas once they were in motion. I wasn't giving her the chance to second-guess the idea of *us*.

"More than alright," I said, "perfect."

And consequences be damned, I kissed her, because I wanted to - and because she needed to be kissed.

CHAPTER EIGHTEEN

Cordelia

I SQUINTED AT THE LITTLE TEA RESIDUE AT THE BOTTOM of my cup and tried to figure out if the random splotches looked more like a donkey or an elephant. According to this website that either meant I was being too stubborn and had to let go - or I'd have to be more patient and just keep holding on.

It could also be an octopus wearing a hat. In which case the octopus would be warning me about my business success. Or something like that.

Groaning, I let the teacup clatter back onto its saucer and closed the website.

Maybe I wouldn't find my answers in the tea Victor made for me. It was some Russian brand I'd never heard of, enough caffeine in a cup to keep me planted in my seat even when my meds wore off, and no discernible taste other than bitter - so once

I poured a bucket of sugar into it, it was basically sweet water with a kick.

Something had changed since my birthday, and the tea leaves lacked clear instructions on handling the situation.

I'd almost expected Victor to completely withdraw from me. Especially when he'd asked me for more time after our kiss in the kitchen. Whatever he had going on, he clearly needed the time. He was almost permanently out of the house. But when he was here, he kept telling me that he didn't want to leave, that he'd rather stay with me, that he was just a phone call away.

He never told me where he was going or what he was doing, and I never asked.

I never asked for the true story behind that phone call in the winter garden either.

I hated this. I hated not being able to confront myself with a simple conversation, a simple truth.

More than I hated being a coward, however, I hated that nobody understood that I didn't have a choice. I couldn't just *switch it off*. I couldn't just *get over myself* or *work through it*. If I even thought of leaving my comfort zone, my chest seized and my lungs constricted and I wouldn't even have the air to speak.

People barely understood that I couldn't leave my house, but at least they were able to comprehend that something bad had happened to me outside. The mental comfort zone was much harder to convey than the physical one.

I glanced at the little red dot next to an email folder dedicated to Silas Whitaker.

The very reminder that I was avoiding the video he'd sent yesterday. I had forwarded the campaign videos to Amani without even looking at them. This one? The big one? I'd have to personally review it.

Detangling my hands from my hair, where they'd been nesting, I grabbed the small camera Silas had left behind for me. It took me a few minutes to figure out. Once I did, I took it to the winter garden and set it up on the table, so I could film myself sitting on the floor between my plants.

"My therapist used to tell me that my brain was neurologically altered by trauma. There is no way to reverse that. That means I will spend the rest of my life in a world that was designed by and for people whose brains work differently than mine. And it's really exhausting. I..." I blinked at the gleaming black lens. "I'm not-" I shook my head and grabbed the camera to switch it off.

I wasn't sure what I'd even meant to do.

There were plenty of mental health advocates out there who were educating people on PTSD.

Maybe we should just invite some of them to our social media channels.

I could talk to Amani about that.

Fitzwilliam traipsed into the winter garden and wove his body through the legs of the table. He blinked at me through tired eyes and let out a tiny meow.

"Hi," I whispered and booped his little nose.

He meowed again.

"I know," I sighed, "we can't all be brave like you."

He climbed into my lap and rubbed his head against the flower-shaped buttons on my cardigan. Del had warned me that her cat was possessed, and I'd seen both her and Victor spot some scratches, but I had yet to meet Fitzi's demons.

"I think they're lying," I told him while I rubbed his big, soft belly, "you're my little sugarplum."

DEL HAD GONE INTO DEEP RESEARCH MODE FOR HER wedding. The kitchen table was completely covered in binders and magazines and various lists she'd printed off the internet.

I'd agreed to her backyard wedding.

She'd persuaded me with Pinterest boards and an endless string of texts, in which she'd pulled all sorts of statistics about the downsides of big weddings. Including the carbon footprint of the wedding industry. At that point, I couldn't say no. I'd end up feeling more guilty about the environment than about Del potentially regretting a small guest list.

"No, I definitely prefer this. I don't care if it looks a bit like a baby shower." She tossed one magazine aside and gently patted a different one, which showed a wedding all in white, pale blue and pink.

"I think it's cute. I like the bows on their dresses." I pointed at the big fluffy bows on the bridesmaids' sweetheart necklines.

"Oh, that would look cute on you. You can actually wear whatever you want. Have I told you yet?" Del flipped through her lists, brows furrowed. "I'm not doing bridesmaids. Not much of a point when it's just eight guests. Brody will be our ring bearer because we want to include her, but that's it."

As always, Brody's name punched me right in the gut, coating my tongue in acid. I was the reason they had to make her feel included. The reason her family had been reduced to-

"I need to talk to you." Victor's voice ripped me from the oncoming thought spiral.

He stopped at the table and his veined hands wrapped tight around the back of a chair. Those threatened to send me down a whole different thought spiral. Because I could still feel his fingers digging into my hips.

"Sure," I breathed.

"I can go," Del said and pushed her chair back.

"It concerns you, too."

"That's ominous," I said.

Victor took a deep breath and looked back and forth between the two of us before finally settling on me. "I'll be gone all weekend."

"What?"

"I'm leaving later tonight. I'll be back as soon as possible."

"No. You can't." My protest sounded weak even to myself.

"I have to."

"What if you don't? What if you just stay?" I asked.

"You know who my family is, right?" Victor's eyes skipped to Del, who nodded, then back to me. "My uncle would use you to punish me, Cordelia. Something small at first, just to send a message. A finger. A tooth maybe."

My spine straightened but I pushed away the images of blood, and tried to process what he was actually saying. Victor's uncle was holding me over his head. Victor had to work for his uncle because he was trying to keep *me* safe.

"Should I be concerned?" Del asked.

"No, you're safe," Victor said, "my uncle wouldn't take on Beckett without good reason."

"Should I be concerned *for the two of you*?"

"I've got it under control."

"Can I just- I need-" I scrambled out of my chair, grabbed hold of Victor's wrist and dragged him to my office. Once the door was closed, I whirled on him. "I need you to tell me it's safe for *you* to go. I have like two or three dozen teeth. I can give up a molar to keep you safe. You don't have to go because of me."

"It's safe for me to go," he said matter-of-factly.

"And now the truth?"

He heaved a deep sigh. "I'm coming back to you, zhizn' moya. Everything in between doesn't matter."

"You've called me that a few times. Zhizn' moya. What does it mean?"

"My life."

"Is that a Russian endearment, like my *honey, baby* or *sunshine*?"

"No." He ran his fingers over the curve of my chin. "You *are* my life, Cordelia. I have no interest in existing without you. In fact, I don't think I could. It's not an endearment. It's a simple truth."

"That's not healthy," I breathed as if I hadn't gone through a full meltdown myself when I had to meet Silas Whitaker without Victor by my side.

"I don't care." His fingertips curved along my jaw to the small hollow below my ear.

"How long is this going to last?" I asked and closed my eyes. "How much longer do I have to wait?"

"I'll try to find out this weekend."

"It's hard," I whispered and leaned into his touch, "I don't even know how to talk to you about what happened on my birthday, because that was the complete opposite of waiting. Well, maybe not *complete*. The *complete* opposite would involve less clothes."

"That was me being selfish. I'm sorry. I shouldn't have done that when I know I can't be with you yet. Not fully. Not the way you deserve."

He pulled his hand away and my eyes flew open. "*You* shouldn't have done that? If I remember correctly, I did the *doing*, you did the sitting."

He smirked, his eyes crinkling just a little bit in that perfect way. "If *I* remember correctly, I told you what to do."

"But before that *I* told *you* to tell me what to do. So it comes back to me initiating."

"Kiss me."

"What?" I glared at him.

"I'm telling you what to do without you initiating it. Kiss me."

"That's not fair," I huffed, "You can't just tell me to kiss you in order to win an argument."

"Cordelia Montgomery, with all due respect, shut the fuck up and kiss me."

The hairs on the back of my neck stood up at his harsh words, and the rough edge to his tone. I'd always hated being told what to do, but when *he* did it... in *that* voice...

"Screw you," I muttered, grabbed his collar and pulled him to me.

I wasn't even pretending to hold back. I kissed him with my lips, my tongue, my teeth. I kissed him in a way that curved my body into his. I kissed him until I couldn't breathe.

"Point made," he rasped, chest rising and falling fast against mine.

"No," I gasped and stole another kiss from his lips, "I've kissed you multiple times without having to be told to. I like kissing you. This kiss just coincidentally happened after you told me to kiss you."

He rasped a laugh, and my eyes fell shut as I soaked the sound in like sunshine. "You win this round," he said, "but one day soon, I'll tell you to get naked and wrap your legs around me and you'll do as I say."

"You know where to find me when you want to test that theory."

"Soon. Just a little more time." He kissed my forehead. "I promise."

CHAPTER NINETEEN

VICTOR

"That job of yours pays well?" Luka asked as he took the exit off the I-90, which meant I was less than 10 minutes from being home with Cordelia.

"Yeah." I'd barely needed a cent of the money over the years, considering Cordelia put a roof over my head and paid for the food. I knew better than to let Luka know that I had half a fortune in the bank by now though. "It's good work."

"Waiting on some rich girl's hand and foot?"

"Sure." The housekeeper, took care of cleaning, laundry and most groceries. That, too, was information I wasn't willing to volunteer though.

"Why?"

I shrugged and tossed the ice pack to the backseat. It had lost its cooling effect hours ago, leaving my face hot and throbbing.

"Come on, what are the upsides? Sell it to me. Because you decided to be a fucking butler instead of getting out of the country. You look like the biggest idiot in the world to me - and we both know that you still have a fully functioning brain in that thick head of yours. At least for the time being."

I didn't particularly care about what my cousin thought of me or my choices, but he had been the one person who had understood why I had to get out. Not just out of the octagon, but *out*. If only he understood that there was better for him out there too.

"She's good, Luka. She's a genuinely good person. It's nothing like what we grew up with." I flexed my jaw. "It's like waking up from a nightmare. You don't realize you were stuck in hell until you sit up in your bed and the world is actually quiet and safe."

"Yeah, no, I think you're full of shit." He chuckled and shook his head. "The real world is hell. You're just escaping into a perfect little dream. Helps that she has boobs and legs, so being her lap dog doesn't seem so bad. It's time to wake up and face reality, man."

He was wrong, but he had spent 30 years being fed this reality. One crappy metaphor wasn't going to deprogram our family's shit out of him. He was right about one thing though. I had to wake up. I had dragged Cordelia into my nightmare. She deserved better.

"Is that why you told your father where I was? Because I didn't take the chance to get out of the country and decided to stay with a woman?"

"I told him jack shit, Vitya."

"You're the only one who knew."

"He doesn't even know that I knew. He'd have my head on a platter if he did." Luka tapped his fingers against the steering wheel. "A couple years ago, your girl bought the house next to hers. Put your name on the deed."

It took a second before his words clicked. "Oh, for fuck's sake. That's public record."

"She screwed up."

"Yeah. Fuck." Cordelia's koi pond ramble about property lines made so much more sense now. I had no idea about the legalities of owning property and hadn't thought much of it. If she wanted a koi pond, she'd make it happen. Except I - Victor Yelchin - actually owned my house and its backyard. "She bought me a fucking house for my birthday." Six years of teacups suddenly looked very silly.

"Sorry, bro."

"If you ever tell her that's how Petya found me, I will scalp you."

"Despite what you might think, I have no interest in ruining your life."

"Then tell me how to get out of this. What does your father want?" I asked, watching the street lights flicker out. The morning was gray and hazy, sunrise covered by a thick layer of clouds.

"I don't know what he's working on, but I think it has something to do with Paris."

"Paris?"

"There's a fight night scheduled for Paris in about two months. You're on the card."

"Against?"

Luka stayed silent as he brought the car to a standstill across the street from Cordelia's house.

"Luka, who am I fighting?"

"Silver."

"Fuck's sake." I ran my hand down my face and flinched at my own rough touch, the cuts on my brow and cheek opening back up. My fingers came away bloody. A little blood would be the least of my concerns though. I had fought Emanuel Silver twice - and he'd knocked me out both times. If he landed another hit like that to my head, I was done. "Is it a one way ticket? Am I coming back in a body bag, guts replaced by drugs?"

"Not if you win."

"Great. Thanks."

"Go home. Get some sleep."

The only reason I didn't push further was that I didn't want to waste another second out here. Maybe I should have just gone to my own house and my own bedroom. My instincts led me to Cordelia though.

The house was quiet, and upstairs only the faint glow of Cordelia's night light spilled out from under her door. It probably would have been kinder to let her sleep, but I needed to check on her. I needed to see her face and know that she was okay. If I'd just walked in, chances were, I'd send her into a panic spiral, so I gently tapped a single knuckle against the door, once, twice.

"Del?" She croaked, sleepy but awake.

"No," I replied and pushed the door open just enough to slip through.

"You're back." Fuck, that little rasp in her voice was cute. Even when I saw her first thing in the morning, she was usually a bit more awake - and I suddenly hated that I wasn't here the very second she opened her eyes, to hear that sleepy voice.

"I'll let you get back to sleep. I just wanted to check on you."

"No, wait." Her bedsheets rustled and a moment later, the bedside lamp switched on. Cordelia's whole body jerked the second she saw my face. Yeah. Not pretty. Especially with the cuts freshly opened again. "Oh my god."

"It looks worse than it is. I'm fine."

"You're bleeding." She untangled herself from her bedsheets, clad in one of her tiny pajamas. Those things were a satin whiff of nothing, masquerading as tiny tops with tiny shoulder straps, and tiny shorts to go with them.

My eyes were squarely focused on her long, smooth legs when Cordelia grabbed me by the wrist and pulled me into the bathroom - which only gave me a perfect view of her ass in those tiny shorts.

I had to get a grip.

My entire body was pumped up on adrenaline and pain. That fight had been over too quickly, and all that built-up tension needed release. If not through my fists...

"Sit," Cordelia ordered and pointed at the edge of her tub. I did as she said, only to be rewarded with another prime view when she bent down to grab her first aid basket from under the sink. Those flimsy shorts were way too tight over her ass when she bowed like that.

I had to adjust my sweats. They left little to the imagination anyway, but fuck.

"Hold still." Cordelia started carefully dabbing at my face, and I barely felt a thing, concentrating on keeping my breathing even. "What happened?" Her hand trembled, holding the bloody gauze.

"I was in a fight."

"What? With who?"

"Not like that. I was in *a fight*. It was on TV for fuck's sake." My harsh tone had nothing to do with her question and everything to do with the fact that I'd been keeping a secret, and now she was parading around in front of me in these scraps of fabric - and I was too fucked in the head to form a coherent thought.

"I thought you'd quit," Cordelia whispered, hand hovering.

"I had."

"That's what you've been training for all this time. You said you weren't doing anything dangerous. You lied to me." Her voice cracked, her eyes taking on a dangerous sheen. Fuck.

"I didn't want you to worry. I'm fine. I'm being careful." Maybe I should have told her about Paris. About the very real chance that Emanuel Silver would land the blow to my head that would finally rattle my brain enough to take me out.

"Victor, you can keep secrets from me, but you can't lie to me about your safety."

"Can we not talk about that right now?" I blinked up at her, the swollen eye blurring half of her into a kaleidoscope of pink and blonde.

"Fine, you're getting a pass for today." She dabbed a fresh piece of gauze against the cut on my cheek and I hissed and jerked away from the sharp sting of alcohol.

"You did that on purpose."

"I did," she chirped. "Sorry not sorry."

"Fuck you," I grunted, and I would have immediately regretted the words if she hadn't giggled.

"Not tonight." She pressed another piece of cotton against my split lip, the sharp scent of alcohol and the sting almost enough to knock me out.

For fuck's sake. She was enjoying this.

"Stop being a bitch," I huffed.

"Stop treating me like I need to be delicately handled." She fluttered her lashes at me and pressed another piece of alcohol-drenched gauze right into the cut on my brow.

I didn't flinch this time. I kept my eyes squarely on hers.

We stared at each other, the air between us crackling with unspoken truths. It was too much tension. In my veins. In the stern set of her jaw. In the room. And it had to go somewhere or we'd implode before we'd even started.

"Kneel down, Cordelia."

"What?"

"On your knees."

She narrowed her eyes at me, that angry storm flashing in them, but she sank to her knees right in front of me. Doing exactly what she was told. Fuck if that wasn't the hottest thing I'd ever seen. "If this is your idea of-"

"Shut up and put your hands behind your back." Her nostrils flared but, again, she did as she was told. I freed my growing erection from my pants and watched her lips tremble as her eyes raked over it. I fisted my dick, a few drops of precum already there for her tongue. "Open that feisty little mouth for me."

She parted her lips - but barely enough.

"Tongue out," I rasped, my dick hard in my hand.

Once she put her tongue out, I placed my tip on it, almost expecting to have to give her more commands, but she started licking off my cum. She moaned, lashes fluttering. Fuck. Her mouth fell open and I rolled my hips forward, pushing into her. She gasped and moaned around my cock but her pink lips closed around it anyway, and she grasped the back of my knees for support instead of jerking back. I gave her a second before I pushed deeper, completely mesmerized by how eager she took my cock. It hit the back of her throat. Cordelia's eyes flew up to me, tears cresting her lashes.

When I pulled back, her cheeks hollowed as she sucked on my dick like it was a goddamn lollipop. Fucking hell. My cock sprang free with a *plop*, and Cordelia gasped for air. Her hand flew to her throat and she swallowed hard, and something clicked. "Have you sucked a dick before, Cordelia?"

"No," she gasped and shook her head.

Well, shit.

Despite her inexperience, her hands tightened around my knees, and she cocked her chin up in a quiet challenge. That hurricane was still raging in her eyes, ready to lay destruction.

"Open your mouth back up, baby. I'll start slow." She nodded and breathed deeply before parting her lips for me again. I pushed in slower this time and gathered her hair behind her head in a makeshift ponytail to wrap around my fist. "Your mouth feels so good, just relax your jaw."

I carefully slid back and forth a few times, using my tight grip on her hair to direct her head to move opposite my pace. "That's it, you've got it." She moaned when my next thrust pushed deeper, and she ran her tongue over me. "Fuck. Yeah. Use your tongue."

That seemed to unlock something in her head because she started doing all kinds of shit to my cock with her mouth. She licked slowly, then flicked her tongue against it. She sucked me in and pursed lips tight around my cock. My thrusts came faster, sliding deeper to a point of gagging her. The more she played with me, the more erratic my movements became.

"That's my girl," I moaned.

Cordelia's hands slid up my thighs and she curled her fingers around the base of my cock, pumping when her mouth was sliding off me. Fuck.

Then she grazed her teeth over my tip and I fucking lost it. I moaned her name and spilled myself down her throat. She spluttered for a second before sinking back on her heels, hand closed over her mouth.

"Swallow," I huffed.

She winced but did as she was told, throat bobbing. Shit. That would have been hot under any circumstance, but that girl was the pickiest eater I'd ever met, and her choosing to swallow my cum felt like getting knighted.

"Fuck, Cordelia, you're going to kill me."

Cordelia wiped her pinky over the corners of her mouth, a small grin quirking across her lips. "Feel better?"

I nodded, still breathless and reached a hand out for her. "Are you alright?"

"Yeah." She let herself be pulled back to her feet and grimaced. "I want to brush my teeth though."

Not what a man wanted to hear after the best blow job of his life, but fair. Especially if she'd never even had a dick down her throat before. "Go ahead. I'll clean this up," I said and collected some of the gauze scattered around me.

While I pulled my pants back up and sorted through the first aid shit, Cordelia plunged a toothbrush into her mouth with just as much fervor as she had taken my dick with. When I'd thrown away all the used gauze and empty wrappers and stored away the first aid kid, and Cordelia was still pulling faces at her reflection, brushing every which angle, I stepped up behind her. Her shoulders stiffened but she met my eyes in the mirror.

I'd never really considered what we looked like side by side. She was tall and lean, but she still just matched my shoulder. Her permanently sun-kissed golden skin stood out against my tattooed chest. Her champagne blonde waves the opposite to my short brown, stick-straight hair.

"Stop staring, weirdo," she grunted around her toothbrush.

"Cordelia?" I wrapped my hands around her waist and pressed a kiss against the back of her head. Her hair smelled like coconut and oranges. "Have you ever been fucked?"

She narrowed her eyes at my reflection, then bent to spit and rinse. I had a feeling the sharp push of her hips against me was *not* an accident. When she whipped her head back up, I barely managed to duck from being head-butted. That woman had a violent streak. Maybe *she* should get in the octagon. "Are you asking if I'm a virgin or if I've ever had dirty sex?"

"Have you ever had *any* sex?"

"No."

Fuck. I let out a long breath. "Got eaten out?"

"No."

"Touched?"

"You're touching me right now."

"You know what I mean."

She shook her head, lips pursed.

"So, when you said that you squirt sometimes..."

"On my own."

Double fuck. "Got it."

"Let me make this clear for you. You were my first kiss and my second kiss, and now my first blow job. I did those things because I wanted to. If I wanted to, I could get on Tinder and get laid like that." She snapped her fingers. "So if you start pitying me-"

"I've never pitied you and I don't intend to start now."

"Good. Why are you smirking like that?"

"I think I'm going to have a lot of fun being your first everything." I bent down to kiss her neck and she trembled, composure slipping for a split-second.

"What makes you so sure that I'll let you?"

I trailed more kisses up her neck to the hollow beneath her ear, her breaths stuttering through her lungs. I shot a glance at our reflection. Her eyes had closed. And I was satisfied with the position of my mouth - so, I sucked her skin beneath my teeth.

"Ow." She jerked in my embrace, nails digging into my wrists, only to dissolve into whimpers. She writhed her hips against me and my dick was ready to go again.

It was over within seconds though and I leaned back to admire the angry red mark I'd left of her neck. "First hickey."

"Are you serious?" She gaped and leaned forward, pushing her hair back to check for herself. "Are you dumb?" She whirled around and whacked me in the shoulder. "Del is going to see that. Tabitha and Defne are going to see that. What do you expect me to tell them, huh?"

"That you went on Tinder and got laid like that." I snapped my fingers, throwing her words back in her face.

"I'm going to bed and if this thing is still there in the morning, you can start looking for a new job, Vic."

"Vic? That's new."

"Rhymes with dick." She stuck her tongue out at me and turned to walk off. I couldn't help myself. I slapped her ass.

She yelped and turned around, wagging her finger at me. "Thin ice."

I finished cleaning up and walked out of the bathroom to find her curled up in bed under a mountain of blankets, that demonic cat lying beside her while she tapped away on her phone.

"Looking up ways to cover a hickey?" I asked.

"No-ouh."

"You're a shitty liar." I laughed and pulled the door open. "I'll see you later, zhizn' moya."

"Bye Vic." She smirked at her little joke but didn't look up from her phone, clearly intent on putting me in my place. I switched her light off, and almost missed her mumbling "Thanks." before I pulled the door shut behind me.

CHAPTER TWENTY

Cordelia

• FRAP SLUTS •

DEFNE · 08:39AM

First everything? EVERYTHING??

DEL · 08:39AM

He said that?

TABITHA · 08:40AM

ooooh the boy is whipped

TABITHA · 08:41AM

I bet he will go down on you everyday if you make your fluttery eyes at him

CORDELIA · 08:42PM

What fluttery eyes?

TABITHA · 08:43AM

you know

CORDELIA · 08:43PM

WHAT FLUTTERY EYES

DEL · 08:45AM

When you want something, you usually look like this: BattingLashes.GIF

CORDELIA · 08:45PM

I don't do that.

DEFNE · 08:46AM

You do but it's ok 🖤 it's cute!

A KNOCK ON MY BEDROOM DOOR STOPPED ME FROM replying to Defne.

"Breakfast!" Victor announced from the other side, then opened the door before I even had the chance to respond. Probably specifically so I didn't get the chance to avoid him.

"Hi," I mumbled, first time using my voice since he left my room three and a half hours ago.

He was fully dressed and his face already looked much better with the cuts closing and the swelling around his eye turning into a plain black bruise. Balancing the breakfast tray on one hand, he made quick work of collecting the glasses and cups off my nightstand to clear a space for it.

"You didn't have to bring me breakfast," I said, "I wasn't going to hide from you."

"I'm checking in."

"Do you want to sit?" I moved my legs aside to give him some space, startling Fitzi awake. The cat blinked at me through tired eyes, then spotted Victor and let out a vicious hiss.

Victor ignored him and smirked at me. "Are you inviting me into your bed, Miss Montgomery? That's very inappropriate."

I rolled my eyes. "I had your dick down my throat a few hours ago. I think we're past the point of propriety."

"My what?"

"Your-" My lips snapped shut before I could repeat the word. "I hate you."

"Here." He handed me the porcelain cup of tea from the tray before actually sitting down on the edge of the bed, right next to my knees. My mattress dipped under his weight, and my stomach tumbled enough for me to lower the tea cup again. Fitzwilliam jumped, claws-first, for Victor's wrist, but Victor just grabbed hold of him with one hand and dropped him off the bed. Sensing a fight he couldn't win, Fitzi dashed out the door.

"Do I ever make fluttery eyes at you?" I asked.

"You mean that puppy gaze when you want something?"

"Really?"

"You do that all the time. I thought you were flirting with me for a week when I started here. Then I saw you do it to everyone. You have a very animated face."

"I do?"

"It's sweet. I like it."

"Oh man. Does everyone think I'm flirting with them?" When he didn't reply, I set my tea aside and dropped back into my pillows, arms raised to cover my face. "If you need me, I'm in the backyard. I'm going to go ahead and bury myself alive."

"Come here." The mattress dipped further as he scooted up to pull at my arms. "Come on, make your fluttery eyes at me."

"No," I moaned, "I don't even do it on purpose."

"Please," he chuckled.

That sound got to me, pulling at the strings in my chest. I lowered my arms only to find him hovering over me. My breath stuttered in my throat, my entire vision suddenly taken up by the calming green of his eyes.

"Like this?" I asked and tried to bat my eyelashes like I wanted something.

"God, you're cute." He crushed his lips over mine. I jerked back, hand on his shoulders to get some distance between us. He'd kissed me. Victor had just put his lips to my lips after calling me cute. Very much a kiss and not an emergency mouth-to-mouth.

"What was that?" Three days ago he had been adamant that my birthday had been a selfish mistake, that he still needed some time. I could take the blow job out of that equation because that had been different. I'd wanted to make him feel physically better and I'd just been so angry, and somehow that had helped.

"What can I say? Fluttery eyes work for me."

"Would you go down on me every single day if I made fluttery eyes at you?" I asked, recalling Tabitha's words.

"Cordelia, you just have to say the word if you want my head between your legs. No fluttery eyes needed." He grazed his lips over mine, not a kiss, just his mouth skimming mine. "Do you want me to eat you out?"

"Uh, no. Actually. Not when your face is all bruised like this."

"Do you have anything else you want to try?" His fingertips skimmed down my neck and over the hickey, and I sighed at the featherlight touch to my collarbone. He followed the lacy neckline of my camisole, sloping down, down, down...

"Ow." A burst of dull pain had me shrinking back from him. "Shit. No. Thanks," I gasped.

"You're hurt." His hand snapped back, his brows furrowed. The angry line above his nose deepened as if I'd kept a vital secret from him.

"No, I'm in pain. There's a difference."

"Why are you in pain?"

"Uhm..." My skin suddenly felt too tight around my muscles.

"Cordelia?"

"Kind of- well- so, it's not-" I slapped my hands into my

175

cheeks, trying to get my thoughts in line, and when that didn't work, I dug my nails in. "It's because my period is due tomorrow."

"I know." Victor gently pulled my hands off my face, holding them in his, and chuckled at my raised brows. "Zhizn' moya, I'm the one who stocks up your tampons and Rocky Road half the time because you don't put them on the shopping list until you've run out. We only get groceries twice a week. I take care of it when it needs to be quick."

"Oh." I hadn't known that.

"Your breasts hurt because you're getting your period?"

"Yeah. They're swollen and every bra is too tight and my boobs feel like they're about to burst."

"Is that normal?"

"Yeah," I sighed, "some people say that it might get better if I ever have a baby and try breastfeeding, but you know..."

"I don't know."

"I can't have kids."

"Shit. I really didn't know that." His fingers tightened around mine. "I'm sorry."

"No, I mean, medically I could. I'm not infertile. I'm just not mom material."

"You're the most caring person I know. Even that cat from hell loves you."

"Moms have to leave their house."

"Why?" His face contorted in confusion as if I'd said something completely outlandish.

"Parent teacher conferences? Picking kids up from school? Taking them to the playground? Going to their friends' birthdays? I can't do any of those things."

"Video call. Driver. Nanny. Father."

"You don't get it," I mumbled and pulled my hands out of his. "It would be so selfish to have a child just because I want one, when I can't- I will never-"

"You founded an entire organization to help people like you.

To create support systems for women who need accommodations. You can make use of those in your own life, too."

"Why are you pushing this?"

"I just think that if you want to be a mother, you should have the chance."

I narrowed my eyes at him. "Do *you* want children?"

"One."

"Why just one?"

He sighed and ran a hand through his hair. "Do you want me to lie or do you want the truth?"

"Truth."

"Two children are more leverage than one."

A flash of pain cracked through my chest and it had nothing to do with period hormones. "By that logic, one child is more leverage than no child."

"It's a balance. You have to figure out what you want even if there's a chance you'll lose it. And what you're willing to live without." Victor reached out and brushed his thumb over my cheekbone. "When I have a child, I will love them and care for them and keep them safe. I want that."

"What if you only have that one child and they don't turn out the way you want them to."

"What do you mean?"

"My father hated what I became," I said, and turned away from his hand, suddenly too aware of how close he was, of the fact that he was in my bed and we were talking about babies.

"Your father was a dick," Victor said.

"A few years ago-" My voice quivered. I closed my eyes, my father's words still ringing in my head. "A few years ago, before you were here, before he got sick, my father suggested that I should have a child. He had the fertility clinic lined up, and a pre-selected list of donors. Everything. At least I would have gotten a vote on whose sperm they'd have shot into me, right?" I laughed bitterly. "He made it very clear that he wanted a grandchild to raise in a way befitting the Montgomery name. I wouldn't have gotten to raise the child. I'm not mom material beyond my DNA, am I? He didn't want someone soft. He wanted someone to take over the company. That's... that's when I moved out and got this place for myself."

"For fuck's sake, Cordelia." Victor climbed over my lap and settled in next to me, so he could pull me into his arms. The second they closed around me, my nerves released a whole body shiver. Victor kissed the crown of my head and whispered, "If he wasn't dead already, I'd put a bullet in his brain for that."

"He even put my future children in his will. He had higher hopes for my unborn offspring than for me."

"Cordelia, our child doesn't have to worry about any of that shit. We will love them, no matter what."

"Oh, it's *our* child now?" I tilted my head back, only then realizing that tears had gathered in my eyes, because Victor was very blurry.

"Seems fitting. First kiss. First blow job. First man fuck your brains out. And first man to father your child. We can discuss logistics later." He leaned down to kiss me with a little too much eagerness. His chest collided with mine, and I shrank back with a pained hiss. "Sorry. Right."

"You want to fuck my brains out?"

"Hmm." His voice rumbled from deep in his chest. "You won't be able to walk the next day."

"You're overly confident in your skills."

"Zhizn' moya, that wasn't confidence. It was a warning."

I rolled my eyes at him even as the muscles low in my stomach clenched at the idea. But that brought back the memory of him sitting in my bathroom with blood on his face. "Part of me is still mad at you for lying to me."

"I know. You have every right to be."

"You should have told me."

"You already have so much on your plate."

"Don't do that. Don't decide for me how much I can or cannot handle."

"Fine." He adjusted his position again to sit right in front of me, my legs slung over his lap. "How much do you want to know?"

"All of it."

Victor didn't hold back. We spent the entire morning in bed, sharing the croissant and tea from my breakfast tray, and Victor told me about his family. What it was like to grow up on a family estate with his cousins. How his uncle had his parents killed when he'd just been a teenager. All the years he'd gotten in the ring because it seemed like the only option. The fight in Paris his uncle wanted him to win.

"At least it makes sense now," I said and reached for his hand.

"What does?"

"You said you wanted to do *this* right but you needed time to get your situation sorted out." I drew his inked knuckles to my lips. "You don't think you have that time anymore, do you? You think you're running out. You think Silver will get in that one punch your doctors warned you about."

"Look-"

"You don't get to sacrifice your own safety for mine, Victor. We'll figure this out, alright?"

He hesitated for a moment, then pulled our linked hands up to his mouth, mirroring my kiss to his knuckles. "Alright."

CHAPTER TWENTY-ONE

Cordelia

VICTOR ONLY GOT A DAY OFF TO REST AND RECOVER before his uncle expected him back. At least now I knew that he only spent his days training or preparing for fights in one way or another. Which was much safer than the endless possibilities I'd been considering.

And knowing everything, my scheduled phone call that Wednesday just got so much easier.

"I understand, but I just can't have you over all the time right now. I have some things to figure out," I said, twirling a pen around on my desk. Didn't even have to tell him how uncomfortable all those cameras made me. I really did have other things to prioritize.

"Did you watch the video I sent you?" Silas asked.

"No, not yet." I glanced up at my screen and the red dot next to the email folder dedicated to him.

"Before you reject my idea, at least give it a chance."

"You are extremely persistent, has anyone ever told you that?"

"You're not going anywhere. I'm not going anywhere. Hell, you can call me three years from now. Just take a look at it."

I shook my head, then when I realized he couldn't see me, I verbalized my reply a bit more eloquently: "Thank you for the campaign videos."

"My pleasure," he said and actually sounded sincere, "I'll talk to you soon."

"Maybe in three years."

I let my phone drop next to the still spinning pen and turned to my computer.

Once I'd told Silas that I wasn't doing his project, it felt like that red email dot had suddenly turned pink. Not at all threatening anymore.

There was more movement in the video than I expected. It wasn't just me sitting at my desk and answering calls. But then it cut to the voice over of me talking about my mother, and the video showed her pictures lining my walls before panning out. It was a montage of my house. My rooms dissected on a micro level. There were detailed shots of the bits and bobs on my bookshelves, a close-up of my hands running over my furniture, a scenic moment of little dust particles dancing in the sun between my living room curtains. All accompanied by my voice, my memories of my mother.

My stomach somersaulted behind my belly button.

I was going to be sick.

VICTOR

"Cordelia?" I jogged up to the park bench, heart still racing. She'd dropped me her location. I'd been in the middle of rewatching the fight from last weekend with Yury when my phone had pinged with a fucking GPS signal.

I'd gone way over the speed limit to get here, assuming the worst.

Cordelia just lifted her head, her blonde hair cascading over a pale blue coat I'd seen Del wear a few times.

"Hi," she whispered, the word escaping with a cloud of breath in the cold air. It had gotten unreasonably cold again with the ground freezing over last night. Of course that was the day she'd leave her perfectly heated house.

"What? How?" I turned from side to side to see if Del was here, or anyone else who might have gotten her out of the house. But it was only her. In the middle of this sad excuse of a park. She'd pulled her knees up to her chest, rolled up into a small ball on this random park bench. And her lips quivered as she looked up at me through watery eyes. "It's okay. Come here." I took a seat next to her, just to hoist her into my lap. Her entire body trembled, either from panic or from the cold. "What's going on?"

"I was going to go for a walk and get ice cream."

Sure. Car windows were freezing over but that would never keep Cordelia Montgomery from her ice cream. Her favorite shop to order from was twenty minutes in the other direction, but she'd made it halfway to the nearest ice cream parlor, which was only a ten minute walk from her house. "I see. Holy shit. You made it so far."

"I can't move."

"What do you mean?"

"My feet are frozen. My legs are frozen. I just can't. I can't go back home. I can't go get ice cream."

I'd seen people paralyzed from one bad hit to the spine, so if she'd tripped or slipped on a frozen puddle... "Can you feel this?" I squeezed her calf, ice cold and only covered in some wool tights, but she nodded. I slid my hand further down and opened her boot to slip my fingers around her fuzzy-socked foot. "How about this?" She nodded again. Well, she wasn't physically paralyzed at least.

"I feel silly," she squeaked.

"You should feel proud. You made it really far." I zipped her boot back up and pulled her hands into mine instead. "Jesus, Cordelia, your fingers are frozen."

"I forgot gloves."

"How long have you been sitting here?"

She shrugged.

"Do you want me to take you home?"

She shook her head.

"Do you want me to take you to the ice cream place?"

She shook her head again.

I leaned back to open my jacket to wrap her up in it too. She nestled into it. Her cold fingers slipped in under my shirt, seeking every bit of warmth she could get. This wasn't quite how I'd imagined getting her hands on my bare skin.

"You smell good," she mumbled.

I chuckled. "It's the same aftershave you get me every year for Christmas."

"I have good taste."

"I agree."

"I'm exhausted." She turned her face, pushing her frozen nose against the hollow of my collarbone.

"I know, zhizn' moya. I've got you." I bundled the jacket

tighter and burrowed a hand into her soft hair, holding her against me. "You can relax now."

Fifteen minutes later a bike courier came to a screeching halt in front of us, making Cordelia's head snap up. "Victor?"

"That's me."

He swung his legs off the bike and opened his cooler box. The paper bag he pulled out had Cordelia sitting up straight, and losing her body folded against mine was only worth it for the way her face lit up at that damn logo.

"Enjoy guys!" The courier laughed as he handed her the bag, before driving off.

"What did you do?" she squealed but she was already digging through the bag, pulling out two massive cups of ice cream and the spoons to go with them.

"You wanted to go for a walk and get ice cream," I said. "You walked here. We have ice cream."

She handed me the plain mint chocolate chip one, and stared at her cup - even bigger than mine - with wide eyes. "It's beautiful," she whispered.

Beautiful was a choice word for 15 ounces of Rocky Road topped with whipped cream, gummy bears and rainbow sprinkles, but the woman knew what she liked. She popped off the plastic lid and dug through the first half at record speed, each icy spoonful melting the tension in her body bit by bit.

"What happened?" I asked.

"I told Silas Whitaker that it wasn't a good time to do his series. I figured if I wanted to do it, we could try it when you're back home permanently." She made a point of staring down her ice cream instead of meeting my gaze. "Then I actually watched the preview he sent."

"And?"

"It was beautiful. But it was suffocating. He captured so much of my world. And then wherever I looked, I saw how it could all be reflected in five seconds of video. It all felt so small."

"I'm sorry." I pulled her against me and kissed her temple.

"And my bangs look horrible on camera," she huffed.

I chuckled and removed the little flower clip that was keeping her bangs out of her forehead. I clipped it to my jacket's collar instead. "They're cute in person."

"I don't like going outside."

"You don't have to."

"I think I'd like to try painting again though. I haven't. Not since my mom died."

"I didn't know your mom painted all the pictures in your house," I said, recalling that interview she'd done with Silas.

"She did," she sighed. "She was great. She had her art in galleries all over the world."

"I love the one in your bedroom. The storm? It reminds me of your eyes."

Cordelia blinked up at me, lips parted. "Yeah," she said after a moment of silence, "it's... she called it Cordelia's Skies. It's a word play." Her face contorted as if she'd just bit into a lemon and she put the spoon down, setting the ice cream on her knees.

"What's wrong?"

"I haven't really talked about her in a while," she sighed, "I talk about what happened to her a lot, but she was so much more than her death."

"I'd love to know more. Whenever you want to talk about her." I brushed her hair behind her ears, finally getting her to look at me.

Cordelia nodded, but the smile on her lips quivered with exhaustion. "Maybe not right now."

"Okay."

"I think you were right. And she was right."

"About?"

"I'm allowed to have fun."

"Yes." The word shot over my lips way too fast. She wasn't just allowed to have fun. She deserved to have fun. She deserved so much more than that.

"But this isn't my idea of fun." She looked around, crinkling her nose at the bleak and icy park. "I don't care for it."

"Let's get you home."

"The fun way, please."

"What's the fun way?"

She grinned and put the plastic lid back on her ice cream. "Piggyback ride."

I laughed. "As you wish."

CHAPTER TWENTY-TWO

Cordelia

THE MORNING AFTER I DECIDED TO VENTURE OUTSIDE, I walked down to the kitchen for breakfast- and froze in the doorway. There was a girl at my table, chewing on a pencil and staring down a sudoku pad.

"Who are you?" I asked, voice surprisingly unwavering.

Her head snapped up, brown curls bouncing. "My name is Irina, ma'am."

"Ma'am?" I narrowed my eyes at her. I blamed my lack of panic solely on the fact that she had big brown doe eyes - and I clearly wasn't quite awake yet. I should have called 911.

"I'm Victor's cousin, ma'am."

My tired thoughts slowly started piecing her words together. Irina. Victor had told me about his cousins: Luka, Natalia and

Irina. She was the youngest in the bunch. "Why are you sitting in my kitchen?"

"I'm waiting for you to wake up, ma'am."

"Okay, cut the ma'am. You're making me feel old." I took a few tentative steps into the room and crossed my arms in front of my chest. "How old are you?"

"Twenty-one, ma-, Miss Montgomery."

"Just call me Cordelia, or nothing at all. And please explain why you're in my kitchen."

"Victor asked me to look after you when he's away," she replied as if that was logical.

Look after me? That girl looked like a puppy sitter at best. "No offense, but..."

"I have a black belt in Karate. My aim with a gun is the best in my family," she interjected. "I'm currently carrying five concealed blades, two of which can cut through bone. I can look after you, trust me. Better than Victor, I dare say."

"Okay..." I swallowed and tried not to stare too openly as I tried to figure out where her tight sweater and jeans were supposed to hide any knives. Victor had plopped his cousin in my house to *look after* me - and her definition of that seemed slightly violent. I tried to recall the first time I met Victor. Had he been just like that? Was that just how the Yelchins were raised? "Can you cook?"

"I can order from any of the 23 Victor-approved restaurants I have saved in my phone."

"Okay." I bit my lip. Part of me wanted to send her back home. Victor was clearly sending me a message. I'd been able to breathe through my panic attack just long enough to send Victor a GPS ping. And now I had a babysitter. Despite that, I felt the muscles between my shoulder blades unclenching. Irina's presence did that.

"Can I ask what we have planned today? Need to drive anywhere?"

"I have a lot of work to get through. So I'll be in my office most of the day." I awkwardly pointed over my shoulder to where my office was.

"Do you prefer for me to be in the same room as you or do you want me positioned outside, by the door?"

"Just within earshot is fine."

She gave a curt nod, and turned back to her sudoku. Well, that warm spirit was definitely a Yelchin family trait then. I grabbed a smoothie from the fridge and disappeared in my office - where I firmly closed the door behind me and Fitzi.

THAT DAY, I GOT THROUGH SO MUCH WORK THAT HAD been piling up, just because I avoided leaving my office. I barely looked up from my computer until Victor knocked against the door and opened it to peer in. It took me three, four, five furious blinks to even get my eyes to focus on him. Maybe I should invest in some blue light glasses. I'd probably break them within a week though. They seemed like a great little thing to fidget with whenever my hair was up.

"You didn't take your meds today," Victor grunted, and it took me a moment to realize he'd been talking.

Yeah, well, I hadn't had breakfast and I hadn't had lunch, so there was no meal that I took my meds with. And once I'd started looking into providing car services for women who couldn't get to our centers themselves, my day just rushed past.

Instead of explaining all of that, I just said, "You could have given me a heads-up regarding Irina."

"You need someone here. I took care of it."

"I don't know her."

He raised his brows in a silent question, because of course my argument didn't make sense. I hadn't known him either before I'd hired him.

"That's besides- I just-" I huffed, grasping at the fleeting thoughts as I tried to verbalize. "You didn't- Gah." I flexed my fists until my nails dug into my palms.

"You're angry with me," he realized.

"Yes. I guess."

He nodded. "I'll get started on dinner."

"That's all you have to say?"

He lifted his arms in a *what do you want me to say* shrug.

"God, you're frustrating. This is all- You can't- Fine. Have it your way. Go make dinner." I let out a strange sound, caught between a grunt and a scream and a sigh.

Victor didn't move away from the doorway, eyes still on me.

"Stop staring at me!" I yelled a little too loud, and got out of my chair a little too furiously, sending it crashing into the wall. It startled Fitzi enough for him to jump off the window and run from the room. Great. Even the cat that viciously attacked everyone was scared of me. I clasped my hands over my face, trying to still my breathing, to calm the blood rushing in my ears. "I'll get used to Irina, okay? I'm fine."

"Cordelia."

"Go!"

"Cordelia."

"Go make dinner." I lowered my hands just enough to see him standing still and staring at me. "What?"

"I hate being away from you. Trust me, if I had a choice, I wouldn't be further than ten feet from you at any given point in time. Once I've taken care of my family, I'll be by your side every second of every day. You're going to wish that you could get rid of me."

"I'd never wish that," I breathed, deflating even at the thought.

"Cordelia." This time his voice was laced with defeat, but he stepped into the room and closed the door behind him. "I need to figure out what Petya wants in Paris. Then I use that to get out of the fight, out of this stupid arrangement."

"How? How do you plan to get out once you have leverage?"

"I'll figure that out when I know what it is. A person can be killed. Money can be burned. We'll see."

"That's a horrible plan."

"I'm working on it." His fingers hooked into the belt loops of my skirt, pulling me closer. "Zhizn' moya?"

"Hmm?" I hummed, my eyes fluttering shut when his thumbs traced the sliver of skin between my skirt and my top. It was such a simple touch, but it stilled every thought in my mind. Everything zeroed in on the twin curves he was drawing.

"What are you in the mood for?"

"Uh... I..." I let out a shaky breath when his thumbs dipped into my waistband, grazing down the slope of my hip bones. Hands wrapped around his biceps, I steadied myself.

"Use your words, Cordelia," he commanded as he tugged the fabric down an inch.

Words required thoughts - and all of mine were occupied by the rough pads of his thumbs pushing against the elastic of my panties. "Yeah, okay."

His fingers stilled and my eyes flew open. He grinned a stupidly smug grin. "Blini?"

Damn him. He was talking about food. What *dinner* I was in the mood for?! I nodded at his suggestion, but my voice came out clogged. "Blini sound good."

"I'll get started."

THE CATCHY POP MUSIC WAS BARELY ENOUGH TO COVER up the buzzing sound. I just hoped the latter didn't carry all the way to the basement, where Victor was swimming laps. In his black swim shorts. With the water pearling off all his muscles.

That mental image did nothing to stifle the hot gasps escaping my throat.

I clutched my free hand over my mouth and tightened my grip on the vibrator. My legs jerked under my blanket, causing my bed to creak, adding to the not-so-subtle sounds.

The memory of Victor's hands inside my waistband mixed with images of him climbing out of the pool. Not swimming, not even jumping in - climbing out, hands wrapped tight around the railing of the ladder, arms flexing as he pulled himself up, water dripping from his hair.

"Oh god," I gasped against my palm. The hot pressure between my legs was mounting higher and higher. I writhed on my sheet, my spine arching off the mattress.

And then that picture of him climbing out of the pool morphed, and the water from his hair was dripping onto my stomach. Cold droplets trickling down the curve of my belly and into my navel as his mouth left a scorching path down, down, down my torso. His teeth and tongue played with me, left a burning red trail on my skin. And then he dipped his head.

I whimpered, bucking against the vibrator, as the pressure became too much to contain.

I tasted him in my throat and I felt him between my legs, and the heat erupted from my core in shakes and moans. Memories and fantasies flashed through my thoughts. They blurred together. Until it was all him. His deep earthy scent. His bottomless green eyes. His strength flexing around my body. Victor. *Victor.*

"Victor," I gasped, right before the world stilled.

Warmth radiated through my limbs as I crashed back into my pillow. Every breath was labor in my lungs. Fingers jittering like fall leaves, it took me a couple of tries to turn the vibrator off before I let myself fully sink into the softness of my bed.

I waited.

And I listened.

Because I'd just come with Victor's name on my lips, and I wasn't sure whether I wanted him to walk in or not.

But the house remained quiet.

CHAPTER TWENTY-THREE

VICTOR

My feet pounded into the whirring machine. The display shot some electronic fireworks across the screen as I added another mile to my total. Even the days I didn't spend at Petya's, I'd started working out more. It was self-preservation. If a hit took me out, it wouldn't be because I hadn't been prepared.

"I can't focus," Cordelia whined as she trotted into the gym. She was pulling an adorable grumpy face that lacked any sort of conviction. Her little pink skater dress and the thick fluffy socks meant she hadn't come down here to work out.

"Want to jump on the treadmill?" I offered, because I knew that whatever I suggested right now, she wouldn't do on principle.

She grimaced. "I'm distracted, not bored to death."

"Okay," I huffed, "what's so distracting?"

"You," she sighed.

"I'm not doing anything."

"I'm distracted by the idea of you."

"The idea of me?" I chuckled and raised my brows at her. "What does that mean?"

"I keep thinking about what it would be like if you went down on me."

My steps faltered, the machine almost catapulting me backwards. "Fuck, Cordelia. Give a man a heads-up."

"Alright, heads-up." She bent over the control panel and slowed the tempo for me. "I want your head between my legs. I don't think I'll be able to focus on anything else until I know what it feels like to have you eat me out."

I cursed under my breath. "Right now?"

She eyed me up and down. "Preferably, but if you'd feel better after a shower, I can wait."

"Shit."

"Is that a yes?"

"Come here." I flipped the main switch on the control panel, the machine dying under my feet.

"I was thinking upstairs..."

"Don't make me repeat myself, Cordelia."

She combed her fingers through that damn golden hair of hers, biting her lip, before ducking under handrail. She slotted into the narrow space between me and the console, big eyes looking anywhere but at me. Her boldness was fading fast.

Fuck, I wasn't sure what was hotter. The confidence to ask for my head between her thighs, or knowing that she was mine alone. Mine first.

"What if I don't like it?"

"Then we stop."

"Okay," she nodded, "how do I- do you need me to-"

Fuck her not looking at me. I wanted her to want this. I kissed her, and after a short flinch, she sighed into my mouth. Her sweet breath mingled with mine and she relaxed against me. Her delicate fingers wove around my neck and down the back of my shirt. Nothing could compare to her hands on me. Her touch was so careful, so gentle, exploring the feel of someone else's skin against hers. She could explore all she wanted. I'd be her goddamn puppet and she could pull every string to test my reactions.

I broke out of the kiss, leaving her gasping.

"Take off your panties." I braced my arms on the handrails, caging her between me and the machine.

"Oh, yeah," she rasped and looked down at her own body, "do you want me to take off the dress?"

"Did I tell you to take off the dress?"

She swallowed and shook her head. With her eyes on me, Cordelia reached up her skirt and wiggled her hips until a tiny piece of peachy fabric slid down to her knees. She stepped out of her panties and held the scrap of lace and cotton up for me. "Like that?"

I took them from her and ran my thumb over the small dark spot in their center. For fuck's sake. "Is that how wet you get thinking about me?"

"Is there always this much talking involved? Or are you actually going to do something?" She ran her tongue over her lips. "Because I wasn't really imagining a Q and A session, you know."

I pocketed her underwear, grabbed her waist and hoisted her up on the console. She let out a surprised gasp but didn't need any direction to open her legs to let me stand between them. "Is this what you want?"

She nodded.

"Are you that desperate to have someone eat your pussy?"

She shook her head. "Not someone. You."

Fuck me. I pushed her dress up. Her thighs twitched around my waist, the little muscle spasm rippling all the way up to her perfect pink pussy, bare and glistening for me. My fists tightened around the bunched fabric of her dress. It took every drop of self restraint in me not to plunge my fingers into her. Not when she was still- fuck, I wasn't sure how far she wanted to go. Cordelia was the first girl I meant to take my time with.

"Fuck, you're beautiful," I rasped through strained lungs.

She let out a little giggle that burrowed right into my chest. "That's a weird thing to say when you're not looking at my face."

"Yeah, I'm not talking about your face, Cordelia," I grinned and dragged my eyes up, "I'm talking about that sweet little cunt, already twitching and getting wet for me. So fucking needy."

"Vic-"

"Shut that pretty mouth of yours." Her lips snapped close at my command and her eyes widened. "You're right. It's not a Q and A. You don't talk unless I tell you to."

Her nostrils flared but she nodded.

I slipped my hands down her perfect, smooth legs and leveraged them over the handlebars of the treadmill. She let out a small whimper, her hands clamping around the console, but that was the only sound from her as I spread her wide open for me.

"I'm starting to think you're so desperate to come on my face, you'll do just about anything I say."

She bit her lower lip, watching, waiting.

"Close your eyes," I said, just to see if she would.

She blinked once, twice, and on the third blink, her eyes stayed shut.

I wrapped her hair around my fist and yanked her head back. The sharp pull wrangled a cry from her lips that turned into a soft moan when I claimed her throat with my mouth. I'd never get enough of the taste of her skin, as sugary as her mouth. "I bet your pussy tastes just as sweet as the rest of you."

One of her hands found my neck, wrapping around the back of it - and pushing down.

"Nice try," I chuckled and plucked her hand off me, planting it back on the machine, "needy little things don't get to make demands. They take what they get."

Before she had the chance to react with a disapproving brow

wrinkle, I tugged her hair back again - and at the same time, let my other hand slide up her thigh until I could part her with my thumb. Fuck, she was hot and wet. And I languished in every muscle twitch as I traced slow curves from her entrance to her clit and back again. Cordelia squirmed, letting out an unintelligible garble of half-formed words. She was blinking rapidly against the ceiling.

"Didn't I tell you to close your eyes?"

"Hffn-" She squeezed her eyes shut, pushing her hips against my hand, seeking more friction than I was giving her.

"Do you touch yourself while thinking about me?"

She nodded.

"Tell me." I flicked my thumb against her clit.

"Yes," she squeaked.

"Yes, what?"

"Yes, I think about you when I use my vibrator."

Vibrator. The word echoed through my brain. Cordelia didn't just fuck her own fingers while thinking about me - she had a vibrator somewhere up in that bedroom, and she plunged it between her legs, imagining it was me instead.

"Look at me," I said, and waited for her glassy gaze to find me, "there's no turning back after this. You let me get a taste, and that's it. I'm not going to walk away. Not ever."

"Good," she whispered, "I want you to stay."

With that, I sank my head between her legs. I kissed my way up the insides of her thighs first, used my lips, my tongue and my teeth to test her reactions. Until finally, I gave in to the intoxicating scent of her pussy, and sank my tongue into her.

"Oh fuck," she cried.

Oh fuck, was right. Her taste dissolved on my tongue even sweeter than I could have imagined - and there was no way in hell I'd ever give this up.

Cordelia

HIS TONGUE WAS INSIDE OF ME. LITERALLY. INSIDE. MY. Body.

It was strange and perfect and overwhelming. And my nerves were buzzing. And my bones were vibrating. And- and- oh god.

My hips bucked and threatened to slide off the treadmill but then Victor's hands dug into my thighs, deep enough to bruise, locking me in place.

He licked - LICKED- along my slit and I let out an ungodly cry.

I'd seen this before. In porn. But seeing it didn't compare to the actual feeling of his tongue flexing and pushing against me.

His teeth grazed over my hot clit. "Victor, please," I whimpered, not even sure what I wanted.

"Shut up, or I'll find a way to make you shut up, Cordelia," he replied, and while his mouth was busy forming words, flicked two fingers against my sensitive bundle of nerves.

"Like what?" I whined.

He huffed, straightening up. I already regretted asking, only because I wanted him - no, I *needed* him to keep going.

I just tracked the flash of peach lace, before he clasped a hand around the back of my neck, locking me in before he shoved my own panties into my mouth. "Be a good girl and hold onto these for me."

"What the fuck?" My reply was muffled, and sounded more like *whah heh huh.*

I could taste myself on the fabric and it sent a strange, blinding rush through all my senses.

Then Victor's mouth was back between my legs, torturing me. He played with me. Fast then slow. Angry then gentle. The pressure in my core built and built, brimming to the edges of what I could survive - only for him to ease up again, giving me a few breaths to simmer down.

"Please," I begged, blinking through a sudden onset of tears, but it sounded more like *pheeh*.

"Fuck," he huffed and straightened again. He pulled the fabric from my mouth, and I worked my jaw for just a second, before his lips claimed mine. If I'd thought my underwear tasted like my own arousal, it was nothing compared to his tongue, coated in it. The guttural moan that escaped me completely ruined the kiss. "Cordelia?"

"Hmm?"

"I told you to shut up."

I nodded, squeezing my eyes shut and shifting my hips against him, needing to feel something.

Instead of giving me what I was desperate for, Victor's arms folded around me and he lifted me off the treadmill. I remained pressed against his chest, my legs nowhere near stable enough to hold me up.

"What are you doing?" I whined.

"If you can't do as you're told, you don't get to come."

"What?" I sounded pathetic.

He slid a hand down my back, over the curve of my cheeks and between my legs. One finger parting me, he gave me one last, slow stroke that had me shuddering against his chest, before he pulled my dress down over my hips again. "Don't worry, you'll learn, zhizn' moya."

"Are you serious?" I pushed my fists into his chest, but he had me in an iron grip against him. I could only crane my neck back to furiously blink up at him. "That's not-"

He silenced me with a kiss - much gentler than before, his lips carefully exploring mine. "For what it's worth," he rasped, breath lingering in the space between our faces, "you taste even better than I imagined."

I shuddered at the meaning of those words. "Do you think about me when you touch yourself?" I asked, throwing his question back.

"I always think about you."

CHAPTER TWENTY-FOUR

Cordelia

IRINA'S STUPID DUFFEL BAG DIDN'T FIT INTO MY LIVING room. It was scuffed leather, slouchy and black. It looked like it belonged to some hitchhiker in an old horror movie. And the fact that I hated it had nothing to do with Irina. Irina was *fine*. Being home alone with her was *fine*. Victor going to Las Vegas to give some official UFC interview about his comeback was *fine*.

It was just that ugly duffel bag. It completely messed up the look of my pretty pastel sofa.

Jaw locked tight, I threw the door of my office shut, leaned my back against it and took some steadying breaths.

Stupid ugly distracting duffel bag.

"This could still make a great political jumpstart, just saying," Amani mused a few minutes later, when we were discussing the campaign videos Silas had sent.

"I'll keep that in mind."

"We'll publish the first video tomorrow."

"Okay."

She rattled on about the platforms and what I should expect coming my way consequences wise. Comments. News outlets. Something... something.... Stupid. Ugly. Duffel. Bag.

"Cordelia?"

"Hmm?"

"Do you need me to send you everything in an email, so you can read through it when you're more focused?"

"I'm sorry." I pushed my nails deeper into my cheeks, trying to pull myself back into the moment. "I think I got most of it."

"There's going to be some attention coming your way. Your face will officially be out there. Are you ready for that?"

"I don't really have a choice, do I?"

"There's always a choice. You can open a center in every state by the end of next year. I mean, you have the money. We can do it all the old-fashioned way. Print more pamphlets. Reach out to social services. We don't need publicity to help people."

I rolled my eyes at her silly attempt at reverse psychology. As if I hadn't thought the whole thing through myself five hundred times already. My discomfort was a small price to pay for the awareness this campaign would generate. And the more women were aware of the foundation, the better. I had been given the chance to help people. What did my discomfort mean in the grand scheme of things?

"I'm good," I mumbled, "I'll be fine."

"Okay, great. I'll basically be awake for the next 72 hours monitoring this, so reach out if you need any help whatsoever, okay?"

"As your employer, I can't condone that. Get some sleep. But as myself? Thank you."

"You got it. Let's tell the world who we are, huh?"

"Sure," I breathed and my eyes dropped back to the small camera Silas had left for me.

After hanging up, I turned the camera over in my fingers and replayed the stupid short video I'd taken in the winter garden the other day. It was silly, but the first thought that popped into my head was that *that* Cordelia had no idea what it felt like to have Victor's head between her legs.

My second thought was that, as of tomorrow, everybody would know who I was and what I really looked like.

And my third thought was that everyone already knew what Victor looked like.

I opened a new browser window and typed in two words I hadn't googled in years: *Victor Yelchin.*

His comeback fight was one of the first results that popped up. I watched it and flinched at every hit Victor absorbed like it was nothing. I watched it again and compared the commentary to the fight itself. I hit play again and listened to it while scrolling the comments excitedly (albeit sometimes rudely) discussing Victor's victory. By the fourth time it played, I kept track of the camera. It clearly favored Victor. He was the star in this fight. To the audience, to the camera man, and to the commentators.

The fifth time I watched it, I turned down the volume and just watched Victor's body move. Covered in ink and sweat, he navigated the octagon like it was his home - and the other guy was nothing but a mouse fated to be trapped. He was astonishing. Biting my lip, I hit play again, and blamed the heat rising to my cheeks on the thick sweater I'd thrown on today.

"Irina?" I called her name when the screen faded to black.

The girl took less than three seconds to swing the door to my office open, hand on the gun on her hip. "Yes?"

"Would you mind picking up some pizza?"

"Victor prepared-"

"I really like this place called Coco's," I said before she could reason her way out of it, "I'll take a four cheese, please. You can get yourself whatever you want." I fished my wallet from my desk drawer and waved my credit card at her.

"Sure thing, Miss Cordelia," Irina said and snatched the card from my hand.

I waited until the door had fallen shut behind her and counted to sixty before I picked up my phone.

CORDELIA · 11:58AM
You're mine.

VICTOR · 11:59AM
Yes

CORDELIA · 11:59AM
I won't let him touch you.

I DIDN'T WAIT FOR VICTOR'S NEXT REPLY. INSTEAD, I scrolled through my contacts and called the one person who could frame a narrative like nobody else. He picked up fast enough to make me think he must have been expecting this call - and he would do just about anything to stay on my good side.

"Silas? I have a proposition for you."

CHAPTER TWENTY-FIVE

Cordelia

THE GLOVED HAND MUFFLED EACH SOUND, BUT I KEPT screaming. Screaming for my mom, for help, for mercy. She didn't move. Of course she didn't move. I'd seen the bullets tear through her chest.

"Grab the girl, Nick."

I was hauled off my feet like I weighed nothing. Like I wasn't supposed to stay with my mom. They couldn't just leave her there.

I kept screaming until something hard came down on the back of my head and knocked me out.

And then there was light. So much of it.

I blinked against my bedroom, shooting upright.

"You're alright. You're fine." Victor's voice barely broke through the images still flooding my mind. The four words that had changed the complete trajectory of my life.

Victor crossed the room but I threw my hands up to stop him before he could touch me. I could still feel the imprint of the gloved hand over my mouth. *"Grab the girl, Nick."*

"Not real. Not real," I mumbled, shaking my head.

"I'm very real, zhizn' moya." He crouched down, tilting his head in search for my gaze, but my eyes were still roaming over every corner of the room. Nobody. Nobody was hiding in the shadows. Nobody was going to grab me.

"Not you," I breathed.

"There's nobody here. It was just a bad dream."

"No," I lowered my shaking hands, "I can hear them even after I wake up, Victor. I don't have nightmares. I have memories."

"But both are just in your mind." He shifted his weight onto the mattress, but it wasn't enough. I wanted him closer. I needed to soak up his warmth.

I scooted aside and lifted the edge of my tangled blanket. Victor didn't need a verbal invitation. He hadn't even settled yet when I slung my arms around him, slotting against his side. I rested my head on his chest, finding the steady rhythm of his heart and letting it slow my breathing.

"You're alright," he whispered against my crown, rubbing slow, soothing circles into my back.

We lay there for a few minutes, until my pulse eased and my thoughts cleared. And I became very aware of the fact that I had invited Victor into my bed and was resting my cheek against his chest. And it didn't feel wrong. Not having him around was worse. This? This was meant to be. Him coming home, lying next to me, his perfect earthy scent engulfing me.

"Did you just get home?" I asked.

"Yes," he replied, voice rumbling low in his chest, "I came straight from the airport, sent Irina off and was about to check on you when I heard you scream."

"I'm sorry, you should go get some sleep," I tried to push off him but his arms locked around me.

"Stay," he said in that tone of his that left no room for protest. I deflated against his chest. My body immediately molded into him again. "That's my girl."

My cheeks heated. *My girl.* I'd told him that he was mine in a text message just a few hours earlier, but that was different. Hearing him say it out loud sent a flutter through my nerves that had nothing to do with my night terrors.

"We can get some sleep right here," he said and reached for the light switches. He only killed the big light though, leaving the room in the faint orange flow of the bedside lamp.

"If you hand me my Kindle, I'll just read while you sleep."

He gently tugged on my braid, forcing me to look up at him. I knew exactly why his brows were furrowed.

"There's just no way I'll fall back asleep. I'm sorry. It's okay, though. You sleep," I patted his hard pecs, "and I'll stay right here."

He leaned down to graze his lips over mine. "I can think of a few ways to tire you out."

A shiver rippled along my spine, just as his hand grazed down my side to the elastic of my shorts. "I don't think that'll work," I breathed.

"I've always hated your tiny pajamas." His fingertip ran a lazy line along my waistband, burning hot against my skin. I sucked in a breath and glanced down at the cute rosy satin set I was wearing. They were covered in floral lace and little purple bows on the straps and waistband. Girly, but not remarkable enough to *hate*.

"Why?" I asked through a clogged throat. His fingertips dipped into my waistband - then stilled when they didn't find another layer of fabric covering my hips.

"Because they're so flimsy, I just want to rip them off. Fuck you until you lose your voice." His hand slid lower and I pushed into him when he brushed down my pubic bone. "Your tiny shorts make it very hard to pretend that I don't want your thighs clenching around me."

"Oh." My eyes squeezed shut and I pressed my face into the soft fabric of his shirt, because his words had sparked a small flame in my lower stomach.

His hand stopped just before touching me where I needed him to. "Look at me."

I shook my head, skin prickling in anticipation of what my defiance would get me.

He gave my braid a sharp tug, forcing my eyes up to him. I sucked in a breath. Something had to be seriously wrong with me because that harsh tone and rough touch just fanned the heat in my core.

"Stop being a dick," I hissed, eyes narrowed, and pushed against his fingers, "first I'm not allowed to open my eyes or make a sound when you go down on me, and now I'm *supposed* to look at you when you finger me? If you want to touch me, touch me already, asshole."

"Care to repeat that?"

"Didn't hear me the first time, *Vic*?"

"I heard you. I'm just making sure you know what you're saying."

"I said, you're being a dick who demands too much considering you've never even made me come."

Victor grabbed me by the waist and hoisted me around like I weighed nothing, draping me over his lap. His thighs pressed into my stomach, and I spluttered out air and nonsensical sounds. Without so much as a warning, he slid his hand up the back of my shorts and dug his fingers into my ass cheek. I knew that he was strong, but being on the receiving end of his strength, without the care he usually took when touching me, was unfamiliar and it ignited a new kind of heat between my legs.

"Are you sure that's what you meant to say?"

"What are you doing?" My voice came out muffled, his legs pressing into my lungs.

I wriggled backwards but before I could move more than an

inch, his other hand clamped down around the back of my neck. He'd locked me down. I squirmed in his lap. I didn't even want to get up. I just wanted his hand to move. To slide a few inches downwards. But shifting my hips did nothing to elevate the dense pressure between my legs.

"Lie still and answer when you're asked a question, Cordelia."

"I don't know," I breathed, already forgetting what he'd asked.

"Do you like acting like a fucking brat?"

"I... I just..."

His hand slipped between my legs, hard knuckles brushing against my most sensitive parts. Heat rushed through me. I squirmed against him, barely able to move.

"Victor," I moaned his name, tilting against him.

"I told you to answer my questions."

"I wouldn't have to act like a brat if you stopped being a dick," I huffed, curling my hands into my sheet as his knuckles rippled over my clit, slowly, one after the other. Pictures of those same knuckles connecting with his opponent's face flashed through my thoughts. It should have turned me off. Instead it pulled another moan from my throat. This was too messed up. I was too messed up. I tried to get up again, but his grip around my neck had me firmly caged in place, and the realization that he wouldn't let go spiked my pulse. "Fuck."

"Not tonight," he chuckled and leisurely ran his knuckles back over my clit in the opposite direction.

It was getting decidedly too hot in here. My cheeks were burning, and my lungs aching and his torturous touch didn't help either. I dropped my head, pressing my face into my sheets. "What are you doing?"

"Teaching you some manners."

"By getting me wet?"

"By showing you that it would pay off to do what you're told - like lying still."

"And I don't get a choice in-hng." He parted me for access,

and one of his fingers ran from my entrance to my clit, pressing down firmly.

"Fuck, you're already so fucking wet, baby. You can call me a dick all you want, but you can't hide how desperate you are to be fucked."

I couldn't even respond. I could only moan as his finger strummed my nerves, and electric sparks zapped through my whole body.

Only for him to pull both his hands back, leaving me breathless.

"Vi- Victor- I-" I started pushing to my knees, limbs trembling. Before I could, his fingers hooked into my shorts and he yanked them down over my ass. I moaned at the rough scrape of fabric against my sensitive skin, and again when his hand dug into my flesh and pushed me back down on his lap.

The thrill of his forceful touch was quickly followed by his rough fingers back between my legs.

"Lie still. I'm not done with you, Cordelia," he rasped, then dipped his index finger into me.

I moaned, any protest fading from my body. He barely pushed into me, but my muscles strained and ached to accommodate him. I had touched myself before - but it was nothing compared to his large hand. I choked on each breath I took as he burrowed deeper.

"That's my girl," he said, and this time the words washed over me like another incinerating touch.

"Victor." My voice was a breathless plea, and then I felt him bottoming out. His finger slid into place perfectly, knuckles brushing against my sensitive flesh. My breath spluttered from my lungs. And just when I thought it couldn't get better than this, he moved inside of me. His finger curled, brushed over a tender spot, and my vision blackened.

I dissolved into moaning mess as he carefully pulled his finger back a little, only to come back and push into that sensitive spot again. My muscles clenched around him but he kept moving undeterred. My bones shattered like glass and my nerves sparked like a fuse and my body was nothing beyond where he touched me. I climaxed, screaming his name from an already sore throat, the pressure bursting from my core. I spilled myself over his lap.

"Fuck, I'll never get over this, zhizn' moya."

His words were a hazy blur as I lay slumped over his thighs, breathing hard into my sheets, but Victor wasn't stopping.

I whimpered and tried to wave at him. He had to know that I had come. I was covered in slick wetness. His finger squelched, pumping in and out of my trembling core.

"Victor." I squeezed my thighs together in an attempt to get his attention, but as a result, I just felt every knuckle of his finger pressing against my sensitive insides, and I moaned, caught somewhere between pleasure and pain.

"I told you to lie still, Cordelia," he responded and gave a poignant harsh thrust, "can you do that?"

"Yes," I gasped. I gripped my sheets with both hands but didn't otherwise move.

It almost felt like a reward for my obedience when his second hand found my swollen clit. My climax hadn't tamed his touch though. His rough fingers thrummed against me violently.

"I don't know if I can- fuck," I squeezed my eyes shut at the heat boiling between my legs. I'd never come twice in a row before but within a few thrusts, I clenched around his finger again. My insides were bursting for him, aching under the deep-rooted pressure built inside me. Until he flicked my clit and the short burst of pain tore me wide open.

He kept going through my climax, and braced his arm over my hips to keep me still while my body rocked under the intense pleasure bursting through me. It felt like drowning. Like my lungs tried and tried with each moan and still couldn't get enough air. Like my body was no longer mine to control.

I rode this orgasm longer than the first one, my overstimulated body caught in the current of it. Until the last wave swept me out of the water, and breath spluttered back into my lungs.

When he finally slipped his finger out of me, I whimpered. It had felt like such a perfect fit that losing his touch seemed wrong.

"So needy." He chuckled. "Still not enough?"

"I-" My voice broke off as another tremor tightened my insides. I wanted more, but I wasn't sure I *could.* My limbs were buzzing. Electricity hummed through my nervous system, making me quiver from my lips to my toes.

"Come here," Victor whispered, gentle hands helping me up until he was cradling me in his lap. Half my braid had come loose, and he carefully brushed the wayward strands from my face. "What do you need right now?"

"I just." I grimaced at my hoarse voice scratching up my throat. "Water."

He leaned back and grabbed my glittering tumbler from my bedside table, giving it a small shake to ensure it wasn't empty before he brought the straw up to my lips.

Greedily gulping down the cold relief, I let my eyes fall shut and my head drop against his shoulder. He lay his lips against the top of my head, whispering something unintelligible in Russian.

"What does that mean?" I mumbled.

"It's the text of a lullaby."

"Oh right, you were trying to tire me out. Good effort." I smiled into the side of his neck, barely even able to keep my eyes open.

He chuckled and placed the tumbler back on the bedside table. "Anything else?"

"Hmm," I thought for a second, "I need your shirt."

"My shirt? This shirt?"

"Yeah."

He started peeling the fabric off his back and I leaned back just long enough for him to undress. When he handed the bundled up shirt to me, I tossed it aside and wrapped my arms around his bare torso instead.

"Perfect," I sighed, letting his warmth and his scent close around me.

"Perfect," he agreed and kissed my forehead.

Victor slid down the mattress again, until we were lying down, my head still resting on his shoulder. He kept one hand wrapped around the nape of my neck while the other drew languid patterns on my thigh.

Despite my body feeling warm and heavy, sleep was impossible. My adrenaline may have been pumping earlier but now my hormones kept my thoughts whirring. Hormones and the unmistakable hard outline pressed against the inside of my thigh. Because I didn't mind. I loved that making me come had gotten him hard. I wanted to feel him again, touch him, see him fall apart. But all of this only had one possible destination - and I wasn't sure if I was ready for it yet. This was the kind of thing you were supposed to be able to ask your mom about. I'd never even gotten *The Talk* - having gotten my sex ed from the internet, and it hadn't bothered me until right this second.

I huffed and traced my fingertip over the feather tattoo on his shoulder, desperate for any distraction. "Do all of your tattoos have meanings?" I asked.

"Mh-mm, no."

I tried to do the math of how long it took to have a tattoo needled into you and how long it took to heal - how many hours he had spent in tattoo studios over the years. "Do you know how many there are?" My finger sloped down his side to where a snake slithered down his ribcage.

"No," he whispered against my hair.

"Do you have a favorite?"

"You pick."

"You want me to pick your favorite tattoo for you?" I giggled. "That makes no sense."

"Whatever you pick."

"I'm trying to get to know you. Stop trying to be romantic." I pushed myself up until I straddled his hips and looked down at his sharply sculpted face, not a hint of amusement in his eyes.

"For fuck's sake, stop moving." Victor inhaled audibly, hands wrapping around my bare hips and digging in hard enough to keep me locked in position. "Look, Cordelia, I had one tattoo with a meaning. Got it covered up."

"Why?"

"It was my first tattoo. I had it done after my parents died. Then I realized how stupid it was to wear my grief on my skin for everyone to see."

"I'm sorry," I swallowed, "so did you get the others for the aesthetic? To look menacing in the ring?" My fingertips brushed down the storm of clouds and lightning on his stomach, his abs tightening under my touch.

"I got them because they reminded me that my body was my own. My uncle could make me throw punches, dictate what I eat, when I sleep, where I go, who got to beat me to a pulp. My skin was my own."

"Oh." My chest deflated, air replaced by a dull ache for him. "Victor."

"So you pick a favorite. It'll be mine because you like it."

"I can do that." I bit my lip, unsure where to start. I knew many of them by heart, from the classic roses on the backs of his hands to the moth wrapping its wings around his neck. And then there were some I had barely caught glimpses of. "Turn over."

He quirked his brows but when I rose to my knees to give him space, he wordlessly twisted under me to give me a better view of his back.

My hands roamed down his shoulder blades, his muscles rippling under my touch. His back was warm and hard and covered in dry branches, birds and ornaments, all coming together in a mosaic of a skull. It was hard to focus on the ink, when Victor made small humming noises while my fingers traced patterns over his skin.

"Victor?" I whispered.

"Hmm."

I flattened myself against his back, whispering a kiss against his spine. "I want you to get a new tattoo. Would you do that?"

"Anything specific?"

"No," I mumbled, kissing the space between his shoulder blades again, "I don't want to choose one of the tattoos that are all yours. They kept you alive. They got you to me. But they're all your past. I want a good one. A happy one."

Victor flipped us over. On my back, with him between my legs, his erection pressed against my center. I whimpered, but he ignored the pathetic reaction he drew from my lips.

"Where do you want the tattoo?" he asked.

I picked his right hand off the mattress, interlacing my fingers with his and turning them over. On that hand, only his middle finger had ink on it, a small dragon. The other fingers were still perfect empty canvases. "Here. So I can see it all the time."

"Anything specific?"

"Something happy."

"Tea cup?"

"Not bad."

"Kittens."

"Better."

"Gummy bears."

"Perfect." I smiled.

He tilted his chin, eyes dropping to our linked hands. "A ring."

"Tha-" My breath left me in a single whoosh. He couldn't mean what I thought he meant. "Wrong hand."

"Russian people wear it on the right hand."

He definitely meant what I thought he meant. "If this is your way of proposing to me..."

"I don't need to propose. We both know this is it."

"So I'm not even getting a ring?"

"You want a ring? I'll get you a ring. But I'm not asking you to marry me. I'm not proposing. There is no question whether or not you will be my wife. We are undeniable."

"A gummy bear on your index finger," I said, "and a wedding band on your ring finger."

"Alright."

"I do want a ring. A wearable one."

"Alright."

"My wedding dress will be pink."

"Alright."

"You're taking my last name," I said. Victor's lips parted but no sound came out, so I continued: "You're going to be part of my family. Mine. Screw your uncle. Screw anyone else who thinks they have any claim on you. You're mine."

He gave me a small smile and a nod. "Alright," he whispered and lifted my top off, before covering my body with his. Skin on skin, any space between us was diminished when he finally sank his mouth over mine again. He fit so perfectly over me, our bodies aligning in all the ways. I wanted to feel more of him. All of him. But when I tried to reach for his waistband, Victor grabbed my hands and pressed them deep into the mattress beside my head.

"Try to undress me again and you're not walking out of here a virgin," he warned and dug his teeth into my lower lip.

I whimpered, at his words and his bite. "I just want to feel you."

Without warning, he viciously rocked his hips into mine. I could feel him. Every inch of him, hard and rough against my center. Only a thin layer of fabric between us. A fresh electric current thrummed up under my skin and I pushed my hips against him, seeking more friction.

"Fuck, Cordelia, how can you-" He pressed his lips together, stopping himself from finishing that sentence.

"What?"

"Nothing."

"What?" I asked, unable to stop the laugh erupting at his deeply furrowed brows. I reached up to smooth out the small wrinkle above his nose. "What's wrong? You look like you're trying to win at chess without cheating."

"Nice," he huffed and playfully snapped at my hand, managing to graze his teeth over my palm, "it's truly nothing. Just me being an idiot."

"Tell me."

"You know what you want. I shouldn't be surprised that you're not shy in bed."

I let out an ungodly cackle. "I'm sorry," I gasped, "oh my goodness, could you imagine? *Oh no, Victor, please, your erect penis is so intimidating. Don't come any closer or I might faint.*"

He laughed. The only thing better than a Victor laugh, I discovered, was a Victor laugh reverberating from his chest into mine.

"You're right. Fuck that." He was still grinning when he leaned back down to kiss me.

"*Oh no, I'm fainting,*" I mumbled into the kiss, "*my poor virgin soul is being corrupted.*"

VICTOR

CORDELIA'S RATTLING BREATH PULLED ME FROM THE half-asleep daze. My arms immediately tightened around her. After hours of talking and kissing and dozing and finding all the ways her body fit against mine, the nervous tremble in her chest ripped through the warm comfort of her bed.

"What's wrong?" I asked.

"Nothing. Go back to sleep."

"You're a shitty liar."

She scoffed and buried her face in the crook of my neck. "The campaign just went out," she mumbled, barely audible.

Fuck. I'd completely missed that. That explained her panicked flashbacks from last night. Of course her nerves were getting the best of her the night before she became the official face of her foundation. She'd spent too many years hiding for it not to affect her.

I caught a glance at the time. Just after 10am. She was off-schedule, and it was my fucking fault. Not only had I kept her in bed, I hadn't made sure to get her breakfast in time.

"I'll go and get your computer," I said but before I could move, Cordelia's arms around my waist turned to stone.

"I've got my phone for emergencies, but I took the day off."

"Breakfast?"

"Can we just stay here for a bit?"

"Of course."

"There's something you should know." Cordelia untangled her legs from mine and sat up. She straddled one of my thighs, and I flashed back to her birthday, when she'd ridden my leg and had come all over my jeans. Except this was better, because she was still naked, and I would never get tired of this. Her body was all soft curve, smooth skin, and fine blonde hairs that made her glow in the sun like a goddamn angel. "It's about Silas."

My mood plummeted. "Don't tell me."

"What?"

"You're naked in bed with me, and you need to tell me about another man? I don't think that's something I want to hear."

"I don't- that's not- I mean, Silas and I aren't-"

I grabbed her by the neck and yanked her down to me, stifling her words with my mouth. She tried to jerk back - and moaned against my lips when she realized I had her in a death grip. Her tongue melted against mine, her hips tilting desperately for friction. Fucking hell. My girl liked to be roughed around a little. No wonder she hadn't kept it together on the treadmill. I'd been too nice.

Without giving her a warning, I tossed her over. Her back hit the mattress, air rushing from her lungs. Positioned above her, I jerked her knee up and dipped one finger back into her warm pussy. Silky and wet, and pulsing for me.

"Victor," she whimpered, "please, I just need you to lis- oh god."

"Mention another man again when you're in bed with me, and I'll ruin you, Cordelia. I don't share."

"Fuck you," she hissed but despite her harsh words, she latched onto my shoulders and thrust her hips against my hand, sliding deeper onto my finger.

"You're already doing a good job at that."

Whatever retort she came up with died on her lips the moment I rolled my thumb over her clit. I watched her flushed face in fascination, tracking all the little reactions I could draw from her with my hand. And just when it looked like she'd caught her breath again, I sank my teeth over her nipple. Cordelia unraveled beneath me.

She could talk a mile a minute and had more thoughts zapping through her brain simultaneously than I would ever comprehend, but when she came, she was all sound. No words, barely even my name. Just soft moans and ragged breaths. And when the trembling stopped, that little hitch in the back of her throat, as if her lungs were trying to gulp down more air than they could hold.

"We should have been doing this for the last six years," I said, smoothing hair from her sweaty forehead.

She giggled, but froze to watch me suck my finger into my

mouth. I wasn't sure what was better, her sweet taste, or her wide-eyed blush. "Victor?"

"Yes, zhizn' moya?"

"You need to let me get this thought out, okay? Be patient with me."

"What?"

"I asked Silas for help- stop making that face." She clutched my jaw, and I forced myself to breathe and wait. "In a few days, there's going to be a *leak*," she made air quotes around the word, "of footage from the video shoot. Of you and me. It's not much because I initially asked him not to film you. But with my campaign out there, and you back in the octagon, we have enough name recognition for the leak to draw attention."

"What the fuck?" I sat back on my heels, raking my hands through my hair. "This has to be the stupidest thing you've ever done."

"Excuse me?" She scooted up and grabbed a pillow to clutch over her bare body as she stared me down.

"People are going to go bat shit. Best case scenario, they'll treat you like a fucking news story. You're already risking your privacy with this campaign, and now you're publicly mixed up *with me* on top of that? Are you trying to put a target on your back?"

"No," she swallowed, "I'm trying to keep you alive. If you disappeared again, that would be on brand. You've done it before. Nobody would look at your uncle twice. I know this isn't much. But it's a story. The heiress who disappeared and the athlete who disappeared. Turns out, they've been cohabitating. It will generate enough attention for now. People will be watching what you do, where you go, who you spend time with."

"For fuck's sake. I don't know whether to be mad at you or kiss you," I sighed, "I'm supposed to keep you safe. My name next to yours is going to be more than gossip, Cordelia. It's a liability."

"I know."

"My family-"

"I know, Victor," she swallowed. "It came down to my comfort zone or you. I chose you."

"I never wanted to make you choose. I don't want to make your life harder."

"You didn't - and you're not. Your uncle is making *our* life harder. You and I are on the same team."

I nodded because there was nothing left to say. She was right. She was on my team. I'd just never played a team sport before. She'd made a move for the team.

Which probably meant Silas was getting his docu series. The Whitakers hadn't built their empire on doling out favors.

"Also both," she said.

"Both?"

"You can be mad at me and kiss me. At the same time. I feel like I would enjoy that." She smiled and sweetly batted her lashes at me. This fucking woman. "I'd also enjoy a shower and some French toast. Not at the same time though."

"You'll be the death of me."

"As your employer, I forbid you to die."

"Yes, boss." I slapped her ass when she climbed off the mattress. She shot me a quick glare over her shoulder before disappearing into the bathroom.

CHAPTER TWENTY-SIX

VICTOR

"ARE YOU TRYING TO GIVE ME A HEART ATTACK?" I almost dropped the plates when Cordelia plopped down at the dinner table in a tiny little crop top and a tinier pair of ruffly shorts. Bloomers. She was wearing bloomers - like she was about to star in some fucked-up 19th century porn.

"Why?" She asked, batting her lashes, all fake innocence.

Instead of telling her what those goddamn bloomers were doing to my heart rate, I leaned around the back of her chair and sank my mouth over her pulse point. Her breathing fluttered, but that didn't quite match the beating in my veins yet. So I scraped my teeth over that little dip right beneath her ear.

"What are you do-hing?" Her voice hitched when I bit down.

"I'm considering having a snack before dinner."

"Did you know that some sharks mate for life? They look all big and mean but they're actually really cute and romantic."

God, I loved the way she came up with these things. "Is that your way of saying I look big and mean?" I asked and leaned back to raise my brows at her.

"Huh? Oh, no, sorry." She swallowed, her eyes squarely on my lips. "Just because male sharks bite the female before having sex. So that's just... sorry... keep going."

For fuck's sake.

Between the bloomers and the sharks, my turn-ons were becoming very confusing. When I bit her, her mind jumped to sex. If she wanted to compare me to a shark, I'd take that.

"Any other interesting animal trivia you want to share?" I asked and lowered my mouth to her throat again. This time, I curled my hand around her neck from the other side. I had her captured between my fingers and my teeth. Under my lips, right beneath her golden, delicate skin, her vein pulsed faster and faster. Wonder what animal wisdom she'd come up with if I... I let my tongue sweep a long, languid stroke all along her vein. It was ridiculous how sweet her skin tasted. Cordelia shuddered and let out a goddamn adorable squeak.

"Oh god, shit, sorry!" Delilah yelped. One of her countless wedding magazines dropped to the floor and skidded halfway over to us.

Cordelia startled and jumped from her chair. "Flip, I'm sorry. Del, stay." She rubbed her neck, where my tongue had just left its mark. "I thought you were at Beck's. I didn't know you were home."

"I did," I mumbled, earning myself an elbow in the ribs. Cordelia didn't have the strength for that to even leave a bruise.

"This is happening now? You two?" Del asked as she picked up the magazine, eyes skipping back and forth between Cordelia and me.

Cordelia opened and closed her mouth twice before I replied for her, "Yes."

"That's great. That's amazing!" Del threw her arms around Cordelia in a quick hug before opening her arms to me, too, and raising her brows in a quiet offer. I sighed and lifted an arm, only for her to throw herself against my side and squeeze my ribcage. *She* had been working out. *That* might actually leave a bruise. It was an oddly validating hug. Not that we needed her approval, but still. "I'm so happy for you guys. Do we need to work out a schedule? We could do a shared calendar app. Or do we revert to the good old sock on the door?"

"What sock?" Cordelia asked.

"She doesn't want to walk in on us having sex," I replied.

"Oh no, Del, no. If I had known you were home," she shot me a withering glare, "this wouldn't have happened."

"Exactly. Sock on the doorknob is like a universal roommate symbol for *someone is having sex in this room*." Del shrugged. "I mean, it's your house, so you can have sex in all the rooms, and I guess I could share *my* schedule with you. It might help if you knew when I was home."

"Potatoes. Oven," I said by way of excusing myself from this conversation and stepped out of Del's embrace.

The second the girls considered me far enough away, the squealing started.

CHAPTER TWENTY-SEVEN

Cordelia

THE CAMPAIGN ROLLED OUT ONE VIDEO AFTER another, and I stayed off the internet. I waited for updates from Amani, and she thankfully kept them very brief and statistical. I only knew when Silas dropped the fake leak because the number of views on our first campaign video skyrocketed, when Amani had expected them to drop.

After that, I canceled the rest of my meetings and switched off my phone. I didn't want to answer anyone's questions about Victor.

All the time I should have spent working that day, I channeled into the plans for my new fish pond.

And when work hours were over, Irina and I spent way too much time trying to order food from five different places without me accidentally seeing my emails. Why on earth did every place require you to confirm a one-off email code nowadays?

An hour later, the living room was decked out in waffles, milkshakes, pizza and various other foods. Between all the styrofoam and paper boxes, the floor was covered with bridal magazines.

"Do you need something blue? Because this is gorgeous," Defne mused, turning over her phone to show off a beautifully arranged cornflower and peony bouquet.

"I have something blue," Del replied, hand reaching for her collar bone and the gold necklace with the small blue pearl on it. I had given that to her the first night we met. "But I like the flowers." She stretched her hand out, and Defne placed the phone in her palm.

Leaning over to get a better look, my eyes caught on the notification that popped up at the top of the screen.

FROMTHEDARKROOM · 07:41PM

My whole bed smells like you.

"OH!" I JUMPED AND QUICKLY LOOKED BACK AT THE magazine in my hands. Clearly, that message wasn't intended for anyone's eyes.

"What's wrong?" Defne asked.

Del chuckled and returned the phone. "Who is FromThe-DarkRoom?"

Defne started grinning. "The guy single-handedly paid for my tuition this semester."

Tabitha let out a loud whistle, and Del said: "Good for you."

I clearly wasn't in on something, but before I could ask, Defne caught my puzzled gaze. "It's a little weird, but I sell worn clothes online. Mostly socks and tights." She pinched at the sheer black tights on her legs and let them snap back into place. "I wear this stuff anyway, and this way, I avoid student loans."

"Do you need money?" I asked.

"No, oh god, Cordy, no." Defne shook her head vehemently. "That wasn't me trying to get your credit card info. I mean, I rely on Delilah becoming my sugar mommy once she has a ring on her finger, but I'm okay. I'm making this work."

Del grinned and shook her head. "Hey, if I'm marrying rich, you might as well profit off it."

"Besides," Defne bit her lip and pulled her shoulders up, "I like feeling wanted, you know? There's some creeps, but they're no worse than the guys on Tinder. This way, I get all the attention and money on top of it."

"Just none of the sex," Tabitha mumbled, then shot me a slightly panicked look, "which is fine, if you don't want sex."

"I do want it..." I hugged my knees to my chest. "I think we're getting there."

"Would you mind if I excuse myself?" Irina asked from where she was standing near the doorway. She had refused to sit with us. But she'd been sticking around religiously on the days Victor was training at his uncle's.

"Sorry, TMI?" I scrunched up my nose. I had neither siblings nor cousins, but I doubted I'd want to hear about their sex lives.

"A little."

"Yeah, I'm okay if you want to leave for a bit."

"Thank you," she said and turned on her heels.

"I mean, I kind of thought you were already doing it, considering that video of him pulling you into the bathroom and then your mic cutting out," Tabitha said.

My spine stiffened. Of course I wouldn't be able to escape the fake leak. Up until now, I had at least been blissfully unaware of which video Silas had picked. "You watched it?"

"We all did," she retorted.

"Did you not check the group chat?" Del asked.

"No, I haven't checked my phone today, but for what it's worth, nothing happened in that bathroom." I looked around the room. God, it was strange to have actual girlfriends to share these things with. I could have used more of that over the years, but this was good. Now was good. "What was it like for you guys? Losing your virginity?"

"Hmm, not great to be honest," Del mused. One would think Tabitha would be the first to speak up about her sex life, but Del had become a lot more relaxed over the last few months. Being with Beck was good for her. She seemed less tense. "I think that's just what happens when you lose it at 15. We were in his bedroom while his parents were out with friends for the night. Took less than 5 minutes, and I spent the entire time wondering if I was doing everything the way I was supposed to be doing it, wondering if his parents would come home early, wondering about the chances of the condom breaking."

"Did it hurt?" I asked.

"A little."

"It doesn't have to," Defne added, "mine was completely pain-free, and I actually had a good night. My ex took his time, so I had like two orgasms before we even got to the actual sex. At that point, I was ready to go."

"Okay, so foreplay," I concluded.

"Lots of lube. Just use lots and lots of lube," Tabitha chimed in. When all of us kept our eyes on her, she groaned. "I technically did it myself, okay? I didn't see the big deal. I wanted to hook up with random guys and I wasn't going to wait around for some dude to stick his meat pipe into me once, just to get the first time out of the way. And what? Have him brag to all his friends that he banged a virgin?! My big sister was really cool about the idea and bought me a dildo when I asked her to. Did it hurt? Sure, but it was also a sparkling, pink silicone dick, so I can't tell you if it'll be different with an actual flesh one."

I blinked as I let her story sink in. "I think you're the coolest person I know."

"Thanks." She held up her tablet with a small boutique's website opened. It showed a lacy empire waist dress fit for a regency romance. "Del, I think I found your dress."

"Gimme," Del's eyes lit up and her hands shot forward.

"ARE YOU SURE YOU WANT TO STAY UP?" DEL ASKED AS she climbed off the sofa, a pile of magazines in her hands.

The others had cleared out earlier, leaving us with too much food and too many haphazard bridal magazines. Del had spent the last hour going through them again with color-coded sticky notes, while I worked on the plans for the pond. We'd have to get that installed in time for the lawn to recover and the new plants to get settled, or the aisle would be a mudslide.

"Yeah, just a little longer." I glanced towards the door. Victor usually didn't come home this late without giving me a heads-up.

"I'll be reading for a while if you need anything."

"You're not going to call Beck?"

"Sure," she grinned sheepishly, "but I like reading while he's on the phone. Just hanging out together."

"I get it," I said, trying to suppress the aching in my voice. Based on Del's sympathetic smile, I didn't do a good job at it.

"I'm sorry. Let me know if there's anything you need, okay?"

Once she was gone, Irina walked in and we cleared away the leftovers. We both stood in front of the loaded dishwasher with puzzled expressions though. Turned out, Irina had grown up with just as much household staff as I had. We watched a YouTube tutorial and immediately failed because we couldn't find the dishwasher tabs. In the end, we left it. Victor or our housekeeper would know how to handle this. Heck, maybe Del would know.

By Irina's third yawn, I sent her to bed.

When I had finalized the list of plants for the pond to make it a welcoming habitat for fishes and frogs and ducks, I finally picked up my phone again. I ignored all the notifications and brought up the only chat that had been quiet all day. Which wasn't like him at all.

CORDELIA · 3:32AM

Are you alright?

At some point, I must have fallen asleep on the sofa, because I woke up to the sound of the coffee machine, my phone stuck in the crook of my neck.

No reply from Victor in five hours.

I rubbed the sleep from my eyes and ran my hands through my tangled hair, then checked the kitchen. Irina greeted me with a tight smile and a nod, clutching her cup of coffee in both hands.

"I haven't heard from him," she said before I could ask.

"Thanks."

"I just texted Luka to be safe. I'll let you know the second he replies."

"Thank you. I appreciate it." I grabbed one of the breakfast smoothies from the fridge, my mind reeling. Despite his crazy schedule over the last few months, Victor had never been gone overnight without checking in with me. He could just be at his own place, next door, sleeping safe and sound - but I knew in my gut that he wasn't. He would have come see me before going to bed. He would already be here for breakfast. "Do I have reason to be concerned?"

Irina weighed her head from side to side, actually considering my question instead of placating me with empty phrases. That alone told me why Victor had positioned her with me. "Not about his well-being," she said eventually, "my father has a plan for him, so he's as safe as can be."

"Then what should I be concerned about?"

Irina sighed and pulled out her phone. When she flipped it around and held it out to me, it was showing tabs upon tabs of news articles, all accompanied by screenshots of my campaign videos, of Victor's fights, and of moments that Silas captured. Victor's hands on my hips as he moved past me. My hands on his arm in the kitchen while he cooked. Our gazes locked in the hallway, and my smile so big, you didn't need a suggestive headline to catch the meaning behind that look.

Warm heat prickled up my neck as I realized how obvious we must have seemed to everyone with a pair of eyes in their head.

"You turned from pawn to player, Cordelia. My father just countered your gambit."

"So you think he's keeping Victor away from me because of this?" I pointed at the phone.

"Yes," Irina's lips twitched into a small smile, "as fucked-up as it is, you probably just became one of the most powerful women on the east coast."

"Excuse me?"

"You made a public move against Piotr Yelchin, and he's accepted your challenge. If he hadn't, Victor would be here," she shrugged and took her phone back, "which means you just automatically made a lot of friends. *Enemy of my enemy* and all that."

"I never wanted anything like that. I just want to look out for Victor."

"Just get me a head-start and a ticket to the Maldives before you start working with the Italians. I'm not getting involved in a turf war."

"The Maldives?"

"No extradition."

I shook off all the questions that began bubbling up with *that* answer. I couldn't let myself get distracted by Irina's personal situation. "What about you? Why are you still here? I mean, you're hired to protect me but if your father thinks I'm challenging him..."

She smirked and reached into her blazer and withdrew a small gun. My spine stiffened at the sight, my pulse rushing in my ears, loud enough to pull me under. I focused on breathing, on staying present, on watching as she slid the firearm across the counter to me.

"I'm laying my weapons at your feet. Symbolically, I mean. I have so many more on me and it would take way too long. Anyway. I won't hurt you, Cordelia. I gave Victor my word that I would look after you, and I keep my word. Just don't ask me to hurt my family."

"I'd never do that. I don't want to hurt anyone. Quite the opposite, actually." I carefully pushed the gun back at her with my smoothie bottle. I didn't even want to touch that thing.

"Okay then," Irina let the firearm disappear under her jacket, "what's your next move?"

CHAPTER TWENTY-EIGHT

VICTOR

THE SECOND DAY WAS THE WORST. WHEN I KNEW I'D walked into a trap, but had no idea how Cordelia was holding up at home. Petya had taken my phone and kept me in line with a single video call to one of his men, just to show me he was sitting in a car with a perfect view of Cordelia's house and a Glock in his lap.

Even if Irina probably could have handled it, I wasn't going to gamble with Cordelia's life just because Petya wanted me to stay at his place. They even took my key fob. Any door I wanted to walk through, I'd need a fucking babysitter for.

I should have known my uncle would pull something like this. He wasn't going to let a few headlines take away his power over me.

The third day, when my concentration in the ring was beyond

abysmal, Luka finally replied to Irina's texts. If his father found out, he'd be lucky to walk off with a few broken fingers. He still sent her a quick update, just to let her - and Cordelia - know that I wasn't hurt.

By day five, an unsettling routine had crept in. I slept in my old bed. I sat in my old chair at the dinner table. I nodded at all the same stories of the glory days that Petya had been recanting for years.

I had to get the fuck out of this place.

Thankfully, the opportunity announced itself on day six.

"You're fighting this weekend," Luka said when he picked me up from the gym to walk me to dinner.

"That's short notice," I replied while trying to remember the fight schedule. The fight this weekend was set for Toronto. That was just across the border. If I got even a moment alone after the fight, I could slip out.

"It's the last one before Paris, so you'll have to win."

"Sure," I replied, barely listening. Once a fight was over, Petya usually didn't care about me for a few days until the cuts and bruises healed enough for me to look pretty in pictures and keep training for the next fight.

When the matches were just fights, no schemes, he just wanted a show pony. Not a bleeding, black and blue, fucked-up piece of meat. Even if I slipped his grasp, he wouldn't give a fuck, not when I was too injured to keep fighting, and too banged-up for triumphantly posed pictures.

He wanted a win? Fine. I'd just have to make it a bloody one.

EVERYONE HUDDLED AROUND ME WHEN I GOT OUT OF the octagon. Yury, Luka, some ringside doctor I didn't recognize, my uncle, his men, some kid taking my gloves. People prodded and rubbed and dabbed and talked. It all blurred together with the adrenaline of the fight still rushing through my veins.

The only crystal clear thought I had was that I had to get out of here.

My eyes roamed the arena, the halls, scanning for exit signs and open doors.

Someone tried to usher me to the first aid room, but I kept barreling for the locker rooms. *Shower.* The second I got in the shower, they'd leave me alone.

I wiped at something on my face and my hand came back covered in blood and vaseline. Before I could wipe again, someone smeared a new layer of vaseline on my cheek bone to stop the bleeding.

"Shower," I mumbled when my locker room was finally in sight, then repeated myself louder, "shower."

"I think hospital would be more appropriate," Luka hissed, low enough not to draw attention.

I shouldered through the door to my dressing room - and stopped dead in my tracks. A slew of people collided with my back, and the fact that I didn't even stumble should have told them all how superficial these wounds were. Not that any of that mattered. Not the blood, not the people, not their jumble of comments or their hands on me.

My eyes met Cordelia's stormy blue gaze across the room when she turned from the big screen in the corner to me.

Cordelia.

Her hands were in her hair, wrapping it around her fingers, twisting it and combing it, while she stayed frozen in place, blinking rapidly. She was trying not to look at the others. People. There were too many people.

"Get out," I barked without taking my eyes off her.

"Vitya, where are your manners?" My uncle shifted next to me, his broad frame moving into my peripheral vision.

"*Please*," I grit through clenched teeth, "get the fuck out."

"You should introduce us to your famous girlfriend," he said and took a step forward.

My hand shot out, making his chest collide with my arm. "Take another step and it will be your last."

That finally got everyone to shut the fuck up, and Cordelia's eyes steadied on me. My words hung in the still air. I didn't fucking care how stupid it was to threaten my uncle in front of everyone. I'd break his goddamn neck with my own hands if he took one more step towards my girl.

"Very well," he finally said and clicked his tongue, "another time."

That was enough for all of them to get their asses moving. I only took my eyes off Cordelia long enough to shut the door and twist the lock.

"What are you doing here?" I asked, confusion and worry mixing with the insane relief of seeing her face.

"I was... I just..." She pressed each word out through labored breaths. Her cheeks were as flushed as if she'd been the one to throw endless punches. "I just came... I mean I wanted..." Every time she started a sentence, her eyes jumped back and forth between me and the door. Fuck.

"Look at me." I crossed the room in a few strides and cradled her soft face in both hands. Drawing my thumbs over her temples in soothing circles, I lowered my voice, forcing myself to sound calmer than I felt. "It's just you and me in here, zhizn' moya. Just us. One room, two people. The outside doesn't matter. We're inside. We're safe."

Her eyes found mine, lashes fluttering fast.

"Just us," I repeated, "alright?"

She took a stuttering breath before swallowing. "Alright."

"What are you doing here?"

"Support," she whispered and glanced down. I hadn't even looked at her clothes before. She was in a skintight green dress that showed off every curve of her body, and scooped low enough that her erratic breathing pushed half her tits over its collar. It had a big black bow fixed right to the center of her chest, as if her cleavage alone wasn't drawing enough attention. It took a second for the colors to click. Green and black, same as my shorts. She was flaunting that body while wearing my colors. Mine.

"Fuck," I breathed.

"Surprise."

"Fuck." I swallowed, the rush of the fight morphing into a thicker, hotter instinct. "Yes."

"So that was your uncle?"

"Don't mention him right now." I dragged my hands down her sides to her waist, her body so soft and warm.

"Victor," her voice broke, and my head snapped up, my hands stilling. Cordelia's lips were trembling and she shook her head, squeezing her eyes shut. "I shouldn't be here."

"I know. I know." I brushed her tangled hair back and kissed her cheek. Her whole body shuddered, and I wrapped my arms around her. She melted against my chest, muscles limp and shaking, only her fingernails digging into my sides, sinking in like claws. "I got you. You're alright."

"That's your blood," she whimpered.

"Hmm?"

She barely nodded towards the mirror on the wall, but I followed her attention to the streak of blood I had left on her cheek with my kiss.

"Sorry. I have to get cleaned up and then I'm getting you out of here."

Her nails dug deeper, another shaky breath rocking her body.

"Okay, don't worry," I whispered, a small grin tugging at my lips as I realized what she meant. Instead of letting her go, I held her tight and walked her into the shower room. Her grip on me didn't loosen until I reached for the shower handle.

"Not the dress." She fumbled for the zipper at the back of her neck. "It's dry-clean only."

"Here." I turned her around by the hips and pulled down the zipper, only to reveal that she wasn't even wearing a goddamn bra. For fuck's sake. I trained my eyes on the crumbling grout between the tiles while she stepped out of her clothes and carried them off. She was inches away from tipping over the edge of a mental breakdown. Even with every cell in my body still in fight mode, still seeking physical release for all this tension, I couldn't dwell on her state of undress.

I tossed my own clothes aside, not giving one shit where they landed or whether they'd get wet.

"You look horrible, by the way," Cordelia whispered when she came back and wrapped her arms around my middle. I could feel every inch of her skin pressed up against me, but I didn't look at her again until the hot water was running, blurring my vision further and easing some of that pent-up tension.

"You should see the other guy," I chuckled and ran my hands up and down her back.

She hummed and I wasn't sure if it was the water or my touch, but her tension seemed to loosen as well. "I did. I watched the whole fight. Why did you go easy on him?"

No need denying anything. Cordelia had probably spent the last few days mainlining every single one of my fights, read the UFC rulebook backwards and forwards, and had spent countless hours on social media to figure out every angle of who and what was involved in fight nights. Cordelia didn't half-ass things. "I knew I had a better chance of coming home to you if I was beaten to a pulp."

Her head snapped up, brows drawn deep. "You're an idiot. You could have gotten yourself killed."

"Worth it."

"No." She shoved against my chest, putting a few inches of distance between us. All the insecurity in her eyes was replaced by hot fury. "You do not risk your life like that. Especially not for a temporary solution. Not when your uncle could just let you go now, then keep you locked up again once you've recovered from this fight."

"Cordelia-"

"You have power now. We have power. You need to stop thinking like your body is the only leverage you have," she hissed and stepped out of the shower stream, water pearling down her smooth skin, "I put on that ridiculous dress and I got in front of the cameras outside. I told these people that I'd have to buy you *makeup* because I didn't want your bruises to distract everyone at the foundation's first open door event next week. I gave them a silly headline, and I gave them a time and place to expect you at."

"What open door event?"

"The one I just pulled out of my *fucking ass*. The one I hope I'll be able to throw together in a few days."

"Come here." I reached for her wrist and pulled her back under the shower with me. "Thank you. You came for me."

"Of course I did," she huffed.

"I don't know how to do this. I never had anything other than my body and my family name."

"You have me now." Cordelia wrapped her arms around my neck and pulled herself up on her tiptoes, until her nose brushed against mine and her sweet breath coated my tongue. "I'll always come for you."

I closed the gap between our lips and devoured her like I was returning from war. Her kiss turned frantic within seconds. Cordelia grasped at my hair and scratched at my skin, bit my lips and pushed herself into me. She was searching her escape in my body.

There was a good chance, I was making the wrong decision here, but I just wanted to help her forget where she was. So I grabbed her by the hips and lifted her up. Those long legs I'd been fantasizing about closed behind my back, locking me in tight. Her thighs around my hips diminished my doubts, and I just needed more.

It wasn't until she started rolling her hips over my throbbing hard cock, that I pulled out of the kiss again.

"We should stop," I grunted, desperately trying to breathe through the steam and her intoxicating scent.

"Why?" She kissed me again and I retuned the kiss for just a moment or two, unwilling to give up the taste of her lips.

"Because your first time won't be in a fucking locker room."

"I know," she huffed, "my first time will be on the fluffy rug on my bedroom floor."

"Of course you have a plan for that," I chuckled. Whether she realized it or not, we were only inches from blowing that plan. All her writhing didn't help either. My cock would end up inside of her just because she'd tilt her hips too far.

"I don't want to stop. Please. Don't make me go out there yet."

"Fuck, Cordelia." My hands still wrapped around her middle, I pulled back just enough for her legs to instinctively fall off my hips before I sharply turned her around. Her ass pressed into me, my cock perfectly nestled between her cheeks. "Put your hands on the wall."

She wordlessly followed command, pressing both palms against the tiles.

The fact that she wasn't even playfully protesting was enough to set my teeth on edge. Cordelia was constantly running on multiple streams of thought, and at least one of them was currently panicking.

"Count down from eighty-thousand," I told her as I reached up and grabbed the detachable showerhead.

"Eighty-thousand," she whispered, her stomach trembling as my free hand slid down over her belly button, and I used the showerhead to run hot water over her peaking nipples. "Seventy-nine thousand nine hundred ninety-nine. Seventy-nine thousand nine hundred ninety-eight. Seventy-nine-hng."

Her breath hitched when I carefully spread her open, exposing her clit without touching it.

"Keep counting," I said, voice rough, and bit her neck. Maybe one of her many mental tabs would jump to shark sex.

"Seventy-nine thousand nine hundred ninety-seven."

I brought the showerhead down to where the water hit the junction of her thighs. Cordelia moaned and bucked back. Her ass pressed flush against me. It was almost too much and I could have exploded right then and there, her soft body tight against mine and the sounds she made for me.

She tried to writhe her hips as I brought the showerhead closer, but my grip around her locked. As much as it was torture, I didn't want a single pocket of air between our bodies.

"Please," she whimpered, craning her neck.

"Keep counting," I growled, knuckles whitening around the handle.

"Seventy-nine thou-oh." Her nails scratched over the tiles and her thighs twitched around my hand. "Seventy-nine thousand nine hun-nnh."

"That's it, baby, you almost got it. What comes after ninety-seven?"

"Seventy-nine thousand nine hundred ninety-six," she breathed, almost voiceless.

"That's my girl." I slipped a finger over her swollen clit, and Cordelia let out another one of her chesty moans that burrowed straight through me. I brought the showerhead right up against her, and with one more flick of my finger, she fell apart. Her knees buckled. Her hands dropped off the wall, only to claw at my arms to keep herself upright. Her neck tilted back, and I caught her mouth with mine, tasting each of her moans as she came undone.

With her orgasm, that white hot cord around the base of my spine wound tighter and tighter. I bit her lip and pushed hard against her backside until my dick was cradled by her ass cheeks. Her trembling muscles were enough to give me that last bit of friction. The one that made the cord snap. The blinding electric shock surged through me until nothing mattered but being as close to Cordelia as humanly possible. I rocked my hips into her and spilled myself over the curve of her ass.

When Cordelia stopped shaking, I dropped the showerhead, and held her against me. She dropped her head back onto my shoulder and blinked up at me, eyes glazed and cheeks flushed. It was the most beautiful thing I'd ever seen. Cordelia Montgomery, thoroughly satisfied and covered in my cum.

"Let's go home," she whispered.

"Sounds good," I agreed.

Fifteen minutes later, Cordelia had fixed herself back up - and I looked worse than I had right after the fight. The bruises were starting to show color and half my face was swelling up to twice its size.

I expected to walk out of the locker room and find my uncle and Luka waiting, instead Silas fucking Whitaker shoved his camera in my face. Cordelia shot me a small smile and took my hand in hers, her slender fingers weaving through mine. "Just until we're in the car. Just keep walking."

I blindly followed her. She took a detour on our way out. My first guess was that she had to take me to visitors' parking, but instead, she led me through the press room. She smiled but she didn't pause for the flashing cameras or the yelling reporters, and I instinctively moved closer, physically putting myself between her and the crowd. Once out the door on the other side, I could see the panic creeping into the tight set of her shoulders and her fast breathing. I wrapped my arm around her middle, and she kept walking.

Down to private parking, and to a glaringly red Porsche.

"With three minutes to spare." Del slapped her book shut and slid off the trunk of her car.

"Didn't pause for interviews," Cordelia mumbled.

"Okay, come on, let's get you home." Del waved us forward

and opened the passenger door. Whitaker took that as his sign and lowered the camera with a sigh.

I walked Cordelia to the passenger side - which had been turned into half a living room. She sat nestled in a fleece blanket with a fluffy pink pillow in her lap. A pair of thick slippers lay to her feet, next to headphones, her iPad and a Dunkin Donuts box. And I counted no less than three bottles and thermos cups.

"What exactly is this?" I asked.

"Comfort," Del quipped, "I figured leaving the house was hard enough. Might as well make the car as comforting as can be."

If I were to believe in soulmates, it wouldn't be because of me. It would be because of them. Del and Cordelia had this strange bond that I could never understand. It was like they took one look at each other and recognized a missing piece of themselves. Cordelia and I were a match forged by circumstance, but they had always been meant to find each other.

"What about all of this," I clarified by circling my finger to include her and Whitaker in my question, "and where's Irina?"

"I'm just following the story." Whitaker shrugged and got in the back seat. He was clearly lying but he wasn't who I was concerned about.

"Get in. I'll explain." Cordelia gave my hand one more squeeze before reaching past me for the door handle.

It wasn't until we were several miles from the arena and both Cordelia and Del stopped constantly checking the rearview mirrors before Cordelia turned around in her seat to face me. "Hi." She offered me an exhausted smile.

"Hi." I scooted forward and ran a finger down the delicate curve of her jaw.

"I couldn't come alone. I can't even drive," she said and nodded towards Delilah behind the steering wheel, "and Del is the best driver I know."

She wasn't wrong. Del was expertly weaving her car through the streets now, just slightly above the speed limit, but that pocket-sized blonde could have probably gone up against Luka in his glory days.

"I didn't know how hard it would be to get you past your uncle," Cordelia continued, "but I figured a camera would be a pretty good shield. Silas Whitaker behind the camera? Practically untouchable. And then leaving Irina at home was mostly about space. Two cars would be a bigger target than one if your uncle was going to cause trouble, and I wasn't sure how hurt you'd be and how much of the backseat you'd need. She put this in my purse though." Cordelia reached for her bag and handed it to me.

The weight already gave it away. I still unzipped it to find a 9mm covered in pink rhinestones. "She gave you a pink gun."

"Yeah," she breathed, the one word rattling through her chest.

"For fuck's sake," I groaned and took the gun before returning her purse. Of course my stupid baby cousin would give a gun to someone who dealt with PTSD from gun violence. "I'm sorry."

"She meant well." Cordelia pulled her shoulders up.

"Not to interrupt, but I need to know if we're gunning for the border or if you need a hospital first," Del asked, shooting me a quick appraising glance in the rearview mirror.

"Border," I said in unison with Cordelia and Whitaker.

I raised my brows at him and he shrugged. "I know a life-threatening wound when I see one."

CHAPTER TWENTY-NINE

VICTOR

I spent three days drifting in and out of sleep in Cordelia's bed. She woke up thrashing and screaming every night, and I knew it was my fault that she was on edge, but between the painkillers and the exhaustion, I wasn't lucid enough to do anything about it. I could only pull her tight against me, keeping her warm and safe until morning light broke.

When my skull no longer felt too small for all the swelling on my face, I finally ventured out of the bedroom. I only left the comfort of Cordelia's scent to follow her melodic voice down to her office.

"I'm sorry for missing that, but you wanted me to get my face out there. It's out there. I thought you'd be happy." That melodic voice currently didn't sound very happy. Cordelia didn't even lift her eyes from the screen when I leaned in her doorway. Her hair was up in a braided bun, her bangs held back by a pair of pink headphones.

"Showing up to her boyfriend's matches worked for Taylor Swift and that football guy," she argued and threw her hands up.

This phone call was about me. Or at least about Cordelia showing up for me. She was getting shit for coming to see me? I pushed myself off the doorframe. Not that I could punch whoever was on the other end of that call through the screen - but I could get their name and location.

"No, I don't want to be- Amani, I was never going to be some political beacon of hope." Cordelia's attention flickered, and she straightened as her eyes caught mine over the edge of her screen. "I gotta go." One mouse click and she pulled her headphones down. "Hi. You're up."

"What's wrong?" I asked, ready to dig through her files for Amani's address. Work was work. I would never fuck with Cordelia's foundation. But I wouldn't let some gray-haired chick in California make Cordelia feel bad about this relationship.

"Nothing." She swung herself out of her chair and walked around her desk, stopping me before I could come dangerously close to Amani's information. "How are you feeling? Are you hungry?" She smoothed careful fingertips over my temple, examining my busted face.

"Shitty liar," I said because the shadows under her eyes were as dark as my bruises.

She scrunched up her nose at me before snaking her arms around my middle and dropping her forehead against my chest. "Fine. Let me rephrase that. Nothing I can't handle."

"You're the one who said we work as a team," I told her, "so what's wrong?"

"I missed some meetings this week because my mind was in a million places."

"Because of me," I assumed.

She nodded. "And Amani is worried about our branding.

Because the video campaign is very soft and heartfelt, and I opened up about my agoraphobia and not really leaving my house in years. Except now there's the pictures from the fight. I didn't just leave my house, it's also quite obvious that-" She groaned in frustration and pressed her face deeper into my chest.

"What?"

"I walk in with my hair in beach waves. I walk out with a wet bun." She leaned back, finding my eyes before explaining further. "They're basically slut-shaming me. I personally don't care, to be honest, because people are just super weird about sex. But I don't understand why it reflects badly on me that I took a shower with my boyfriend after he won a *professional* fight. But Amani says it will have a negative effect on the foundation and diminish the very serious work we do for women who need to get away from their *domestically* violent partners. Like, that violence exists in two completely different contexts. So what if you punch a guy in the octagon and then I sleep with you?" She groaned. "At least we don't have to go to that open door event, because our attendance would be too distracting."

"I'm sorry."

"I just want to help. What does it even matter who I sleep with?" She ran her hands through her hair, a red flush spreading up her neck. "Not that I even slept with you. We had fun but we didn't have sex. I'd be less annoyed if I had actually earned the negative consequences through my actions. I'm just getting consequences based on presumptions. Do people really always just bang one out? No nuance? Nothing between kissing and jumping each other's bones? It's stupid. It's just- anyway- food- you haven't eaten in two days." She tried to push past me, angled for the kitchen.

"Hold on, come here." I sighed and cradled her face in my hands. "I'm sorry."

"It's not your fault."

Maybe she really believed that, but she was fighting my battle for me, and it was turning her life upside-down. She could be so much more than tabloid fodder. "What did you mean, you were never going to be a political beacon of hope?"

"She thinks I could have a political career if I wanted to."

"Do you want to?"

"No. What's the point? Human trafficking is illegal. Kidnapping is illegal. Domestic abuse is illegal. These women suffer anyway." Cordelia shook her head. "I'll stick with direct action, and I think I can do more than what I'm already doing. You actually inspired me."

"I did?"

"The Theresa Montgomery foundation has been focused on helping women, right? There's many men who go through the same things. That trauma alters your brain chemistry. It doesn't matter whether you've had one traumatic event or went through years of abuse." She ran her hands over my chest and traced the inked lines on my neck. "The support needs most men experience are systemically different, so it won't be easily integrated into the foundation, but it would be a new branch."

"I love you." The words slipped from my mouth lighter than air. Loving Cordelia was easier than breathing.

"Good," she laughed, some of the tension easing from her brows, "or our wedding would have been very awkward."

"Wedding?"

"I told you I'd be wearing a pink dress. You didn't think you could get out of it just because you got kidnapped by your uncle, did you?"

"I love you," I said again and kissed her.

"Good," she giggled into the kiss, so I moved from her lips to her neck, "or raising our future child together could have been very awkward."

I pushed her back against her desk. "I love you," I whispered against her skin as I undid the buttons of her blouse and kissed my way down to her collar bone.

"Good," she said, her breath hitching, "or asking you to move in could have been really awkward."

I loved hearing all her plans for me, for us. I wondered just how many I could draw from her before she'd lose the ability to form full sentences. Pushing her blouse off her shoulders, I moved my mouth down to her quivering chest. "I love you," I whispered into the dip between her breasts.

"Good," she whispered, "or our honeymoon in the Caribbean would have been very awkward."

"Honeymoon?" I chuckled and lifted her onto the desk. Some folders and pens clattered to the floor, but neither of us cared. Instead, Cordelia's beautiful long legs immediately fell open for me, her plaid skirt riding up to expose the soft flesh of her thighs.

"My family has a small private island in the Bahamas. I've not been there in fifteen years, but we'll get to use Beck's jet in exchange for him and Del getting married here."

"Of course you already have that figured out," I chuckled and knelt down between her knees, so I could kiss my way up her thighs, "I love you."

"Good," she breathed shakily when my mouth connected with the top of her thigh, "or it would have been very awkward for me to tell you that I love you, too."

VICTOR WAS MAKING THE MEMORIES MORE BEARABLE. They still rattled me. I wasn't sure if there was ever going to come a point when I wouldn't start screaming at the image of my mother's body hitting the ground, when I wouldn't start crying when I heard the four words that sealed my fate *"Grab the girl, Nick."*, or when I wouldn't feel like suffocating under a leather glove.

But when I woke up, Victor was there. He pulled me against him. He kissed my forehead and ran his hands through my hair and down my back until my breathing slowed down.

Every day became a little easier.

Victor started moving around the house. He cooked and meal prepped. He inventoried the entire kitchen and put labels on the cupboards, so I'd find every little thing in his absence. Irina only left once she was sure Victor was well enough to care for both of us. We kissed, and we played chess, and we kissed, and we watched the new Earth Day documentary on Netflix, and we kissed.

"I leave you alone for a week," Victor chuckled when he brought me a cup of tea in the winter garden.

"Too soon." I shot him a withering glare. "Besides, Irina was here. She helped. She's nice. But I couldn't focus on anything when you were gone. So I just..."

"Turned into Monet?" He gently lifted a flowery canvas to reveal the one behind it. That one was a speckled version of the winter garden: blue skies, white beams, plants upon plants, and my small gurgling fountain. Victor looked up from the canvas and narrowed his eyes at that corner of the room, figuring out the exact angle I must have painted from.

I should have probably looked into a better place to store these. The sun coming in from all angles wasn't going to be kind on them, especially not now that it was getting warmer by the day.

"Painting helped. I know my mom was always trying to make it exciting and fun," I ran my hand along my speckled easel, "but it helped me stay calm. It was comforting."

"I understand." Victor came up behind me and wrapped his arms around my middle, drew me against his chest. The way his body cocooned around me was a whole different kind of comfort.

"That's how I used to feel about fighting. Like the rest of the world didn't exist. I just focused on the constraints of the octagon."

"And now?"

"Now I feel it when I'm with you." He kissed the back of my head. "Zhizn' moya."

My life.

"Do you think we're too codependent?"

"No."

"You didn't even think about that."

"I don't need to." He kissed my neck. "I won't doubt our relationship just because it's not ordinary. You said that our brains are altered by trauma, right?"

"My therapist technically said that, but yes."

"We've both been turned into people who function differently. We depend on each other because we have to, and because we can. I think that makes us lucky."

"Lucky," I smiled and turned in his embrace, "I do feel incredibly lucky to have you, Victor. Don't ever forget that."

The doorbell cut off any response he had for me, his body immediately turning rigid. "Are you expecting anyone?"

I shook my head. Anyone who needed a key had one, and I had yet to catch up with Silas.

Victor pulled me into the kitchen and firmly closed the door to the winter garden before telling me to stay put. I waited and listened to the short exchange at the front door. I didn't recognize the other voice. Then the door fell shut and the house quiet before I could question it.

"Bike messenger," Victor said as he came back, carrying a small cardboard box. "I need you to sit down with your back to me."

"Why?"

"Because Petya sent this and I don't know what's in it." His eyes narrowed and his head swiveled. "Where's Irina?"

"I don't know." Dread seeped through my stomach. It only

took one or two old mafia movies to guess the horrible contents of that box. "She's been staying at your place. She might just be next door." I stepped up behind Victor, snaked my arms around his waist and buried my face between his shoulder blades. "I won't look. Open it."

I listened to the rustle of the cardboard and to Victor's still breathing, and felt his tense muscles ease in my embrace.

"It's fine," he said, "it's an invite."

Without letting go, I ducked under his arm to stand by his side as he lifted the silver-foiled card from the box. There was no envelope. Why would you send an invitation card in a- I yelped and squeezed my eyes shut before I could even fully register the bloody sight beneath the card.

"Fuck," Victor hissed and shuffled me behind his back again.

Severed finger.

That had been a finger. Cut off. Blood dried and crusted now, but there had been enough to make it clear that the finger had been freshly separated from the hand when it got packaged.

Victor closed the box again and turned around, cradling my face in his hands. "I'm sorry, Cordelia. I'm so sorry. Are you alright? Look at me."

I blinked up at him, the concern in his bright green eyes enough to elicit a trembling smile. "I'm alright." I waited for the nausea to hit, but it didn't come. I supposed that was the advantage of seeing blood splatter every time I closed my eyes. "Do you think that's Irina's?"

"I don't know. I'll have to take another look." He smoothed the hair away from my face, eyes still searching my features for a hint of wrongness. "Tell me what's going on in your head."

"I keep waiting to feel horrified. Or sick. It's a horrible, sickening thing." I crossed my arms in front of my chest. "Something must be *very* wrong with me not to feel worse than startled."

"Zhizn' moya." He chuckled and gently kissed me. "My uncle

253

cuts off someone's finger and sends it to us by bike messenger, and you think something is wrong with *you*?"

"I feel like I should be throwing up. That would be the normal reaction."

"I have to take another look."

I nodded and glanced at the box. "I want to see."

"Are you sure?"

"I owe that much to whoever this finger belongs to. It was sent to us as a message. They... they deserve to have that sacrifice honored."

Victor's hand wrapped around the back of my neck and he pulled me to him just to lay a kiss to my forehead. "I love you."

"I love you," I replied and kissed his biceps. "Now show me the finger."

He flipped the box open again. The card already lay discarded to the side, so the finger was right there, out in the open. White skin, black polish, small and slender enough to belong to a woman. A slim silver ring rested between the knuckle and the blunt and bloody edge of the finger.

"It's Irina," Victor confirmed.

"How do you know?"

He pointed at the swirl etched into the ring. "That Y is the family seal. She's being excommunicated," he slid the card across the counter, "and we're invited."

CHAPTER THIRTY

Cordelia

WE HAD A WEEK TO PREPARE AND IT STILL WASN'T enough. I barely slept. Irina was hurt because of me. She was getting cut from her family, literally, because she'd stayed to look after me when her father had taken Victor. She hadn't stopped me from taking Victor home. My actions kept putting people in danger.

The guilt was festering in my gut. I threw up the morning before we left. It didn't help that I had to get into a car I'd never seen - apparently my old car had died and Irina had given this one to Victor. Just rubbing in that all these things were happening out of my control.

I blacked out for most of the drive. I didn't even remember how we got from the car to the long table in Piotr Yelchin's backyard. The cheery white flowers and streamers mocked me along-

255

side the warm sunshine and chirping birds. Spring was in full bloom when the day would have called for dark skies and raging storms.

Victor's hand was wrapped around mine in my lap, all ink and veins contrasting against my fluffy skirt.

I kept my eyes on that.

Last time I'd left my house, I had focused on his fight. It had been enough to keep my mind occupied.

But my memories were mixing with anxieties today, all blood and violence - and not the UFC-controlled kind.

"And to Cordelia Montgomery, our very special guest of honor."

My head snapped up at the mention of my name. Victor's uncle stood at the head of the table, a hand clamped over Irina's shoulder, the other raised in a toast.

"Or maybe not so special," he continued, "seeing her used to be such a rarity, but her face is practically everywhere these days, isn't it?" He smirked and Victor's hand tightened.

I took a trembling breath and forced a smile as I raised my own glass. "Can never have too much of a good thing," I said, my voice surprisingly steady.

Piotr's eyes flashed but he just smiled and continued: "To Irina and Cordelia."

Everyone chimed in as they toasted to both of us. I set my glass back down without drinking and met Irina's eyes. She grinned and winked, as if she wasn't sitting there with a bruised hand that seemed to just begin to scar. At least she seemed otherwise unharmed. Losing one finger to break free from her father didn't seem so bad, right?

One finger for a fresh start?

No matter how hard I tried to tell myself it was a small price to pay, my stomach remained sour. I'd failed her. She should have just stayed in my house. She would have been safe there.

I blinked, the outline of a familiar blood stain flashing behind my lids. When I opened my eyes again, lunch was somehow over. A waiter carried my untouched plate off. This wasn't good. I hadn't been bleeding time like this in many years. Logically, I knew it was my brain trying to protect me - but it was doing a really poor job if it put me on autopilot in front of two dozen deadly men, hiding guns in their designer suits.

"Come with me." I glanced up and did a double-take at the man standing behind Victor's chair. They looked so much alike. Victor was older, broader and tattooed, but their bone structure was incredibly similar. That had to be Victor's other cousin, Luka. "We have an hour."

"I'm not leaving her," Victor said.

"No shit. I meant both of you. Come on."

I let Victor pull me to my feet. He carried most of my weight with his arm around my middle and I realized that's how I must have gotten from the car. I glanced at him as he led me through the gleaming smooth house and up the stairs.

"You're alright," he whispered and squeezed my waist without his eyes ever leaving his cousin.

Luka eventually scanned his key fob at a door at the end of the hallway. Irina was pacing inside. A gorgeous tall brunette was watching her. Based on those two looking like carbon copies of one another too, I'd say that was Natalia. A blond man stood by the window, vaguely familiar, sipping from a flask as he stared at the guests outside.

"Cordelia," Victor sighed and positioned himself behind me, both hands wrapping around my middle. The way he steeled his embrace made it easy to lean into him, let his strength hold my body as I forced my brain to stay with me, to let me process this. "These are my cousins. You've already met Irina. Luka, Natalia, and her husband Daniel."

"What are we all doing here?" I asked and curled my hand around my arm. I pressed my nails down hard until my skin ached, hoping to stay present. I had a bad habit of doing that to my cheeks when I sat at my desk - but this was more important than zoom meetings. I'd draw blood if I had to.

"I'll do a lot for our family but I'm not ready to denounce Irina," Natalia said. From the corner of my eye, I noticed her husband taking another swig. "I didn't stay mad at her for more than a day when the little psycho burned my American Girl Doll collection. I'm not starting now."

My jaw clenched at Natalia's use of 'psycho' but this probably wasn't the time or place to start educating her on language.

Luka sighed and rubbed the bridge of his nose. "This is so fucked up."

"You're all on borrowed time," I said. All heads swiveled towards me and I winced, only for Victor to tighten his embrace on me. "Take it from someone whose father only cared about money and legacy. You're cogs in a machine. Not family. Not to him."

"Yeah babe, that's why it's called family business, not family love fest." Natalia rolled her eyes at me. "Some of us just suck it up and do what's expected of us."

"You can't have it both ways. You can't play by your father's rules and not expect him to enforce them on your sister."

"This isn't helping," Irina grunted and stopped her pacing to glance at me. "Look, we never assumed we'd die of old age. We know what we were born into, okay? But the second I walk off this property without my family's protection, I'm dead. Not how I saw this going."

"You're coming with us," Victor replied without missing a beat.

I nodded in agreement. "You'll be safe as long as you stay at my place. You know how secure my house is."

"No offense, but I don't want to spend the rest of my life in your house, Cordelia." Irina crossed her arms over her chest.

"If I may offer a different perspective," Daniel capped his flask, "it seems to me that all problems started with her." He tilted his head towards me, and I stiffened.

Victor straightened behind me, his grip loosening. He'd steadied me for my benefit, but I had watched his body move through enough fights. The videos were burned into my brain. I knew the subtle stance adjustments.

Luka held up a hand in front of me and Victor, turning his attention to his brother-in-law. "The girl just ended up in the middle of it all by association. Just like you."

Daniel dragged his eyes from Luka to his wife and pursed his lips, but didn't say anything else.

"Luka," Victor said, voice low.

They looked at each other, quietly tilting their heads and having a conversation none of us were invited to, until Luka subtly shook his head.

"What was that about?" I whispered.

He kissed the top of my head. "I'll tell you later, zhizn' moya."

Luka flexed his jaw and looked back and forth between Victor and me. "Fine," he huffed, "fine. We don't drag the girls into it. Paris."

"Excuse you?" Irina waved her bandaged hand through the air. "We're already in it."

"I'm not," Natalia mumbled. Before anyone could say anything about that, Daniel took her hand and gently pulled her out of the room.

"Still," Victor said, his arms tightening around me again now that Daniel was gone, "we shouldn't discuss it *here*. Irina, you'll come with us for now. Luka?"

"I'll let you know."

"Then it's settled." Victor loosened behind me. "Come on, Cordelia. There's something I want you to see."

One glance between the cousins and Luka sighed and tossed Victor his key fob.

I thought I'd had wordless communication with Victor down, but these two operated on another level.

Victor took me to a room just a few doors down the hallway. The room was fairly simple compared to all the modern touches everywhere else. A bed pushed into one corner with a mirror next to it, a small desk under the window, a chest of drawers covered in faded stickers with a small TV on it, and a punching bag in the corner. *Oh.*

"This is your room."

He hummed in confirmation.

I turned from him to the chest of drawers, where I let my fingers glide over the stickers. Most of them were UFC-branded in some way. The others all seemed to be souvenir stickers from different places. Las Vegas was there a lot, but some of them were from much further away, Brazil, Australia, the Emirates. "Have you been to all these places?"

He nodded.

"For fights?"

He nodded again.

He'd been all over the world. Maybe he'd still be collecting stickers if his brain hadn't taken him out of the ring. "Do you miss it? Traveling?"

"No," he smirked, "those are all airport souvenirs. I never got to see much of the places I visited."

"If you want to, we can figure that out, you know? You can send me postcards." I smiled. "You'll just have to learn how to express your love for me in all the different languages."

He chuckled and kissed my forehead, then pointed at one of the Las Vegas stickers. "I love you." Then he pointed at an Ontario one. "I love you."

"Very funny."

"I love you," he said again while pointing out an Australian one.

"You're just proving that colonialism is horrible."

"I'm proving that I'm already in the only place that matters." He leaned down and kissed me, his lips rough against mine. His tongue nudged mine, and he didn't stop kissing me until I gasped for air, cheeks flushed and pulse racing. "I love you."

"Uh-huh." My brain tried to come back from *nice, more, yes, good*, to the present. "Are you going to tell me what you and Luka just agreed on?"

He shook his head. "Not here. The walls have ears."

"Okay, fine," I pursed my lips and wandered from the dresser to the punching bag, "did you ever pin your uncle's face on this?" I pushed my fist into the worn leather, coming up against a deceptively hard surface. Good thing I hadn't swung for it.

"Like this." Victor's fingers closed around mine and he rearranged my fist, placing the thumb loosely against the side rather than tucked away. "And no. Imagined it though."

He stepped around behind me and guided my arm into position. "Hit."

I followed command and swung my fist into the bag. "Ow! Flip! That hurts!"

"Ideally, you'd be wearing gloves."

"And then it doesn't hurt?"

"Less and less with each hit."

"I'll leave the punching to you." I turned and almost collided with his chest. Victor didn't move out of the way. He just stared down at me, green eyes moving fast, tracing every inch of my face. "What? Do I have something on my face?" I wasn't even sure if I'd eaten anything. Let alone something that could ruin my makeup.

"No," he shook his head, a small smirk playing out over his lips, "you're here. It's strange."

"I'm not doing too good," I confessed, "I'm not... I can't..."

"I know." He wrapped the end of my braid around his fingers. "What can I do?"

"Right now I'm okay, but outside, with people, I'm dissociating. I'm on auto-pilot and I have no idea what I've said or done for most of the day."

"I know."

"How? This hasn't happened in years."

"It actually happened last year. After Julian Beckett." I flinched at the name, but Victor continued. "When we had to take Del to the hospital, I wasn't going to leave you behind. You came with us to the hospital, and then you spent the night at my place."

"I don't remember that."

Victor tipped his head as if to say *case in point*.

"What happened?"

"Nothing. You took a shower, borrowed some sweats and fell asleep on the sofa. But you had the same look in your eyes. It's like part of you has vacated your body. It's... scary."

"Scary? Why? Do I look like a zombie?"

"No, it's scary because I don't know where you go. I'd follow you anywhere, but I can't do that when you disappear like that. I don't know how to get you back."

"You could try kissing me."

He quietly raised his brows.

"I don't really know how to explain it, but when you kiss me, my brain gets very quiet. It's like all the buzzing of the world just stops, and I can only feel you."

"Like this?"

Victor leaned down and brushed his lips over mine, testing, teasing. My eyes fell shut. On my next quivering inhale, he stifled my breath with his mouth on mine. And the world fell quiet. My body fell quiet. Just a very low, warm hum thrummed through my chest when I tasted him.

"Yeah," I replied breathlessly, "like that."

Victor barely let me get the words out before he kissed me again. In one swift move, he picked me up and my legs closed around him on their own accord. *This* made sense. Even if the world was derailing, this - his hips pressed against mine and his tongue in my mouth and his heartbeat hammering against my chest - made sense.

At least until my back hit his mattress. These sheets smelled nothing like home.

"We probably shouldn't," I mumbled

"Are you here with me?" Victor's mouth hovered above mine. "Does this help?"

"Yeah."

"Then let me make you feel good, Cordelia."

"Oh goodness." I gasped when Victor's hands slid down my torso. His knuckles grazed over the thin sliver of skin between my top and my skirt, leaving a hot trail in their wake. Whether this was a good idea or not, I craved his touch.

His kisses travelled down my neck and I raked my fingers into his hair. I wanted to lock him against me. Keep the warmth and the weight of his body pressing down on me.

"Victor," I whimpered, wriggling to get a better angle under him.

His mouth closed over the little hollow at the base of my throat. "Still here with me?"

My thoughts were beginning to swim - but in a good way - and I merely managed a strangled sound.

Victor's mouth moved lower and lower, his lips leaving a burning path down my throat and chest.

"I... oh god... I mean..." I squirmed at a sudden sharp pain. It shot through the right side of my chest. Closing my fists, I tugged at his hair like my life depended on it.

Victor let out a low hum of appreciation.

"No. Let me, ow, hold on...." I fumbled at his face until he leaned back enough to let me sit up. Confusion wrinkled his forehead. Not bothering with an explanation, I worked the bow-shaped brooch on my chest until the needle sprang free. There was no trace of blood, but I had an angry red scratch across my chest. Definitely not what this pin was made for. I tossed the thing aside with a grimace. Only to catch a glance of myself in the mirror behind Victor. Two minutes on his bed, and my braid was tousled and my cheeks were flushed.

"Oh, that's..." I looked different. My reflection wasn't perfectly controlled on the outside just to hide the chaos on the inside. "Different."

"Hmm?" Victor glanced over his shoulder, following my gaze.

"I look different."

"You look exactly like I see you," he replied.

"What?" I laughed. "Horny and feverish?"

"Someone who isn't afraid to take what she wants, no matter what it looks like to the outside world."

"You really think that?"

"I do." He kissed my throat again, and I watched his back muscles move in our reflection.

"You're gorgeous," I whispered.

In response, he lifted off my shirt and kissed the space between my breasts.

I could see the heat rising in my body. The red flush spreading over my skin like a wave of lava. I could watch exactly what Victor was doing to me and it was exhilarating in its own right to see.

"How's this? Still helping?" Victor asked and lowered himself to the floor between my legs. I wasn't sure where to look. At him and his beautiful thick lashes lowered to look at me? Or at his reflection as he spread my knees and fit himself so perfectly between them?

"Yeah," I mumbled, completely entranced.

"You like watching, zhizn' moya?" he asked.

I swallowed and nodded.

"Keep your eyes on the mirror." He pushed his hands up my skirt until his fingers curled around the waistband of my panties. "Lift your hips for me, baby."

I watched my own body move for him as I pushed my ass off the mattress, giving him the leverage to pull my panties down.

"Fuck, you're so gorgeous," he said and I whimpered at those few little words - because I could see exactly where he was focusing his attention when he said them.

"Victor," I whispered, pleading for him to continue.

He wordlessly bunched my skirt up, baring my pussy to him. "Gorgeous," he repeated, hot hands running down my thighs to my knees. He had them hooked over his shoulders in a split second. "I fucking love your legs."

"Oh god," I whimpered, because each of his words was a hot breath tickling over my delicate skin, "god, please."

"God's not here, Cordelia. He can't help you."

"*Victor*. Please." I ran my hands through his hair again.

"Beg," he commanded.

Beg. The word echoed through my mind, then plummeted straight down my center.

"Please," I breathed.

"You'll have to do better than that, zhizn' moya." He chuckled, then blew on me. The air hit my wet folds like a ghost touch, sending a shiver down my spine.

"Fuck," I hiccuped, "please Victor. I need to feel you. Please, I beg of you, just touch me."

It didn't take more than that for him to delve forward, his tongue flicking against my sensitive flesh. I let out a loud moan and bucked against him.

I could see my reflection, flush and desperate, clinging on to Victor like my life depended on it. Meanwhile Victor's arms flexed as he gripped my hips. His shoulders rippled with every move as he devoured me.

Each flick of his tongue against my clit fanned the fire that was building fast and ruthlessly in my center.

I moaned and tried to move against him, but he had me clamped into a death grip, keeping my hips exactly where he wanted them as he tortured me with his mouth. He grazed his teeth over me and thrust his tongue into me, driving me to a breaking point. Only to then ease up again and give me a few breaths of respite.

My cheeks bright red, my dazed reflection looked back at me from the mirror.

"Please," I whimpered, breathing shallow.

"Beg," he growled.

"Please," I croaked, "please let me come. I need to come. I can't... I need to."

He let out a hum of appreciation, then dove forward with more force than should have been possible. I was almost knocked back to the mattress, but his hands on my waist kept me steady.

He pushed his upper body against my hips at the same time as his arms pulled me into him. My thighs clenched around him as his tongue struck deep. I was wound all around him. Tighter and tighter and tighter.

Then he sucked my clit into his mouth and it was over. The tension snapped from my body. Limbs shaking, I fell over a deliciously hot edge and back into the soft sheets. My body jerked against his grip until the aftershocks quaked through me. It wasn't until I whimpered his name that he let go and crawled over me.

"Can we just stay in here?" I asked.

"Yes."

"Really?"

"No, but I don't care."

DESPITE HIS WORDS, WE HAD TO LEAVE HIS ROOM eventually. We picked up Luka and Irina from her room, then ventured back outside.

Being a little more present than before only made the afternoon weirder. People were acting like this was any regular family gathering. Servers circulated with champagne flutes and canapés, and nobody seemed to care that Irina was scared for her life.

"So what do you do?" I asked, blinking at the gray man in a

sharply cut suit, who had approached us to congratulate Victor on his fight.

"Cordelia." Victor spoke my name like a warning.

"It's quite alright, Vitya," the man laughed, only to meet my puzzled stare, "that's not a question people ask around here, honey."

I didn't even blink at his condescending tone, but Victor's hand tightened around mine.

"Okay, fine, don't tell me about your boring job then," I replied, each word dripping with sarcasm. If he thought I'd be intimidated by vague insinuations and a condescending attitude, he could go straight to hell and meet up with my dad.

"I get the girls." His voice had taken on a sharper edge. Someone had a bruised ego...

"What does that mean?" I asked and made sure to sound extra disinterested, fumbling with the bow pinned to my top.

He huffed and straightened his spine. "I get the girls for Piotr's whore houses. I get them out of Russia and I get them here. The young ones, the pretty ones, are all mine. They make him good money."

Despite my best efforts, I still flinched at his reply. *The young ones.*

"See, honey, not as boring as you think," the man laughed before I had the chance to come up with a reply.

"I think she's heard enough, Lev," Victor said, voice dropped low.

"Besides, that's not impressive. That's just disgusting," I said.

"You should teach your woman to show some respect for your family."

"*She* is with me. And *you* aren't family. Which means you should be the one showing her some respect."

Lev grunted, clearly unhappy with that response. "Yeah? How about I respectfully offer her a job? She's pretty enough."

"Excuse me?" My voice sounded strangely distant in my own

ears, and I clutched Victor's hand tighter, trying to stay present, trying to listen.

"I said, you're pretty enough, honey. My boys will fix that attitude in no time."

Nausea swept through my gut. Not on *my* behalf, but for all the girls - the pretty ones, the young ones - that this man was talking about. All the girls who might need their attitudes *fixed*.

Victor shifted beside me. "They brought out the cake."

"What?" I rubbed a hand over my tight chest, blinking up at Victor who had half-turned to me.

"Look, they brought out the cake," he repeated and nodded at the set-up behind me.

I followed his gaze to the decked-out table, where people were slowly taking their seats again. Smack in the middle of it was a huge, three-tiered cake, fit for a wedding, covered in fondant and gold leaf.

The gunshot tore through my eardrums first. The loud blast behind me made my breath hitch and my muscles cramp. Before my mind could even put together the sound and its meaning, Victor's hands wrapped around the back of my neck and my waist. He pushed me forward without room to budge.

"Keep walking," he murmured low and pressed a kiss against the back of my head.

"Did you just-" I couldn't even bring myself to say it.

"Keep walking," he repeated.

I blinked and blinked and tried to starve off the darkness at the edge of my vision, tried to push down the images of blood. Red stains on white shoes.

"You're alright, zhizn' moya," Victor whispered. He snaked his whole arm around my waist, taking some of my weight.

As we got closer to the table, Luka jogged towards us, hands thrown up. "Seriously? Today of all days?" Exasperated. Not shocked.

Maybe the gray man wasn't dead. But he hadn't screamed. If he'd just been hurt, he would have made a sound, right?

"He threatened her."

"A kneecap would have done just fine," Luka groaned, staring past us. The rest of the guests were staring, too. At least most of them. Some were sipping champagne like nothing was wrong. How fucked-up did you have to be to ignore a man getting shot?

"I was making a point."

"Yeah? You plan on making a point of scrubbing his brains off the lawn, too?"

I flinched. Victor kept pushing me forward, wordlessly walking me past Luka. He maneuvered me into my seat and crouched next to it, his eyes searching mine. "Panic attack?"

"No."

"Want me to kiss you?"

I dragged my eyes away from his. My attention caught on the angry red welt across my chest, where the pin had scratched me the last time he'd kissed me. Minutes ago? Hours ago? Time suddenly felt kaleidoscopic, not linear.

"No kissing," I mumbled, "just cake."

"Cake?"

"Cake."

"Okay, let's get you cake."

He shoveled a mountain of cake onto my plate. Every tier was supposed to be a different flavor, so I got a slice of each. They all tasted like sand in my mouth.

"Cordelia?"

"Hmm?"

My gaze swiveled to Victor. It was dark. How was it dark? Where was everyone? My spine snapped up straight.

Not again.

"Where's Irina?" I asked.

I'd missed it. Victor had talked me through the whole process only for me to black out.

Irina cleared her throat behind him and awkwardly waved at me with both hands - both now bandaged. One missing a finger, the other visibly branded under all that gauze. No matter which hand she was doing business with, nobody would mistake her for being part of her father's business anymore.

That was my fault. Both of those bandages were because of me. If I hadn't left the house, Victor wouldn't have felt guilty about leaving me alone, and he wouldn't have asked her to look after me. If I'd stayed home, Irina would have been alright. I kept making these stupid, selfish decisions, and everyone else was getting hurt.

"Can we go home now? I'm craving some real food," Irina said, pursing her lips at the remnants of cake and caviar on the table. "I need a burger and a beer."

CHAPTER THIRTY-ONE

VICTOR

It only took Cordelia a shower and a night's rest to get her bearings back. She didn't want to talk about Irina's excommunication, and I didn't push her for it. After that, weeks passed in a blur. Irina moved into the bedroom across from Del's. I went back to training. Cordelia handled one phone call after another for her foundation. Even when I came home at night, her voice carried through the closed office door more often than not.

Despite the routine of it all, Paris hung over us like a countdown.

There was only one way this would end and it was with a bullet between Petya's eyes. Luka would take over for his father. It was as barbaric as it was easy. Kill the boss, become the boss. Nobody would even bat an eyelash as long as it was Luka himself who killed his father. The business would stay in the family. There would only be a skeleton crew with us in Paris, so finding an unguarded moment wouldn't be hard either.

Cordelia knew as much, but she insisted that she couldn't just sit back and wait for Paris.

She scheduled the pond construction, and told Del to stay with Beck to avoid the noise. Del didn't even bat an eyelash before packing some bags.

One morning, before I headed off to training, she set up social accounts. The only picture she posted was a group shot from her birthday party. As soon as her friends reposted it, people followed her in droves. It helped that the campaign - and especially the leaked footage - had gotten so much attention, because everyone was desperate for another glimpse at the elusive Cordelia Montgomery.

At some point, training ran long and I was late for dinner *once*, and she posted a video telling everyone. It was ten cute seconds of her pouting into the camera, but Luka's phone blew up with notifications. He managed some official accounts in my name, and Cordelia's followers flooded them all.

Petya played it old school. He posted a van outside Cordelia's house, clearly visible from her office. A quiet threat.

Cordelia started posting a "Fitzi's view from his window seat" photo every morning. A cat picture to everyone else - a public *'everyone can see you'* to my uncle.

Organized crime only worked as long as it was conducted behind closed doors - and Petya hadn't considered that the girl who had kept her whole life a secret was willing to turn him into a public spectacle. She was a goddamn force and she didn't even realize just how much power she was wielding.

Meanwhile, she tasked Irina with overseeing the construction in the backyard. It kept her busy enough while she was hiding, and ensured that no worker went unvetted or even thought about entering the house.

As much as Cordelia amazed me, her sleep schedule worried

me. It had started with waking up screaming every single day. Then she started tossing and turning all night. With one week left before I'd leave for Paris, she was avoiding sleep altogether.

I couldn't stop her memories from haunting her, but I wasn't letting her shoulder this alone. So I wasn't getting any sleep either. We played chess, watched TV, swam in the pool. I even posed for a portrait for three fucking hours. Anything and everything to keep her mind busy.

"I think I might try baking a cake later," Cordelia mused while she stashed her empty plate in the dishwasher. Without me here all the time, she was picking up so many small tasks she'd probably never even had to think about in the last 30 years.

"I actually have plans for us tonight."

"Board games?"

"No."

"Friendship bracelets?"

"No, and I wouldn't accept a *friendship* bracelet from you anyway."

"Matching tattoos?"

I opened my mouth to say no, but the idea of having a permanent mark on her body wasn't unappealing.

"A teacup and a teapot," she quipped.

"Hmm?"

"I think those would be cute partner tattoos. In purple or pink. That way it stands out between all your others."

"We're not getting tattoos tonight."

"Oh. Okay." She narrowed her eyes at me. "Do I have to keep guessing?"

"I'm taking you on a date."

"I don't think-"

"We're staying here, but it's a real date."

"A date?"

"Like a normal couple."

"Oh. *Oh.* We're a couple." A big smile spread on her tired face. "I'm in a *couple* with you."

"You have thirty minutes to get ready. I'll pick you up by the stairs at eight."

"Oh shit," I hissed and closed my eyes for a second, willing my pulse back into its regular rhythm. One look at her and I was going into cardiac arrest.

"You didn't tell me how to dress. I had to wing it." She grinned down at me from the middle of the stairwell. "I've never been on a date with anyone else."

"And you never will be," I said and held my hand out for her, "but feel free to put this on for any of our future dates."

"You like?" She did a wobbly little twirl at the bottom of the stairs. Her shiny light pink dress was almost the exact soft shade of her skin, except for its blue seams. It hugged her chest tight like a corset, while its skirt flared out. As she twirled, that tiny little skirt lifted just enough for me to catch a look at a pair of lacy white fabric underneath.

"Yeah, baby, I like," I huffed, feeling the heat rush down my center.

Cordelia giggled and raised her brows at me.

"What did I say?"

"I'm usually a lot less dressed when you call me *baby*."

Not that I'd noticed it, but considering her panties had been on my mind when I'd said it, she was probably right.

"Let's go before I decide to show you just how much I like that tiny dress."

"Do I need shoes?" Cordelia wiggled her fuzzy socked toes at me.

"No, you'll be fine."

I led her through the kitchen and the winter garden filled with paintings. She already narrowed her eyes at the backyard through the windows. Before she could start puzzling it out, I swept her up into my arms. No need for her to get those socks dirty.

She laughed as I carried her over to the pond and set her down on the picnic blanket on the lawn. I didn't even get a word out before she dropped to her knees and started fumbling with the waiting cooler box.

"Are we having ice cream?"

"No." Her excitement almost made me wish I did have ice cream in there. "Careful, don't tip it."

Kneeling behind her, I released the little plastic snaps on either side of the box.

"Can I open it?" She clasped her hands together. So giddy, it was beyond cute. It triggered a weirdly possessive, violent response in my brain - and I nipped at her bare shoulder to get the tension out somehow.

"Mm-hmm," I agreed without easing my teeth off her skin.

"I'm being careful," she reassured me and gently lifted the lid off. "Is that-"

"Fish."

"Fish?" Her fingers trembled when she lifted one of the plastic bags from the box and held it up against the last rays of sunlight. The bright orange goldfish inside whirled around.

"The pond should be ready for them to move in."

"What do I do?" Cordelia looked over her shoulder at me, eyes big.

"We let the plastic bags float and add some pond water every ten minutes."

"I can't believe you got me fish." She beamed and handed me the first bag before lifting another one from the box. "Are they all goldfish? Do they need specific foods? Or plants? I have to go grab my phone."

"Why do you need your phone?" I asked and held her by the elbow before she could get up with a plastic bag in each hand.

"Because the water needs to have a certain pH-level, right?"

"Don't worry," I said as I caught on, "you don't have to look it up. I'll show you how to test and adjust it."

"Where did you learn that?"

"I do know how to use Google."

"Sorry, that came out wrong." She lowered the plastic bags back into the cooler and turned to me. Her delicate hands curved around my jaw, soft and sweetly coconut-scented. "You got me fish, and you learned how to take are of them for me. Thank you."

"Anytime," I brushed her hair behind her ears and kissed her. It only took a millisecond for me to realize she wasn't kissing me back. I sighed. "You want to put the fish in the pond right away?"

"Yes, I do." She grinned and whirled back around.

Thirty minutes later, Cordelia stood ankle-deep in the pond, cupping water into plastic bags. She was fixating on the fish but her nose was turning bright red. Maybe we should have waited a few more weeks to do this. As soon as the sun was down, temperatures still dropped quickly.

"Just warm up for five minutes."

"I'm plenty warm," she sing-sang.

I reached for her paling fingers and she swatted me away.

"Stop being annoying or I'm sending you back inside," she warned.

"Try sending me away. I'd like to see how that goes for you."

"Ooh, I'm so scared. Is the big bad man going to be mean to me? Is he going to make me put my socks on? Boohoo."

"Come here." I grabbed her hand the moment she'd tied up the plastic bag. She tried pulling out from my grasp, but it was too firm. She finally looked at me. Her lips were turning blue, for fuck's sake.

"Leave me alone. Go inside if you're cold."

"Cordelia, come here."

My shoes sank into the first inch of water. I wrapped my arm around her middle and hauled her back.

"What are you doing?" She protested and slapped at my arm. "The fish need-"

"The fish need *nothing* for the next ten minutes. Just let them get used to the water."

I tried to just set her down on the blanket, but her jittering knees folded right up, and she plopped to the ground with a grimace.

"Fuck," I muttered.

"I'm not leaving them." Cordelia glowered up at me, all that stormy determination in her eyes.

"Fine." I slipped my suit jacket off and knelt down to wrap her up. She sniffled, brows still drawn deep. "What's wrong?"

"I'm not a child."

"I know that."

"I'm also not being stubborn just to annoy you." She flexed her shaking fingers, then pulled the sleeves over her hands to wrap them up.

"I know that, too." I sat down in front of her, pulling her legs into my lap and rubbing some life back into them. "I'm not complaining, am I?"

She looked past me at the pond. "I know that I'm not easy to spend a lot of time with. I'm really trying not to be so self-centered all the time."

"Excuse me?"

"I got really excited about the fish and I want to make sure they're happy and they're safe, and I snapped at you, and I ruined our date." Her voice clogged up. "I'm so sorry."

"*Oh*. No, stop. You didn't ruin anything." I lifted my hands from her legs to her cheeks, just in time for my thumb to catch a tear. She couldn't actually believe all of that, could she? "I love spending time with you, zhizn' moya. It's incredibly easy, actually. I will happily let you ignore me, so you can take care of hundreds of fish for hours on end. I got these fish because I knew they'd make you happy."

"But I-" She hiccuped as her throat closed up.

Fuck. Cordelia crying like this was a whole new pain. I'd seen her cry before, but not because of me. Nothing like this. Her brows were quivering and her breaths were barely making it to her lungs, and no sound came across her lips.

"I didn't pull you out of the pond because I thought you were being too self-centered."

"I told you to leave me alone. On our date." She reached for her hair, realizing too late that her hands were still bundled up.

"So? I know that had nothing to do with me. I can read you, Cordelia. For six years, I've spent almost every minute of every day getting to know you." I peeled her fingers from the sleeves, and I picked up a strand of her hair to wrap around her index finger. Because I did know her. Her shoulders immediately eased a little as she started winding the hair through her fingers. "Which means I put food in front of you, and I buy your tampons, and I pull you out of freezing ponds. Because you're not even self-centered enough to monitor your own bodily functions."

She blinked at me, eyes still glassy. "My heart is beating really fast. That's a bodily function."

"Just try to take some deep breaths."

"No, that's not it." She shook her head. "You make my heart beat really fast, Victor. I love you so much, sometimes it feels like my heart can't keep up with it. I don't know what I did to deserve you in my life."

"Don't worry. That feeling's mutual." I leaned in for a kiss, but she sucked in a deep trembling breath before our lips could touch. "Do you want to release the fish first?"

"I do," she whispered.

"Okay, give me a second."

I scooted back and took my shoes and socks off, before dragging the picnic blanket - and Cordelia with it - to the edge of the water. I got in myself this time, gathering all the plastic bags in front of Cordelia.

"Thank you." She untied the knot on the first bag. She was swallowed whole by my jacket, her hair had dropped to the mud, and her face was still flushed from crying - but in the faint purple evening light, she was the most beautiful thing I'd ever seen. Her eyes flicked up, sensing my stare. "You have to get one, too."

"Okay." It took me a second to drag my gaze away. Then I followed her example and waited for the signal.

"3, 2, 1." She tipped the plastic bag and released her fish, and I was too busy watching a big smile replace all the tears and pain from before to remember my own fish until she yelled, "Victor!"

"On it."

My fish scurried from the plastic bag and into the depth of the pond.

I was better at keeping up with her pace for the next few fish, until all of them were exploring their new home.

"You can kiss me now," Cordelia said as I stepped out of the pond, legs of my pants soaked, incapable of feeling my toes.

"Oh, can I?"

"I'll allow it." She grinned and fluttered her lashes at me in that silly way she did that punched me right in the chest every time.

"Let's get you inside to warm up first."

"You have to carry me back anyway," she grinned smugly while putting her socks back on, "you might as well carry me kissingly."

"Alright, come here." I waited for her to push herself up - only to scoop low. I threw her over one shoulder, and she screeched. Her arms flailed through the air for a hold, but I had my hands already wrapped around her waist and her thigh, keeping her safe and steady.

"Victor," she gasped, finally stilling when I took a few steps.

"Kissingly, huh?" Her ass was right next to my face, and that tiny skirt didn't do much to conceal anything anymore. I had to. Giving her exactly two seconds to protest my question, I laid my lips to her cool skin.

The tension spluttered from her body. It would have been hilarious how limp she fell if it hadn't been for her thighs jerking and pressing together. That told me exactly where her mind had gone.

I kissed the undercurve of her ass again. Her breath hitched and her muscles twitched.

Fuck me.

If I had spent even two seconds thinking this through, I would have guessed as much. Thinking about her wants and needs was second nature by now - just not this kind of want and need.

"What are you doing?" She asked breathlessly when I slid my hand up her thigh, fingers brushing up against those tiny panties.

"Date's not over, zhizn' moya," I replied and crossed the threshold into the house.

"Will you set me down already?"

"Nope."

"Nope? What are you? Five?"

This time, I sank my teeth into her flesh, and Cordelia's whole body shuddered around me.

I didn't put her down until we got to her bathroom. Her face was red and her hair a mess, and I never wanted to get my hands on her body more.

"What are we doing?"

"Unless you want to lose your virginity while reeking of fish and pond water," I unbuttoned my shirt, "I suggest we take a shower first."

She stilled, eyes flicking between the open door to her bedroom, to the shower, to me, back to the bedroom - again and again.

"I need to call Del."

"Right now?" I tossed my shirt over the sink and reached for Cordelia's hands.

"I-" Her eyes started skipping again.

"If you're not ready, we can wait."

"I'm ready. I'm so ready. But I'm not prepared. I should do that now. If I get in the shower first, then I can't call her afterwards, because we're going to have fun in the shower, right? I want you to do the showerhead thing again, so then it would be really weird to take a break after that and call Del and *then* have sex."

"Del can *prepare* you? Do you need to talk anything through? Is that a girl thing?"

"What?" Cordelia furrowed her brows. "No. I mean that Del probably has condoms. I don't. I'm not prepared for that specific *bodily function*. Go figure. So if I call her now, I can get condoms from her room, and then we can take a shower."

I parted my mouth, but instead of replying, I just opened the medicine cabinet behind the mirror. The box of condoms was exactly where I'd left it.

"What? When?"

"The day you asked me to go down on you on the treadmill. I wasn't sure how fast you'd get there, but I figured we'd need these."

"Oh," a perfectly melodic laugh bubbled from her chest, "you are so getting lucky tonight."

"If you think this is impressive, just wait until you find the lube in your nightstand."

"You put lube in my nightstand?" Before she could spin around to run and check, I caught her by the elbow and pulled her back against me. She collided with my chest with a little *oomph*.

"You can search for that later," I promised and slid my jacket off her shoulders. It landed in the sink with my shirt. "Let's see how wet I can get you first."

"Are you making puns?"

"If that's what it takes to get your attention long enough to get you naked." I unzipped her dress and pulled it off, then made quick work of her panties, too. I'd never get tired of this. Her perfect raindrop tits, or the dip of her waist like a handle made for my hands only, or those fine blonde hairs that made her entire skin glow in the light. Just looking at her felt like a sacrilege, because there was no way her body was meant for my mortal eyes.

"My turn," she breathed and reached for my belt. She bit her lip as she worked the leather, and I couldn't take it anymore. I wrapped her hair around my hand and pulled. The only opening I needed was the moment she gasped, and I sank my mouth over hers. This time, Cordelia kissed me back. Lips, tongue and teeth, as desperate as mine.

The rest of my clothes dropped to the floor and I pulled her into the shower.

With the hot water coming down on us, her hands were all over me. I hummed into the kiss, leaning into it. We had been touching - *she* had been touching for weeks. Exploring my body, and all the reactions she could draw from it. And she was getting way too good at it. As if I wasn't ready to go whenever I got a taste of her sweet skin anyway.

One brush of her fingertips along the underside of my cock, and I was damn close to exploding.

"Fuck." I pushed myself harder against her hand.

"Not yet." She laughed, only to do her little finger trick again. It sent an electric hot bolt down my spine.

"Let's leave that for later." I groaned and pulled her hands up to the shower rail. "Hold onto that."

"But I want to-"

"Hands on the damn rail, Cordelia."

"Fine," she huffed.

I let my hands explore her body. Her eyes fell shut and her breath hitched as my fingertips coasted down her wet skin. Her stomach trembled when I dragged my thumbs over her peaking nipples, and her thighs twitched when my hands slid over her hip bones. All the while, those damn cute little sounds slipped from her lips.

It was fucking fascinating, the ways she reacted to me.

Part of me still couldn't believe that I was allowed to touch her like this. How on earth had I gotten lucky enough to be the one she wanted?

I kissed my way from her collar bone down her chest and the dip of her navel. When I sank to my knees, Cordelia's eyes fluttered open a little, and she looked down at me through her thick lashes. Her eyes dark blue and her cheeks bright pink.

I tilted my chin in a silent question and she nodded. *Alright? Alright.*

With that, I ran my hands up curved calves and thighs, so fucking perfect. "Spread your legs."

"I feel like, if you have to tell me to spread them, you're doing something wrong."

"Have it your way," I chuckled and grabbed hold of her knee. I yanked it up and over my shoulder, prompting Cordelia to yelp and grapple for a better hold on the rail. I bit the inside of her thigh before she could steady herself and she squeaked and jerked. If it hadn't been for my hands around her hips, digging into her ass, she would have toppled over.

"Asshole," she hissed and crinkled her nose.

I bit her again, gentler this time, dragging my teeth over her soft flesh. The muscles between her legs twitched, her perfect pink pussy pulsing in anticipation. "Don't talk like a brat if you can't handle the consequences, zhizn' moya."

"I don't have much of a choice when you take so long. I just want you to- fuck."

She shivered around me after I caught the sensitive skin right above her pussy between my teeth. "You don't want to wait? Then ask for what you want."

"Eat me out," she huffed, chest rising and falling fast.

"Ask nicely." I grinned at her scowl. Impatient little thing. I was struggling to hold out myself. The scent of her arousal clouded my senses until nothing but her twitching pussy filtered through. My dick was rock hard and ready to claim her. But I waited, even when she wriggled, even when she let out a frustrated moan that pulsed right through my cock.

"For god's sake, fine," she whined, "eat me out, *please*."

"You can do better than that."

She squirmed, thighs twitching.

"Can you please fuck me with your tongue? Please."

"That's my girl."

I buried my face between her thighs, parted her lips with my tongue and lapped up every delicious drop of arousal. Her hips bucked against me, meeting every hungry stroke of my tongue. I flicked it against her and thrust into her. And I savored every moan and every twitch of her muscles around me.

"More, please, more," she whimpered while I sucked on her clit until it was swollen red.

"Since you begged so beautifully." I leaned back just enough to watch her pussy flutter when I sank a single finger into her in one quick stroke. Cordelia choked on her voice and her entrance gripped me tight enough to stop me from moving. Eyes torn open, she glanced down. Mouth ajar, but no more words coming out, just small breathy moans.

I rolled my thumb over her clit and her hips shuddered, just enough to give my finger a little leeway. Her walls pulsed around me with every small thrust, gripping me tight each time I was down to the knuckle.

When her thighs started twitching, I delved forward again. Two more strokes of my tongue against her clit, and Cordelia's writhing turned into a full-body tremble. Her pussy frantically clenched and unclenched, and each breath came with a desperate moan. I brought the tip of a second finger against her tight entrance, barely pushing in, and my girl unraveled.

When her body stilled around me, I waited for that one hitched sound to let me know she was finished, before I pulled my hand back. My mouth stayed right where it was, my tongue slow and gentle against her.

"Victor," she croaked.

I only shot a glance up to make sure she was still gripping the shower rail. She was. So, in one move, I grabbed her second leg and threw it over my other shoulder.

"Oh my god," she gasped and clenched her thighs.

If being smothered by her thighs around my face was how I'd die, I'd go happily. But maybe not today. Leveraging my shoulders against her, I pushed her back until her hips were lodged between the wall and my face, giving her just enough hold for her legs to fall open again. That was all I needed to let my tongue sweep down the length of her fold.

One of her hands raked through my hair, gripping it in her fist, and the sharp tug on my scalp spurred me forward. The harder my tongue worked against her, the tighter her fingers wound through my hair, and the louder her moans echoed from the tiles.

Her second climax stirred up fast, body twitching around mine. Her other hand burrowed into my hair, and I had to steel my grip around her hips to stop us from toppling over as she rocked against my face.

Legs clenched around my head and fists jerking on my hair, Cordelia fell apart a second time, so consumed by feeling - not thoughts - that I barely got enough room to breathe.

I had that effect on her. Me. And it was a better win than any knockout or any championship belt.

She winced when I finally untangled myself. Even when I stood, I kept my hands wrapped around her middle, because her knees were still jittering.

"I…" She huffed out a long breath, glazed eyes searching mine. "Uh…"

"Need a minute?"

"Uh-huh." She nodded, shaky lips pulling into a smile.

I looped my arms around her waist and pulled her against me, absorbing her weight and her warmth. While her body trembled through the aftershocks, Cordelia kept her face buried in the curve of my neck, and I traced soothing circles between her shoulder blades.

The spark returned to her eyes when she pulled me out of the shower a few minutes later. "That's not the kind of shower head thing I had in mind, you know. But no complaints. That certainly was shower head." She grinned, and snatched the towel from my hand. "Let me."

She smoothed the towel over my body and I leaned into her careful touch. She dabbed at my chest and used her free hand to trace the inked lines on my skin. Every muscle fiber inside me clenched for her touch, craving the next as soon as her hands lifted off me. But when her hands dropped low and she cupped my dick through the towel, I grabbed her wrist and cuffed them behind her back with one hand.

Her eagerness to get her hands on me was going to drive me insane.

"Later," I said.

"When later?"

"When you've come on my dick once or twice. When I'm no longer worried that your first time is going to suck because you've already jerked me off."

She squinted and crinkled her nose, clearly not quite happy with my response. "Fine. Ugh. Stupid fucking virginity. I can't wait to get rid of it." She twisted out of my grasp and snatched a condom from the bathroom cabinet, before marching straight to her bedroom. "Are you coming, or what?"

The impatience really did something to my brain. Cordelia

wanted to have sex with me. There was no back and forth, no games, no quit-pro-quo. Being chosen, being wanted like that, eased off all the weight from years of feeling like I only mattered when I won a fight. Cordelia was stitching me together without even trying.

I followed her to the bedroom and furled my arms around her middle from behind. Her spine had gone tense, and her fingers were twirling a wet strand of hair. I kissed her shoulder, waiting for whatever end result her whirring mind would produce.

"Maybe I just like my vibrator."

"Do you want to get it? You can show me what you like."

"No, sorry," she shook her head and turned in my embrace to blink up at me, "I have a plan."

"I know."

"My plan never included you. I mean, sometimes I thought about you when I thought about the plan, but it wasn't *you*. I don't know what you like when you're having sex. And I don't know if I will like the way you fuck me. Maybe you'll hate the plan. Maybe we're not compatible. Maybe, at the end of the day, I just like my vibrator."

"Cordelia, I just made you come twice on my face. You'll *love* the way I fuck you."

"Okay, but do you even like missionary? Because I know you like my legs more than you like my tits, so if we have to change the plan, figure out some positions you like, I'd rather do it now and then enjoy the sex - and not pause in the middle because you're not feeling it."

"Shut up and let me fuck you according to your plan."

"I'm not stalling to be a brat. I'm trying to be considerate."

"I'm good with your plan." I tightened my arms around her until my dick pressed deep into her lower stomach. "I don't give a shit about where you want me to fuck you, or which position you want to try. Bend over, sit on me, whatever. I want *you*, Cordelia. Let me have you."

Cordelia bit her lip and watched me closely, as if I might take my words back any second.

"Rug or bed?" I asked just in case she'd changed her plan.

"I just-"

"Rug or bed?"

"Rug, please." A small smile played over her lips as her shoulders loosened. She brought my hand up to her face and kissed my knuckles one after the other as she sank to the floor and tugged me down with her. Condom tossed aside, Cordelia positioned herself in a specific direction on the rug, then pulled me on top. She'd thought this through exactly and I was more than happy to kneel between her knees and play along.

"Hi," she whispered once she seemed happy with the way we were positioned.

"Hi," I replied with a smile.

"Can you do it slowly?" Her voice had gone quiet and small. "I don't know if that's actually possible or if you need the momentum to get inside. But if you could do it slowly, because I'm scared it will hurt, that would-"

I silenced her worries with a slow kiss. I kissed her until I felt her anchor beneath me. "I can do slow."

"Good. Okay. Thank you."

I gave her another quick, reassuring kiss before leaning back to grab the condom. I didn't get the chance to even take it out of the wrapping, because Cordelia snatched it from my hands.

"I'll do it," she said without room for protest. Whoever preferred sex without condom had never seen her long, elegant fingers work one. Just watching her unwrap it made my mouth run dry. It took her a moment to position it on me, but *fuck* when she rolled it down the length of my dick. Her fingers curled around me perfectly, a happy little smile on her lips.

"Cordelia," I huffed, jerking forward into her hand.

She let out a delighted giggle. Way too fucking cute considering all the things I wanted to do to her. "Is this right?" She asked and tapped her thumb against the pulsing head of my cock.

"Yeah, but you're not losing your virginity if you keep playing with me like that." I directed her hand off my cock and kissed her pouting mouth. Using my weight to push her back down on the rug, I lined myself up with her pussy.

She was writhing against me, all warm and wet, letting me slide up and down the length of her slit. The traction had my muscles tightening, ready to pounce. I moaned her name into her mouth and reached down to work her open for me.

"Wait," she gasped out of the kiss, grasping my face in both hands, "I think I changed my mind."

"Shit, okay, hold on." I stilled above her, muscles tense and trembling. "Fuck, give me a second."

"No, I mean, I still want this. Can you do it fast though? Like ripping off a band-aid."

"Are you comparing your hymen to a band-aid?"

"Yes," she giggled, "I think-"

Her words were cut off by a pained squeal when I plunged into her with one hard thrust. Her back arched for the ceiling and her eyes screwed shut.

She was so fucking tight, her inner walls clenched around my dick in a death grip.

"Victor," she gasped.

"I know, baby." I leaned down to kiss her, stifling the whimper she let out at the small shift of my hips. "You've got this."

"Don't move. Can you give me a moment please?" Her voice was so quiet and quivering, I was close to calling it quits. That would require moving though, and I was more focused on staying still.

"Does it hurt?"

"Yeah."

"I'm going to pull out."

"No, wait." She shifted, hands on my shoulders, and shot me a trembling smile before looking down at where our bodies connected. "Okay, go, but not all the way."

She wanted to watch. Fuck, if that didn't send another tremor through my hips. I selfishly wanted to throw her legs over my shoulders and drive into her hard enough to make it worth watching. Instead, I reminded myself that she was probably just curious, so I eased out of her inch by torturous inch.

"Huh." She let out a little surprised sound while her brows moved in that little confused wave usually reserved for Disney princesses.

"What's wrong?"

"Nothing."

"Shitty liar."

Cordelia's lips quivered when I sank back into her, but her eyes remained solely trained on my cock disappearing in her pink pussy. Despite how damn tight her walls gripped me, her insides were soaking wet from our shower, allowing me to burrow deep.

"Oh, snap." She gasped when I hit a tender spot inside her, but her gaze still didn't leave my cock.

"Want me to get you a mirror, so you can see from all angles?" I asked, moving slowly, only half-joking.

"I just didn't think," she huffed and reached a hand between our bodies. Using two fingers to part herself, she revealed an unobstructed view of how exactly my dick fit into her. Holy shit. My next thrust was a quick and hard jerk, caused entirely by that view, and it wrangled a sharp hiss from her throat.

"Didn't think what?" I groaned.

"I didn't think it would feel this right to have you inside me. It's painful, but it doesn't feel wrong at all." She blinked and dropped back onto the rug, her hands wrapping around my shoulders, and her stormy eyes finding mine. "Feels like you belong there."

"Hate to be the one to break it to you, but that's literally what your pussy was made for."

"Very funny."

"I'm not kidding, baby." I grabbed the back of her knee and yanked it up, allowing my next thrust to hit even deeper. Cordelia let out a glorious sound caught between a moan and a cry. "Your cunt takes my cock so well because that's its purpose. You were fucking made for me."

Her lips dropped open, twitching with every blow I delivered, but her eyes narrowed on me as that feisty defiance took hold in her. "If you're that sure of yourself, you better prove it."

"Oh, I think the way your needy little pussy is dripping for me is proof enough."

"That had nothing to do with your dick. You got me wet with your fingers and your tongue, *Vic*." Her new nickname for me earned her another violent thrust, this one hard enough to push her body higher on the rug. She gasped but then pinched her lips together before another sound could come out, glaring at me. "Asshole."

I chuckled. "Careful or I'll have to fuck that attitude out of you."

Cordelia's breathing was growing faster, and her nails dug into my arms. "You can try," she gasped, "but you'll fail."

"You're a fucking bitch when you're horny, Cordelia." I couldn't help but laugh because this was so different from the Cordelia the rest of the world got to see, reserved just for me, and it made me want to fuck her senseless.

I leaned back and yanked her second knee up. With both her legs hooked over my arms, I grabbed hold of her hips and pulled her against me. Her ass came off the floor, and I knelt before her, charging at her like I had a fight to win. She yelped and flinched, and I didn't ease up for a second. "Trying hard enough for you?" I growled.

She couldn't get a word out, her vocabulary reduced to deep, reverberating moans.

When her thighs twitched, I slowed down, repositioning myself above her.

"Don't stop," she gasped.

"Oh, I have no intention of stopping anytime soon," I stole a breathless kiss from her lips, "until I've proven that you're just a needy little whore, desperate to have your cunt filled with cock."

Her walls clenched tight at those words, but she raked her hands through her hair in a tell-tale show of her racing thoughts. I may have gone one step too far.

"Slut," she said, earning herself a puzzled glance from me, "not whore. Whores have sex for money. If anything, I'd be a slut."

Fuck. Me.

"Is that what you are? A desperate slut?" I pulled out and ran the crown of my throbbing cock over her clit. She shuddered under me.

"Well, you've not proven it yet."

I didn't need to be challenged twice before I delved back into her. She was a writhing mess underneath me within minutes, and again I eased up when I felt her legs twitching around me.

Cordelia let out a protesting little moan.

"She sounds like a slut," I whispered as I nipped the sensitive spot beneath her ear, while she caught her breath.

I leaned back, putting as much distance between us as possible without actually pulling out, moving painfully slow. Her hands became frantic, reaching for me, roaming over her chest, finding her clit, and I pressed them deep into the rug above her head.

"She moves like a slut."

Steadying myself with my hands in hers, I picked up my pace again. The tension in my own hips coiled tight, as I chased her to another edge of her climax, only to pull out at the last second.

"Fuck's sake," she groaned, pulling her hands from mine and running her fingers down her reddened, glowing face, "Vic."

"Mouth like a slut," I replied and dipped two fingers past her lips. I delved them deep, and her eyes blew wide as she choked.

Both her hands closed around my wrist. I didn't pull back, locking her chin with my palm, waiting for her to adjust to the fingers down her throat before I unceremoniously shoved my cock back into her. She bucked and squealed, nails digging into my wrist.

Her legs started twitching within a few thrusts and this time, I didn't stop. Spurred on by her muffled sounds and her tongue lapping at my fingers. I fucked her until her body broke out in shivers, until she squirmed and arched, and her tight cunt pulsed around me uncontrollably. Something wet hit me, and my brain took a second longer than my hot-pulsing dick to realize that she just came all over me.

When the orgasm was through with her, I pulled my hand from her mouth and claimed it with mine instead. Her kiss was tired, but my tongue took its fill of her.

"Comes for me like a slut," I groaned against her lips.

My own pace turned erratic; my thrusts turned careless. The tension drawing down my center drove me further and faster and blinded my vision. Until the cord snapped, and I bucked and spilled myself. She gasped, her inner walls tightening again, draining every last drop from me. "Milks my dick like a slut," I huffed and ran my hand over her glowing cheeks, picking sweaty strands of golden hair from her skin.

"Victor."

"Cordelia." I trailed kisses along her jaw, across her cheekbone, up her temple.

"That was…" She trailed off and shook her head.

"Are you still hurting?" I directed her thighs apart with careful fingers, just enough for me to detangle myself, lean back and assess the situation.

"I'm good," she sighed.

Despite her words, a spot of bright red blood tainted her rug. At least she didn't seem to be bleeding anymore. Still. I'd been rough with her. She would have deserved to lose her virginity on a goddamn bed of rose petals, being worshipped.

"Are *you* alright?" she asked.

"Let me go get something to clean up," I said, but before I could detach myself further, Cordelia's hand shot out and caught my wrist. I let myself be pulled back to her. Her nose crinkled as she shook her head at me. I wasn't going anywhere. To drive the point home, she wrapped her legs around my waist again, caging me in.

"What's wrong?"

"You're bleeding, zhizn' moya. Fuck. I'm sorry. I should have been more careful."

"Are you kidding?" She giggled. "It was perfect."

"What?"

"I'm not that fragile. You won't break me by shoving your fingers in my mouth."

"That's not-"

"Do you want to see the porn I watch to get myself off? Because it's not 'sweet lovemaking with my blushing bride' or whatever you might be thinking of." I must have stared a little too hard because she rolled her eyes at me. "Oh, what did I say now? Yes, I watch porn. Is that it?"

"You're so fucking perfect."

She pulled a strand of my hair down. It stretched all the way down into my vision. I'd only let it grow this long because my uncle hated it, but Cordelia playing with it was an even better reason. She used it like she used her own hair while sorting through her thoughts, and I could get addicted to her fingers fidgeting around my scalp.

"Thank you," she whispered finally when her hands slipped from my hair to my neck.

"Anything. Always."

She leaned up to give me a quick kiss, but her eyes remained shut when she sank back to the floor.

"Come on, let's get you in bed."

"What if I want to go again?" She asked without even opening her eyes.

"Not tonight."

I somehow managed to detangle us just enough to lift her into bed, take care of the condom, switch the lights off and climb in next to her. She hummed her '*not quite sure about this*'-hum and fumbled for my hand on her stomach. She repositioned it, pulling it up her body and cupping it around one of her breasts.

"That's better," she whispered.

Fuck, I loved this woman and her weirdly specific mind.

CHAPTER THIRTY-TWO

Cordelia

"WHAT IF I JUST DON'T LET YOU LEAVE?"

Victor had a plane to catch, but part of me couldn't let go. It was the very same part that kept me rooted on his lap, hands stemmed onto his chest to press him into my mattress. The other more logical part of me only made for like 5% - so maybe my hair and my toes.

"Then I'll be dragged out of the house and if I'm not killed, I'll probably have my hands cut off."

I narrowed my eyes at him. "Couldn't think of a nicer way to say that?"

"You told me not to coddle you," he shrugged, "so I'm not."

"Fine," I sighed, "but I don't trust Luka. We need a backup. Maybe I should come with you. I managed Canada. I can do France."

"Why don't you trust Luka?" His brows shot up as if he hadn't been the very person to tell me that I couldn't trust his cousin.

"He betrayed you before when you thought he'd have your back. He told your uncle about you living here with me." Something unspoken passed behind his eyes, there and gone in an instant. "What?"

"Nothing." His expression shut down, locking me out of his thoughts. "We can trust Luka."

"You're keeping things from me again." A startling cold shock ripped through me. It felt like being pushed into the pond outside on an icy day.

He didn't even deny it.

I shuffled backwards to the far end of the bed.

"Tell me," I said.

"I can't." He pushed himself up, his hands ghosting over his chest where mine had just been.

"Why?"

"Because I don't want to hurt you. I *never* want to hurt you."

"I don't want you to hurt me either." My throat tightened as a dozen scenarios threatened to push their way into my thoughts. "If you don't stop keeping things from me, Victor, this will never work. We're partners or we're nothing at all."

"Cordelia, please," he grit out.

"I know you've done horrible things. I know that. Whatever you're keeping from me-"

"It's not something *I* did."

I froze.

"Me?"

"Yes."

"What did I do?" My voice was merely a whisper.

"Zhizn' moya."

"Victor, tell me."

"You're brilliant. You take on so much responsibility." His

placating words did nothing to stop the dread from souring my stomach. "You have big plans and even bigger ideas. And they all come from such a good and pure place. You play by the rules and it's not your fault that there's plenty of people out to exploit that."

"I don't follow."

"You bought me a house for my birthday."

"Because I wanted you to have your own space. I didn't want you to feel suffocated."

"I know. You see? Kindness." He crossed the mattress, hands wrapping around my ankles, thumbs already drawing soothing patterns, when I still didn't follow.

"I bought you a house."

"Yes."

I bought the house next door. No. I bought *him* the house next door.

"It's public record."

"Luka never told his father where I was."

"I did."

"Unintentionally, yes."

There was no electric shock to my nervous system, no exploding pain in my chest. There was nothing at all. My body just ceased to feel. Numb and nonexistent as I realized what I'd done.

I hadn't wanted to stifle him. I'd wanted to keep him in my life so badly that I bought him a house before he could find out that I was too much to be around. I hadn't done that for him. I hadn't done that out of kindness. I'd done that for *me*.

"Cordelia?"

Just like I'd hired Delilah for *me*. So I could stay at home. If I hadn't hired her, if there hadn't been two Cordelias, Julian Beckett wouldn't have tried to kill me.

"Cordelia."

"I caused all of this. First I put Del in danger by making her take on my name, and now you. I did that. I fucked up. If Julian

Beckett- If you had- He could still be alive. He got in over his head with your family, and then I threw him for a loop with Delilah, and he could still be alive. He'd hopefully be in jail, but Brody would still have a father."

"Don't do that. His death is on my hands. Nobody else's. I pulled the trigger."

"Everything I did, every stupid decision I made, led to that moment. I come up with these stupid impulsive things. I cost Brody her father."

"He made the deal with my uncle. He tried to take your father's company away from you. He put himself in danger."

"Your uncle knew you were here because of *me*. Julian wouldn't have- If *I* hadn't-" I couldn't get enough air into my lungs. Couldn't get my tongue to move fast enough to convey everything that needed to come out. "How could I be so stupid? I did that to her. I keep trying to do the right thing, and it's all wrong. Irina, too. I did that. And that man. That man you killed because he threatened me. He wouldn't have threatened me if I hadn't pushed him. I keep doing that. I keep pushing. Everything I do hurts people."

"Cordelia, slow down."

I couldn't. The words kept tumbling. "My mom didn't want to go that day. She had those days when she said her outside batteries were drained, and this was one of them. But I was so excited for my first dress for my first dance. I had stayed up late and I had printed out a map with the exact plan for the day, which dress shops in which order, where we'd get lunch. I made an itinerary with pretty fonts, and I planned our outfits for us, down to the matching white shoes. I made all of those plans and she came with me and she died."

"She was killed. *You* didn't kill her."

I heard his words, but I couldn't stop the train I was on. My thoughts bulleted down the rails. "I keep making impulsive plans and people keep getting hurt. I make all the wrong decisions. I can't do this anymore. I can't- I can't- I can't breathe." I squeezed my eyes shut because it was all too much. Too much light, too much pain, too many mistakes. But all that waited for me behind closed lids was blood. So much blood on the ground. It soaked through my shoes. *Grab the girl, Nick.*

A hand inched up my chin, ready to cover my mouth and fill my nostrils with the scent of leather, but for the first time in my life, I swung my fist at the man.

"Fuck," Victor groaned.

My eyes flew open. Blood. Actual blood. On the bedsheet, dripping from his nose. "I'm sorry. Oh my god. Oh god. I hit you." My voice was a breathless squeak. I hurt him. I'd actually physically hurt him.

"Come here." He stretched one hand out while wiping the blood off with the other.

"No, please. I don't want to hurt you." I inched away from him and sank to the floor. I couldn't even trust myself around him anymore. I'd hurt him. I'd hit him. Oh god.

"Come here, Cordelia." He slid off the mattress and climbed over me, caging my hips in.

"Please Victor, I don't know what's real, please-" He stifled my words with his mouth on mine.

It wasn't slow and it wasn't gentle. Victor took my mouth like he had a claim to stake. Everything zeroed in on that kiss, until my mind was his teeth and his tongue and his taste. His hands were in my hair, around my neck, and grasping at my face, pulling me into him. He consumed every wild and racing thought. And when he finally let me breathe, I was nothing but air and kiss.

"You and me," he rasped, "real."

A sob broke from my chest and Victor kissed me again, more careful this time. He took my hand and, after using his other hand to unbutton his shirt, slid it over his chest. "Do you feel this? This is real. The only reason it's beating is because you hired me. I'd be dead without you."

"You'd be on an island in South Asia, relaxing on the beach."

"I'd be breathing, but I'd be dead, *zhizn' moya*. Do you not hear me telling you again and again? You are my life."

CHAPTER THIRTY-THREE

VICTOR

THE PRIVATE JET REEKED OF CIGAR SMOKE AND THE perfume of the busty ginger in my uncle's lap. God knew where he'd left his wife, but she wasn't coming to Paris. I dropped into a seat as far away from Petya as possible, one that still allowed me to keep an eye on the entire plane.

Three men surrounded my uncle, none of which I knew personally. Yury shuffled in, dragging the same small silver suitcase he'd been logging to all my matches over the years.

I only glanced down at my phone once, just to check if there were any messages. None. It was wrong to leave Cordelia, but it would have been worse to stay. I had to trust Irina and Del to keep her safe for a few days, while Luka and I took care of Petya.

Worse than the bruised nose she'd given me, was the pressure ache in my chest. I shouldn't have told her about the house right before taking off. I shouldn't have told her about the house. Period. I'd thought it was bad when she was shutting down and left her body on autopilot, but that didn't compare to the panic in her eyes. She'd been so scared. And not of anything out there, not of anyone who could harm her, of herself. That was the worst part. I couldn't keep her safe from herself.

The speakers crackled to life when the pilot announced that we were ready for take-off, and I whipped around to see the flight attendant latching the door.

"Where's Luka?" I asked, not directing my question at anyone in particular.

The dread slammed me in the stomach before anyone even responded.

"He's sitting this one out," Petya replied, fondling his plaything's zipper.

Fuck.

I bit my tongue just in time to keep the curse down and keep my face still. I felt his eyes on me. Whether he knew exactly what we had planned or he just thought Luka and I were getting too close, I wasn't going to give him the satisfaction.

Instead, I turned to the window and watched Boston turn into a tiny cluster of lights before clouds overtook the view.

I was screwed.

I didn't have a gun with me. Even if I did, there was no guarantee Petya's men wouldn't put a bullet in my brain milliseconds after I'd shot him. Their loyalty might have just extended to Luka. I was too much of a wildcard.

Shifting my seat back, I closed my eyes as a slow panic crawled through my bones. I needed Cordelia's brilliant scheming mind to make it out of this alive. But if I called her and told her, chances were she'd shut down again. If I didn't make it back from Paris, she'd find a way to blame it on herself. I couldn't keep doing this. I couldn't keep making her life harder just because mine had been fucked up from the start.

I opened my eyes again to take stock of everyone on the plane.

I'd gone into this deal with my uncle prepared to die for Cordelia. Now I had to figure out how to survive for her.

CHAPTER THIRTY-FOUR

Cordelia

"Why is your communications manager calling me of all people? How did she even get my number?" Del stormed into my bedroom, door banging into the dresser behind it. She let out a quiet "Oh." - probably when she realized that I was hiding under my covers with the curtains shut.

"You're my emergency contact," I mumbled, pulling my blanket down just enough to look at her.

"Really? Not Victor?" Del asked as she opened curtains and windows to let in some light and air.

"Well, no. He goes where I go. Usually. So if I was in a car crash, he would have been next to me." I tried keeping her on the sidelines, but Del was in the loop. She knew where Victor was right now.

"She sounded serious," Del sighed and knelt down beside my bed.

"Add failure to run charity foundation to my long list of short-comings." I wasn't entirely sure how many meetings I'd missed over the last few days, but I just didn't have the mental space to deal with all these people and all their emails and all the decisions. Today, I just hadn't logged in at all. Hadn't even gotten out of bed after staying up late until I knew Victor's plane had landed. Not that I would be of much use even if I logged in. No matter what I did, someone always got hurt.

"I'm here to help," Del plucked a few stray strands from my face, "what do you need right now? Just to make it through the next few hours."

"I need..." I needed to get out of bed. I needed for the world to stop for a moment and just let me get my bearings. I needed Victor home, happy and healthy. I needed him to be okay. I needed him safe. "I need to talk to someone."

"I think that's a great idea. Therapy can be-"

"Have you seen Irina? I have to go." I struggled against the mountain of blankets as I sat up.

"Right now?"

"Yes."

"Didn't you say that Irina needs to lie low?"

"Right. You're right." Irina couldn't take me where I needed to go.

"I'll take you. Come on."

"THIS IS WHERE YOU GREW UP?"

"Yeah." My breath lodged in my throat as I got out of the car and let my eyes trail over the house. I hadn't been back here since

I'd moved out, hadn't even come back when my father was dying. I'd let the lawyers take care of everything afterwards.

When we walked in, the furniture was covered in cloth, the walls were bare, and the rooms just smelled faintly of dust. All the paintings and antiques had gone to museums. The rest, I didn't really care for.

"It's huge," Del whispered into the stillness.

"I hate this place," I muttered. It was big enough to completely forget there was a girl living in a room somewhere on the third floor. Old enough to forget the many mothers and daughters that had played in the halls.

"Then why do you keep it?"

"This way." I flipped through my keys while I led her through the house.

It took some force and shoulder strength for the backdoor to spring open and let us outside. The backyard was eerily dead and alive at the same time. The fountain was dry and crumbling, but moss and grass were sprouting through the cracks. The pool house lay dark, and the pool inside empty, but a beehive had formed in the gable. Only a year and nature was reclaiming its space.

"How old is this place?"

"Almost 150 years now," I replied as I led her around the pool house and down a small pebbled path.

"Sometimes I forget that your family is like... old money."

"Gun powder."

"What?"

"Gun powder." I stopped in my tracks and Del almost ran into me, all wide-eyed and in awe of the grounds and the buildings. "My family's fortune goes back to the civil war. Got another good boost in the First World War. Then they turned the image around in the twenties and became hoteliers. But the *old money*? I got that because my ancestors profited from people killing each other. Sure, you can call them merchants, or suppliers, or manufacturers, but my ancestors were *war profiteers*. My father didn't deserve a dime of it, and neither did any of my ancestors." I glanced back at the house, poking into the sky with its steep roofs and many chimneys. "I hope they're rolling over in their graves while I give it all away."

"I had no idea," Del mumbled.

"I *really* hate guns."

"Makes sense."

I sighed and tried to offer her a small smile before I started walking down the path again. It curved around a big old birch tree with leaves lush enough to hide the mausoleum. There were no plants snaking up the marble walls and no insects nesting in its crevices, because this was the one place I'd hired proper maintenance for. The inside was flooded in rainbow light thanks to a spotless stained glass window, and a small potted flower arrangement bloomed right in front of my mom's grave.

"The reason I haven't sold this house," I said and traced the words *'loving mother'* with my fingertips. "I'm selfishly too sentimental."

"I don't think that's selfish, Cordelia," Del said and stepped up beside me, wrapping an arm around my waist. "It's completely normal to be sentimental."

Maybe she was right, but my sentimentality came attached to a couple million dollars worth of real estate. There was no point in starting an argument though, not when Del was just trying to comfort me.

"Could you give me five minutes?" I asked instead.

"Of course. I'll go for a little wander, but I have my phone if you need me."

"Thanks."

I waited until her steps had scrunched up the gravel far enough for her to be out of earshot before I let out a deep sigh and closed my eyes.

"I don't know how this works," I whispered, letting my fingernail catch on the etched grooves of her birthday. "I don't know if you can see me, or hear me, or if you've been reborn and you're a teenager somewhere on the other side of the world. And I know this is just another selfish thing, but I really wish you were here with me."

Memories of this place replayed in my mind. Memories of Mom catching me when I jumped into the pool. Of Mom running down the long hallways and hiding in doorways and alcoves as I ran after her. Mom digging through the soil as she planted an apple tree in the backyard, explaining that our family was very lucky to have inherited this home and it was our responsibility to make sure we left it better than we got it.

The images were interrupted by the echo of a gunshot and I opened my eyes before the blood from that day could stain the good memories.

My gaze flicked to the other date right next to Mom's birthday.

"It's so strange. I see you almost every night, but I've actually spent more of my life without you than with you." I dropped my hand and leaned back against the wall, my eyes roaming over the other graves. Dad's was right next to Mom, and right underneath them was an empty slot, covered by a blank stone. That one had been reserved for me from the day I was born. Another empty one waited beside it, reserved for whoever was dumb enough to tie themselves to me.

"He makes me feel safe, you know? Everything is always chaos. Sometimes it seems like the whole world is going up in flames, but it just keeps on turning. Everyone just keeps going about their lives, as if all of the violence and all of the hate was completely normal, as if it didn't affect them. But I can't ignore it. It's always there. Everything is always there." I tapped my fingers against my forehead. "But he makes it go away, even just for a little bit. I can breathe when he's there."

The air in my lungs trembled up my throat and my eyes

burned, the next words already festering in my mind. But I had to get them out.

I had to tell her.

"I think I have to let him go. Everything I do ends up hurting people. If I hadn't made you come dress shopping with me, you wouldn't be in this place. Victor has gone through so much because of me. He doesn't deserve that. I don't think he realizes how much it's going to cost him if he stays with me. I can't do that to him. I can't keep hurting him."

"You're wrong."

I jumped at the sudden interruption. A large silhouette crowded the doorway, and for a second, the cheekbones, the sharp jawline, I thought maybe... but where Victor wore tattoos on his skin, a long silver scar ran down Luka's neck.

"What are you doing here?"

"Shit, you really need better security, you know?" He leaned back against the doorframe and lit a cigarette.

"You can't smoke in here."

"Fine. I'll smoke *out here*." He huffed blue smoke out into the backyard.

I blinked, but nobody else appeared behind him. There was no logical way they could have landed in Paris, killed Luka's father, and already be back here. That was humanly impossible. Which meant...

"You didn't go to Paris."

"Nope."

"You left Victor alone?" I'd known we couldn't trust him. My stomach lurched because Victor didn't have a backup. And while he was alone in Paris - I was alone in a small crypt, and Luka was blocking the only way out.

"My father told me to stay. I could only push back a little without him getting too suspicious, but it looks like that was for the best." Luka took another drag and grimaced. "There may or may not be two dead Russians in your driveway."

"What?"

"You didn't think my Dad would just let you play your little social media games without trying to retaliate, did you? Victor's about to be useless to him, so you were fair game."

I blinked. "You killed your father's men to protect me?"

"Yup." He sighed and waved for me to follow him when he hopped down the stairs of the mausoleum. "Let's find your friend before she spots the bodies, and then it's time you learned the truth about Victor."

CHAPTER THIRTY-FIVE

VICTOR

Petya had confiscated my phone the second the airplane had touched ground, but this was too far. His whole entourage had herded me into the hotel room but fuck this. He could lock me in this room for all I cared, but sharing it with my trainer like I was a teenager on a field trip?

"Money running out?" I raised my brows at the second bed in the room. Yury threw his suitcase on it, and didn't heed me any attention as he started his whole hotel routine. Apparently that hadn't changed over the years. *Fresh shave, fresh breath, fresh socks.* "Or do I need a babysitter?"

"You have a tendency to run off, son." Petya stepped aside to let Yury disappear in the bathroom.

"Where would I run? We're in France, for fuck's sake."

I hated that my frustration was showing, and I hated how Petya smirked and shrugged. "I'm not taking the risk."

"What are we doing in Paris? What am *I* doing in Paris?"

"Vitya, you are irrelevant."

"What?"

My uncle's dark eyes dropped to Yury's silver suitcase, opened on the bed, then shifted to the bathroom.

I stayed still. The faucet was still running but there was no other noise, no break in the water stream.

Before I even had the chance to go for the bathroom door, two of my uncle's men shouldered their way past him with two large UFC duffels. In a perfect fucking world full of butterflies and rainbows, I wouldn't have clocked it immediately. But I'd grown up with this. Two duffels, because Yury's body wouldn't fit in one.

Fuck.

"What the hell did he do?" And why the fuck did they have to get rid of him in Paris?

Just as I mentally prepared myself for cleaning up Yury's blood for the rest of the night, the door to the connected room opened and Yury walked in. Which made no fucking sense. Yury had gone to the bathroom.

"Zdraviya zhelaju." Yury saluted my uncle. Except it wasn't Yury. The voice didn't match. Same height, same built, same face with the groove down the chin.

"Victor, Yury. Yury, Victor," Petya chuckled, clearly pleased with his showmanship.

He'd switched them.

"I don't even want to know who you are," I told the man who had obviously undergone enough surgery to look like my trainer of twenty years.

"Did you ever look at Yury's eyes, son?" Petya asked, and I hated myself for checking the *new* Yury's eyes. Blue, except for a patch of dark brown in his left eye. I'd seen the same eyes a million times. It had freaked me out the first time I'd seen them as a kid,

313

because it had looked like Yury's pupil was leaking into his iris. I hadn't thought about them in years.

The pieces clicked together in time with the unmistakable chop of a butcher's knife in the bathroom.

Just like that, twenty years of loyalty to my uncle had become replaceable. Yury became nothing but a couple dismembered body parts about to be scattered in the Seine. Because he was a genetic rarity, and someone just as genetically rare had enough money to pay for a new identity and a new life.

My mask must have slipped again because Petya started grinning from ear to ear.

"You and Luka always think you're more important than you are, like the main character in an action movie." He shook his head. "But I have to thank your little girlfriend for the idea. Switching places with someone who looks like her? Genius."

"So you don't even need me to fight. You just needed to trick Yury into coming to Europe."

"Eh." He pulled his shoulders up. "You fight Silver, I don't have to worry about making sure you keep your mouth shut. He'll put you in the ground for me. Like I said, you have a bad habit of running off."

"Well, we both know that you don't like people running off."

Petya clicked his tongue. "Still sulking over your dead parents like you're a little boy. Your father would be ashamed."

"My parents tried to leave. I doubt my father would be ashamed that I tried to do the same."

"Grow up," he snarled, "I got rid of your father because he tried to kill me and take my place. At least he had ambitions. You're just going to die like a coward."

Cordelia

"Guys, you do realize I'm on your side, right?" Luka leaned back in his chair and crossed his arms over his chest.

"Don't look at me. There's a million places I'd rather be." Irina threw up her hands but she didn't leave the kitchen. I wasn't quite sure whether she stayed for my protection or for Luka's, but she was also the only person not sitting down. She was ready to pounce if need be.

"It's fine," Del reassured him, "we're just here to listen. Tell him we're just here to listen." She nudged Beck in the side, and he scowled.

"Depends on what he has to say," Beck replied dryly. His eyes were trained on Luka, but his arm was draped over Del's lap.

"Well, first of all, I really just need to talk to her," Luka quipped and pointed two finger guns at me, "so this isn't any of your business. No offense."

"You made it my business," Beck answered and tilted his chin in a quiet challenge. "Your father's men were on the Montgomery estate while my fiancée was there. That means your family feud is putting my family at risk."

Another pang of guilt shot through my gut. I hadn't even thought that part through. The men who had been sent after me could have easily mistaken Del to be their target. My actions had put her at risk. Again.

"Anyway," Luka huffed and turned to me, "as I said before, you're wrong. My father isn't putting Victor through all this crap because of you. I mean, shit, *you're* not even going through all this crap because of you."

"Don't tell me it's all your father's fault. Victor tried that already."

"No, actually," he ran a hand over the scar on his neck, "this all goes way back to my uncle, Victor's father. He married my dad's little sister to be a proper part of the family, but he was my dad's best friend way before that. The two of them were like brothers. Until the day uncle Nikolai decided he would be the better boss. He planned a whole coup. Just needed the funds to flip a few business partners, and get the right people to turn a blind eye when he'd shoot my dad."

"Victor's dad tried to overthrow your dad?"

"He never got that far." Luka's body stilled and his gaze remained zeroed in on me. "Nikolai needed twenty million. Turns out, you weren't worth that much to your dad."

Grab the girl, Nick.

"You know better than anyone that your kidnapping was a fucking disaster. Killing your mother turned up the heat on Nikolai and his right hand man. Then your dad negotiated for days. By the time Nikolai got the four million, my father had already gotten wind of everything."

"Victor told me your father killed his parents because they tried to leave."

"They did. Four million would have been enough to run." Luka glanced up at the ceiling. "And he didn't kill them. He had them killed. Important distinction. Just in case you're filming this."

"What? No. The cameras were only here for- Never mind." I raised my hands to press my fingernails into my cheeks, just to stay focused, but before I made it that far, an orange landed in my palms. I glanced up at Irina who just shrugged. I dug my fingernails into the fruit's thick skin instead. "Victor doesn't know any of this, does he?"

"No. He was in Vegas the week you got kidnapped. His trainer took him to some big fight night. With him out of town, it was the perfect chance for Nikolai to act without Victor being a liability. And after it was over, it was easier for my dad to keep Victor in check as long as he thought his parents were killed just for running, not for fucking mutiny."

"And you?"

"I was fourteen at the time. Young enough to worship the ground beneath my father's feet. Not old enough to legally drive. Certainly not old enough to be sentenced if I accidentally ran my uncle's car off the road."

"You killed Vitya's parents?" Irina gasped.

"I did."

"Dad had you kill his own sister?"

Silence unfolded in the kitchen as we all sat with the truth.

"You've been trying to make up for it for years." I set the orange down and brushed my sticky hands off on my skirt. "Six years ago, you sent Victor here to hide. You arranged for him to leave the country, but he stayed with me. And at Irina's excommunication, you heard what he called me. That's why you agreed to kill your father."

"Not just him. My family owes you, too. I figured if Victor worked security for the girl his father once kidnapped, that would somehow cancel out a small percentage of the debt."

"I need to…" I couldn't breathe. My throat was being wired shut. "I need… I need…"

"You need to go Paris," Irina said, "before Dad figures out what Luka did today. It's going to be history repeating itself."

"I can't."

"Just live stream the whole thing," Irina said.

"I can have the jet ready in an hour," Beck offered.

"No, no, I can't. Every single time I try to help, things go wrong. I *literally* can't. People die wherever I go."

"Have you not been listening?" Irina grunted. "Our fathers - yours, mine, Victor's - they set up the game board for us years ago.

God, I'm so tired of this. It's time we wipe their pieces off the board."

"She's right," Del whispered and reached over to squeeze my hand, "you and Victor got caught up in a fight that has nothing to do with you. I mean, have you ever killed someone?"

"What? No. Of course not."

"Have you ever given the order to kill someone?"

"No."

"Okay. Have you willfully made decisions *knowing* they would get someone killed?"

"No, but they still-"

"You're not a butterfly causing a tornado." Del shook her head. "Free will is a thing. People make decisions that have nothing to do with you. Last year, when Julian tried to take over your dad's company by force, that was his choice. He decided to hurt you and me. That decision cost him his life. You *personally* had nothing to do with that. In fact, we're pretty sure he's hurt someone else before." She bit her lip and looked over her shoulder at Beck. He nodded without taking his eyes off her. "He got away with it once, so he decided to try again. This time, Victor just stopped him before it could end badly for either one of us. Julian's the one who chose violence. Not you."

"So what? I just have really bad luck?"

"Well, you were born with a big fat diamond spoon in your mouth," Irina grabbed the orange and stated peeling it, "so that kinda stacked the odds against you as a target for violent extortion."

"I don't know if I can do this," I whispered, "I don't even know what to do."

"I'm coming with you," Irina said, "I did promise Victor that I'd look after you, and I've always wanted to see the Sistine Chapel."

"Dude, that's not Paris," Luka muttered.

"What's the Paris one?"

"Notre-Dame, but that burned down. Like, you can't go."

"It burned down? What? When?"

"Guys, please." I was about to say something unkind when Luka smirked and nodded at me. Oh, *they were good.* My chest tightened as I finally understood how Victor and his cousins had survived all those years. "We're not going sightseeing in Paris."

CHAPTER THIRTY-SIX

VICTOR

MY UNCLE KEPT MY PHONE UNDER LOCK AND KEY, AND I didn't get a second unsupervised. Even when I went to the goddamn bathroom in the hotel restaurant, one of Petya's men stood outside the stall. Whatever it took to keep his 6-foot-tall Russian secret.

New Yury kept quiet. He didn't speak. He showed up wherever Old Yury would have been expected to go. His posture was slightly off, but he'd clearly studied Old Yury because his gait matched almost to a tee. Former military, I assumed. Maybe politics if he couldn't just disappear on a fake passport.

I wouldn't have particularly cared - but New Yury's existence meant I didn't have Old Yury to get me ready for the fight. Even if he'd been a link in my uncle's chain around my neck, Old Yury had been my trainer all my life. He knew how to get me through fight nights alive. That was probably why Petya had made the switch the second we'd arrived. My chance of making it through had slimmed considerably without my trainer.

He was hoping Emanuel Silver would kill me.

I zoned out through most of the pre-fight press conference. I was racking my brain for the next time I'd get two minutes alone with my uncle. I wouldn't need more than that to get close enough to break his neck without earning myself a bullet in the brain.

I'd been scared of running away from him for half my life. He'd kept me on a leash with a lie, perfectly delivered with two urns. That sick bastard had wanted me under his control by any means necessary.

Maybe it was purely practical, or maybe he'd been scared that I'd follow in my father's footsteps and could actually pull off the coup.

I glanced down at the ink needled into the back of my hands, reminding me of how I fought tooth and nail to feel like I had any semblance of control over my own life. My attention didn't snap back to the press room until the moderator announced the next question was for me. My gaze met Silas Whitaker's. For once, he wasn't holding a huge camera but his phone was angled at me. It was stupid but my eyes immediately roamed the room for a head of blonde hair. Of course she wasn't here.

"I'm following a story from a few months ago," he announced to the whole room as if the people here didn't know exactly whose footage had put Cordelia and me on the map.

I noticed a shuffle from the corner of my eye. No doubt Petya was about to cut off the conference.

I leaned into the mic before anyone could interrupt. "I'm assuming this has nothing to do with how I'm about to kick Silver's ass, and everything to do with Cordelia Montgomery."

My reply got a few chuckles from the reporters but everyone was waiting for Silas' actual question.

"Are the rumors true that Cordelia's pregnant? Is that the reason she couldn't be here tonight?"

What the actual fuck? Pregnant? I'd never been more grateful for the ability to keep my face still.

The rest of the room wasn't as good at that. Pens scratched on paper, cameras flashed to capture this moment. People were taking note. People were interested in my answer.

This wasn't Silas asking.

This was Cordelia giving me a chance to speak.

I could take back the narrative.

My eyes found the big official online stream camera with its flashing red light.

"There are so many rumors out there, Silas. I heard one that involved you, me, Cordelia and a hot tub. There's even a rumor that my uncle is involved in human trafficking and that he keeps using my team to smuggle criminals out of Russia. Did you hear that one?" Something clattered just behind the stage but I didn't turn. "Just today I heard a rumor that he replaced my trainer Yury with an almost identical looking man, but he's standing right there, so you judge for yourself. Apparently you can tell by the ears. Ear shapes are almost as unique as fingerprints." There were some angry Russian curses being flung my way. But I was live on the internet. If he put a bullet in me. he'd not get away with it. Cordelia had fearlessly wielded the public eye for months. It was my time to brave whatever consequences doing the right thing would get me.

"All I can say is that most rumors hold a kernel of truth, just not the hot tub ones. So I have no Intention of letting Silver get to me tonight, and I have no intention of ever fighting again *after* tonight. I'll focus on staying healthy enough to be with my fiancé and my family."

Some more cameras flashed, and reporters leaned into each other, chattering. I hoped that was enough. Announcing my retirement during my comeback year, insinuating that Cordelia and I had a family together... That had to get enough eyes on this.

I stepped of the stage and out of sight of the cameras and reporters. Some official with a clipboard was yapping about where to go and pointing each of us to our locker rooms. A hand clamped around my arm before I reached the clipboard lady.

My uncle's nostrils flared as he yanked me to the side. He wasn't even strong enough for that, but the three men behind him, plus New Yury, didn't exactly leave me much choice.

"If Silver doesn't put you in the ground tonight, I'll make it look like he did," Petya hissed.

"Okay."

"If your father could see you," he spat, as if he wasn't the very reason that my father couldn't see me right now.

"This way please, Mr. Yelchin, we're on a tight schedule," the woman with the clipboard called out.

I bared my teeth at my uncle and yanked my arm free. "If Silver doesn't put me in the ground tonight, you'll end up wishing he did."

I had about three hours before I was expected in the octagon. I'd never prayed a day in my life, but as I walked down the arena hallways to my locker room, I sent a plea to any deity listening that three hours were enough for Silas Whitaker to publish the interview video, and get law enforcement down here.

CHAPTER THIRTY-SEVEN

Cordelia

"I'M AS SAFE HERE AS I WOULD BE AT HOME. I'M AS SAFE here as I would be at home. I'm as safe here as I would be at home," I whispered my new mantra over and over and over again. If Irina or Luka were tired of hearing it for the last ten hours - intermittent only by the sleeping pills I took on the plane - they didn't show it.

I knew I was lying to myself but even the repetition of those ten words helped a little. If only to stay present enough to voice them, present enough to get to Victor.

"See?" Luka huffed. "Told you it burned down."

"Oh yeah," Irina quipped, "that's some shitty scaffolding though. You'd think they'd make it prettier for this kind of monument, right?"

My eyes flicked up to Notre Dame on the other side of the

river, illuminated by street lamps and the flashing red lights on the construction cranes. Catastrophic images of flames and dark plumes slithered into my mind like smoke, and I immediately pulled my gaze back to the fraying end of my braid. I wrapped blonde strands around my finger until my skin turned bright red. "I'm as safe here as I would be at home. I'm as safe here as I would be at home."

Our car stopped across the street from the Accord Arena. I'd studied the building's plans online, but from here, it just looked like a strangely geometric hill of grass. Way too serene for the bloodshed about to happen inside.

"Get out," Irina barked at Luka.

"Seriously?"

She kicked his shin in response, and only turned to me when he was out on the sidewalk. "You have sixty seconds to ramble or cry or throw up, because once we walk through those doors, you need to be switched on, got it?"

I nodded and took a shaky breath.

"Got it," I whispered.

"Okay, go." Irina grabbed my bag and pulled out hairbrush and makeup before getting to unraveling my braid.

I wasn't sure what she expected from me. It wasn't like I could flip a switch and go through a quick sixty second panic attack and then feel magically better. The panic was always there. Just beneath the surface.

I could, however, watch Luka light a cigarette and scratch the scar on his neck, and remind myself that our fathers had sent us down an impossible path. His. Mine. Victor's. This wasn't about me, and everything that their actions had put me through. This was about *us*. We deserved better than this. All of us.

"Done." Irina capped the lipgloss she'd just put on me and tossed it back into my purse. "Let's go."

I wordlessly got out and let Irina fix my dress, tug the silky purple bow at its front into place, and press my overstuffed ruffly pink bag into my lace-gloved hands. She and Luka had agreed that I had to look as girly as possible if I wanted to get us in the same room with their father. So I was all boob and lace and pastel tonight.

The two of them got us into the building and backstage and I just concentrated on staying upright in my heels. We didn't stop until we were around the corner of a long hallway at the top of the arena. The VIP suite wasn't hard to spot. No other door had three security guards positioned outside.

"This is as far as I go," Irina said and waved her branded hand through the air.

"Thank you," I sighed, "go find Victor. We've got this."

"Good luck," she said before taking a door that very clearly said *Staff Only.*

Once the door fell shut behind her, Luka placed a hand on my shoulder and nodded once for reassurance. "Here we fucking go."

"We've got this," I repeated. If only to make myself believe it a little more. If only because speaking the words out loud kept me rooted in the moment enough to pay attention as we walked down the hallway. I bit my lip and stared at my feet and hoped that was enough to look small and vulnerable.

"You're not supposed to be here," one of the security guards said when we stopped at the VIP suite, and Luka's hand stiffened on my shoulder.

"Yeah, I've never been much good at doing what I'm supposed to do," Luka chuckled.

"What's she doing here?" one of the other guards asked. No beating around the bush with these guys.

"I know Dad's pissed at me, okay? It's why I brought a little present. Get myself back into his good graces."

"A little present?" I let my head snap up. "Is that what you call kidnapping me?"

"Will you shut up about the kidnapping already? *Fuck me.*"

"No, thank you."

"Yeah, we'll see about that later. I can think of a dozen ways to keep your mouth busy," Luka bit back in a tone that actually made me flinch. No acting chops required.

I almost believed him. The guards definitely believed him. They all chuckled. The guy in front of us raked his eyes over my naked legs before he stepped away from the door. Luka's hand was steel around my arm as he pulled me through, hard and fast enough to make me stumble in these damn heels. If it hadn't been for his grip, I would have face-planted on the gleaming wood floors in the VIP suite. This way, I could get a good look at the large windows on one end of the room, overlooking the arena, the bar lining the corner, and the bright and modern seating area on the other side of the room.

When I got to that seating area, my steps actually faltered and Luka groaned as he kept me upright.

"Silas." The man slumped back over a chair looked almost nothing like Silas. Half his face was bloodied and swollen, his usually perfectly-styled hair hung limp, and even the camera on the floor had come apart in a thousand shards. If I hadn't spent a whole week with him, I might not have recognized him.

Silas Whittaker groaned and blinked, clearly trying to focus on me.

"What are you doing here?" I hissed.

"Following the story."

Fuck. I hadn't planned on him being here. I hadn't planned on him getting himself beaten up. For what story, exactly? This? Me? Victor?

"Explain yourself," Piotr Yelchin didn't bother with faux niceties this time as he pushed himself off the bar, rolling his wrist to swirl ice cubes around in his drink. He was in a gray pinstripe suit and shiny grey leather shoes.

Another man stood at the bar - short gray hair and striking blue eyes - and I recognized him from countless videos. But Yury,

Victor's trainer, should have been with him. He should be preparing Victor for a fight, not sipping drinks with Petya.

Luka offered his father the same story he'd told the guards at the door.

Beyond the windows, the arena roared, illuminated by spotlights and phone cameras flashing. Two women were laying into each other in the octagon. When I tugged in that direction, Luka let me go. I flattened a palm against the glass panes. Even if the cold barely sank through my thick lace gloves, I could still *feel* the arena. It trembled like a frenzied heartbeat. Wherever Victor was, wherever he was feeling this tremor coursing through the arena, I hoped Irina got to him. I needed her to get to him.

"Well, what the hell am I supposed to do with her, huh? You never think twice, do you? Fucking moron."

I saw Luka's eyes twitch in the reflection of the glass. I turned back around just as he pulled a gun from beneath his jacket. It was wrapped in a plastic bag.

"This has Vitya's fingerprints all over it. We can make it look like a murder suicide. You already have the guy who's been lurking around her house. Might as well throw him into the mix, too. Tragic love affair and all that."

"Oh, that's fucking great," Silas chuckled, then groaned and readjusted his position. We had to get him to a hospital.

"Alright, maybe not such a moron." Petya clicked his tongue and sipped his drink, regarding me over the rim of his glass. "You don't want to run away screaming, Barbie?"

"I'm wearing heels too high to run and the fight is too loud for anyone to hear my screams."

"Smart girl," he chuckled.

"Smart enough to propose a deal."

"A deal?" He laughed and sauntered over, swirling those damn ice cubes in his drink. "You're in no position to offer me a deal."

"If that's what it takes to stay alive." I swallowed and forced myself to meet his cold eyes. "Last I checked, you lost a supplier.

Lev? The last man who threatened me and wound up dead." I shot a glance at Luka that hopefully looked menacing enough. "He was one of the men who delivered you girls to work in your brothels, right? He said your other *suppliers* weren't half as good as him."

"Did he?" Petya raised his brows at me.

That wasn't enough. I needed confirmation. I needed him to say it. I glanced down at my big bow and all my ruffles, before popping my glossed lips at Petya. "Uh-huh, like, that's literally what he said. He could have been, like, totally lying. I kinda don't think so though."

His icy eyes dropped to my mouth. Pink and pouty and perfectly underestimateable. "He did always bring in the prettiest girls."

Yes. Exactly. I needed more of that.

"Well, if you're looking for hookers..."

"Are you offering?"

"Very funny. Do you want some or not?"

I needed him to spell it out. Say it. If he just said the words, we'd have him.

"Alexei has been struggling to get good meat," Petya said, and my stomach coiled tight at these girls being described as meat. "Do you have connections to Russia that I should know about, Miss Montgomery?"

"I have a country-wide organization that deals with thousands of young women in desperate need of jobs."

"Cordelia, stop," Silas muttered from the other side of the room.

"Stay out of this, Whitaker," I hissed, because I just needed Victor's uncle to say something incriminating. Something we could use against him.

"Piotr," the man by the bar straightened and nodded at the window.

Behind me, the crowd roared and bright lights flashed into the

VIP suite. There was only one reason Piotr Yelchin should look out these windows right now, and it chased goosebumps up my neck.

I turned to see Victor cutting his path down the crowd, clad in his shorts and a sports jacket. He didn't look up, didn't perform for the camera, didn't high-five the audience, like I'd seen him do in some older fight videos. No idea who those people surrounding him were, but none of them were Irina. She hadn't gotten to him. He didn't know I was here. He didn't know that he didn't have to fight.

"No, no, no," I muttered, hands wrapping around the straps of my bag until my knuckles turned white. "No, he can't fight. He'll die." Panic seeped through every word. "Silver's too fast. He'll die. Where's Irina? She was-"

"Irina?" Piotr's voice could have cut glass. "You brought your sister?"

My breathing stilled.

I'd fucked up.

I whirled around and somehow everything happened all at once. Luka tore the gun from the plastic bag. His father pulled his own piece from inside his suit. And in the corner, Victor's trainer sprang into motion. Within a split-second, my mind showed me how the next moments would play out in perfect slow motion. Luka pointing the gun at his father and firing, being tackled from behind, bullet missing its target. His own father would shoot him. None of us would walk out of here.

I'd fucked up.

For once, I didn't think, and I didn't hesitate. I just *knew* what had to happen. My body *knew* what to do. My hand was in my bag, curled around cold metal and pink rhinestones, and my thumb flicked the safety off before I'd even pointed the gun. I didn't even pause to take aim. I fired.

My arm jerked around the kick back of the gun, and the shot echoed in my ears.

But for a moment, nothing happened. Nobody paused. Luka aimed for his father, and his father aimed for him, and Yury was halfway across the room.

And then Piotr Yelchin dropped to the ground.

"Hide your gun, Cordelia," Luka hissed and swung his arm around. With the barrel of Luka's gun pointed straight at his head, Yury stopped dead in his tracks.

Piotr Yelchin lay still. Perfectly, unbreathingly still. And dark crimson blood pooled fast from the hole in his neck. Not crimson. I mentally flipped through the catalog of colors I'd been painting with. Perylene maroon. Piotr Yelchin bled perylene maroon from his arteries.

"Cordelia, put it the fuck away. Now."

Something about Luka's tone got through enough to let my hand drop back into my bag - just in time for the door to burst open. The three security guards had their own guns drawn. All of them immediately zeroed in on Luka.

Furious Russian was exchanged. It didn't matter though because the crowd behind me was making the window at my back tremble.

"I have to go," I muttered. Nobody looked at me. I glanced between Silas and Luka and Piotr's body. Logically, I knew how much blood a human contained. I'd never seen someone bleed out though. The maroon pool was growing, inches from my feet. "I have to go."

When still nobody looked at me, I took a step, only for the damn heels to wobble. Or maybe it was my legs. My knees seemed to tremble like loose flower petals on a windy day. I kicked off the stupid shoes and they landed in the puddle of blood with a splash. Perylene maroon spatters on opera pink vinyl. I could file that away as another image of shoes to haunt me. For now, I had to get out of here.

"I'm going to get Victor," I said to nobody in particular as I inched towards the door and the three men with guns.

"Let her go," Luka said, probably in English for my benefit.

Two of the men kept their handguns pointed at Luka, but the third one, the one closest to me, lowered his arms and stepped aside. He'd listened to Luka's command.

Kill the boss, become the boss, as long as it stays in the family. That's what Victor had told me.

I shot one last look back at Luka, feet planted in the gleaming red lake of his own father's blood, before I ran. My socked feet pounded into the ground as I sprinted down the corridor. Shadows lurked around the corners of my vision, but I grit my teeth and focused on the pain in my wrist from shooting a gun, on the twisting ache in my stomach from killing a man, on the throbbing in my ankles because I'd worn high heels to a gun fight. I focused on the hurt to stay present as I barreled past some redheaded woman carrying a big bucket of popcorn out the elevator. The popcorn sprayed through the air and she yelled at me, but I was in the elevator and I pressed the button for the arena floor often and hard until the elevator doors finally fucking closed.

Piotr Yelchin was dead and Victor didn't have to fight.

His uncle was dead and I could take him home.

He was free and he didn't know it.

And those red numbers on the elevator didn't change fast enough.

I paced the elevator because I had to keep moving, running my hands through my hair, and muttering the next steps to myself. "Out the elevator, to the right. Second door. Out the elevator, to the right. Second door."

As soon as the little bell rang and the doors slid open, I sprinted out, sharp right turn, second door. And I froze.

People. The arena was filled with hundreds if not thousands of people. I stood at the side exit of block B, with roaring stands to either side of me, dozens upon dozens of rows filled with individual people. It was one thing to hear a crowd, but these were actual... this was a whole arena full of... and it was in Paris and...

"Keep walking." A hand wrapped around mine and tugged me forward. I looked down at Irina's burnt skin. "Don't look at them. Look at me." I did and once my eyes found hers, the next few steps were a little easier. "I didn't make it in time. I'm sorry. It's a maze back there. It's good that you're here, because that means we're going to stop the fight, okay? We'll tell them it's a family emergency. Just stay that pale."

"Irina, I can't. There's too many- we're outside. It's loud. It's so loud. And there's lights. I can't."

"Look at me."

I wanted to, but I couldn't, because she tugged me a few more feet forward and then there was the octagon. Just like when he kissed me, everything besides Victor fell away. He was all ink and muscle, and he was moving fast to keep up with Silver's fists.

Victor's biggest strength in the ring was that he knew he could take a beating. He never flinched. He was never nervous even when it looked like his opponent was leading the scoreboard. He stayed upright through hits that would take other fighters down. He outlasted, and then he struck.

The problem was that Emanuel Silver hit twice if not three times as fast as other fighters. Which meant outlasting him was twice if not three times as dangerous for a man with a ticking time bomb in his skull. And Victor already sported a bleeding cut on his forehead.

"He's tired," I mumbled, not sure if Irina heard me over the roar of the crowd. Not sure if it mattered that I could see the slope in his right shoulder being off by half an inch.

"...family emergency. Do you know who this is?" Irina was yelling at some guy with the official UFC logo on his shirt. I hadn't even noticed that she'd started talking to him. But looking at him, meant looking at the other men in the same uniform behind him, and there were too many, and that meant we were outside, where there were people - and I flicked my eyes back to Victor.

Everything else fell away again, and I watched Victor lead Emanuel in circles through hit after hit. That was good. If he kept their feet moving, Emanuel would tire faster without actually doing damage. Something else was off, beyond the angle of Victor's shoulder. I narrowed my eyes at the two men, covered in sweat and blood.

"Cordelia, walk!" Irina yanked on my arm and I stumbled forward, being pulled off to one corner of the Octagon. She started yelling at someone else, but I watched Victor keep his arms up to block any hits flying at his head. He was trying to keep himself safe. He was trying to stay alive. Silver was trying to win, one fist after the other.

"He's not using his legs."

"Are you listening? It's the last round. They're not stopping."

I blinked at Irina and at the big clock behind her telling me that this would go on another four excruciating minutes. Four minutes in which one bad hit could take Victor out.

"Victor isn't letting a single hit through, but his lower half is wide open," I said, "Silver's not even trying to land a kick."

"What?" Irina grimaced.

She wasn't watching and she wasn't thinking fast enough. I twisted my wrist from her grip and beelined for Victor's side of the octagon. A cameraman swung around and I barely dodged his equipment. My socks stuck to some spilled drink on the floor. But I kept my eyes on Victor. Because Emanuel Silver *wasn't* fighting like he was trying to win. He was fighting like he was trying to stay on his feet.

"Kneecaps!" I started yelling when I was two corners away. "Kneecaps!"

Victor's body slammed into the corner post. I ducked under the arm of some guy trying to herd me back.

"Victor, the kneecaps!"

Someone's hand wrapped around my arm, and another memory of being grabbed threatened to well up. I whipped my hair back, and the man behind me spluttered at the blonde whip. Surprised just enough for me to wrestle free and close the last few feet.

"Kneecaps, *Montgomery*, kneecaps!"

I saw the exact moment he heard me. His right shoulder lifted that half inch. He was back in the fight. One beat later, Victor dropped low, and cross-jabbed Emanuel Silver in the knees. Left, then right, and the whole man collapsed like a Jenga tower.

Victor was on him in a split-second, knees, fists, elbows. Silver tried to twist out, but Victor shoulder-barreled his face into the floor. Emanuel grunted, face turning red, and he gave one last shove before the air spluttered from his lungs.

Three little finger taps and it was over.

The referee pushed Victor back.

People flooded the octagon and Victor shoved all of them away, twisting, eyes searching, until they found me. A perfect, secret, small Victor-smile stole its way onto his lips as he started towards my side of the cage. And then he stopped moving. His fall wasn't like Silver's, all momentum and pain. Victor's entire body went slack as if someone had flipped a switch. He dropped. Lifeless. Blood trickling from the cut on his brow.

One hit in the head. That's all it would take.

CHAPTER THIRTY-EIGHT

VICTOR

Whoever claimed dying was peaceful was a fucking liar. It was being poked and prodded. It was sirens. It was people screaming. Dying was pain. It was your muscles burning and your bones splintering while you were stuck in darkness. Or maybe that was already purgatory, because the burn ended, and then everything fell silent.

You didn't get to see life flash by one last time.

Your brain didn't trick you into thinking your loved ones were waiting in the light. Nobody was waiting for you when you died. Nobody went through it with you.

Dying meant leaving her behind.

Dying sucked.

CHAPTER THIRTY-NINE

VICTOR

Living smelled like coconut and oranges. Living smelled like Cordelia. It felt like her, too. Like her fingertips tracing patterns across my skin, like her lips pressed against my mouth, and her hair tickling my collar bone as her body curved around mine.

Living was fucking perfect.

"Victor?" Cordelia's breathing trembled.

I blinked against the bright light and blurry shapes. My eyes didn't focus. Cordelia was next to me, but only in streaks of colors. Outlined by the glow of a window, golden hair like a halo around her form.

"Zhizn-" My voice crumbled like old stone.

"It's okay, don't speak. Your throat might be sore from the intubation."

Her fingers brushed over my cheek and I jerked back. I hadn't seen her touch coming.

"Sorry, sorry, are you in pain?" She fumbled around beside me, but I couldn't make out what she was holding. "I'll call the nurse."

"I..." I swallowed against the burn in my throat. Intubation. Nurse. They'd gotten me to a hospital. Cordelia was at the hospital. I had ended the fight and I'd gone down anyway, and Cordelia was at the hospital where I had been intubated, and she was calling a nurse, and I couldn't see her. I couldn't make sure she was okay. I couldn't-

"Calm down. Breathe," Cordelia whispered, barely audible over some incessant beeping. "You need to calm down, Victor. You're alright. You're alright, I promise. And I'm fine. I'm not hurt."

"I can't-"

"Ah, I see Mr. Montgomery has woken up, yes? That's very good. Beautiful." A woman with a thick French accent said, but I couldn't make out her shape, her bright orange hair and blue clothes, until she stood right next to Cordelia's shape. "Mr. Montgomery, can you understand me?"

Mister Montgomery?

Cordelia squeezed my hand.

"Yes," I rasped.

"Perfect. Can you tell me how many fingers I'm holding up?" She raised her hand. I saw that much. There were shadows. Shapes. Maybe a ring glinting in the light. Three fingers. Four. Or maybe all of them. "Can you count them for me?"

Cordelia squeezed my hand again when I didn't reply.

"I can't see."

"Okay. No need to worry. I will get the doctor."

Cordelia waited until the nurse was gone before she spoke. "I'm sorry. I told them you're my husband. Otherwise they wouldn't have let me stay. They wouldn't have given me any information. I couldn't let you get brain surgery and wait in some hotel nearby. So you're Mr. Montgomery now. If it makes you feel any better, even the Parisians know my family by name, so everyone's been giving you the very best of care. I bet you'll even get the red jell-o, not the green one."

She was rambling. I tried to follow her train of thought, but my own mind was still sluggish.

"Just tell me," I rasped.

"It was a brain bleed. A fairly minor one, thankfully. They got you out of that arena and into surgery so fast. But it still damaged your visual cortex."

The arena. She'd been there. "You're in Paris."

"I told you. I'll always come for you."

"Petya? The press conference?"

"He's dead. Your uncle's gone for good." Her hand slid up my arm and onto my chest. "And Yury, or whatever his actual name is, is in custody for assaulting Silas Whittaker, and because it turns out, ears are sort of like fingerprints, huh? Makes it easier to catch internationally wanted criminals."

I could barely make out the shape of her pink lips, but I heard the relieved smile in her voice.

"Learned that from one of your documentaries."

"You spoke up. You found out what was going on, and you used the dozen of cameras trained on you. You spoke up against your uncle." Her fingertips feathered over my temple. "I'm so proud of you."

"I should have done that much sooner. We wouldn't-"

"No, you don't get to do that. *We* don't blame ourselves anymore for the things they put us through and the people we've become because of them. We just move forward now."

"Who's *they*?"

Cordelia was saved from replying when the door clicked open again.

"Mr. Montgomery, my name is Dr. Pelletier, it's nice to officially meet you." Just like the nurse, I couldn't make out the doctor until she stepped up beside the bed. She was a blur or beige and white from head-to-toe, but it seemed like she was flipping through my chart. "How are you feeling?"

For a while - it could have been thirty minutes or three hours - I answered questions, got tested and examined, and listened to the same medical bullshit over and over again. Even with the promise of some improvement over the next couple of weeks, it all boiled down to this:

Brain, permanently fucked.

When my eyelids got too heavy to keep open, they told me to rest as if I had a choice in the matter. My body was forcing me to.

As soon as the door clicked shut, the mattress dipped under Cordelia's weight. She arranged my arm to drape around her shoulders as she snuggled in, head on my chest. It felt like a routine move, and it took me a second to realize that she *had* routinely been sleeping like this. I'd felt her next to me before waking up.

"How long have I been out?"

"Four days. Your cousins have been on food delivery duty and the nurses feel sorry enough for me to keep bringing me tea. Apparently there's a rumor that I'm pregnant."

"And my uncle's really dead?"

"Yeah," she breathed, "I shot him. If anyone asks, it was Luka. But I shot him, so I know that he's really, very dead."

"Cordelia-"

"You should rest now. The doctor told you to rest. We can talk about it tomorrow."

I wasn't getting a choice, neither from her, nor from my weak brain pulling me into a deep slumber before I could utter another word.

"You knew?"

"Uhm," Cordelia sucked in a breath, "for the last few days, yes. Luka told me right before coming here."

It was easier to tell with daylight streaming through the windows, how she turned her head back and forth between Luka and me. I couldn't read her expression but I could still see her perfect storm blue eyes. "Okay."

"I told you, I owe you more than a fucking car. I'll owe you for the rest of our lives. Well, the rest of your life. Looks like you'll drop dead way before me, bro."

"Shut up," Cordelia hissed and whipped around.

"Ow. Fuck. Maybe you should get in the ring, huh?"

"It's okay," I said again and reached out for Cordelia's hand. She wove her fingers through mine instantly. This was the only thing that mattered. Even knowing that it was my father who haunted her, Cordelia was here. She chose me, against all odds, again and again. And I would have never known her if it hadn't been for my cousin. "You don't owe me anything, Luka."

"Can you just keep us out of everything from now on, please?" Cordelia added. "We're moving on. Maybe you should, too. You do cars, right?"

"Yeah, I do cars," Luka chuckled and I knew him well enough to know that he was *not* moving on, "speaking of moving on, where is that awful bow?"

"It's not awful."

"Got it." Luka moved around my bed and I pushed myself up on the mattress. He grabbed a big purple something from the side table. "How do I switch it on?"

"What's that?"

"My pin," Cordelia replied, "one of them. Silas helped me modify them."

"Silas?" I asked, only for Luka to click his tongue at me.

"Seriously, if you didn't have a huge bandage on your head, I'd smack you. You and every straight man who gets so easily distracted by boobs. I thought you shot Lev because he realized Cordelia was recording the excommunication."

"I don't-"

"I've been filming. Here," Cordelia grabbed her pin from Luka and placed it in my palm, all ruffles and ribbons, "there's a small camera here." She gently turned it over until I could feel the small, smooth surface. Even holding it up to the light, all I could see was purple with a small dark dot. It could have been a button for all I knew.

I racked my brain, trying to remember what she wore when she came to my uncle's house. There *had* been a huge bow on her chest. She'd thrown it aside right before I'd gone down on her. And when she'd shown up to my fight in Canada, she'd worn another bow - and hadn't let me pull her into the shower with her clothes on.

"Cameras on your chest? The whole time?"

"I've been told I have a great cleavage, so I figured I'd put it to good use."

"Fuck," I breathed, at a loss for words. Cordelia, who had panic attacks at the idea of being filmed just a few months ago, was wielding cameras like swords.

"Silas has the footage, and so does Del. I CC her in on everything."

"Of course you do," I chuckled.

"Switch it on for me," Luka said, "and then I need you to sit on the video for like two weeks, so I can get my shit together and get out of the country."

"Maldives?" Cordelia asked.

"I was thinking Beijing," he replied.

"I hear they have great cars in China."

"Great cars, and great asphalt."

Cordelia pointed her pin at Luka, and for a split second I wanted to ask her to wait - and ask him to stay. I'd lost six years with him. Seeing Cordelia at ease with him just drove home how much we might have missed out on. But Luka was always going to be Luka.

"Ready?"

"Yep."

"Recording."

"My name is Luka Yelchin," Luka bent down, leveling his face with Cordelia's pin camera, "and my father is Piotr Yelchin. He's pulled some shady shit over the past couple of years. I don't have proof, so you're just going to have to take my word for it. I'm of sound body and mind, and am recording this testimony voluntarily. Let's see... I guess we can start with the money laundering."

CHAPTER FORTY

Cordelia

"Del, if you don't stop fussing-" Victor shut up
the second Beck cleared his throat from the driver's seat.

"You didn't have to come pick us up," I said.

"Of course we did." She rolled her eyes at me while smoothing
out the fluffy blanket she had thrown over mine and Victor's laps
as if the sun wasn't cooking the car. "I'm not letting you take a
cab."

The sentence hung in the air for a moment. It contained so
much. I couldn't drive. Victor's sight had gotten slightly better the
last few days but the doctors had still called it legally blind, unable
to drive. Luka and Irina were gone to pick up the pieces of their
family. Our only alternative would have been a cab.

"Thank you," I finally said.

"Okay, you get this, and you get this." Del pulled a large plastic bag from the passenger seat and handed Victor a pack of mint chocolates and me a rocky road chocolate bar. "Next up, I have mango-pineapple, wild berries, or ginger-carrots." She produced a handful of smoothie bottles.

"I'll take mango," I said.

"I'm good," Victor grumbled, clearly not used to being the doted on in the backseat.

Del made a disappointed little sound, which prompted Beck to twist around and glare at Victor. I wasn't sure if Victor could quite tell the sour expression he'd caused. "Pick a fucking smoothie, Yelchin."

"Ginger," Victor said and opened his palm.

Del beamed when she handed over the bottle and I couldn't help smiling right along with her. This was going to be our life now. We got to be with our friends, and bicker over smoothie bottles, and eat chocolate.

The second we took off, I closed my eyes and I leaned into Victor's shoulder. He pressed a kiss to the top of my head and ran his hand along my arm until he found mine to squeeze. "Almost home, zhizn' moya."

"Before we get there, I should tell you that the chairs by your office window will need replacement," Del said, "because I was trying to get Fitzwilliam into his carrier and take him to Beck's. He literally clawed himself away from me and almost took down the curtains too."

"Oh, he must have been so confused. Is he okay now? Does he like his new home?"

"Sorry, that wasn't clear. I tried and failed," Del said, "I don't think he'll leave willingly."

"We can ask his vet about sleep meds. That should make it easy to put him in the box. Or maybe we can get him a different box, because he might just associate that one with the previous times he was taken from a home he'd gotten used to." I was on my phone and looking up pet carriers in an instant.

"What if he stayed?"

"With us?"

"Yes," Del smiled over her shoulder at me, "if you'll have him."

"Of course," Victor said before I could. I silently raised my brows at him, only to remember that he could no longer easily read my expressions. But when I opened my mouth to speak, he said, "You love that cat. I'll live with the scratches."

"And you won't miss him?"

"Of course I'll miss him, but I'll come visit all the time. And this means we can get Brody the fluffy curly guinea pigs she's been asking for."

"Brody's not getting a pet," Beck interjected.

"Oh, come on. No little kid keeps a hamster alive. Sad but true. You can't fault her for that."

"Plenty of children are responsible and keep their pets happy and healthy. You showed me those videos of the little boy and the octopus he built a whole tank for."

"Yeah, and the octopus died, smart-ass." Del poked her tongue out at him. "Besides, she's sixteen. She can handle guinea pigs."

I let my eyes fall shut again and leaned into Victor.

Brody wanted guinea pigs. So simple. So sweet. Despite everything her father had put us through, she was still living the kind of life that made a girl want to adopt fluffy curly guinea pigs.

The thought had me smiling against Victor's shoulder, but I was too tired to partake in the conversation. For the first time, the exhaustion of the last few days seemed to take root in my bones. I wanted to sleep. Not just nap. Curl up in my bed, pull the blanket up, and sleep for a few days.

I blinked and I was in Victor's arms and we were halfway up the stairs.

"Don't trip," I mumbled and buried my face in the crook of his neck.

"Not happening. I know this house like the back of my hand."

Next time I blinked, I was in bed with Victor's body curved

around my back and Fitzwilliam curled up against my front. Dim sunlight turned the whole room pink, and I didn't know if it was sunrise or sunset.

I blinked again, and sat up straight because the bed was empty. The spike in my pulse only shallowed out immediately because the bathroom door stood slightly ajar and the shower was running. Victor wasn't gone. He was just in the next room.

My whole body was tingly and stiff, and my tongue felt like sandpaper. Judging by the bright daylight outside, I'd been in bed for at least 24 hours. I grabbed the glitter tumbler from my night-stand and let out a relieved sigh when ice cold water hit my tongue - not stale water from a week ago. Victor had refilled it on the off chance I'd wake up thirsty.

Straw still between my lips, I climbed out of bed and forced my creaky wooden limbs to get me to the bathroom. Just in time to see Victor get out of the shower with a towel slung around his hips, droplets of water still running down his sculpted pecs and clinging to the sharply cut arrow muscles above his hip bones. His hair had been buzzed short in the hospital, so when he ran his hand through it now, a thin mist sprayed around him. The sight made me forget that I was drinking, and I choked on the next sip of water.

Victor raised his brows at me, the smallest of grins tugging on his lips.

"I was just…"

"Uh-huh."

"Oh, be quiet," I grumbled, heat rushing to my cheeks, "I've seen you naked before."

"Come here." Victor leaned against the counter, all glistening skin and green eyes, and my legs moved on their own accord. I had absolutely no say in the matter. He freed the cup from my grasp and set it down before his hands pulled my face to his. "Good morning."

"Hi," I whispered.

Victor kissed me without caution or hesitation. His lips and tongue and teeth claimed me and I barely had the air to gasp. My lungs filled with air that was his, and my mouth flooded with his taste. And I kissed him back. I pulled at his waist and I bit his lip, because he was *here*, and he was alive, and I was never letting him go again, and I was never going to get enough of him.

"I'm keeping you," I rasped, breathless.

"I'm yours to keep," he replied.

Our mouths crashed into each other again, and then I was walking backwards. Victor led us out of the bathroom and toward the bed without ever coming up for air. His hands slipped up my shirt, strong fingers folding around my waist, and I froze. Victor's grasp immediately loosened.

"I'm still in airplane clothes," I muttered against hist lips, "airplane underwear, airplane leggings. I've been wearing these for two days."

"I'm trying to get you out of them."

"I'm probably all sweaty."

No wonder he'd taken a shower. I should have been taking a shower. The airplane was one thing, but the hospital hadn't exactly been a spa holiday either. I hadn't even brought a razor to France.

"Lift your arms."

"I'm hairy."

"Lift your fucking arms, Cordelia."

The gruff note in his words sent a warm shiver down my spine. I complied, and Victor pulled my shirt and bralette top off in one move. I expected him to keep kissing me and touching me, but he paused with my clothes in his fists. His gaze roamed down my torso, brows quivering. Any worries about my clothes or my shaving routines evaporated because Victor looked at me and his eyes couldn't focus.

"Here," I whispered and reached for his hand. He let me direct his fingers to my chest until they brushed over my nipple. My breath trembled as I moved his touch down the dip of my sternum to my other breast.

"It just looks different."

"I know."

"Lie down." The command lacked some of the strength from before, but I still sank back onto the bed, propped up on my elbows, knees dangling off the side.

Victor dipped his fingers into my waistband and pulled off my leggings and panties, kissing each ankle before letting them sink down again. As he stood between my legs, and let his eyes travel up and down my body, the nervous tension trickled from his face. Others might have thought he was apathetic. They just didn't know him well enough to read the little sideways tilt of his chin or the crinkle in the corner of his left eye. Nothing compared to being looked at like that. He was stealing my breath without even touching me.

"I love you," I said and watched the corner of his mouth twitch ever so slightly.

"We'll have to do something about that."

"I'm sorry?"

"You're usually a little meaner when you're horny."

"Oh, excuse me for having feelings for the man I want to spend the rest of my life with."

"That's more like it." He tossed his towel aside, giving me a perfect view of his mounting arousal. God, he was so beautiful. Every inch of him was perfectly chiseled and sloped. I'd pick up sculpting, just to immortalize him. My fingers itched to reach out and touch him, but I waited for him to climb onto the mattress with me. His thick thighs knocked mine up and apart as he moved over me.

"I'm not fragile," he echoed the words I'd used after our first time, "only adjusting."

"Okay." I swallowed, feeling his hard length press against my center. My hips shifted up against him on their own accord because I needed to feel him, needed him as close as I could get him. "Kiss me."

"No," he huffed, holding perfectly still as I tried to gain any sort of traction under him.

"Then touch me."

"No."

"Victor, please." I sounded pathetic and I didn't care. I slung my hands around his neck for leverage against him, or to pull him to me - or anything. But Victor didn't budge.

"So impatient." He smirked and kissed the inside of my wrist. "So needy." He kissed my other wrist.

I tried bucking my hips into him again, but this time, he spread a hand over my lower abdomen and pushed me deep into the mattress. Despite the distance between our bodies, I still let out a moan at the mere pressure. "Do you like torturing me?"

Victor leaned down slowly, dark lashes lowering over his eyes just before his lips brushed over mine. "Yes," he whispered, and kissed my jaw.

"I hate you."

"You're wriggling and begging me to touch you because you hate me, huh?" He kissed a path along my jaw to the small spot behind my ear, and all the air spluttered from my lungs. "You hate that?"

"I hate you," I repeated weakly because he still wouldn't kiss me.

"Let me see how desperate you are to be fucked by the man you hate." His voice was a low rasp by my ear.

Leaving a scorching hot path, Victor's hand trailed down my stomach and dropped into the space between my legs. Without any playful teasing, he dipped two fingers into me. I choked on my own voice. The sudden stretch to my insides set my body ablaze, each nerve firing heat through my systems.

"You're so fucking tight," he breathed, and pushed his fingers deeper, "tight and soaking wet for me, baby."

"Vic-" His name dissolved into a wordless moan as he pushed all the way in, my insides pulsing around his knuckles. I tried to tilt my face to him, tried to get his lips within kissing distance, but all I got was his teeth cutting punishment into my neck. I stilled with a whimper. "Asshole."

"Want to know one of my favorite things about making you come?" He flicked his tongue over his bite mark, sending a shiver through me. That shiver in turn made me tighten around his hand, prompting another wave of heat.

"I hate you," I whined and sank my nails into his shoulders, "stop playing with me. Man up and fuck me already."

"One of my favorite things..." he continued undeterred, sliding his fingers out just an inch, only to curl them inside me. My vision blurred. My heart stilled. I moaned, throwing my head back. "...is when you stop talking."

"Fuck you," my voice was barely a raspy squeak anymore, "I'll talk however much I w-ah." Victor's fingers slipped out of me, only to fill me a moment later in a harsh thrust.

"What was that?" Victor finally leaned back, his emerald eyes on me, with a small crinkle between his brows.

"I'll talk-" My words were cut off again, because he dragged his thumb over my clit, and every bone in my body started shaking.

"Yes?"

He tortured me with his fingers flicking and curling. I was a mouse and he was the cat chasing it through the room for fun before going in for the kill.

"I'll- I- I..." Thoughts and words incinerated in the heat that washed through me. It furled under my skin, seeking a way out. I grabbed the sheets, and I wasn't sure if I was pushing against him or away from him. One way or another, I needed to extinguish the fire in my blood before it burned me up.

"You were saying?" Victor stilled and unsheathed his fingers excruciatingly slow.

Nothing. I was saying nothing. I was just *needing*.

I shook my head, nose brushing over his and clawed at his arm to make him continue.

"There she is, my needy little slut, so eager to spread her legs for me."

He delved his fingers back into me, and hit that spot that made my pussy tighten, and my stomach cramp, and my spine arch. The fire washed over me, burned my skin and singed my bones. I moaned and I thrashed, and I dropped over the deliciously painful edge, letting the fire consume me whole.

"The way you come... it's fucking addicting." Victor gently leaned his hips sideways to keep my shaking legs spread as he freed his hand. I jerked with each knuckle slipping from my tender opening.

"Kiss me," I croaked, "please."

Victor must have heard the small hitch in my voice. He shifted his weight, leaning onto the arm he'd just had between our bodies, and using his clean hand to smooth my bangs from my face. "Need a break?"

I shook my head. "Just a kiss."

This time, his mouth was careful. His lips teased mine, letting me open for him at my own pace. With my eyes closed, I savored the taste and the slow caress of his tongue.

He was home and he was mine and he made me feel alive.

My stomach cramped again, this time not from climaxing, but with a loud rumble. "Ow." I grimaced.

"I think you do need a break," Victor chuckled and tried to lean back, but I kept my hold on him firm.

"I can eat later," I said, but my stomach let out another gurgle, gnawing at itself.

"Up you go." Two strong arms wrapped around my back and lifted me off the mattress. I yelped, barely reacting fast enough to wrap my legs around Victor's waist before he started walking.

"I'm naked!"

"Yes."

"It's a shared household. Sock-on-the-door kind of rules."

"Not really," he said and started jogging down the stairs like it was nothing, "Del is practically living with Beckett, and Irina is gone. It's just you and me now."

"Okay but- we can't just- that's not how-" I had never left my room naked. Potentially as a toddler, running away from diapers. Then again, I'd also never lived in a house without staff. "Do you want me to pay you?"

"For the sex?" Victor set me down on the cold kitchen counter. "No, that comes free with the marriage license."

"We're not married yet."

"Fine, you can pay me for all the sex we have before we get married, but not after." He opened the fridge, closed it again, shook his head, then reopened it and started going through the contents with careful hands.

"On paper, you're still my employee, but we're a couple now, and that's weird and complicated."

"Okay, I quit." Victor spread out everything he needed to make sandwiches on the counter beside me. "It's not complicated."

"Okay, but still. Obviously everything that's mine is going to be yours someday, but what about until then? Do you want a credit card? Pocket money?"

"I don't need your money."

"Victor, will you let me take care of you please?"

"You can always take care of me." He leaned over to press a quick kiss to my shoulder. "But I don't need your money. Luka cleared my uncle's accounts before leaving. He transferred every cent I made in the octagon over the years. Fighting and winning against Silver in my comeback year would have been enough to retire on. You're marrying a filthy rich man, Cordelia Montgomery."

"Oh."

"Don't tell me you only like your men poor."

"No," I scoffed, "I just realized that you're profiting of your uncle's death."

He hummed in understanding and laid down the butter knife. Hands on my knees, he stepped up in front of me. "You killed someone, Cordelia."

"I'm aware."

"Are you?"

"What do you mean?" I picked up his hands and intertwined my fingers with his.

"I think I'm still waiting for your reaction."

"I don't have one, and I'm okay with that." When he only raised his brows at me, I sighed and slid towards him until my knees caged his hips. "I know it's bad. I know that I took a life. If you think of me differently now, that's okay. I'm okay with being different, but I'm also the same. The idea of leaving this house again makes me want to throw up. Back in Paris, I didn't sleep for more than twenty minutes at a time, and when I did, I still saw the same memories flash before my eyes. It's always my mother. Maybe it's always going to be that way. But at least when I wake up now, I know it's over. Your father, who killed my mom, is dead. Luka's father, who had your father killed, is dead. And my father, who's responsible for me being locked up for days instead of hours, is dead. It's over."

"No wonder you slept for 24 hours straight."

"I need you to understand that I'm at peace with what I did. Maybe this makes me a really terrible person, but I think the world is a better place because all of these men are dead."

"I agree," he ran a hand through my hair, "and I don't think that makes us terrible people."

"Just vigilante murderers."

"Maybe." He smiled a perfect little Victor smile and shrugged. "If you're alright with that, I'm alright with that."

"I'm alright."

"Alright."

CHAPTER FORTY-ONE

VICTOR

"THANK YOU," CORDELIA CHIMED AND TOOK A FOLDER from me.

We were sat on the floor of her office and she kept furiously typing into her computer. I sorted another stack of loose paper into a folder. The text was too blurry for me to read, but I could still help work through the two-foot-tall stack of files.

Besides a couple million, Luka had also sent over some books. No ledgers and nothing that had any real value to a judge. Certainly nothing the government would help with. Just names. Dozens of names of women, their children, and their families both here and in Russia. All the women my uncle had shipped here to be exploited.

Which meant, after officially ending my employment with Cordelia Montgomery, I was now working for the Theresa Montgomery foundation. Mostly as a translator for the Montgomery Estate Women's Shelter.

Cordelia had consulted with her team for days. A few of the women had chosen to go back to Russia, but most of them had nothing to go back to - which had made them easy targets in the first place. A few had larger families here and got their individual needs taken care of through the foundation. But most of the women were young and single. Some of them weren't even legally allowed to drink yet. Some of them had kids from some asshole who paid fifty bucks for a quick fuck in the back of a van.

None of it was pretty.

But Cordelia had turned her family's estate into a group home in the blink of an eye. She wanted to keep them together. This way, they could at least keep the small community they had built under my uncle's control. Especially because a handful of them didn't even speak a lick of English, which was where I came in.

"I hope you're calling with good news," Cordelia angled her laptop, presumably so her caller could see me sitting next to her.

"Hi guys," Amani's voice piped from the speakers, "I do have good news. The documentary on Victor's uncle is going online on Sunday. I just saw the final cut and it looks like we're completely in the clear. Victor's been pushed to the sidelines in an 'oh, he also has a nephew in sports' kind of way, and you're only briefly mentioned as Victor's girlfriend."

"Perfect," Cordelia said and smiled over her shoulder at me, "sounds like Silas found his story."

It helped that my uncle's death had gotten a lot of attention from the news. Even those who had never heard of Piotr Yelchin until two weeks ago, had probably studied his Wikipedia article now. Which meant Petya was a far more interesting subject for Silas to study than Cordelia was.

As long as the news kept reporting that Luka had shot his father and had since fled the country, I didn't care about any of it. Cordelia just deserved her peace now.

"The other thing," Amani said, "is that we should really take this chance to talk about the women's shelter. It will tie in great with the documentary. You can make an official statement. We can probably get Silas to film you, too."

"No," I said before Cordelia had the chance.

"Excuse me?" Amani replied.

"I said no."

"And you speak for Cordelia now?"

"No, he doesn't, but he knows the women in the shelter better than anyone." Cordelia reached over to squeeze my hand. "If he says no, it's a no."

"This isn't just about the shelter, it's about the whole foundation. I mean, we're just getting control over the situation with our Florida center. The good publicity of you picking up the pieces after Piotr Yelchin's death would really help our image."

"I don't care," Cordelia said, "this isn't a publicity stunt."

"I know that," Amani scoffed.

"I'm also not setting myself up for a political career." Cordelia leaned forward, one arm braced on my lap. "These women don't need my face trending on their For-You-Pages, reminding them of what they've gone through. They want to move forward, and it's our job to help them with that. This isn't some trolley problem. The foundation isn't going to collapse if we don't profit from the documentary. We're not going bankrupt. We just keep going. And we don't ever put publicity above the needs of the people we help."

I let a hand slide up Cordelia's spine, resting it between her shoulder blades. Just to silently offer my support even if she might not need it.

"I know this might sound harsh to you. I'm sorry. I went along with the video campaign because it only affected me, but gave us the chance to help many more women. You're great at what you do. But you don't work for me. You don't even work for the administration of the foundation. You work for the women who need our help."

"Right." Amani audibly swallowed on the other side of the screen. I had very little sympathy for her left after having witnessed how the whole campaign took its toll on Cordelia. "I'm sorry."

"It's okay," Cordelia said and leaned back, shifting into my hand, "if you want to talk about it more, we can schedule a proper call next week."

"I'll think about it," Amani said. The computer made the little swooping noise of a call ending and Cordelia sagged against me.

"Did she hang up on you?"

"Yeah," she sighed and dropped her head to my shoulder, "she didn't look happy."

"You did the right thing." I pressed a kiss to the crown of her hair, inhaling her sweet summery scent. "I know that was hard."

"Thank you. And thank you for saying no. You're really good at this, you know?" She tilted her head back and gave me a quick, innocent kiss. "The girls at the shelter are all swooning over you."

"Swooning?"

"So handsome. So nice. So attentive. Always knows the right thing to say. Never raises his voice to make a point."

"Hmm," I nudged my nose against hers, "almost like I have a few years experience in handling a woman with a complicated past."

"You've never *handled* me," she scoffed and sat upright.

"I handled you just this morning."

"I damn well hope you don't handle any other women like you handled me this morning."

"Don't worry, you get special treatment, zhizn' moya."

"Good," she chuckled and leaned in to press her lips against my cheek, "next file, please."

CHAPTER FORTY-TWO

Cordelia

"THE STAFF HAS CLEARED OUT," VICTOR SAID OUTSIDE the bathroom door. "One hour until the wedding."

"Thanks," I breathed shakily, staring at my strange reflection.

"What's wrong?"

"Nothing."

"You're a shitty liar, even behind closed doors."

"I- I just- you can't be mad, okay?"

"Why would I be-" Victor stepped into the room, and his words died on his tongue as he took in the evidence of my massacre. The counter was covered in magenta dye, glitter, and hair strands. Instead of saying any more, he lifted his hand and his brows, waiting until I nodded my permission before he touched my hair. My breath got lodged in my throat as he ran his fingers through my attempt at a pink balayage. Glitter rained down, on

359

the floor, on my PJs, on his suit. "Why would I be mad?" he repeated, voice soft and low, and he leaned in to kiss my cheek.

"It's pink."

"I like pink"

"And short."

"It's only a little shorter," he countered, fingers sliding down my hair to where it stopped at my collar bone, "did you cut it yourself?"

"Yeah," I pointedly glanced at the sink. Half my hair piled up in it.

"Do you like it?"

"I do," I whispered. "Do you still think I'm pretty?"

"That's what you're worried about? Zhizn' moya, you're the most beautiful woman in every room. Nothing can change that." Victor shook his head. "But if you're asking for my input? All I care about is that it's long enough for me to do this." He wrapped my hair around his fist and yanked it hard. My head snapped back, giving him the perfect angle to close his mouth over mine. I quietly moaned into the kiss, caught between the force of his mouth and the strain on my scalp.

"The glitter is going to get everywhere," he grunted. He pulled his hands from my hair and held them up to the light. The glitter refracted in thousands of little rainbows. Even if he couldn't see every glitter particle, the light spectacle was hard to miss.

"Don't worry. That's just for the wedding."

"I'll look like I fucked the tooth fairy." Before I had the chance to reply, his mouth crushed into mine again and he pushed me against the door. "Beautiful," he whispered before his lips moved to my jaw. "Beautiful." He kissed my neck. "Beautiful." His teeth grazed over my collar bone. "Beautiful." His mouth dipped to the space between my breasts.

"Victor," I gasped, arching into him. Goosebumps broke out along my arms, every little hair on my body desperate to be closer to him.

"Beautiful," he said again, and pulled my top aside to close his lips over the peak of my breast. Heat seared through my veins and I grasped onto his hair as my knees buckled.

"I need to get dressed," I insisted weakly.

He let go of my breast, my nipple coming free with a *pop*. When he rose to his full height, his eyes had taken on that dark determined shade that made my stomach twist in anticipation. "Turn around."

"I have to get ready," I said, knowing fully well what my protest would earn me.

His hands wrapped around my arms, and with one rough twist, I was spun 180 degrees. Grabbing a fistful of my hair, Victor pushed my face against the door. Cold wood kissed my cheek, but did nothing to distinguish the heat in my blood. All hard muscle and ridges, Victor pushed his body against mine, caging me in. "Put your hands on the door, Cordelia," he growled, his lips ghosting over my ear.

My pulse spiked at the strength he was submitting me to. If I opened my mouth, I wasn't sure I'd be able to form words. So instead, I just nodded and flattened my palms against the door.

"That's my girl." If he noticed the shiver rolling down my spine at those last two words, he didn't let it show. "Now push your hips back."

I wriggled, my face still pressed to the door, but he gave me just enough space to tilt my lower half into him. The soft material of his pants did nothing to cover the hard length pushing against the curve of my thigh.

With one swift move, he pulled my shorts down. They dropped to the floor and I kicked them off to the side.

"Fuck," he grunted, mouth frozen against my neck, hand hovering just over my hip bone.

"What?" I gasped.

"Spread your cheeks for me."

"What do you-" Before I could finish my question, he grabbed my hands and brought them back to the curve of my ass. My breath stuttered in my throat. "I don't think I'm ready for that."

"Baby, I'm just figuring out how to fuck you without making you sparkle from the inside. Spread those cheeks, so I can see your pussy."

"Oh," I breathed. I hadn't even considered that body glitter might not be very safe *inside* your body. Made sense. Victor pulled back a little to work his pants, and I tried to adjust my grip to bare myself to him.

"You're so fucking beautiful," he rasped right before he clamped his hands around my waist and pushed himself into me in one sharp thrust.

"Oh damn you, *Vic*." I winced, my lower stomach seizing around the strain.

"That's it." His thumbs rubbed slow circles into the base of my spine, soothing my tense muscles.

"Did you come here to give me a massage or will you fuck me already?" I hissed.

Victor chuckled, only to deliver a thrust hard enough to slam my face against the door. My inner walls tightened, heat and pain bleeding into each other. I just had time to flatten my palms against the door again before the next harsh blow came. This one wrangled a deep moan from my chest.

"Look at you," he pulled back, and stilled, "you're dripping wet for me already."

"Don't stop," I whimpered.

"So desperate." Victor thrust forward again, and didn't stop this time. My entire body rocked, cheek pressed against the door as he drove faster and deeper. The force of his body crashing into mine almost took out my knees, but he just tightened his grip around my waist. Fingertip-sized bruises probably bloomed under my skin as he held me steady.

"Yes, oh god," I whimpered. The pressure welled up inside me, hot and thick and unbearable, and I squeezed my eyes shut.

"Open your eyes," Victor growled. He grabbed my hair and yanked my head around, forcing me to face the mirror. My scalp tingled and a hot wave prickled down my entire body. "Look at what a needy little slut you are for me."

I blinked at the girl with pink hair, with the flushed cheeks and glassy eyes. I watched her whole body jerk as a mountain of a man, covered in tattoos, rammed into her. She wasn't delicate or put together, or even naked. She was half-dressed and sparkling and getting exactly what she craved.

"Fuck. Yes," I gasped and watched myself fall apart. I watched how my legs jittered as the heat mounted in my core. How my spine curved when the pressure pushed against my insides. And how my muscles lost all hold, when the dam finally broke, and a wave of searing pleasure, so hot it almost hurt, swept over my nerves.

I felt *him* from the roots of my hair to the tips of my toes.

I felt *me* from the roots of my hair to the tips of my toes.

Victor kept me upright through my orgasm, until I was nothing but a trembling mess of aftershocks. My release dripped down my thighs. I blinked against the blinding haze and grasped at his arms, tightly wound around me to keep me on my feet.

"You're perfect, zhizn' moya," he rasped against the curve of my ear. I shivered, because that girl in the mirror hadn't looked anything like what I would have considered perfect just a few months ago. But she was. And we were.

"I love you," I croaked an craned my neck to kiss him. Victor's lips came close, but hovered over mine as he groaned, deep green eyes boring into me. His hips snapped forward for one last breathless thrust, before he spilled himself in me.

We stood slumped against the door for a moment, breathing hard and fast.

"Let me have a look at you," Victor rasped. He kissed my bare shoulder, then gently lifted my silky top off.

"Victor." My breath hitched. His touch grazed over my waist, where he'd just gripped me like steel, but now his fingertips were featherlight. The part that sent a shiver down my spine, however, was the fact that he hadn't pulled out. With even the smallest move, my oversensitive muscles seized around him again.

"I need you to stop squeezing my dick unless you want to go for round two."

"I would stop squeezing if you pulled out."

"If I pulled out, I wouldn't be inside you anymore."

"Yes, that's the logical order of things," I laughed - and immediately choked on the sound, when my entire body constricted and I was reminded of the thick length lodged inside me.

"Fine, don't move," he huffed and slowly pulled back. I sucked in a breath but otherwise managed to stay very still as he freed himself. A moment later, his breath fanned out over my ass while he knelt behind me and gently wiped a towel up the insides of my thighs. "I love your legs," he whispered and kissed the spot he'd just cleaned.

"I love your hands," I replied and let my forehead sink against the door again, let my eyes flutter close as he cleaned both our releases off my legs.

"Yeah? If there wasn't so much glitter on them, I would-"

"No," I cut him off, "I mean, I love that too, but I guess, it's because you go from gentle to rough so easily. It's not just words, and it's not just the way you fuck me. I love your hands because when we have sex, you touch me purely for pleasure. There's no reverence or caution or love in those touches, and it feels amazing."

"Cordelia," Victor sighed and stood. He gently turned me around, towel abandoned on the floor, hands curved around my cheeks. "Every single time I touch you, I touch you with love. Don't ever forget that."

"I just meant-" My voice hitched when both his hands grabbed my hair and yanked my head back, exposing my throat.

"This is love." Victor rasped, lips running along the underside of my jaw, "because I know you hate when people treat you like you're made of glass. It's love because you trust me more than I trust myself - when I've only ever used my body for destruction."

I swallowed, my throat bobbing against his mouth.

"It's love because when I touch you like that, neither of us hides who we are."

"I take it back," I breathed, "but it only makes me love your hands even more."

"Good," he chuckled, his fists flexing, teasing my scalp.

"Now I need you to stop touching me like this, or we won't actually make it to the wedding."

OUTSIDE, A SMALL AISLE WAS COVERED IN PINK FLOWER petals from the winter garden to the pond. I'd somehow ended up adopting four white ducks last week, who were all paddling away in the sun. Meanwhile, Beck waited by the edge of the water with the officiant, standing under an arch of blue flowers. He was clad in a gray coattails and a pale blue cravat, looking exactly like the English lord from one of Del's historical romance novels.

Four rose gold chairs on either side of the small aisle led towards the pond. The front rows were reserved for Del's mom and grandma on one side, Brody and Isaac on the other side. Victor and I took our seats behind Del's family.

"Have you seen Defne?" Tabitha dropped into the chair across the aisle from me. Her pixie cut stood off in all directions and her mascara and lipstick were smudged.

"I think she's helping Del maneuver her dress in the bathroom. Why?"

"I'm holding onto her phone, and it's been ringing off the hook." She pulled a small compact from her purse and started reapplying her mauve lipstick, rubbing at the smudged corners.

"Tabitha," I narrowed my eyes at her disheveled appearance, "did you just have sex in my house?"

"No," she scoffed, "what kind of heathen do you take me for? I just had sex in a car parked outside your house."

I didn't even get the chance to reply because Defne breezed towards us and plopped into the chair on Tabitha's other side. "Okay, she's ready. Here we go," she huffed.

"I shut this off because some New York number keeps calling." Tabitha dropped the phone in Defne's lap.

"Did you pick up?"

"No," she scoffed, "I was busy."

My eyes flicked to Brody who was cackling and scratching at a stain on Isaac's shirt collar that looked an awful lot like mauve lipstick. "Tabitha-" I started, only to immediately turn the other way when the music started spilling from the speakers.

Del stepped out of the winter garden in a beautiful empire waist dress. Thin white lace was layered over opalescent satin and hundreds of small blue pearls shimmered in the sunlight. It wasn't a traditional wedding dress, more like something out of a regency movie, but it was whimsical and romantic and completely *her*.

My eyes skipped from her to Beck, who was watching her every step with the biggest smile I'd ever seen on him. Not one of those perfectly polite smiles, but a big, bright, honest smile. And the second Del was within reach, his hands were around hers, and he pulled her in for a kiss. An impossible kiss because both of them were smiling too much.

The ceremony was short and sweet, and instead of exchanging vows, they exchanged letters that they silently read. Considering how public their relationship had started, this was perfect, and it was all theirs.

The other side of the backyard was set up with a large table, covered in pink and blue flowers and pearls, and when everyone crowded around it after the ceremony, Victor wordlessly took my hand under the table. He soothed my nerves without me even having to glance his way.

I laced my fingers through his and scooted my chair a little closer to him.

"Alright?"

"Yeah," I breathed and leaned into him, soaking up his warm, grounding scent, and letting my head rest on his shoulder for a moment. It would have been a lie to say that I liked having a large group of people in my space, but Del was beaming, and our friends were laughing, and the huge piece of cake in front of me oozed caramel, and I was sitting next to the man I wanted to spend the rest of my life with. "More than alright."

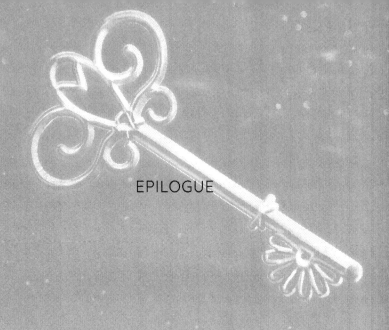

VICTOR

"TRY THIS ONE." I PLACED A SPARKLING PINK THERMOS cup on the side table next to Cordelia. At least I'd learned my lesson not to let her see the green and brown smoothies anymore. The color alone made her throw up.

"No, thank you, I'm good." She placatingly patted my arm. Despite the bronze tan she'd curated, there was no warmth in her cheeks.

My vision had improved over the past year, but I still needed a lot of light to make out any details. Right now, the bright summer sun just drove home how bad Cordelia had gotten, because I could make out the dark purpling shadows under her eyes, and the ghostly paling of her lips.

"You're a shitty liar, zhizn' moya." I climbed onto the winter garden chaise behind her, legs slotting around her hips.

368

"I'll just end up sick again."

"Just try it."

"This never would have happened without you, you know?"

"I know."

I grabbed the cup and held the straw up to her lips. She huffed but finally gave in, taking a small sip. Then cautiously another one. Until her hands folded over mine and she greedily gulped down half the cup.

"Slow down," I chuckled.

"It's the mint. The mint is good," she whispered, eyes closed.

"Good. Just give it a minute to settle."

"I never really saw myself going on a honeymoon - but this has to be close to the worst case scenario. We're not at the beach. I'm sick all the time. And we're not even having crazy newlyweds sex."

"We'll go to the beach next year," I promised.

"And then we still won't be having crazy newlyweds sex, because we'll be up all night feeding the baby. Plus, we won't be newlyweds anymore."

She'd spent weeks preparing for the private island honeymoon. It was going to be her first trip *outside* since Paris last year. Instead, her first trip had been to the hospital because two weeks before the wedding, she'd been unable to stop throwing up.

We'd postponed the party, but we still got married on paper. Partially for the baby. Mostly because we just didn't want to wait.

"You want to have crazy newlyweds sex? We can have sex right now."

"I promise you, the second your dick presses against my insides, I'm throwing up again."

"Come here." I set aside the pink smoothie cup and pulled her back against my chest. One hand on her stomach, I used the other to massage her palm. I'd learned more about acupressure in the last few weeks than I ever thought possible. The constant discomfort had her on edge more often than not, but hit a few pressure points and Cordelia was humming and melting against me. "Feel better?"

"Mm-hmm."

"You won't miss out on anything. We have time. This is just delaying us by few months. And then we'll have a beautiful baby, with your gorgeous eyes, and my mother's red hair, and tiny hands and tiny feet. And we'll take them to the beach, let them dip their toes in the ocean, and we'll build sandcastles. Or whatever it is families do at the beach."

"We're having a *baby*." She tilted head, nudging my chin with her nose. "I mean, I knew that's what was happening. Condom breaks, get knocked up, have a kid. But it's an actual child, like, a little human person."

"Yes."

"We're going to be a *family*. We can play ball in the backyard, and read picture books, and have birthday parties. We can do watercolors at the kitchen table and hang pictures on the fridge and sing lullabies. We can do all of that." Cordelia sat up straight and turned to me. When she sniffled, I brought my hand to her face just in time to catch a tear with my thumb. "Happy tears," she quickly clarified.

I leaned in to kiss her, tasting the salt on her lips. "We're going to be a boring married couple with a house, a cat and a baby."

"We get to be boring now," she whispered and kissed me again, smiling against my lips, "perfectly boring."

"Perfectly boring," I agreed.

Rapunzel and her prince are free.

It's time for Snow White to meet her new roommates.

ACKNOWLEDGMENTS

I can't believe I'm writing acknowledgments in my second book!

That means, first and foremost, I have to acknowledge YOU. Yes, you, reading this. I wouldn't have made it this far without every single one of my readers. I love connecting with all of you online. Don't ever stop being the most amazing, loving and considerate group of people I've ever known.

Thank you - always and every time - to PB. I love rearranging my bookshelves with you.

To Bethany, Victor's wife, his original fangirl, who loved him when he was just a thought in my brain. In my first acknowledgments, I said we should reduce our 2am phone calls. Technically, we did. They just last until 3am now.

To Imi because this book wouldn't exist without you. Thank you for asking for more chapters, for listening and cheering and nagging and reading and setting up my Notion schedule. And thank you for your extra Eras Tour ticket. (It was the motivation I desperately needed.)

To Caden for always believing in me and for shouting "Oh my god, is that bestselling author Dilan Dyer?" when I walked into the bookshop. I can't wait for Book Lovers!

To my amazing beta readers: Annabel, Courtenay, Edith, Imi and Romie, who rolled with my erratic schedules, who made sense of this book when I couldn't, and who helped me make Victor even more swoon-worthy. I couldn't have done it without you.

To the loving and welcoming and funny romance community, who have gotten me through the infamous second-book-block with their never-ending advice and support. Special thanks to

Amelie, Ava, Carly, Elliot, Grace, Hailey, Jen, Ki, Lisina, Meg, Ruby, Soraya, Stephanie, Summer, Zarin (and I'm probably missing a few author names, I'm so sorry!) - because online friends are real friends. I'm so grateful for all of you.

And to **Channing Tatum**. Thank you for producing *Magic Mike's Last Dance*. Bet you didn't think the grumpy 60-year-old butler would inspire a whole romance book, did you?

ABOUT THE AUTHOR

Dilan is the bestselling author of the Princess Crossover series. Constantly on the move, she has lived in countless cities across five countries and dreams of a camper van to take her life on the road. She just needs to find one big enough for her pets, her vintage tea cup collection and her staggering TBR.

Having outgrown her slut phase, Dilan now channels her thirst in spicy romance novels with swoon-worthy HEAs.

X x.com/authordilandyer
instagram.com/authordilandyer

Made in the USA
Coppell, TX
24 July 2024

35152029R00214